Berry and Co

NOVELS BY DORNFORD YATES

The "Berry" Books

THE BROTHER OF DAPHNE
THE COURTS OF IDLENESS
BERRY AND CO
JONAH AND CO
ADELE AND CO
AND BERRY CAME TOO
THE HOUSE THAT BERRY BUILT
THE BERRY SCENE
AS BERRY AND I WERE SAYING
B-BERRY AND I LOOK BACK

DORNFORD YATES

Berry and Co

WARD LOCK LIMITED
LONDON

ISBN 0 7063 1676 2

First published in Great Britain 1920.
This edition published in 1976 by Ward Lock Limited,
116 Baker Street, London W1M 2BB

Designed by Humphrey Stone
Text set in Intertype Baskerville
Printed by The Compton Press Ltd.
Bound by Leighton Straker Ltd.

To my Customers

There are some old-fashioned tradesmen who send their customers cards, well printed in copperplate, on which they "beg to thank" them for their "continued patronage"—a highly respectable practice, now falling into disuse.

I have no such elegant cards: and, if I had, I should not know where to send them, because I cannot tell who my customers are. But I beg that they will believe that I "esteem" their patronage very high and that I mean what I say when I offer them, one and all, my "respectful compliments and thanks".

DORNFORD YATES

January, 1936

Contents

BERTRAM PLEYDELL
(of White Ladies, in the County of Hampshire)

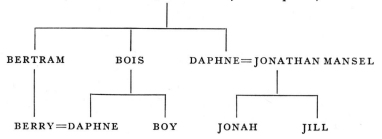

BERTRAM BOIS DAPHNE=JONATHAN MANSEL

BERRY=DAPHNE BOY JONAH JILL

CHAPTER I

How Will Noggin was Fooled, and Berry Rode Forth against his Will

"Who's going to church?" said Daphne, consulting her wrist-watch.

There was a profound silence.

My sister turned to Jill.

"Are you coming?" she said. "Berry and I are."

"I beg your pardon," said her husband.

"Of course you're coming," said Daphne.

"Not in these trousers. This is the first time I've worn them, and I'm not going to kneel in them for any one."

"Then you'll change," said his wife. "You've plenty of time."

Berry groaned.

"This is sheer Bolshevism," he said. "Is not my soul my own?"

"We shall start," said Daphne, "in twenty minutes."

It was nearly half-past ten in the morning of a beautiful summer day, and we were all taking our ease in the sunshine upon the terrace. It was the first Sunday which we had spent all together at White Ladies for nearly five years.

So far as the eye could see, nothing had changed.

At the foot of the steps the great smooth lawn stretched like a fine green carpet, its shadowed patches yet bright with dew. There were the tall elms and the copper beech and all the proud company of spreading giants—what were five years to them? There was the clump of rhododendrons, a ragged blotch of crimson, seemingly spilled upon the green turf, and there the close box hedge that walled away the rose-garden. Beyond the sunk fence a gap showed an acre or so of Bull's Mead—a great deep meadow, and in it two horses beneath a chestnut tree, their long tails a-swish, sleepily nosing each other to rout the flies; while in the distance the haze of heat hung like a film over the rolling hills. Close at hand echoed the soft impertinence of a cuckoo, and two fat wood-pigeons waddled about the lawn, picking and stealing as they went. The sky was cloudless and there was not a breath of wind.

The stable clock chimed the half-hour.

My sister returned to the attack.

"Are you coming, Boy?"

"Yes," said I. "I am."

Berry sat up and stared at me.

"Don't be silly," he said. "There's a service this morning. Besides, they've changed the lock of the poor-box."

"I want to watch the Vicar's face when he sees you," said I.

"It will be a bit of a shock," said Jonah, looking up from the paper. "Is his heart all right?"

"Rotten," said Daphne. "But that doesn't matter. I sent him a note to warn him yesterday."

"What did you say?" demanded her husband.

"I said, '*We're back at last, and—don't faint—we're all coming to Church to-morrow, and you've got to come back to lunch.*' And now, for goodness' sake, go and change."

"But we shall perspire," said Berry. "Profusely. To walk half a mile in this sun is simply asking for it. Besides——"

"What's the car done?" said Jonah. "I'm going, and I can't hurry with this." He tapped his short leg affectionately. "We needn't take Fitch. Boy or I can drive."

"Right oh," said my sister, rising. "Is ten-minutes-to early enough?"

Jonah nodded.

"This," said Berry, "is a conspiracy for which you will pay. Literally. I shall take the plate round, and from you four I shall accept nothing but paper. Possibly I shall——"

Here the girls fell upon him and bore him protesting into the house and out of earshot.

"Who's going to look after the car while we're in church?" said I.

"There's sure to be somebody ready to earn a couple of bob," said Jonah. "Besides, we can always disconnect the north-east trunnion, or jack her up and put the wheels in the vestry or something."

"All right. Only we don't want her pinched." With a yawn I rose to my feet. "And now I suppose I'd better go and turn her out."

"Right oh," said Jonah, picking up his paper again.

I strolled into the house.

We were proud of the car. She was a 1914 Rolls, and we had bought her at a long price less than a week ago. Fresh from the coach-builder's, her touring body was painted silver-grey, while her bonnet was of polished aluminium. Fitted with every conceivable accessory, she was very good-looking, charming alike to ride or drive, and she went like the wind. In a word, she did as handsome as she was.

It was eight minutes to eleven as we slid past the lodge and on to the Bilberry road.

Before we had covered two furlongs, we swung round a corner to see a smart two-seater at rest by the dusty hedgerow, and a slight dark girl in fresh blue and white standing with one foot on the step, wiping her dainty fingers on a handful of cotton-waste.

"Agatha!" cried Daphne and Jill. "Stop, Boy, stop!"

Obediently I slowed to a standstill, as my lady came running after us.

"You might have told me," she panted. "I never knew you were back. And I am so glad."

"We only arrived on Friday, dear," said Daphne, and introduced Berry and me. Jonah, it appeared, had met Miss Deriot at tennis in 1914.

"But you had your hair down then," he said gravely.

"It's a wonder I haven't got it down now," said Miss Deriot. "Why didn't you come along ten minutes earlier? Then you could have changed my tyre."

"And why are you driving away from church?" said Jill.

"One of the colts has sprained his shoulder, and we're out of embrocation; so I'm going to get some from Brooch."

"I'll come with you," said Berry eagerly, preparing to leave the car. "I don't like to think of you——"

"Nonsense," said Daphne, detaining him.

"But supposing she has another puncture?"

"Yes, I can see you mending it on a day like this."

"It's very kind of you," said Miss Deriot, with a puzzled smile.

"Don't thank the fool," said my sister "If I thought he'd be the slightest use to you, I'd send him; but he only wants an excuse to get out of going to church."

"Poor jade," said her husband. "I am a knight, a simple starlit knight, a Quixote of to-day. Your brutish instincts——"

"Carry on, Boy," said Daphne. I let in the clutch. "And come over this afternoon, Agatha, and we'll tell you all about everything."

"Yes, do," cried Jill.

"All right," said Miss Deriot. "So long."

Three minutes later I was berthing the car close to the lich-gate in the shade of sweet-smelling limes, that made a trembling screen of foliage within the churchyard wall.

As luck would have it, Will Noggin, once a groom in our service and now a trooper of the Dragoon Guards, was leaning lazily against the grey wall, taking his ease. As we drew abreast of him, he stood to attention and saluted, a pleased grin of recognition lighting his healthy face. We greeted him gladly.

"Glad to see you're all right, Will," said Jill.

"Thank you, miss."

"Aren't you going to church?" said Daphne.

"Not to-day, m'm. I'm on leave, and I've 'ad my share o' church parades i' the last four years, m'm."

We all laughed.

"Well, if you're not going," said I, "we want some one to keep eye on the car."

"I'll do it gladly, sir."

"Right oh! She's a pretty piece of goods isn't she?"

"She is that, sir," said Will, visibly impressed.

As I followed the others into the porch, I glanced back to see our sentinel walking about his charge, bending an appreciative gaze upon her points.

They were singing the *Venite*.

On the ledge of our old pew lay a note addressed to "Major Pleydell" in the Vicar's handwriting. When Berry had read it he passed it to Daphne, and I was able to read it over her shoulder.

DEAR MAJOR,

Sometimes in the old days you used to read the Lessons. I think we should all like it if you would do so to-day; but don't, if you don't want to.

Yours very sincerely,

JOHN BAGOT.

In a postscript the writer named the appointed passages of Holy Writ.

So soon as the first Psalm had started Berry stepped to the lectern, found his places and cast his eye over the text. Before the second Psalm was finished, he was once more in his place.

Doors and windows were open as wide as they could be set, and the little church was flooded with light and fresh warm air, that coaxed the edge from the chill of thick stone walls and pillars, and made the frozen pavements cool and refreshing. Mustiness was clean gone, swept from her frequent haunts by the sweet breath of Nature. The "dim, religious light" of Milton's ordering was this day displaced by Summer's honest smile, simpler maybe, but no less reverent. And, when the singing was stilled, you overheard the ceaseless sleepy murmur of that country choir of birds and beasts and insects that keeps its rare contented symphony for summer days in which you can find no fault.

My impious eye wandered affectionately over familiar friends —the old oak pews, almost chin-high, the Spanish organ, the reluctant gift of a proud galleon wrecked on the snarling coast ten miles away, the old "three-decker" with its dull crimson cushions and the fringed cloths that hung so stiffly. A shaft of sunlight beat full on an old black hatchment, making known the faded quarterings, while, underneath, a slender panel of brass, but two years old, showed that the teaching of its grim forbear had not been vain.

For so fair a morning, Bilberry village had done well. The church was two-thirds full, and, though there were many strange faces, it was pleasant here and there to recognize one we had known in the old days, and to learn from an involuntary smile that we had not been forgotten.

It was just after the beginning of the Second Lesson that we heard the engine start. There was no mistaking the purr of our Rolls-Royce. For a second the girls and Jonah and I stared at one another, panic-stricken. Then with one impulse we all started instinctively to our feet. As I left the pew I heard Daphne whisper, "Hsh! We can't all——" and she and Jonah and Jill sank back twittering. Berry's eyes met mine for an instant as I stepped into the aisle. They spoke volumes, but to his eternal credit his voice never faltered.

I almost ran to the porch, and I reached the lich-gate to see our beautiful car, piloted by a man in a grey hat, scudding up the straight white road, while in her wake tore a gesticulating trooper, shouting impotently, ridiculously out-distanced. Even as I watched, the car flashed round a bend and disappeared.

For a moment I stood still in the middle of the road, stupefied. Then I heard a horn sounded behind me, and I mechanically stepped to one side. Fifty yards away was the two-seater we had encountered on our way to church.

Frantically I signalled to the girl at the wheel. As I did so, a burst of music signified that the Second Lesson had come to an end.

"Whatever's the matter?" cried Miss Deriot, as she pulled up.

"Somebody's pinched the Rolls. Will you——"

"Of course. Get in. Which way did they go?"

"Straight ahead," said I, opening the door.

We were well under way before I had taken my seat. As we came to the bend I threw a glance over my shoulder, to see four figures that I knew standing without the lich-gate. They appeared to be arguing. As we turned the corner a stentorian voice yelled—

"The Bloodstock road, sir! I can see their blinkin' dust."

Perched on one of the lower branches of a wayside oak, Will Noggin was pointing a shaking finger in the direction he named.

*   *   *   *   *

We were less than three miles from Bloodstock when the off hind tyre burst. Miss Deriot brought the car to the side of the road and stopped in the shadow of an old barn.

"That," she said, "has just done it."

I opened the door and stepped down into the road.

"It means a delay when we least want it," said I ruefully.

"Worse. I've had one burst already, and I only brought one spare wheel."

I whistled.

"Then we are indeed done," said I. "I'm awfully sorry. Heaven knows how far you are from your home. This comes of helping a comparative stranger. Let it be a lesson to you."

My companion smiled.

"I don't mind for myself," she said, "but what about your car?"

I spread out my hands.

"Reasons dictates that I should foot-slog it to Bloodstock and try and get the police moving; but I can't leave you here."

"You can easily, but you're not going to. I don't want to sit here for the rest of the day." She pointed to the barn. "Help me to get her in here, and then we'll push off to Bloodstock together."

A hurried reconnaissance led to the discovery of a little farmhouse, and two minutes later I was making urgent representations to the owner of the barn. To our relief the latter proved sympathetic and obliging, and before we again took to the road the two-seater was safely under lock and key.

"And now," said Miss Deriot," how did it happen?"

"The theft? I can't imagine. We left that fool who yelled at us in charge. I suppose he left her to get a drink or something. This is only the fourth time we've had her out," I added gloomily.

"Oh, I say! Never mind. You're bound to get her again. Look at that meadow-sweet. Isn't it lovely? I wish I could paint. Can you?"

"I painted a key-cupboard once. It was hung, too. Outside the stillroom."

"Pity you didn't keep it up," said Miss Deriot. "It's a shame to waste talent like that. Isn't it just broiling? I should love a bathe now."

"I hope you don't wear stockings in the water," said I.

Miss Deriot glanced at her white ankles.

"Is that a reflection?" she demanded.

I shook my head.

"By no manner of means. But there's a place for everything, isn't there? I mean——"

We both laughed.

"That's better," said my companion. "I couldn't bear to see you so worried this beautiful morning."

"My dear," said I, you've a nice kind heart, and I thank you."

"Don't mention it," said Miss Deriot.

From the crown of her broad-brimmed hat to the soles of her buckskin shoes she was the pink of daintiness. Health was springing in her fresh cheeks, eagerness danced in her eyes, energy leapt from her carriage. Had she been haughty, you would have labelled her "Diana", and have done with it; but her eyes were gentle, and there was a tenderness about her small mouth that must have pardoned Actæon. A plain gold wrist-watch on a black silk strap was all her jewellery.

"We'd better strike across the next field," said Miss Deriot. "There's a path that'll bring us out opposite *The Thatcher*. It'll save us about five minutes."

"You might have been born here," said I.

"I was," said Agatha. She nodded towards a beech wood that stood a furlong away. "The trees hide the house. But we left when I was seven, and only came back to the County five years ago. And here's our field."

The five-barred gate was padlocked. I looked at my companion.

"Shall I get over, advance ten paces, and gaze into the middle distance? Or aren't you that sort?"

Miss Deriot flung back her head and laughed.

"I'd rather you gave me a leg up," she said.

With a hand on my shoulder and a foot in my hand, she was up and over in an instant. I vaulted after her.

"You know," I said, "we ought to perform, you and I. With a painter's ladder, a slack wire, and a little practice, we should do wonders. On non-matinée days I might even lift you with my teeth. That always goes well, and no one would know you were as light as a rose-leaf."

"Seven stone three in the bathroom," said Agatha. "Without stockings. Some rose-leaf."

We were going uphill. The meadow through which we were passing sloped to an oaken fence, stoutly constructed to save the cattle from a perilous fall. For on its farther side the ground fell away sheer, so that at this point a bluff formed one high wall of the sunken road for which we were making. *The Thatcher,* I remembered, stood immediately opposite to the rough grass-grown steps, hewn years ago for the convenience of such passengers as we. There was a little stile set in the fence, and as I swung myself over I glanced down past the edge of the bluff and into the road below.

In the little curved space that fronted the inn the Rolls was standing silent and unoccupied.

I must have exclaimed, for Agatha was over the stile in an instant, and asking me what was the matter. Then she saw, and the words died on her lips. Together we stood spell-bound.

The door of the inn was shut, and there was no one in sight.

My first impulse was to dart down the steps, beat upon the door of the tavern, and confront the thief. But valour yielded to discretion. The great thing was to recover the car. I had but a slip of a girl with me, the spot was a lonely one, and it was more than likely that the highwayman was not working alone. Besides, Agatha must not be involved in any violence.

I turned to my lady.

"You stay here. I'm going to take her and drive straight to the police station. I'll pick up some police and come back just as quickly as ever I can."

Miss Deriot shook her pretty head.

"I'm coming with you," she said. "Carry on."

"But, my dear——"

"I often wish I wasn't so obstinate." She spoke meditatively. "But we're all like that. Mules aren't in it with the Deriots," she added, with a dazzling smile.

"Neither, apparently, are cucumbers," said I, and with that

I began to descend the rough stairs, stepping as delicately as I could.

Half-way down I turned to look at my companion, and at that moment the step upon which I was standing gave way. The scrambling sounds which proclaimed my fall were followed by the rasping protest of yielding cloth, and I came to rest six feet from the road at the expense of a pre-War coat, which had caught the corner of one of the unplaned risers. All had been so still, that in that hollow place the noise could not have failed to attract the attention of any one who was within earshot, and I lay for a moment where I had fallen, straining my ears for the sound of footsteps or voices.

"Are you all right?" whispered a soft voice above me.

I turned my head and nodded. Miss Deriot, standing with clasped hands, heaved a sigh of relief and prepared to continue her descent.

Gingerly I stepped down into the sandy road and started to cross it a-tiptoe.

Facing towards Bloodstock, the car presented her off side to us.

With the utmost caution I proceeded to negotiate the two spare wheels and clamber into the driver's seat. As I sat down, Miss Deriot slipped in front of the bonnet and round to the near side. She was opening the high side-door and my foot was on the self-starter, when I heard the murmur of voices.

We were not a second too soon.

The moment I had started the engine there was a cry, followed by the clattering of heavy shoes upon cobbles, and as the car slid into the road a man in a grey hat came tearing out of the inn's courtyard, waving his arms and yelling like one possessed. Hard on his heels came pounding his supporters, three of them, all bellowing like bulls.

So much I saw for myself. Agatha, kneeling on the seat by my side, kept me informed of their movements till we swept out of sight.

"He's simply dancing. The one in the grey hat, I mean. Now he's shaking his fist at us. Oh, he's mad. He's thrown his hat on the ground. O-o-o, Boy, he's trying to kick one of the others. Oh, I wish you could see. . . ." The merry voice dissolved into peals of laughter.

Then the road curled, and Agatha turned left about and settled herself by my side.

"How did you know my Christian name?" I demanded.

"Your sister used it this morning. You see, I've forgotten your other, and I can't keep on saying 'you'. But I won't do it again."

"Please, Agatha."

"Deriot. One 'r'. I say, you've torn your coat properly."

"It feels as if it was in two pieces," said I.

"If it wasn't for the collar, it would be," said Agatha. "Never mind. Bare backs are still fashionable. And what's a torn coat, when you've got the car again?"

"You're right," I agreed. "You'd hardly believe it," I added, "but I can tell from the feel of her that some stranger's been driving."

"I can believe it. After all, a car's just like a horse."

As she spoke, we sped into the market square of Bloodstock. The police station stood in Love Lane, a couple of streets away.

Here a disappointment was in store. The sole representative of the Law was a station sergeant in his shirt-sleeves and a state of profuse perspiration. Between his lips was a penholder, and he held a telephone receiver to his left ear. In an adjoining room the bell of another telephone was ringing violently in long regular spasms, while, somewhere quite close, a dog was giving ceaseless vent to those short sharp barks which denote impatience of detention.

A sudden elevation of the sergeant's eyegrows invited me to state my business, but before I had spoken two sentences he shifted the penholder from his mouth and shook his head.

" 'Fraid I can't 'elp you at the moment, sir. That's the third car what's been stole in this distric' this mornin'. There's a 'ole gang of 'em about. Every one excep' me's out after 'em now. 'Eaven knows when they'll come in. An' there's that other telephone goin' like mad, an' the Chief Constable's lef' his bull-dawg tied up there, an' 'e won't let me within six foot of it." He turned to blare into the mouthpiece. " 'Ullo! 'Oo *are* you? 'Oo *are* you? Wot! Oh, I can't bear it. 'Ere, for 'Eaven's sake, 'old the line." He set down the receiver, shook the sweat out of his eyes, and sank on to a stool. "Another blinkin' car gone," he said hoarsely. "I dunno wot's the matter with the world. I wish I was back in France."

* * * * *

Love Lane was a narrow street, so I did not attempt to turn the car, but drove on and presently out of the town by back streets on to the Bilberry road.

It would have been better if I had telephoned to White Ladies before leaving Bloodstock, to announce my recovery of the car; but I was expecting to be back there so soon that it seemed unnecessary.

Indeed, it was only when we were once more under way that I thought of the colt and the embrocation, to say nothing of my lady's two-seater, now standing helpless in the gloom of the wayside barn.

"I tell you what," said I. "We'll drive to the barn and pick up the lotion, and then I'll take you home. Then I can run your chauffeur back to the barn with a spare cover, drop him there, and push off to White Ladies."

"I can improve on that," said Agatha, with a glance at her wrist. "It'll be past one by the time we get home, so you must stay to lunch. You can telephone to White Ladies from there. And afterwards I'll go back with you—I was to come over this afternoon, wasn't I?—and we can drop the chauffeur at the barn on the way. And he can come for me in the evening."

Agatha was living at Broadacre, a fine old place on the edge of the forest itself, and thither we came without incident, just as an old-fashioned gong was summoning the household to meat.

Admiral and Mrs. Deriot were kindness itself. First I was given a long, cold, grateful drink. Then the old sailor led me to his own chamber and ministered personally to my wants. My coat was given to a maid to be roughly stitched, and when I appeared at luncheon it was in a jacket belonging to my host. Our story was told and retold, the lawlessness of the year of Grace 1919 was bewailed, and a violent denunciation of motor-thieves was succeeded by a bitter proscription of the County Police.

In the midst of my entertainment I remembered that I had not telephoned to White Ladies, but the servant sent to make the connection was informed by the Exchange that the line was out of order.

"I expect it's fused," said I. "With Berry at one end and that station sergeant at the other, the strain must have been fearful."

* * * * *

It was half-past two before we were once more in the car. On the back seat sat the Deriot's chauffeur, holding a spare wheel between his knees.

It did not take us long to reach the barn, and, so soon as we had once more unearthed the farmer, authorized him to suffer the chauffeur to remove the two-seater, and discharged our debt for "accommodation", I turned the Rolls round and headed for White Ladies.

"She's certainly a beautiful car," said Agatha, as the Rolls sailed up a treacherously steep gradient on top. "It's like being in a lift."

"And, but for you, we might never have seen her again. Shall I give you a stamp album, or would you like to drive?"

"D'you really mean that?" said Miss Deriot.

I shot her a glance. There was no mistaking the eagerness of her parted lips and the sparkle of her gay brown eyes. By way of replying I brought the car to a standstill. A moment later we had changed places.

"It's awfully kind of you," said Agatha delightedly, as she let in the clutch. "I've always wanted to drive a Rolls. I hope I shan't hurt her."

"You'll do her good," said I. "I watched you in the two-seater. You've got beautiful hands."

"Thank you, Boy."

"Now you shall have a stamp album as well. Go carefully here. There used to be a wasps' nest in that bank, but it's closed now, same as the German banks. What a war!"

"But I don't collect stamps."

"Then she shall have a dog. What about a Sealyham to sleep on your bed and bite the postman?"

"I'd love one," said Agatha.

"And you'll sit up in bed in the morning, with your hair all about your eyes, and smile at him, and he'll growl back at you—I can just see you."

"Thanks awfully. But you're wrong about my hair."

"Is it never unruly?"

"Only by day. I wish to goodness I could wear it down."

"So do I. Then we could all sit on it when the grass was wet. At the moment there's a particularly beautiful tress caressing your left shoulder. And I think you ought to know that the wind is kissing it quite openly. It's all very embarrassing. I hope I shan't catch it," I added cheerfully.

Miss Deriot made a supreme effort to look severe.

"If you do," she said uncertainly, "I shall drive straight into the horse-pond."

" 'Sh!" said I reprovingly. "You oughtn't to jest about such things. You might catch it yourself. Easily." Here we passed the horse-pond. "You know you'll never be able to look fierce so long as you have that dimple. You'll have to fill it up or something. I suppose it's full of dew every morning now."

Without a word Agatha slowed down, turned up a by-road, and stopped. Then she proceeded to back the car.

"What on earth is she doing?" said I.

She turned a glowing face to mine.

"Going back to the horse-pond," she flashed.

I laid a hand on her arm and she stopped.

"My dear, if you must have a bath, you shall have one directly you get to White Ladies. I'll turn on the water for you. But let me beg of you——"

"If I go on, will you promise to behave?"

"Faithfully."

"And fold your arms and sit like a groom all the way?"

"I suppose you couldn't make it a footman. Then I could stand on the petrol tank. However, as it's your birthday——"

I folded my arms with a sigh. Instantly Agatha leaned towards me with a dazzling smile.

"Good Boy," she said in a caressing tone. "Now he shall have a stamp album."

"But I don't collect stamps."

The smile deepened. But for her red mouth, her little white teeth would have been the prettiest things in the world.

"Well, I'd thought of a stamp album," she said slowly. "However, as it's your birthday——"

A minute later we were back in the main road.

* * * * *

By my direction Miss Deriot drove straight to the stables, and left the car standing in the middle of the yard.

As we walked round to the front of the house, "We won't tell the others that we've found her just yet," said I. "We'll hear what they've got to say first."

"Perhaps they're all out looking for her," said Agatha.

"Not all. Daphne's sure to be here somewhere."

As I spoke we rounded a clump of laurels to see the lady in question comfortably ensconced in a deck-chair upon the lawn. By her side was Jill, seated upon a cushion, one little foot tucked under her, nursing the other's instep with her slim, brown hand. On a rug at her feet lay Jonah, his chin propped between his two palms and a pipe in his mouth.

All three were gazing contentedly across the grass to where the drive swept wide to the foot of the broad grey steps. *There stood a handsome Rolls-Royce, the facsimile of the one from which we had just alighted.*

With a great gasp Agatha stopped dead, and I recoiled as from a spectre. Instinctively we clasped one another.

"It's all right," I whispered. "I've seen it too. It'll go away in a moment. Shows what imagination will do."

"But—but it's real!" cried Agatha.

"Real enough, my lady," said Jonah's voice. He seemed to be speaking from a great distance. "And I'll bet you never expected to see her again so soon," he added, looking at me with a smile.

"To tell you the truth," said I, "we didn't."

As in a dream I watched a dazed and stammering Agatha made welcome and set in a chair by my sister's side. Somebody—Jill, I fancy—led me to the rug and persuaded me to sit down. Mechanically I started to fumble for a cigarette. Then I heard Jonah talking, and I came to my senses.

"We thought you'd be surprised," he was saying, "but I didn't think it'd take you like this. After all, there's nothing uncanny about it."

"But I don't understand——"

"Listen. Will Noggin was sitting in the car when he heard a crash, and there was this fellow lying in the middle of the road, about fifty yards away, with a push-bike beside him. Naturally Will jumped out and ran to his help. The man seemed to be having a fit, and Will was just loosening his collar, when he heard the engine start and saw the Rolls moving. He left the chap in the road and ran like mad, but he was too late. Nobody ever saw the fellow with the push-bike again. Of course he was one of the gang, and his fall was a put-up job to get Will out of the way. Pretty smart—what?

"Well, you hadn't been gone five minutes when Fitch arrived on his motor-bike. He'd come to bring us a can of petrol, for after we'd left he remembered the tank was almost empty.

"That gave me a bit of hope. If they stuck to the main road you were pretty well bound to catch them, for Fitch swore they'd never get five miles. But, of course, they might turn off. So I thought the rest of us had better follow and search the by-roads for all we were worth. So I sat on Fitch's carrier with the can under one arm, and Daphne commandered the curate's push-bike and sent Berry after us."

"Isn't he back yet?" said I looking round.

"Not yet," said Jonah, with a grin.

"And doesn't he know she's found?"

"That pleasure is still awaiting him. Well, Fitch was right. We left the Bloodstock road for the second time at Dew Thicket, and at the foot of the hill there she was, dry as a bone, but as right as rain."

"Abandoned?"

"Apparently. Anyway, there was no one in sight. I sent Fitch after you and drove her home. Fitch had a burst directly he'd left me, and had to walk back to Bilberry."

"Is that all?" said I.

"Well, it's enough, isn't it?"

"Not nearly," said I, rising to my feet. "Kindly accompany me to the stables."

"What d'you mean, Boy?" cried Jill.

" 'Sh!" said I. "Come and see."

In silence I led the way, Agatha treading solemnly by my side. As we turned under the archway that led to the stable-yard—

"You see," I said carelessly, "we, too, have met with some success."

The Rolls was standing where I had left her, waiting to be backed into the garage.

My sister gave a cry and caught at Jonah's arm. Jonah started violently and smothered an exclamation. Jill put one hand to her eyes, as if to brush away a vision.

There was a long silence.

At length I turned to Jonah.

"I fear that you were hasty, brother. A moment's reflection will show you that you and Fitch have spoiled some poor car-owner's day. Let me suggest that you return your ill-gotten gains to the foot of the hill beyond Dew Thicket without delay. As a matter of fact, I know the police are very concerned about this theft. It was the fourth in this district this morning."

Fitch came forward, touching his hat.

"It's a mistake anybody might make, sir. They're as like as two pins." He pointed to the car. "She's the spit of ours, she is."

"Don't be silly," said I. "I admit they're exactly alike, but that's ours."

Fitch shook his head.

"Different chassis number, sir, to say nothing of the number-plates."

I stared at him. Then—

"Nonsense," I said sturdily.

"It's a fact, sir. The one in the front's ours. I'm afraid you've stole somebody else's car."

* * * * *

We had returned to the front of the house and were wondering what to do, when our attention was attracted by a sudden outburst of cries and the noise of a car's tyres tearing at the road. This lay but a hundred odd yards away on the farther side of the brown stream by which the lawn was edged. For the length of a cricket pitch the hedgerow bounding the highway was visible from where we stood, and as this was not more than four feet high, we were able to observe a scene which was clearly but the prologue to a drama in which we were presently to appear.

Under the explosive directions of a man in a grey hat, who was standing upright and holding on to the wind-screen, frantic efforts were being made to turn what seemed to be a small touring car. Even as we looked, a savage gesture in our direction suggested that our friend was identifying the Rolls by our side as stolen property for the benefit of four individuals who crouched timorously behind him. To my consternation I observed that these were no less than an inspector and three constables of the County Police.

The next minute the car had been turned round and was being driven rapidly back to our lodge-gates.

"Leave them to me," said Jonah quietly. "Go and sit down on the lawn, all of you. I'll fix them."

* * * * *

"That's the fellow," said Grey Hat, in a shaking voice, "and that's his accomplice." He pointed a fat hand at myself and Agatha in turn.

"I beg your pardon," said Jonah. Grey Hat turned and looked him up and down. "Were you wanting anything? I mean, I live here."

"I don't know who you are," came the reply. "But that's my car, and those are the people who stole it."

"One thing at a time. My name's Mansel."

"I'm the Chief Constable of the County."

"Good. Now, about the car. I was under the impression that it was mine."

"Don't try and bluff me, sir," roared the other. "You know perfectly well that that car was stolen from the outskirts of Bloodstock only a few hours ago. You're a receiver, sir, a common——" He checked himself with an effort. "Inspector!" The officer addressed came forward and saluted. "Caution the three of them."

"Hadn't you better identify your property first?" said Jonah. "I mean, I don't want to interfere, but if it's a question of our arrest——"

The inspector hesitated, and the Chief Constable's face took on a darker shade of red. He was a coarse-looking man, generously designed and expensively over-dressed. For a moment I thought he was going to strike Jonah. Then he caught a heavy underlip in his teeth, turned on his heel, and strode to the Rolls-Royce.

He cast a proprietor's eye over her points. Then he stepped behind her as though to come to her other side. The next second he was back and shaking his fist in Jonah's face.

"So you've had the infernal audacity to alter the number-plates, have you?" he yelled. "Thought to bluff me, I suppose. You impudent——"

"One moment," said Jonah steadily. "Without looking at the dash, tell me your chassis number. Your chauffeur should know it."

"One double seven eight," came parrot-wise from the lips of the gentleman referred to.

"Thank you," said Jonah.

Grey Hat almost ran to the Rolls, tore open the bonnet, and stared at the dash—stared. . . .

We waited in a silence so charged with expectancy as to be almost unbearable.

At last the Chief Constable straightened his back. His eyes were bulging and his face redder than ever. Twice he essayed to speak without success. Then—

"I said it was my car," said Jonah placidly.

For a moment Grey Hat stood glaring at him. Then, muttering something about "a mistake", he started to lurch towards the police car. As the officers turned shamefacedly to follow their chief, Jonah's parade voice rang out.

"Stop!" At the word of command, master and men alike stood where they were. "My friends and I have been openly accused of felony and threatened with arrest."

The Chief Constable swallowed before replying.

"I was mistaken," he said quickly. "I—I apologize."

"You mean to say you believed that to be your car?"

"I did."

"Why?"

"It's exactly like it."

"There must be some difference."

"There's no difference at all. If mine were here, I'd defy you to tell them apart."

"Do you seriously suggest that I shouldn't know my own car?"

"I do."

"And that such a mistake on my part would be excusable?"

"Certainly."

"Thank you," said Jonah. "That excusable mistake was made this morning. My car was stolen and sought for. Your car was found. If you will accompany me to the stables, I shall be happy to restore it to you at once."

Grey Hat started forward, his face transfigured with excitement and relief.

"You mean to say——" he began.

"Come sir," said Jonah icily. "I feel sure that the ladies will excuse your withdrawal."

* * * * *

It was half an hour later, just when we were finishing tea, that a cry from Jill made us all turn to follow her gaze down the curling drive.

Twenty paces away was Berry, plodding slowly in our direction, wheeling a tired-looking bicycle. His clothes were thick with dust, his collar was like a piece of wet rag, and on his face there was a look of utter and profound resignation.

As we started to our feet—

"Don't touch me," he said. "I'm leading in the Marathon race. The conditions are fearful. Competitors are required not only to walk, but at the same time to propel a bicycle, the hind tyre of which must be deflated. You're only allowed five falls, and I've used four of them." With a final effort he reached the edge of the lawn and laid the bicycle gently on its side. " 'How we brought the good news from Aix to Ghent,' " he continued. "Yes, I see the car, but I'm not interested. During the last five hours my life has been so crowded with incident that there is no room for anything else. Isn't there a cycling club about here I can join? I've always fancied a grey sweater."

"Did I hear you say that you had fallen, brother?" said I.

"You did. Four times were these noble limbs prostrated in the dust. The first time was when the handle-bars came off. Oh, it's a beautiful machine." Solemnly he waited for the laughter to subside. "But she doesn't turn easily. If my blood counts, there are at least three corners in the County that are for ever England. And now will somebody fetch the Vicar? I shan't last long. And some drinks." He stretched himself upon the grass. "Several drinks. All together in a large vessel."

Jill fled, weak with laughter, to execute his commands. Berry proceeded to remove his collar and tie.

"I can't think," he said suddenly, "why they call them safety bicycles. I suppose it's because they strike only on the box." He turned to Daphne. "Since I left you this morning, woman, I have walked with Death. Oh, more than once. Of course I've walked without him, too. Miles and miles." He groaned. "I never knew there was so much road."

"Didn't you do any riding?" said Jonah. "I know they're called push-bikes, but that's misleading. Lots of people ride them. That's what the saddle's for."

"Foul drain," said my brother-in-law, "your venomous bile pollutes the crystal flood of my narration. Did I ride? That was the undoing of the sage. When he recovered consciousness for the second time, it was to discover that the chain was missing and that the back tyre was windless. In my endeavours to find the chain I lost myself. That reminds me. I must put an advertisement in *The Times* to the effect that any one returning a bicycle-chain to White Ladies will be assaulted. I have no desire to be reminded of to-day. If anybody had told me you could cover about fifty miles of open road in England without meeting anything but road-hogs, who not only failed to stop when I hailed them, but choked and blinded me with their filthy dust, I should have prayed for his soul. And not a pub open!"

He stopped to watch with a glistening eye the approach of Jill, bearing a tankard in one hand and a large jug of some beverage in the other.

"What is it?" he said.

"Shandy-gaff."

"Heaven will reward you, darling, as I shan't." He took a long draught. "And yet I don't know. I've got an old pair of riding-breeches I don't want, if they're any use to you."

There was a shriek from Agatha and Jill.

"Is anybody going to church?" said Daphne, consulting her wrist-watch.

Berry choked.

Gravely I regarded him.

"Run along and change," said I. "And you can return the curate his bicycle at the same time. Besides, a walk'll do you good."

"Don't tempt me," he replied. "Two hours ago I registered a vow. I shall drink no water till it is accomplished."

"Let's hear it," said I.

"To offer no violence to a fool for six months," said Berry, refilling his tankard. "By the way, you'll have to be very careful when you take off my boots. They're very full of foot this evening." He sank back and closed his eyes. "You know I never look at the almanac, but before I was up this morning I knew that this was a blue-letter day."

"How?" said his wife.

"I left a stud within the bath, and heard Jonah find it." He spread out a dramatic arm.

"And he thereon did only sit,
So blind he couldn't see,
And then the fat-head yelled and swore,
Not at himself, but me."

CHAPTER II

How Daphne Wrote for Assistance, and Mr. Holly was Outbid

"Blow this out for me, Boy, there's a dear."

The sun was streaming into the library, in a cage upon the broad hearth there was a blazing log fire, and the appointment of the breakfast-table was good to look upon.

So also was Jill.

Installed behind the cups and silver, my cousin made a sweet picture. Grave eyes set wide in a smiling face, a pile of golden hair crowning her pretty head, the slenderest throat, from which the collar of a green silk coat fell gracefully on either side—so much a cunning painter might have charmed faithfully on to canvas.

But the little air of importance, of dignity fresh-gathered that sat so naïvely upon her brow—this was a thing nor brush nor pencil could capture, but only a man's eye writing upon a grateful heart.

It was but three days since Daphne had left White Ladies for London, and grey-eyed Jill reigned in her stead. Berry had accompanied his wife, but Jonah and I had stayed in the country with Jill, lest we should lose a note of that echo of summer which good St. Luke had this year piped so lustily.

But yesterday the strains had faltered and died. A sour east wind had risen, that set the trees shivering, and whipped the golden leaves from their galleries, to send them scudding up the cold grey roads. Worse still, by noon the sky was big with snow, so that, before the post office was closed, a telegram had fled to London warning my sister to expect us to arrive by car the following afternoon.

Jill renewed her appeal.

Above the little spirit lamp which she was holding hovered a tiny flame, seemingly so sensitive that a rough word would quench it for ever. When I had kissed my cousin, I blew steadily and fiercely from the south-west. Instantly a large tongue of fire flared half-way to where Jonah was eating his porridge and knitting his brows over *The Times*.

Jill's hand began to shake.

"You wicked child," said I. "You knew——"

"Oh, Boy, but it's so silly. We had to leave it for you. Jonah nearly burst himself just now, trying."

"Thing's bewitched," said Jonah calmly. "The more air you give it, the fiercer it burns. I'd sooner try to blow out a hurricane lamp."

"Nonsense," said I, taking a deep breath.

At the end of the round—

"Yes," said Jonah. "Do you mind blowing the other way next time? It's not my face I'm worrying about, but this is the only copy of *The Times* in the house."

Jill was helpless with laughter, so I took the lamp away from her and advanced to the fireplace.

"I'll fix the swine," I said savagely.

Two minutes later, with a blast that almost blew the lamp out of my hand, the flame was extinguished in a flurry that would have done credit to a whale. As I straightened my back—

"Well done, Boy," said Jill. "There's a letter for you from Berry. Do see what he says. Then I'll read you Daphne's."

"Read hers first," said I. "Strange as it may seem, I entered this room to eat."

"Right oh!" And in her fresh little voice my cousin began to read.

Jill Darling,

The sooner you all come up the better. Everything's ready and Berry's more than I can manage alone. His shoulder was aching last night, but when I wanted to rub him he said he was a kind of Aladdin's lamp, and wouldn't be responsible if I did. "Supposing a genie appeared and formed fours, or the slop-pail rolled aside, disclosing a flight of steps." Result, to-day in Bond Street he turned suddenly to look at a passing car, and had a seizure. He just gave a yell as if he'd been shot, and then stood stock still with his head all on one side. Of course I was horrified, but he said he was quite all right, and explained that it was muscular rheumatism. I stopped a taxi and tried to make him get in, for people were beginning to look. Do you think he would? Not a bit of it. Stood there and said it was a judgment, and that he must stay where he was till it had passed. "That may not be for years. They'll put railings round me after a bit, and people will meet at me instead of the Tube. You will be responsible for my meals, some of which you will cook on the spot. I'll have a light lunch to-day about 1300 hours." One or two people stopped, and I got into a taxi just as a man asked him if he was ill. "Brother," said the fool, "my blood tests are more than satisfactory. A malignant Fate, however——" When I asked him if he was coming he told the man I was taunting him, so I just drove home. The Willoughbys brought him back in their car quarter of an hour later. Madge said she'd never laughed so much in her life, but I can't bear it alone. Mrs. Mason is at last reconciled to the idea of an electric cooker, and your new curtains look sweet. Come along. Love to you all.

Daphne.

"Berry's version should be engaging," said Jonah. "Slip along with that porridge."

"Don't hustle me. Gladstone used to masticate every mouthful he took seven million times before swallowing it. That's why he couldn't tell a lie. Or am I thinking of Lincoln?"

The hostility with which my cousins received the historical allusion was so marked that it seemed only prudent to open my brother-in-law's letter without further delay.

I did so and read the contents aloud.

DEAR BROTHER,

Your constant derision of human suffering has satisfied me that the facts I am about to relate will afford you the utmost gratification. Natheless I consider that for form's sake my wife's brother should know that I am in failing health. This morning, whilst faring forth, as is my wont (pronounced "wunt"), upon a mission of charity, I was seized with an agony in the neck and Old Bond Street just opposite the drinking-fountain. Believing it to be appendicitis, I demanded a chirurgeon, but nobody could spell the word. The slightest movement, however, spelt anguish without a mistake. My scruff was in the grip of Torment. Observing that I was helpless, the woman, my wife, summoned a hackney carriage and drove off, taunting and jeering at her spouse. By this time my screams had attracted the attention of a few passers-by. Some stood apparently egg-bound, others hurried away, doubtless to procure assistance. One fool asked me if I was ill. I told him that I had been dead for some days, and asked him if he knew of a good florist, as I wanted them to send no flowers. Had it not been for Madge Willoughby, I should have been there now.

Organized bodies of navvies are slowly but surely ruining the streets. No efforts are made to stop them, and the police seem powerless to interfere.

There is no room in London. I never remember when there was. But don't you come. The air is the purer for your absence, and your silk hats seem to fit me better than my own. My love for Jill is only exceeded by my hatred of you and my contempt for Jonah. I have much more to say, but I have, thank Heaven, something better to do than to communicate with a debauched connection, whose pleasure has ever been my pain, and from whom I have learned more vicious ways than I can remember. For I am by nature a little child. Just before and after rain you may still see traces of the halo which I bought at Eastbourne in '94. My gorge is rising, so I must write no more.

BERRY.

"What's muscular rheumatism?" said Jill, gurgling with laughter.

"Your muscles get stiff," said Jonah, "and you get stuck. Hurts like anything. I've had it."

"Now you know," said I, selecting a sausage. "Will you be ready by half-past eleven (winter time) or must we lunch here?"

"I'm ready now," said Jill. "But you and Jonah said it was indecent to start earlier."

"So it is. We shall get to Pistol comfortably in an hour and a half, and if we start again at half-past two, we shall be in London for tea."

Jonah rose and limped to the window.

"I'll tell you one thing," he said. "It's going to be a devilish cold run."

* * * * *

Jonah was right.

We sat all three upon the front seat, but even so we were hard put to it to keep warm. The prospect of a hot lunch at Pistol was pleasant indeed. Jonah was driving, and the Rolls slid through the country like a great grey bird, sailing and swooping and swerving so gracefully that it was difficult to believe the tale which the speedometer told. Yet this was true enough, for it was not a quarter to one when we swept round the last corner and into the long straight reach of tarmac, at the top of which lay the village we sought.

Pistol is embedded in a high moor, snug and warm, for all its eminence. The moor itself is girt with waving woods that stretch and toss for miles, making a deep sloping sash of foliage which Autumn will dye with such grave glory that the late loss of Summer and her pretty ways seems easier to bear. Orange and purple, copper and gold, russet and crimson—these in a hundred tones tremble and glow in one giant harmony, out of which, at the release of sun, come swelling chords so deep and rich and vivid that the sweet air is quick with stifled music and every passing breeze charged to the full with silent melody.

We had left this girdle of woodland behind us and were within half a mile of the village, when some activity about the gates of a private house attracted our attention. A little knot of men stood arguing in the roadway, three cars and an old fly were berthed close to the hedge, while a good-looking landau was waiting for a furniture van to emerge from the drive.

The next moment we were near enough to learn from a large poster that "the entire contents of Cranmer Place were to be sold by auction" this day, "including a quantity of valuable antique furniture," and with one accord Jill and I called upon Jonah to stop.

"What for?" said the latter, as he brought the car to a standstill. "Don't say you want to go and watch the rector's wife bidding against her conscience and the draper for a what-not."

"Such," said I, "is our intention." I hoisted myself to my feet and, opening the door, descended stiffly into the road. As I helped Jill to follow me, "You push on to *Highlands*," I added, "and order the lunch. We'll only stay a minute or two."

"And you never know," said Jill, "we might see something priceless."

Jonah shook his head.

"Depend upon it," he said, "the oleographs have gone to Christie's, same as the fumed oak. Only the dud stuff's left. However, have it your own way." With a sigh, he let in the clutch. "If you're not there by a quarter past one, I shall begin."

Jill slid an arm through mine, which she squeezed excitedly.

"I'm sure we shall find something, Boy. I just feel it. It always happens like this. You see, it isn't as if we were looking for a sale. We've just run right into one. And last night I dreamed about cretonnes."

"That settles it," said I, as the Rolls glided out of our way and we started to cross the road. "All the same, Jonah's probably right. But I love a sale. I'm afraid it's curiosity more than anything."

Catalogues were handed us at the front door, and we passed into a fine square hall, where a dresser and a large gate-table, each conspicuously labelled, declared that the late occupant was a man of taste.

"Two very fine pieces, sir," said a voice. "Coming up this afternoon." I turned to see a short stout man in a 1907 bowler and two overcoats, which he wore open, regarding the furniture with an appraising look. With difficulty he extracted a card from an inside pocket. "If you're thinkin' of buyin' anythin', Major, that's me card, an' I'll be very 'appy to ac' for you."

"Thanks, I don't think——"

"All right, Major, all right. Only if you should, I'm always about," he added hastily, turning away in response to cry which had risen for "Mr. 'Olly". "Comin', comin'!" he cried, making for what I took to be the drawing room.

I slipped his card into my pocket and we passed on.

The tallboy chest was standing alone in its dignity at the top of the broad staircase.

The moment I saw it I knew it was good stuff. And Jill gave a little cry and began to chatter, till I laid my hand on her arm with a warning pressure.

"Hush," I said quickly, "don't give it away. Of course they all know it's good, but we needn't seem over-anxious. Try and look as if you thought it might do for the harness-room if it was enamelled."

"O-o-oh, Boy."

Such chests may be handsome and—rarely—elegant, but this was dainty. Standing upon short cabriole legs, it was small, but of exquisite proportions, and had been built, I judged, in the reign of Queen Anne. The walnut which had gone to its making was picked wood, and its drawers were faced with oyster-shell and inlaid with box. Their handles were perfect, and, indeed, the whole chest was untouched and without blemish, shining with that clean lustre which only wax and constant elbow-grease can bring about.

When I had examined the piece as carefully as I dared, I winked at Jill and descended into the hall.

Mr. Holly was awaiting us.

Casually I addressed him.

"There's a tallboy at the top of the stairs, labelled 207. I'm not crazy about it, but it's about the right size for a recess in my bedroom. If you like to buy that for me on a five per cent. basis——"

"Certainly, Major." He wrote in a fat notebook. "Lot 207. An' ow' 'igh will you go?"

I hesitated.

"I'll go up to a hundred pounds. But the cheaper you get it, the better for you. Understand?"

"I'm there, Major. Will you be coming back?"

"No. But there's my card. You can telegraph to that address this evening, and I'll send you a cheque."

"Very good, sir."

A minute later we were walking along the road towards *Highlands* and, while Jill was talking excitedly, I was considering my own recklessness.

As we entered the grounds—

"Don't say anything about it," I said. "Let it be a surprise."

* * * * *

The first person I saw, as I entered the lounge of the hotel, was Berry.

"Do you mind not asking me why I'm here?" he said languidly. "I've just finished telling Jonah, and repetition always wearied me."

"Your movements have never interested me," said I. "All the same, I thought you were in the grip of Torment."

"I was and shall be. For the nonce——" He turned to a tall dark girl who was leaning against the chimney-piece, watching us curiously. "Let me introduce my brother-in-law. Carefully kept from me before marriage and by me ever since. Both the ablative case, I believe, but what a difference? So rich is the English tongue."

The girl threw back her head and laughed. I observed that she had nice teeth.

"Name of Childe," she said in a sweet voice. "After all, we can't expect him to remember everything. Wasn't my brother in your regiment?"

"I knew I'd seen you somewhere," said I. "The last time you were on a towel, leaning against a bottle of hairwash. That was in Flanders in 1916."

"That," said Berry, "will do. Miss Childe and I came here to lunch, not to listen to maudlin memories of the Great War. Did I ever tell you that a Spaniard once compared me to that elusive bloom to be found only upon the ungathered apricot?"

"How much did you lend him?" said I.

"Perhaps he knew more about ferns," said Miss Childe.

"Blind from birth, I suppose," said Jonah's voice.

My brother-in-law rose to his feet and looked about him with the expression of one who has detected an offensive odour.

"He was a man of singular insight and fine feeling," he said. "At the time of his outburst I was giving evidence against him for cruelty to a bullock. And now, for goodness' sake, somebody collect Jill and let's have some lunch."

* * * * *

"As a matter of fact," said Miss Childe, "I've come down to get some butter and eggs. They're usually sent, but the housekeeper's ill, and, as I was going spare, father suggested I should run down and pick them up."

Her voice sounded as if she was speaking from afar, and I knew that I must call up all my reserves of will-power if I was to remain awake.

"But Berry's with you, isn't he?"

"Yes, Your sister came to lunch yesterday and happened to mention that he wanted to go to Pistol to-day, so I offered him a lift. He's much nicer than any chauffeur."

"But whatever did he want to come to Pistol for?"

"Ah." From a great distance I watched Miss Childe's brown eyes take on a look of mischief that seemed at home in its bright setting. "He wouldn't tell you and he didn't tell Captain Mansel the truth, so I shan't give him away." She looked at a tiny wrist-watch. "And now I must be going. We want to start back at half-past three, and I've twenty-five miles to do before then."

"May I come with you?"

"Certainly. But——"

I stepped to where Jill was scribbling a note.

"We needn't start before half-past three," I said. "Will you wait for me?"

She nodded abstractedly.

Jonah was dozing over a cigarette. Berry had disappeared.

Three minutes later I was sitting in a comfortable coupé, which Miss Childe was driving at an unlawful speed in the direction of Colt.

"You drive a lot, don't you?" flashed my companion.

"A good deal."

"Then I expect you hate being driven by a stranger?"

"Not at all. Sometimes, of course——" I waited for us to emerge from between two motor-lorries and a traction-engine. As we were doing over forty-five, the pause was but momentary. "I mean——"

"That you're being frightened to death?"

"Not to death. I've still got some feeling in my right arm." We dropped down one of the steepest hills I have ever seen, with two bends in it, at an increased speed. "You keep your guardian angel pretty busy, don't you?"

A suspicion of a smile played for a second about my lady's lips.

"The only thing I'm really frightened of is a hansom cab," she affirmed.

"Try and imagine that there are half a dozen round the next

corner, will you?"

The smile deepened.

"Is your heart all right?" she demanded.

"It was when we started."

"But I know this road backwards."

"You needn't tell me that," said I. "We should have been killed long ago if you didn't. Seriously, I don't want to abuse your hospitality, but we're going to have kidneys for breakfast to-morrow, and I should be sorry to miss them."

"Are you fond of kidneys?"

"Passionately. I used to go out and gather them as a child. In the morning and the meadows. Or were we talking of haddock?"

Miss Childe hesitated before replying.

"I used to, too. But I was always afraid of their being toad-stools. They're poisonous, aren't they?"

"Deadly. By the way, there are six hansoms full of toadstools at the cross-roads which I observe we are approaching."

"I don't believe you."

I was wrong. But there was a waggon full of logs and a limousine full of children, which were rather worse.

We proceeded amid faint cries of indignation.

"What do you do," said I, "when you come to a level-crossing with the gates shut?"

"I don't," said Miss Childe.

I was still working this out, when my companion slowed down and brought the car to a standstill in front of a high white gate bearing the legend "Private", and keeping a thin brown road that ran for a little way between fair meadows before plunging into a swaying beechwood.

"Anything the matter?" I asked.

Miss Childe laid a hand on my arm.

"Be an angel," she said in a caressing voice.

"Certainly," said I. "With or without wings?"

"And open the gate, so that——"

"I know," I cried, "I know. Don't tell me. 'So that the auto-mobile may pass unobstructed between the gate-posts.' Am I right?"

"How on earth did you know?"

"Instinct." I opened the door and stepped backwards into the road. "I'm always like this before eating kidneys," I added.

As I re-entered the car—

"Now we can let her out," said Miss Childe contentedly. "It's such a relief to feel there's no speed limit," she added, with a ravishing smile.

As soon as I could trust my voice—

"I shouldn't think your chauffeurs live very long, do they?"

"On the contrary, they grow old in our service."

"I can believe you," said I heartily. "I myself have aged considerably since we left *Highlands.*"

By this time we had flung through and out of the beechwood, and the car was storming past stretches of gleaming bracken, all red and gold and stuck with spreading oak trees, that stood sometimes alone, sometimes in groups of two or three together, and made you think of staring cattle standing knee-deep in a golden flood.

The car tore on.

"We're coming to where I used to gather the mushrooms," my companion announced.

"Barefoot?"

"Sometimes."

"Because of the dew?"

She nodded.

I sighed. Then—

"Up to now I've been feeling like a large brandy and a small soda," I said. "Now I feel like a sonnet. What is your name, and who gave you that name?"

"I'm sure that's not necessary. I've seen a sonnet 'To a lady upon her birthday'."

"As you please. Shall I post it to you or pin it to a tree in Battersea Park?"

Miss Childe nodded her head in the direction in which we were going.

"That," she said, "is the house."

At the end of a long avenue of elms I could see the bold flash of windows which the afternoon sun had set afire, and a moment later we swept by the front of an old red mansion and round into a paved court that lay on its farther side.

Here was a door open, and in front of this my companion brought the car to a standstill.

I handed her out. She rang the bell and entered. I followed her in.

"Like to look round the house?" said Miss Childe. "We've given up showing it since the Suffragettes, but if you could give me a reference——"

"Messrs. Salmon and Gluckstein," said I, "are my solicitors."

My lady pointed to a door at the end of the flagged passage in which we stood.

"That'll take you into the hall," she said. "I'll come and find you when I've seen the servants."

I saluted and broke away in the direction she had indicated.

* * * * *

There was a closet that opened out of the great gallery. No door hung in the doorway, and I could see china ranged orderly against the panelling of the walls. I descended its two stairs, expecting to find it devoted to china and nothing else. But I was wrong. Facing the window and the sunshine was a facsimile of the tallboy chest which I had coveted so fiercely two hours before.

I gazed at it spell-bound.

"It's very rude to stare," said a voice.

I turned to see Miss Childe framed in the doorway.

Her gown was of apricot, with the bodice cut low and the skirt gathered in loops to show her white silk petticoat, which swelled from under a flowered stomacher so monstrously, that the tiny blue-heeled slipper upon the second stair seemed smaller than ever. Deep frills of lace fell from her short sleeves and a little lace cap was set on her thick dark hair.

I swallowed before replying. Then—

"It's a lovely chest," I said lamely.

"Picked wood," said Miss Childe. "Flogged once a week for years, that tree was."

"Flogged?"

"Certainly."

Suddenly the air was full of music, and a jubilant chorus of voices was singing lustily—

> "A woman, a spaniel, and a walnut-tree,
> The more you beat them, the better they be."

As the melody faded—

"I told you so," said Miss Childe. "What about the butter and eggs? Will you pay for them, or shall I have them sent?"

I handed her the largest one pound note I have ever seen.

"Thanks," she said shortly. "Change at Earl's Court."

A peal of boy's laughter floated in at the open window.

"Who's that?" said I.

"Love," said Miss Childe. "The locksmiths are here, and he's laughing at them. I think it's rather unkind myself. Besides——"

A burst of machine-gun fire interrupted her.

As the echoes died down—

"You smell of potpourri," said I.

"Probably. I made three bags full this morning. Bead bags. Do you mind putting some coal on the fire? If there aren't any tongs, use the telephone."

There was no fireplace and no coal-scuttle, so I took off my right boot and put it in the bottom drawer of the tallboy instead.

"Number, please," said Miss Childe, who had entered the closet and was standing a-tiptoe before a mirror to adjust a patch beneath her left eye.

"Lot 207," said I.

"Line's engaged," said Miss Childe. "Didn't you see it in *The Times*?"

By the way of answer, I threw a large plate at her. She seemed more pleased than otherwise with the attention, and began to pluck the delicate flowers with which it was painted and gathered them into a nosegay. In some dudgeon, I blew a small jug of great beauty on to a carved prie-dieu, to which it adhered as though made of some slimy substance.

"Cannon," said my lady. "Shall I put you on?"

"I wish you would. It's rather important."

"You're through."

"Tallboy speaking," said a faint voice. "Tallboy, Tallboy."

"How d'ye do?" said I.

"Ill," said the voice, "so ill. All these years I've carried it, and no one knew——"

"Pardon me," said I. "I only put it there five minutes ago. You see, the fire was almost out and——"

"Measurements tell," said the voice. "But they never do that. They polish my panels and lay fair linen within me, and great folk have stood about me telling each other of my elegance, and once a baby child mirrored its little face in one of my sides. And all the time measurements tell. But they never do that."

A sigh floated to my ears, a long, long sigh, that rose into a wail of the wind, and a casement behind me blew to with a shaking clash.

Somewhere a dog was howling.

On a sudden I felt cold. The sunshine was gone, and the chamber had become grey and dismal. Misery was in the air.

A stifled exclamation made me look round.

My lady had backed shrinking into a corner, one little hand pressed to her heart, and in her hunted eyes sat Fear dominant. The sweet face was drawn and colourless, and her breath came quickly, so that it was grievous to mark the flutter of her smooth white chest.

Mechanically I turned to seek the cause of her terror.

I saw a powerfully-built man standing square in the closet's doorway. His face was coarse and red and brutal, and his small black eyes glowed with an ugly twinkle as he surveyed his quarry. Upon the thick lips there was a sinister smile, which broadened hideously as he glanced at the nosegay held betwixt his finger and thumb—the little nosegay that she had gathered so lightly from the painted plate. A wide-skirted coat of red fell nearly to his knees and hid his breeches. His short black periwig was bobbed, and a black silk tie was knotted about his neck. Stockings were rolled above his knees, and a huge tongue thrust out from each of his buckled shoes. And in his left hand was a heavy riding-whip whose handle was wrought about with gold. This he kept clapping against his leg with a smack and a ghastly relish that there was no mistaking.

Again that phantom chorus rose up and rang in my ears—

> "A woman, a spaniel, and a walnut tree,
> The more you beat them, the better they be."

But the jubilant note was gone, and, though the tune was the same, the voices were harsh, and there was a dreadful mockery of woe in the stave that made me shudder.

My lady heard it too.

"No, no, Ralph. You do me wrong. I plucked them myself. Who is there now to send me posies? And I am sick—you know it. The last time——" The hurrying voice faltered and stumbled piteously over a sob. "The last time I was near spent, Ralph. So near. And now—— You do not know your strength. Indeed—— Oh, Ralph, Ralph, what have I done that you should use me so?"

The bitter cry sank into a dull moan, and, setting a frail white arm across her eyes, she bowed her head upon it, as do weeping children, and fell to sobbing with that subdued despair that spells a broken spirit.

My lord's withers were unwrung.

For a moment he stood still, leering like some foul thing that feasts on Anguish. Then he let fall the nosegay and took the whip in his right hand. . . .

And I stood there frozen and paralysed and dumb.

Posing his victim with a horrible precision, the monster raised his whip, but it struck a pendant lantern, and with an oath he turned to the gallery, where he should find room and to spare for his brutality. At this delay my lady fell upon her knees, in a wild hope, I think, to turn her respite into a reprieve, but the beast cried out upon her, struck down her outstretched hands, and, twisting his fingers in her soft dark hair, dragged her incontinently out of the closet. The little whimper she gave was awful. . . .

And I stood there paralysed.

Five minutes, perhaps, had passed, slow-treading, pregnant minutes, when my lord reappeared. He stood for a moment listening at the top of the stairs, his chin on his shoulder. Then he stepped lightly down. His vile face was pale and his eyes shifted uneasily. The devil looked out of them yet, but Fright looked with him. Two paces brought the fellow before the tallboy. He put up his hands as if to pull open a drawer, when something about the whip he was holding caught his attention. For a second he stared at it, muttering. Then, with a glance at the doorway, he thrust the thing beneath the skirt of his coat and wiped it as it had been a rapier. . . .

Again he made to open a drawer, but the spell under which I lay seemed to be lifted, and I shot out a hand and clapped him on the shoulder.

For all the notice he took, I might not have been there. The more incensed, I shook the man violently. . . .

* * * * *

"Repose," said Jonah, "is one thing, gluttonish sloth another. And even if you have once again over-estimated the capacity of your stomach, why advertise your intemperance in a public place?" He lifted his hand from my shoulder to look at his watch. "It's now ten minutes to three. Do you think you can stagger, or must you be carried, to the car?"

I sat up and looked about me. Except for Jill, who was standing a-tiptoe before a mirror, we were alone in the lounge.

"I've been dreaming," said I. "About—about——"

"That's all right, old chap. Tell Nanny all about it to-night, after you've had your bath. That's one of the things she's paid for."

"Don't be a fool," said I, putting a hand to my head. "It's

important, I tell you. For Heaven's sake, let me think. Oh, what was it?" My cousins stared at me. "I'm not rotting. It was real—something that mattered."

" 'Orse race?" said Jonah eagerly. "Green hoops leading by twelve lengths or something?"

I waved him away.

"No, no, no. Let me think. Let me think."

I buried my face in my hands and thought and thought. . . . But to no purpose. The vision was gone.

* * * * *

Hastily I made ready for our journey to Town, all the time racking my brain feverishly for some odd atom of incident that should remember my dream.

It was not until I was actually seated in the Rolls, with my foot upon the self-starter, that I thought about Berry.

Casually I asked what had become of him.

"That's what we want to know," said Jill. "He motored down here with Miss Childe, and now they've pushed off somewhere, but they wouldn't say——"

"Childe!" I shouted. "Miss Childe! I've got it!"

"What on earth's the matter?" said Jonah, as I started the car.

"My dream," I cried. "I remember it all. It was about that tallboy."

"What—the one we saw?" cried Jill.

I nodded.

"I'm going to double my bid," I said. "We simply must have it, whatever the price."

Disregarding Jonah's protests that we were going the wrong way, I swung the car in the direction from which he had come, and streaked down the road to Cranmer Place.

A minute later I dashed into the hall, with Jill at my heels.

The first person I saw was Mr. Holly.

"Has it come up yet?"

I flung the words at him, casting strategy to the winds.

"It 'as, Major, an' I'm sorry to say we've lorst it. I never see such a thing. There was a gent there as meant to 'ave it. 'Cept for 'im, there wasn't a bid after twenty-five pounds. I never thort we'd 'ave to go over fifty, neither. Might 'a bin the owner 'isself, the way 'e was running us up. An' when we was in the eighties, I sez to meself, I sez, 'The one as calls a nundred first 'as it. So 'ere goes.' 'Eighty-nine,' sez 'e. 'A nundred pound,' sez I, bold-like.

'Make it guineas,' sez he, as cool as if 'e was buyin' a naporth o' figs. I tell you, Major, it fair knocked me, it did. I come all of a tremble, an' me knees——"

"Where's the fellow who bought it?" said I.

"I'm afraid it's no good, Major. I tell you 'e meant to 'ave them drawers."

With an effort I mastered my impatience.

"Will you tell me where he is? Or, if he's gone, find out——"

"I don't think 'e's gorn," said Mr. Holly, looking round. "I 'alf think—— There 'e is," he cried, suddenly, nodding over my shoulder. "That's 'im on the stairs, with the lady in blue."

Excitedly I swung round, to see my brother-in-law languidly descending the staircase, with Miss Childe by his side.

"Hullo," he said. "Do you mind not asking me why I'm here?"

"It's not my practice," said I, "to ask a question, the answer to which I already know." I turned to Mr. Holly and took out a one pound note. "I'm much obliged for your trouble. 'Not a bid after twenty-five pounds,' I think you said." I handed him the note, which he accepted with protests of gratitude. "You did better than you know," I added.

"May I ask," said Berry unsteadily, "if this gentleman and you are in collusion?"

"We were," said I. "At least, I instructed him to purchase some furniture for me. Unfortunately we were outbid. But it's of no consequence."

Berry raised his eyes to heaven and groaned.

"Subtraction," he said, "is not my strongest point, but I make it eighty pounds. Is that right?"

I nodded, and he turned to Miss Childe.

"That viper," he said, "has stung the fool who feeds him to the tune of eighty pounds. Shall I faint here or by the hat-stand? Let's be clear about it. The moment I enter the swoon——"

"Still, as long as it's in the family——" began Jill.

"Exactly," said I. "The main thing is, we've got it. And when you've heard my tale——"

"Eighty paper pounds," said Berry. "Can you beat it?"

"That'd only be about thirty-five before the War," said Miss Childe in a shaking voice.

"Yes," said I. "Look at it that way. And what's thirty-five? A bagatelle, brother, a bagatelle. Now, if we were in Russia——"

"Yes," said Berry grimly, "and if we were in Patagonia, I suppose I should be up on the deal. You can cut that bit."

Miss Childe and Jill dissolved into peals of merriment.

"That's right," said Berry. "Deride the destitute. Mock at bereavement. As for you," he added, turning to Jill, "your visit to the Zoo is indefinitely postponed. Other children shall feel sick in the monkey-house and be taken to smell the bears. But you, never." He turned to Miss Childe and laid a hand on her arm. "Shut your eyes, my dear, and repeat one of Alfred Austin's odes. This place is full of the ungodly."

* * * * *

My determination to carry the tallboy chest to London in the Rolls met with stern opposition, but in the end I prevailed, and at six o'clock that evening it was safely housed in Mayfair.

To do him justice, Berry's annoyance was considerably tempered by the strange story which I unfolded during a belated tea.

The house and park which I had seen we were unable to identify, and the Post Office Guide was silent as to the whereabouts of Colt. But the excitement which Daphne's production of a tape-measure aroused was only exceeded by the depression which was created by our failure to discover anything unusual about the chest.

We measured the cornice and we measured the plinth. We measured the frame and we measured the drawers. But if the linear measurements afforded us little satisfaction, the square measurements revealed considerably less, while, since no one of us was a mathematician, the calculation of the cubic capacity proved, not only unprofitable, but provocative of such bitter arguments and insulting remarks that Daphne demanded that we should desist.

"All right," said Berry, "if you don't believe me, call in a consulting engineer. I've worked the blinking thing out three times. I admit the answers were entirely different, but that's not my fault. I never did like astrology. I tell you the beastly chest holds twenty-seven thousand point nine double eight recurring cubic inches of air. Some other fool can reduce that to rods, and there you are. I'm fed up with it. Thanks to the machinations of that congenital idiot with the imitation mustachios, I've paid more than four times its value, and I'm not going to burst my brains trying to work out which drawer would have had a false bottom if it had been built by a dipsomaniac who kept fowls. And that's that."

Tearfully Miss Childe announced that it was time for her to be going, and I elected to escort her as far as the garage. As we stepped on to the pavement—

"I know a lot more about you than you think," said I. "I never told you all half what I dreamed."

"What do you know?"

"Oh, nothing momentous. Just the more intimate details of your everyday life. Your partiality to mushrooms, your recognition of Love, your recklessness, pretty peculiarities of your toilet——"

"Good Heavens!" cried Miss Childe.

"But you wouldn't tell me your name."

"False modesty. Seriously you don't mean to say——"

"But I do. Nothing was hid from me. Your little bare feet——"

A stifled scream interrupted me.

"This," said Miss Childe, "is awful." We turned into the mews. "What are you doing to-morrow?"

"Dictating. You see, there's a dream I want recorded."

"I shall expect you at half-past one. We can start after lunch. I've a beautiful hand."

"I know you have. Two of them. They were bare, too," I added reflectively.

With a choking sound, Miss Childe got into the car.

"Half-past one," she said, as she slid into the driver's seat.

"Without fail." I raised my hat. "By the way, who shall I ask for?"

Miss Childe flung me a dazzling smile.

"I've no sisters," she said.

Moodily I returned to the house.

I entered the library to find that the others had retired, presumably to dress for dinner. Mechanically I crossed to the tallboy, which we had so fruitlessly surveyed, and began to finger it idly, wondering all the time whether my dream was wanton, or whether there was indeed some secret which we might discover. It did not seem possible, and yet . . . That distant voice rang in my ears. "Measurements tell, measurements tell. But they never do that." *What?*

A sudden idea came to me, and I drew out the second long drawer. Then in some excitement I withdrew the first, and placed it exactly upon the top of the second, so that I might see if they were of the same size. *The second was the deeper by an inch and a half.*

I thrust my arms into the empty frame, feeling feverishly for a bolt or catch, which should be holding a panel in place at the back of where the first drawer had lain. At first I could find nothing, then my right hand encountered a round hole in the wood, just large enough to admit a man's finger. Almost immediately I came upon a similar hole on the left-hand side. Their office was plain. . . .

A moment later, and I had drawn the panel out of its standing and clear of the chest.

My hands were trembling as I thrust them into the dusty hiding-place.

*　*　*　*　*

"Hullo! Aren't you going to dress?" said Jonah some two minutes later.

But I was still staring at a heavy riding-whip whose handle was wrought about with gold.

CHAPTER III

How a Man may Follow his own Hat, and Berry took a Lamp in his Hand

"What are you doing this morning?" said Daphne.

Berry turned to the mantelpiece and selected a pipe before replying.

"I have," he said, "several duties to discharge. All, curiously enough, to myself. First, if not foremost, I must hire some sock-suspenders. Secondly, I must select some socks for the sock-suspenders to suspend. Is that clear? Neither last nor least——"

"As a matter of fact," said his wife, "you're going to help me choose a present for Maisie Dukedom. Besides, I've got to go to Fortnum and Mason's, and I want you——"

"To carry the string-bag. I know. And we can get the chops at the same time. We'd better take some newspaper with us. And a perambulator."

"Tell you what," said Jonah, "let's all join together and give her a Persian rug."

"That's rather an idea," said my sister. "And they wear for ever."

"You're sure of that, aren't you?" said Berry. "I mean, I shouldn't like her to have to get a new one in about six hundred years. I like a present to last."

Before Daphne could reply—

"How d'you spell 'business'?" said Jill, looking up from a letter.

"Personally," said I, "I don't. It's one of the words I avoid. If you must, I should write it down both ways and see what it looks like."

The telephone bell began to ring.

"Wrong number, for a fiver," said Jonah. "They always do it about this time."

Berry crossed the room and picked up the receiver. We listened expectantly.

"Have I got a taxi! My dear fellow, I've got a whole school of them. Would you like a Renault or a baby grand? What? Oh, I'm afraid I couldn't send it at once. You see, I've only got one boy, and he's having his hair cut. I can post it to you, and I should think you'll get it to-morrow morning. No, I'm not mad. No, I'm not the cab-rank, either. Well, you should have asked me. Never mind. Let's talk of something else. I wonder if you're interested in rockworms. . . . I beg your pardon. . . ." Gravely he restored the receiver to its perch. "Not interested," he added for our information. "He didn't actually say so, but from the directions he gave concerning them—happily, I may say, quite impracticable——"

"Talking of telephoning," said Jonah uncertainly, "don't forget we've got to ring up and say whether we want those tickets."

"So we have," said my sister. "Wednesday week, isn't it? Let's see." She fell to examining a tiny engagement-book, murmuring to herself as she deciphered or interpreted the entries.

I continued to survey the street.

It was a dark morning in December, and we were all in the library, where there was a good fire, warming ourselves preparatory to venturing abroad and facing the north-east wind which was making London so unpleasant.

The tickets to which Jonah referred would make us free of the Albert Hall for a ball which promised to surpass all its predecessors in splendour and discomfort. No one was to be admitted who was not clad in cloth either of gold or silver, and, while there were to be no intervals between the dances, a great deal of the accommodation usually reserved for such revellers as desired rest or refreshment was being converted into seats to be sold to any who cared to witness a pageant of unwonted brilliancy. The fact that no one of us had attended a function of this sort for more than five years, and the excellence of the cause on behalf of which it was being promoted, were responsible for our inclination to take the tickets, for, with the exception of Jill, we were not eager to subscribe to an entertainment which it was not at all certain we should enjoy.

At length—

"I suppose we'd better take the tickets," I said reflectively. "If we don't want to go, we needn't use them."

"Oh, we must use them," said Daphne, "and we've got nothing on on Wednesday, as far as I can see."

Berry cleared his throat.

"It is patent," he said, "that my personal convenience is of no consideration. But let that pass. I have no objection to setting, as it were, the seal of success upon the ball in question, provided that my costume buttons in front, and has not less than two pockets which are at once accessible and of a reasonable capacity. I dare say they weren't fashionable in the fourteenth century. No doubt our forefathers thought it a scream to keep their handkerchiefs in their boots or the seat of their trousers. But I'm funny like that. Last time I had to give the fellow in the cloakroom half a crown every time I wanted to blow my nose."

"You four go," said Jonah. "I always feel such a fool in fancy dress."

"If you feel anything like the fool you look," said Berry, "I'm sorry for you."

Jonah lowered *The Sportsman* and surveyed the speaker.

"What you want," he said, "is a little honest toil. I should take up scavenging, or sewerage. Something that appeals to you."

"I agree," said Daphne. "But you can't start this morning, because you're coming with Jill and me to choose the rug." She turned to me. "Boy dear, ring up and take those tickets, will you?"

I nodded.

The spirit of reckless generosity which is so prominent a characteristic of "Exchange" was very noticeable this morning. The number I asked for, which was faithfully repeated by the operator, was Mayfair 976. I was connected successively to Hammersmith 24, Museum 113, and Mayfair 5800. After a decent interval I began again.

"Kennington Road Police Station," said a voice.

"Kennington or Kennington Road?" said I.

"Kennington Road. There ain't no Kennington."

"Ain't—I mean, aren't there. I always thought . . . Never mind. How are the police?"

"I say this is Kennington Road Police Station," replied the voice with some heat.

"I know you did. I heard you. Just now. If you remember, I asked you if it was Kennington or Kennington Road, and you said——"

" 'Oo *are* you?"

To avoid any unpleasantness I replaced my receiver.

Two minutes later, after an agreeable conversation with "Supervisor", I arranged to purchase five tickets for the Gold and Silver Ball.

* * * * *

"This," said the salesman, spreading a rug upon the top of a fast-growing pile, "is a Shiraz."

"I suppose," said Berry, "you haven't got a Badgerabahd?"

"I never came across one, sir."

"They are rare," was the airy reply. "The best ones used to be made in Germany and sent to Egypt. By the times the camels had finished with them, they'd fetch anything from a millionaire to a foxhound."

This was too much for Jill's gravity, and it was only with an effort that Daphne controlled her voice.

"I think that's very nice," she said shakily. "Don't you?" she added, turning to me.

"Beautiful piece of work," I agreed. "Some of it appears to have been done after dinner, but otherwise . . ."

"The pattern is invariably a little irregular, sir."

"Yes," said Berry. "That's what makes them so valuable. Their lives are reflected in their rugs. Every mat is a human document." With the ferrule of his umbrella he indicated a soft blue line that was straying casually from the course which its fellows had taken. "That, for instance, is where Ethel the Unready demanded a latchkey at the mature age of sixty-two. And here we see Uncle Sennacherib fined two measures of oil for being speechless before mid-day. I don't think we'd better give her this one," he added. "Shebat the Satyr seems to have got going about the middle, and from what I remember——"

"Haven't you got to go and get some socks?" said Daphne desperately.

"I have. Will you meet me for lunch, or shall I meet you? I believe they do you very well at the Zoo."

The salesman retired precipitately into an office, and my sister besought me tearfully to take her husband away.

"I might have known," she said in a choking voice. "I was a fool to bring him."

"Let's play at bears," said her husband. "It's a priceless game. Every one gets under a different rug and growls."

Resignedly Daphne retired to the sofa. Jill sank down upon the pile of rugs and shook silently. Observing that we were unattended, another salesman was hurrying in our direction. Before he could launch the inevitable question—

"I want a dog licence and some magic lanterns," said Berry. "You know. The ones that get all hot and smell."

There was a shriek of laughter from Jill, and the unfortunate assistant looked round wildly, as if for support.

Clearly something had to be done.

I stepped forward and slid my arm through that of the delinquent.

"Enough," said I. "Come and devil the hosier. If you're not quick all the socks will be gone."

My brother-in-law eyed me suspiciously.

"And leave my baggage?" he demanded, pointing to Daphne. "Never. This is a ruse. Where is the manager of the emporium? I dreamed about him last night. He had brown boots on."

I consulted my watch before replying.

"By the time we get to the Club, Martinis will be in season."

"Do you mean that?" said Berry.

"I do."

"And a small but pungent cigar?"

I nodded.

He turned to the bewildered salesman.

"Please attend to these ladies. They want to choose an expensive-looking rug. Preferably a Shiraz. No doubt they will be safe in your hands. Good morning."

On the way out he stopped at a counter and purchased one of the prettiest bead bags I have ever seen. He ordered it to be sent to Daphne.

* * * * *

The omnibus was sailing down Oxford Street at a good round pace, but it was the sudden draught from a side street that twitched my hat from my head. I turned to see the former describe a somewhat elegant curve and make a beautiful landing upon the canopy of a large limousine which was standing by the kerb some seventy yards away. By the time I had alighted, that distance was substantially increased. In some dudgeon I proceeded to walk, with such remnants of dignity as I could collect and retain, in the direction of my lost property. Wisdom suggested that I should run; but I felt that the spectacle of a young man, hatless but otherwise decently dressed and adequately protected from the severity of the weather, needed but the suggestion of impatience to make it wholly ridiculous. My vanity was rightly served. I was still about thirty paces from my objective, when the limousine drew out from the pavement and into the stream of traffic which was hurrying east.

As my lips framed a particularly unpleasant expletive a bell rang sharply, and I turned to see a taxi, which had that moment been dismissed.

"Oxford Circus," I cried, flinging open the door.

A moment later we were near enough for me to indicate the large limousine and to instruct my driver to follow her.

As we swept into Regent's Park, I began to wonder whether I should not have been wiser to drive to Bond Street and buy a new hat. By the time we had been twice round the Ring I had no longer any doubt on this point; but my blood was up, and I was determined to run my quarry to earth, even if it involved a journey to Hither Green.

More than once we were almost out-distanced, three times we were caught in a block of traffic, so that my taxi's bonnet was nosing the limousine's tank. Once I got out, but, as I stepped into the road, the waiting stream was released, and the car slid away and round the hull of a 'bus from under my very hand. My escape from a disfiguring death beneath the wheels of a lorry was so narrow that I refrained from a second attempt to curtail my pursuit, and resigned myself to playing a waiting game.

When we emerged from the Park, my spirits rose and I fell to studying what I could see of the lines of the limousine, and to speculating whether I was being led to Claridge's or the Ritz. I had just pronounced in favour of the latter, when there fell upon my ears the long regular spasm of ringing which is a fire-engine's peremptory demand for instant way. Mechanically the order was everywhere obeyed. The street was none too wide, and a second and louder burst of resonance declared that the fire-engine was hard upon our heels.

The twenty yards separating us from the limousine were my undoing. With a helpless glance at me over his shoulder, my driver pulled in to the kerb, and we had the felicity of watching the great blue car turn down a convenient side street and flash out of sight.

The engine swept by at a high smooth speed, the traffic emerged from its state of suspended animation, and in some annoyance I put my head out of the window and directed my driver to drive to Bond Street.

I had chosen a new hat and was on the point of leaving the shop, when a chauffeur entered with a soft grey hat in his hand. The hat resembled the one I had lost, and for a moment I hesitated. Then it occurred to me that there were many such hats in London, and I passed on and out of the door. Of course it was only a coincidence. Still . . .

Opposite me, drawn up by the kerb, was the large blue limousine.

The next moment I was back in the shop.

"I rather think that's my hat," I said.

The chauffeur looked round.

"Is it, sir? 'Er ladyship see it on top o' the canopy just as I put 'er down at the Berkeley. 'Wilkins,' she says, 'there's a 'at on the car.' 'A 'at, me lady?' says I. 'A 'at,' says she. 'Fetch it down.' I fetches it down and shows it 'er. 'An' a nice noo 'at, too,' she says, 'wot must have blowed orf of a gent's 'ead, an' 'e on top of a 'bus, as like as not.' Then she looks inside and see the initials and the name o' the shop. 'Take it back where it come from,' she says. 'They'll know 'oose it is.' 'Very good, me lady,' said I, an' come straight down, sir."

I took off the hat I was wearing and bade him read the initials which had just been placed there. He did so reluctantly. Then—

"Very glad to 'ave found you so quick, sir. Shall I tell them to send it along? You won't want to carry it."

"I'll see to that," said I, taking it out of his hand. "Why didn't it blow off your canopy?"

"The spare cover was 'oldin' it, sir. Must 'ave shifted on to the brim as soon as it come there. I don't know 'ow long——"

"Best part of an hour," I said shortly, giving him a two-shilling piece. "Good day, and thanks very much."

He touched his cap and withdrew.

A wrestle with mental arithmetic showed me that the draught which I had encountered nearly an hour before had cost me exactly one and a half guineas.

Ordinarily I should have dismissed the matter from my mind, but for some reason I had no sooner let the chauffeur go than I was tormented by a persistent curiosity regarding the identity of his considerate mistress. If I had not promised to rejoin Berry for lunch—a meal for which I was already half an hour late—I should have gone to the Berkeley and scrutinized the guests. The reflection that such a proceeding must only have been unprofitable consoled me not at all, so contrary a maid is Speculation. For the next two hours Vexation rode me on the curb. I quarrelled with Berry, I was annoyed with myself, and when the hall-porter at the Club casually observed that there was "a nasty wind", I agreed with such hearty and unexpected bitterness that he started violently and dropped the pile of letters which he was searching on my behalf.

A visit to Lincoln's Inn Fields, however, with regard to an estate of which I was a trustee, followed by a sharp walk in the Park, did much to reduce the ridiculous fever of which my folly lay sick, and I returned home in a frame of mind almost as comfortable as that in which I had set out.

It was half-past four, but no one of the others was in, so I ordered tea to be brought to the library, and settled down to the composition of a letter to *The Observer*.

I was in the act of recasting my second sentence, when the light went out.

By the glow of the fire I made my way to the door. A glance showed me that the hall and the staircase were in darkness. It was evident that a fuse had come to a violent end.

I closed the door and returned to my seat. Then I reached for the telephone and put the receiver to my ear.

"What an extraordinary thing!" said a voice. "And you've no idea whose it was?"

"Not the slightest," came the reply. There was a musical note in the girlish tone that would have attracted any one. "There it was, on the top of the car, when we got to the Berkeley. It wasn't such a bad hat, either."

"Excuse me," said I. "It was a jolly good hat."

A long tense silence followed my interruption. At length—

"I say, are you there, Dot?"

"Yes," came the reply in an excited whisper. "Who was that speaking?"

"I've not the faintest idea," rejoined the first voice I had heard. "Somebody must have got on to our line. I expect——"

A familiar explosion severed the sentence with the clean efficiency of the guillotine.

"Isn't that sickening?" said I. "Now we shall never know what her theory was."

"It's all your fault, whoever you are. If you hadn't butted in——"

"I don't know what you mean," I retorted. "I was ushered into your presence, so to speak, by *la force majeure*. French. Very difficult."

"Well, when you heard us talking, you ought to have got off the line."

"I should have, if you hadn't started disparaging my head-gear. I repeat, it was a hat of unusual elegance. It had a personality of its own."

"But it wasn't your hat we were discussing."

I sighed.

"All right," I said wearily. "It wasn't. Have it your own way. Some other fool followed a silver-grey Homburg twice round the Park this morning. Some other fool——"

A little gasp interrupted me.

"But how did you know my number?"

"I didn't. I don't. I never could have been about to should. Negatives all the way. It's just chance, my dear. Chance with a Capital J—I mean C. D'you mind if I smoke?"

Her reply was preceeded by a refreshing gurgle.

"Not at all," said my lady. "D'you mean to say you chased us all that way?"

"Further. And if it hadn't been for that fire-engine——"

"I remember. Wilkins turned down a side-street."

"Exactly."

"What a shame. Well, if you go to your hatter's you'll get it again."

"Your ingenuity is only equalled by your consideration. Isn't that neatly put? You see, I'm writing a letter to *The Observer*, and, when I get going, I can just say things like that one after another."

"How wonderful. But I'm afraid I'm interrupting you, and I shouldn't like to deprive Humanity——"

"You name," said I, "is Dot. But I shall call you Mockery. And if you're half as sweet as you sound——"

"Good-bye."

I protested earnestly.

"Please don't say that. We've only just met. Besides . . . why was Clapham Common?"

"Clapham what?"

"No, Common. Why was Clapham Common?"

"Well, why was it?"

"I can't think, my dear. I thought you might know. It's worried me for years."

There was a choking sound, which suggested indignation struggling with laughter. Then—

"I've a good mind to ring off right away," said Dot in a shaking voice.

"That would be cruel. Think of the dance you led me this morning. More. Think of the dances you're going to give me on Wednesday week."

"Oh, you're going, are you?"

"If you are."

"What as?" she demanded.

"A billiard-marker in the time of Henry the Fourth. And you?"

"I can't rise to that. I'm going as myself in a silver frock."

"Could anything be sweeter? A little silver Dot. I shall cancel the body-snatcher—I mean billiard-marker—and go as Carry One. Then we can dance together all the evening. By the way, in case I don't hear your voice, how shall I know you?"

"A dot," said my lady, "is that which hath position, but no magnitude."

"Possibly," said I. "It hath also a dear voice, which though it be produced indefinitely, will never tire. All the same, in view of the capacity of the Albert Hall, you've not given me much to go on."

"As a matter of fact, each of us is going as a parallel line. And that's why I can tell you that I like the sound of you, and—oh, well, enough said."

"Thank you, Dot. And why parallel lines?"

"They never meet. So long."

There was a faint chunk.

My lady had rung off.

Heavily I hung up my receiver.

When the others came in, I was still sitting in the dark at the table, thinking. . . .

*　*　*　*　*

The bitter wind reigned over London for seven long days, meting untempered chastisement to its reluctant subjects, and dying unwept and gasping on a Monday night. Tuesday was fair, still by comparison and indeed. The sun shone and the sky was blue, and the smoke rose straight out of its chimneys with never the breath of a breeze to bend it, or even to set its columns swaying over the high roofs. There was a great calm. But, with it all, the weather was terribly cold.

That rare beauty which Dusk may bring to the Metropolis was that evening vouchsafed. Streets that were mean put off their squalor, ways that were handsome became superb. Grime went unnoticed, ugliness fell away. All things crude or staring became indistinct, veiled with a web of that soft quality which only Atmosphere can spin and, having spun, hang about buildings of a windless eve.

As Night drew on, Magic came stealing down the blurred highways. Lamps became lanterns, shedding a muffled light, deepening and charging with mystery the darkness beyond. Old friends grew unfamiliar. Where they had stood, fantastic shapes loomed out of the mist and topless towers rose up spectral to baffle memory. Perspective fled, shadow and stuff were one, and, save where the radiance of the shops in some proud thoroughfare made gaudy noon of evening, the streets of Town were changed to echoing halls and long, dim, rambling galleries, hung all with twinkling lights that stabbed the gloom but deep enough to show their presence, as do the stars.

So, slowly and with a dazzling smile, London put on her cloak of darkness. By eight o'clock you could not see two paces ahead.

On Wednesday morning the fog was denser than it had been the night before. There was no sign of its abatement, not a puff of wind elbowed its way through the yellow drift, and the cold was intense. The prospect of leaving a comfortable home at nine in the evening to undertake a journey of some two miles, clad in habiliments which, while highly ornamental, were about as protective from cold as a grape-skin rug, was anything but alluring.

For reasons of my own, however, I was determined to get to the Ball. My sister, whom nothing daunted, and Jill, who was wild with excitement, and had promised readily to reserve more dances than could possibly be rendered, were equally firm. Jonah thought it a fool's game, and said as much. Berry was of the same opinion, but expressed it less bluntly, and much more offensively. After a long tirade—

"All right," he concluded. "You go. It's Lombard Street to a china orange you'll never get there, and, if you do, you'll never get back. None of the band'll turn up, and if you find twenty other fools in the building to exchange colds with, you'll be lucky. To leave your home on a night like this is fairly clamouring for the special brand of trouble they keep for paralytic idiots. I've known you all too long to expect sagacity, but the instinct of self-preservation characterizes even the lower animals. What swine, for instance, would leave its cosy sty——"

"How dare you?" said Daphne. "Besides, you can't say 'its'. Swine's plural."

"My reference was to the fever-swine," was the cold reply. "A singular species. Comparable only with the deep-sea dip-sheep."

"I think you're very unkind," said Jill, pouting. "Boy can walk in front with a lamp, and Jonah can walk behind with a lamp——"

"And I can walk on both sides, I suppose, with a brazier in either hand. Oh, this is too easy."

"We can but try," said I.

"You can but close your ugly head," said Berry. "If you want to walk about London half the night, looking like a demobilised pantaloon, push off and do it. But don't try and rope in innocent parties."

To this insult I made an appropriate reply, and the argument waxed. At length——

"There's no reason," said Jonah, "why we shouldn't go on like this for ever. If we had any sense, we should send for Fitch and desire his opinion. It's rather more valuable than any one of ours, and, after all, he's more or less interested. And you can trust him."

Now, Fitch was our chauffeur.

Amid a chorus of approval, I went to the telephone to speak to the garage.

I was still waiting to be connected, when—

"Is that the Club?" said a voice.

"No," said I. "Nothing like it."

"Well, there's a bag of mine in the hall, and——"

"No, there isn't," said I.

"What d'you mean?" was the indignant retort.

"What I say. Our hall is bagless."

"I say," said the voice with laboured clarity. "I say there is a bag in the hall. A BAG. Hang it all, you know what a bag is?"

"Rather," said I heartily. "What you put nuts in. An uncle of mine had one."

The vehemence with which the unknown subscriber replaced his receiver was terrible to hear.

Ten minutes later Fitch entered the room.

"Can you get to the Albert Hall to-night, Fitch?" said Daphne.

"I think so, madam. If we go slow."

"Can you get back from the Albert Hall to-morrow afternoon?" said Berry.

"If I can get there, sir, I can get back."

"How long will it take?"

"I ought to do it in 'alf an hour, sir. I can push along in the Park, where it's all straight going. It's getting along the streets as'll take the time. It's not that I won't find me way, but it's the watchin' out for the hother vehicles, so as they don't run into you."

"Bit of an optimist, aren't you?"

"I don't think so, sir."

"Thank you, Fitch," said Daphne hastily. "Half-past nine, please."

"Very good, madam."

He bowed and withdrew.

Triumphantly my sister regarded her husband.

"At making a mountain out of a molehill," she said, "no one can touch you."

Berry returned her gaze with a malevolent stare. Then he put a thumb to his nose and extended his fingers in her direction.

* * * * *

The unfortunate incident occurred in the vicinity of Stanhope Gate.

So far we had come very slowly, but without incident, and, in spite of the fact that we were insufficiently clad, we were nice and warm. For this, so far as Berry and I were concerned, two footwarmers and a pair of rugs were largely responsible, for the elaborate nature of our costumes put the wearing of overcoats out of the question. A high-collared Italian cloak of the shape that was seen in the time of Elizabeth made it impossible for me to wear a *surtout* of any description, and I was reduced to wrapping a muffler about my neck and holding a woollen shawl across my chest, while Berry, in that puffed and swollen array, which instantly remembers Henry the Eighth, derived what comfort he could from an enormous cloak of Irish frieze which, while it left his chest uncovered, succeeded in giving him a back about four feet square.

Hitherto we had encountered little or no traffic, and an excellent judgement, coupled with something akin to instinct, on the part of Fitch had brought us surely along the streets; but here, almost before we knew it, there were vehicles in front and on either side. Hoarse directions were being shouted, lanterns were being waved, engines were running, and a few feet away frantic endeavours were being made to persuade a pair of horses to disregard twin headlights whose brilliancy was adding to the confusion. Berry lowered the window.

"What about it, Fitch?"

"Well, sir, I'm just opposite the gate, but it's rather awkward to slip across, in case I meet somethin'. If I 'as to pull up 'alf-way, we might be run into."

"Which means that one of us must guide you over?"

"It'd be safer, sir."

By a majority of three it was decided that Berry should enact the *rôle* of conducting officer. Jonah had a cold, and was sitting on the back seat between the girls. I had no coat, and required the services of both hands if I was to hold my shawl in position. Only my brother-in-law remained. He did not go down without a struggle, but after a vigorous but vain appeal "to our better natures", he compared himself to a lion beset by jackals, commented bitterly upon "the hot air which is breathed about self-sacrifice", and, directing that after death his veins should be opened in the presence of not less than twelve surgeons, as a preliminary to his interment in the Dogs' Cemetery, opened the door and stepped sideways into the roadway.

His efforts to remove the offside oil lamp, which was hot to the touch, were most diverting, and twice he returned to the window to ask us to make less noise. At last, however, with the assistance of Fitch, the lamp was unhooked, and a moment later our absurd link-boy advanced cautiously in the direction of the gate.

Fitch let in the clutch.

We must have been half-way across, when a lamp of extraordinary power came gliding up on the near side, confusing all eyes and altogether effacing our guiding light.

Fitch applied his brakes and cried out a warning. Instantly the lamp stopped, but its glare was blinding and our chauffeur was clearly afraid to move.

In a flash I was out of the car and holding my shawl over the face of the offender. At once Fitch took the car forward. As I fell in behind, I heard Berry's voice.

"Thank you. I hope I didn't jostle your 'bus. Yes, I am completely and utterly lost. No, I don't mind at all. I'm going to bale out the drinking-trough and sleep there. And in the morning they'll take me to the Foundling Hospital. Hullo. That's done it. Blind me first and then run me down. What are you? A travelling lighthouse or an air-raid? Want to get to Cannon Street? Well, I should go round by sea, if I were you. . . . Well, if you must know, I'm Mary Pickford about to be trodden to death in *Maelstrom* or *Safety Last*. You know, you're not racing your engine enough. I can still hear myself think. . . ."

His voice grew fainter and stopped.

Vigorously I shouted his name. A cold draught, and we swept in to the Park. Fitch pulled up on the left-hand side.

"Berry, Berry!" I shouted.

In the distance I could hear voices, but no one answered me. . . .

In response to my sister's exhortations I re-entered the car, and drew a rug over my shivering limbs. The others put their heads out of the windows and shouted for Berry in unison. There was no reply.

For a quarter of an hour we shouted at intervals. Then Jonah took the other lamp and returned to the gate. He did not reappear for ten minutes, and we were beginning to give him up, when to our relief he opened the door.

"No good," he said curtly. "We'd better get on. He's probably gone home."

"I suppose he's all right," said Daphne, in some uneasiness.

"You can't come to any harm on foot," said I. "Everything's going dead slow for its own sake. And when I last heard him, he was having the time of his life. Incidentally, as like as not, he'll strike a car that's going to the Ball and ask for a lift."

"I expect he will," said Jill. "There must be any amount on the way."

"All right," said my sister. "Tell Fitch to carry on."

Twenty minutes later that good helmsman set us down at the

main entrance to the Albert Hall.

* * * * *

The conditions prevailing within that edifice suggested that few, if any, ticket-holders had been deterred from attending by the conditions prevailing without. The boxes were full, the floor was packed, the corridors were thronged with eager shining revellers, dancing and strolling and chattering to beat the band, which was flooding every corner of the enormous building with an air of gaiety so infectious that even the staid Jonah began to grumble that the dance would be over before the girls emerged from the cloakroom.

The Field of the Cloth of Gold cannot have presented a more splendid spectacle. True, there was nothing of the pageant about the function, neither were Pomp and Chivalry among the guests. But Grace was there, and Ease and Artlessness, lending the scene that warmth and life and verity which Form and Ceremony do not allow.

The utter hopelessness of encountering my lady of the limousine was so apparent that I relegated a ridiculous notion which I had been harbouring to the region of things impossible, and determined to think about it no more. For all that, I occasionally found myself scanning the crowd of strangers and wondering whether there was one amongst them whose voice I knew. It was during one of these lapses that I heard my name.

"Who have you lost?" asked Maisie Dukedom, all radiant as a gold shepherdess.

"Dance with me," said I, "and I'll tell you."

She glanced at a tiny wrist-watch.

"I promised I wouldn't stay more than an hour," she said, "and I ought to be going. But I want to thank you for that beautiful rug. If I give you the next, will you get the car for me as soon as it's over?"

"If you must go."

She nodded, and we pushed off into the rapids.

"And now, who is it?" she demanded.

"I thought you were going to thank me for the rug."

She made a little grimace of impatience.

"The best way I can thank you is to tell you the truth. Jack and I went to buy a rug at Lucifer's."

"That's where we got yours."

She pinched my arm.

"Will you listen? We must have got to the shop directly you'd left. The one you'd bought was still lying there. We both thought it feet above any other rug there, and, when they said it was sold, I nearly cried. We were so fed up that we said we wouldn't get a rug at all, and went off to look at bookcases and chests of drawers. I didn't get home till six, and, when I did, there was your present. Are you satisfied?"

"Overwhelmed."

"Good. Now, who's the lady?"

"That's just what I can't tell you. I know her voice, but not her countenance. Her name is Dot—Lady Dot. She drives in a blue limousine and she's here to-night."

Maisie assumed a serious air.

"This," she said, "is terrible. Does your life depend upon finding her? I mean . . . it's worse than a needle in a bundle of hay, isn't it?"

"Infinitely."

"You can wash out the limousine, because you won't see it. And the voice, because you won't hear it. And her name, because she won't be labelled. There's really nothing left, is there?"

Gloomily I assented.

"I'm sorry," said Maisie. "I'd like to have helped." The music slowed up and died. "And now will you see me off?"

We made our way towards the exit.

I had found her footman and sent him to summon the car, and was standing within the main entrance, when a familiar figure began with difficulty to emerge from a car which had just arrived. Berry. Having succeeded in projecting himself on to the steps, he turned to hand his companion out of the car, as he did so presenting to the astonished doorkeepers a back of such startling dimensions that the one nearest to me recoiled, for all his seasoning.

I was wondering who was the muffled Samaritan that had brought him along, when the chauffeur leaned forward as if to receive instructions when to return. The light of the near-side lamp showed me the genial features of that communicative fellow who had restored my grey hat some nine days before.

Tall and slight, his mistress turned to the doorway, and I saw a well-shaped head, couped at the throat by the white of an ermine stole. Dark hair swept low over her forehead, an attractive smile sat on her pretty mouth, and there was a fine colour springing in her cheeks.

She looked up to see me staring.

For a moment a pair of grey eyes met mine steadily. Then—

"Is the car here?" said Maisie over my shoulder. "Hullo, Berry" Suddenly she saw his companion. "Betty, my dear, I thought you were in Scotland."

Under pretence of arranging her wrap, I breathed into her ear—

"Introduce me."

She did so without a tremor.

"And give him the next dance for me," she added. "I've just cut one of his, and he's been most forgiving."

"Too late," said Berry. "I have not wasted the shining thirty minutes which I had just spent in Lady Elizabeth's luxurious car. She knows him for the craven that he is."

"I must judge for myself," said my lady, turning to me with a smile. "He's given you a terrible——"

The sentence was never finished, for Berry turned to look at somebody, and Maisie noticed his back for the first time. Her involuntary cry was succeeded by a peal of laughter which attracted the attention of every one within earshot, and in a moment my brother-in-law found himself the object of much interested amusement, which the majority of onlookers made no attempt to conceal.

My lady fled to her cloakroom. Hastily I escorted Maisie, still helpless with laughter, to her car.

I returned to find Berry entertaining a large audience of complete strangers in the vestibule with a fantastic account of his experiences at Stanhope Gate. Concealing myself behind a pillar, I awaited Lady Elizabeth's return.

"Yes," said Berry. "Betrayed by my accomplices, I found myself, as it were, a shred of flotsam adrift in the darkling streets. Several people thought I was the Marble Arch, and left me on the left. Others, more discerning, conjured me to pull into the kerb. Removing from my north instep the hoof which, upon examination, I found to be attached to a large mammal, I started to wade south-west and by south, hoping against hope and steering by the Milky Way. Happily I had my ration-card, and I derived great comfort from its pregnant directions, which I read from time to time by the smell of the red-hot lamp which I was bearing. . . ."

Here my lady appeared, and I led her into the corridor and on to the floor.

As she had promised, she was wearing a silver frock. One white shoulder was left bare, and a heavy fringe, that swayed evenly with her every movement, made the slim line of her dress still more graceful. Silvery stockings covered her gleaming ankles, and she was shod with silver shoes.

For a little we spoke of Berry, and she told me how he had boarded her car and respectfully begged her compassion. Then I spoke of the bitter wind which had blown us about so inconsiderately, before the fog had come to lay upon us stripes of another kind.

"I lost my hat one day." I added casually.

At that she jumped in my arms as if I had stabbed her, but I took no notice, and we danced on.

Deliberately I recounted my loss and my pursuit, only omitting my encounter with her chauffeur.

"I happen to know," I concluded, "that the lady of the limousine is here to-night. Before the ball is over I shall have danced with her."

"But you've never seen her," she protested.

"I know her voice."

She laughed musically.

"Aren't you a bit of an optimist?" she queried.

"I don't think so. And she's just sweet."

"But if you don't know her name, how can you hope——"

"Her name," I said, "is Dot."

The hand upon my shoulder shook slightly.

We danced on.

At length—

"That's not very much to go on," said Elizabeth.

I sighed.

"Don't discourage me," I said. "When I find her, d'you think she'll give me the seven dances she said she would?"

"O-o-oh, I never . . ." She choked and began to cough violently, so that I drew her out of the press and into a vacant corner. "I never heard of such a thing," she continued ingeniously.

"You wicked girl," said I. "Why was Clapham Common?"

For a moment she looked at me speechless. Then she began to laugh tremulously. . . .

With a crash the jazz came to an end. Almost immediately another orchestra took up the running, and the strains of a valse rose up, plaintive and tempting.

I looked at my lady.

"Have I earned my dances, Dot?"

She hesitated. Then—

"Carry on, Carry One," she said.

CHAPTER IV

How Nobby came to Sleep upon my Bed, and Berry fell among Thieves

Thoughtfully I read the letter again.

> . . . It nearly breaks my heart to say so, but I've got to part with Nobby. I'm going to India to join Richard, you know, and I'm sailing next week. I think you'd get on together. He's a one-man dog and a bit queer-tempered with strangers—all Sealyhams are. But he's a good little chap—very sporting, very healthy, and a real beauty. Let me know one way or the other, and, if you'd like to have him, I'll send him round with his licence and pedigree.
>
> Yours very sincerely,
>
> JOSEPHINE CHILDE.
>
> P.S.—He's always slept on my bed.

The letter had been forwarded to me from London, for I was spending the week-end in Leicestershire with the Scarlets.

I looked across the flagged hall to my host, who was leaning against a table with a hunting horn in each hand, listening critically to the noise he was making, and endeavouring to decide upon which of the two instruments he could wind the most inspiring call.

"Live and let live," said I. With a grin Bertram suspended his operations. "Listen. I've been offered a Sealyham."

"Take him," was the reply. "Your guests will regret it, but you won't. They're high-spirited and they're always full of beans. Hard as nails, too," he added. "You'll never kill him. Tell me." He brandished the horn which he held in his right hand. "Don't you think this sounds the best?" With an effort he produced a most distressing sound. "Or this?" Putting the other to his lips, he emitted a precisely similar note.

"There's no difference at all," said I, crossing to a bureau. "They're equally painful. They do it rather better at level-crossings on the Continent."

"It is patent," said Bertram, "that you have no ear for music."

"All right," said I, making ready to write. "You try it. The hounds'll all sit up and beg or something. I suppose it's too much to expect to find a pen that'll write here," I added, regarding uneasily the enormous quill with which the bureau was decorated.

"That's a jolly good pen," said Bertram indignantly. "Every one says so."

I grunted my disbelief.

"Which end shall I use?"

"I recommend the right one," rejoined my host with ponderous sarcasm. "But, as I have yet to meet any one who can read your writing, I don't suppose it matters."

"I have often deplored the company you keep," said I, and with that I selected a large sheet of paper and wrote as follows—

Dear Miss Childe,

I'd like to have Nobby very much. I'm awfully sorry for you, but I'll be very kind to him for both your sakes. The reference you give him is most satisfactory. I suppose he'll want one evening a week and every other Sunday. And will he do in the front steps and spoil the knives? Or only ruin the boots? I beg your pardon. For the moment I was thinking of the cook who nearly engaged us. Only she wanted a pension after six months' service. It was very nice of you to think of me. I'll write you a proper letter when I send you a receipt. I return to Town to-morrow.

Yours very sincerely,

. . . .

P.S.—He shall always sleep on mine.

As I was addressing the envelope, the butler entered the hall. I gave him the letter, and he promised to see that it was dispatched that day. A knowledge of Bertram's household suggested this precaution.

* * * * *

As I had told Miss Childe, on the following day I returned to Town. It was the last Monday but one before Christmas, and Jonah's birthday. To do the latter honour, we were to dine all together at Claridge's and go on to an entertainment, presented in a house in which smoking was permitted, and of such a nature that you gained rather than lost by arriving late.

I reached home with sufficient time only to bathe and dress, and it was not until we were half-way through dinner that I learned that my letter to Miss Childe had borne immediate fruit.

"By the way," said Daphne suddenly, "did the servants give you that message from Josephine Childe?" I shook my head. "It was down on the telephone block, but I suppose you were too hurried to look at that. 'Miss Childe's compliments, and Nobby will be round this evening.' " Hardly I suppressed an exclamation. "We're all mad to know what it means. Berry scents an intrigue and says it's a cipher."

"Worse," said I. "It's a dog."

"A dog?" cried Daphne and Jill together.

"A dog. You know. A small quadruped. Something like a cat, only with hair."

"I know," said Berry excitedly. "I know. I've seen pictures of them."

"Fools. Both of you," said my sister. "What's she giving you a dog for?"

I explained the nature of the transaction.

"I have every reason to believe," I concluded, "that he will become one of us."

The others exchanged meaning looks.

"Is he any particular breed?" said Berry. "Or just a pot-pourri?"

I braced myself with a draught of champagne before replying. Then—

"He's a Sealyham," I said.

Uprose a damnatory chorus.

"I do hereby protest," said Berry. "A barbarous breed, notorious for its unprovoked ferocity. Peaceable possession of our tenement will be unknown. Ingress and egress will be denied us. Substantial compensation will be an everyday affair. Any more for the Pasteur Institute?"

"Rot," said I. "You're jealous."

"They've awfully uncertain tempers," said Daphne. "Maisie Dukedom had one, and it went down and bit a new cook, who'd just come, before she'd got her things off. They had to give her five pounds, put her up at an hotel for the night, and pay her fare back to Bristol. And she had wonderful references."

"Instinct," said I. "The dog saw through her. They ought to have been grateful."

"Truth is," said Jonah, "they're a bit too sporting for London."

"Look here," said I, consulting my watch. "At the present moment the poor little dog is probably fretting his soul out in the servants' hall. So we'll have to keep him to-night. If he's the ravening beast you say he is, he shall be fired to-morrow. If not, I shall stick to him. That's fair enough, isn't it?"

"He's going to be a darling," said Jill. "I'm sure of it."

Before we left for the theatre, I telephoned home and spoke to the butler.

"Is that you, Falcon?"

"It is, sir."

"Any dogs come for me?"

"Only one, sir."

"Is he all right?"

"Seems a little unsettled, sir, and—er—suspicious. He was rather short with Fitch, sir, when he come in, but he had his leggin's on, sir, so there's no harm done. He's all right with me, sir."

I thought of the Dukedoms' cook and moistened my lips.

"See that he has a run on the lead before you go to bed," I said as nonchalantly as possible, "and then put him upstairs on my bed."

"Very good, sir."

I returned to the lounge.

"Has the little bit of Heaven arrived?" said Berry.

I nodded.

"Casualties?"

"Nil," said I. "Everything in the garden is lovely."

"No doubt," said Berry. "And the servants' hall? I suppose that's a shambles."

"Don't be silly," said I. "He's as good as gold."

"There you are," said Jill staunchly.

"Cupboard love," said Berry. "You wait till we come in. I shouldn't be surprised if he concentrated on me. They always aim high. It will be your duty," he added, turning to Daphne, "to suck the wound. That is a wife's privilege."

"The best thing," said Jonah, "is to hold a cigarette-end to the place."

"I beg your pardon," said Berry.

"Well, an iron takes such a time to heat."

In a voice shaken with emotion my brother-in-law stated that he should regard any such treatment as a treacherous and aggravated assault upon his person.

"Don't let there be any mistake about it," he concluded. "I'm not going to have any amateur life-savers burning holes in my body in the hope of being recommended by the Coroner's jury. If I've got to die, I'll just go mad in the ordinary way, thank you. I wonder who I shall bite first," he added pleasantly.

"Don't you worry," said I. "Think what hydrophobia means."

"What does it mean?"—suspiciously.

"A horror of water," said I. "You must have had it for years."

*   *   *   *   *

We left the theatre about eleven o'clock.

We had just come in, and I was disrobing in the hall—Berry was speaking to the chauffeur—when an exclamation from Jill, who was on the point of following Daphne and Jonah into the library, made me look round.

On the top step of the first flight of stairs stood a little white dog, regarding us squarely. He might have been painted by Maud Earl. His ears were pricked, his little forefeet placed close together, his tail was upright. A gas officer would have said that he was "in the alert position".

"Hello, Nobby," said I. "How goes it?"

At the sound of his name the terrier put his small head on one side with an air of curiosity as evident as it was attractive.

"What a darling!" cried Jill.

As she spoke I heard a latch-key inserted, and the next moment Berry pushed open the door.

Breathing out threatenings, the darling streaked down the stairs and across the hall to the new-comer's feet, where he stood with his back arched, one forepaw raised, and bared teeth, emitting a long low snarl, while there was a look in the bright brown eyes which there was no mistaking.

My brother-in-law stood as if rooted to the spot.

Jill began to shake with laughter.

"What did I say?" said Berry remaining motionless. "Can't enter my own house now. It's all right, old chap," he added, gazing at Nobby with a winning smile. "I belong here."

His statement was not accepted. Nobby, who was clearly taking no risks, replied with a growl charged with such malevolence that I thought it advisable to interfere.

I addressed myself to the terrier.

"Good man," I said reassuringly, patting Berry upon the

shoulder.

Jonah contends that the dog construed my movement as an attempted assault, which it was his duty to abet. In any event, in less time than it takes to record, the growl culminated in that vicious flurry which invariably accompanies the closing of jaws, there was a noise of torn cloth, and with a yell Berry leapt for and reached the bookcase to which he adhered, clinging rather than perched, after the manner of a startled ape.

A roar of laughter from me and long, tremulous wails of merriment from Jill brought my sister and Jonah pellmell upon a never-to-be-forgotten scene.

The four of us huddled together, helpless with mirth, while Berry, calling upon Sirius, clung desperately to the bookcase, and Nobby, clearly interpreting our merriment as applause, stood immediately below his victim, panting a little with excitement and wagging his tail tentatively.

"After all," said my brother-in-law, "what is Death? A b-b-bagatelle. Excelsior. Of course, I ought to have a banner, really. Just to wave as I fall. Two and a half guineas these trousers cost. Think of the dogs you could get for that. Excelsior. Seriously, I should get him a set of false teeth and keep them locked up. It'll save in the end. Yes, I know it's side-splitting. I'm only sorry I haven't got a tail. Then I could hang from the electric light. As it is, what about calling off the dog? Not that I'm not comfortable. And the air up here's lovely. But——"

With an effort I pulled myself together and laid a hand on Jill's shoulder.

"Here," I said, nodding in Berry's direction, "here we have the Flat-footed Baboon, an animal of diverting but vulgar habits. That between its eyes is its nose. The only other known specimen is at Dartmoor."

"D'you mind not talking?" said Berry. "I'm just thinking out your death. They say pressing is very painful. Or would you rather call off the mammal?"

I picked up Nobby and put him under my arm.

"You know, you're wicked dog," said I.

For a moment his bright brown eyes met mine. Then with a sudden movement he put up a cold black nose and licked my face. . . .

Before we retired that night, Berry had admitted that Nobby had his points, Nobby had accepted from Berry a caviare sandwich, and I had handed my brother-in-law a cheque for two pounds twelve shillings and sixpence.

* * * * *

It had been arranged that we should spend Christmas with the St. Martins in Wiltshire, and we were to make the journey on the twenty-third. High festival was to be held at Red Abbey, a fine old place with mullioned windows and a great panelled hall that smacked of revelry and Christmas cheer even in summer-time. On Christmas Eve there was to be a dance, on Boxing Day a tenants' ball, and on Christmas Day itself the house-party of twenty souls was to essemble for dinner correctly attired after the manner of children of tender years.

So far as clothes could do it, the spirit of childhood was to be recaptured that night. Guests had been put upon their honour to eschew evasion. Kilts and sailor suits had been forbidden, as was any suit or frock which was not the monopoly of juveniles. Hair was to be worn down, monocles and jewellery were banned. The trappings of Dignity were to be rigidly put off, and Innocence courted with appropriate mockery. The composition of the house-party, which had been carefully chosen, promised an entertainment of more than ordinary interest.

On all three evenings dance music was to be discoursed by a famous coloured band, whose services had long ago been retained for the occasion.

A long-standing engagement made it impossible for Berry to accompany us from London. On Tuesday he must leave Town for Hampshire, but time-tables were consulted, and it was discovered that he could travel across country on Christmas Eve, and, by changing from one station to the other at the market town of Flail, arrive at Red Abbey in time for tea.

"We can take your luggage with us," said Daphne. "You've got all you'll want for the night at White Ladies."

It was half-past nine o'clock, and we were all in the library, resting after labours of the day.

Berry from the depths of the sofa grunted an assent.

"All the same," he added, "I must take something. Beard-eraser, for instance, and a clean neckerchief. Same as when you enlist."

"Everything you can possibly want's there already. Mrs. Foreland knows you're coming, and she'll put everything out."

"I have a weakness," replied her husband, "for my own sponge. Moreover, foolhardy as it may seem, I still clean my teeth. The only question is, what to put them in."

"What's the matter with your pockets?" said I.

"Nothing at present," said Berry. "That's why I shall want your dispatch-case."

"Nothing doing," said I. "I refuse to subscribe to my own inconvenience."

"Self," said Berry bitterly. "Why wasn't I born selfish? I've often tried, but you can't bend an oak, can you? Anybody can have my shirt at any time." Languidly he regarded his cuff. "No. Not this one, but almost any other. My life has been one long unrecognized sacrifice. And what is my reward?" He looked round about him with pitying eyes. "Poor bloated worms, you little know the angel that labours in your midst." His own being finished, with a sigh he took his wife's newly-lighted cigarette from the ash-tray which they were sharing. "I had a dream last night," he added comfortably.

"What about?" said Jill.

"I dreamed," said Berry, "that I was a pint of unusually broad beans. Several people remarked upon my breadth. After spirited bidding, I was secured by no less a personage than The McAroon himself, to whom I gave violent indigestion within twenty-four hours. Pleased with this attention, the laird erected in my memory a small bar at which the rankest poison could be obtained at all hours by asking in Hebrew for ginger ale. Which reminds me. I haven't taken my medicine." Meaningly he regarded the tray which had just been placed upon a side-table. "The doctor said I mustn't move about after meals, or I'd mix it myself. As it is . . ."

He broke off and looked round expectantly.

"Idle brute," said Daphne. "I wonder you aren't afraid to—— Where's my cigarette? I only lighted one a moment ago."

"Perhaps it's behind your ear," suggested her husband. "Perhaps——"

"Where's the match you lighted that one from?" demanded his wife.

"Woman," said Berry indignantly, "you forget yourself. Besides, I didn't use a match. I kindled it by rubbing two sticks together. Same as they do in Guano, where the jelly comes from."

Here a diversion was caused by the opening of the door sufficiently to admit a slightly damp white ball with a black spot, which projected itself into the room as if possessed. Nobby.

Exhilarated to frenzy by the reflection that at least four days must elapse before any one could be bothered to bathe him again, the terrier took a flying leap on to the sofa, licked Daphne's face, put a foot in Berry's eye, barked, hurled himself across the room to where Jonah was playing Patience, upset the card-table, dashed three times round the room, pretended to unearth a rat from the depths of Jill's chair, and finally flung himself exhausted at my feet.

"I suppose this is what they call 'animal spirits'," said Berry. "Or 'muscular Christianity'."

"It is well known," said I, "that exercise after a bath is most beneficial."

"No doubt," was the icy reply. "Well, next time I put my foot in your eye, assume that I've had a bath and call it 'exercise', will you?"

"Have you written to the St. Martins," said Daphne, "to say that you'll be a day late?"

"I have. The masterpiece is on the writing-table, awaiting insertion in an envelope."

I picked up the letter and read aloud as follows—

MADAM,

I am disposed to refer to your invitation to make one of the house-party due to assemble on the 23rd instant.

I am to say that a malignant Fate has decreed that I shall not dignify your hovel before the evening of the following day.

The feeling of profound disappointment which this announcement will provoke should be tempered by the reflection that you are fortunate indeed to have secured so enchanting a personality for your festivities, which, however hopeless they may appear, cannot fail to be galvanized into some show of life by my inspiring presence.

My luggage and the four ungrateful parasites who have so long battened upon my generosity will arrive on the 23rd, as arranged. One of the latter has stealthily acquired a mongrel, which, provided he can obtain the necessary permit, he proposes to bring with him. My protests against this abuse of hospitality have been received with that vulgar insolence which I have, alas, learned to expect.

I am to request you to remember that I am visiting you incognito, as the Duke of Blackpool, and that at this season it is my practice to consume a mince-pie and a bottle of beer before retiring.

I am, Madam,
Your obedient Servant,
BERRY PLEYDELL.

"Outrageous," said Daphne, "perfectly outrageous. However, there's no time to write another, so it had better go. Boy, be a dear and answer that invitation for me."

"This lecture thing?" said I, holding up a gilt-edged card.

My sister nodded.

"We'll have to go, I suppose."

In a flowing hand I wrote as follows—

Major and Mrs. Pleydell have much pleasure in accepting the Countess of Loganberry's kind invitation to attend Professor La Trobe's lecture on the 3rd of January.

When I had read this aloud—

"What an interesting subject!" said Berry. "We shall enjoy ourselves."

* * * * *

Three days later I was in the act of fitting a new blade to my safety-razor, when Berry entered the room fully dressed.

"I'm just off," he said, "but you may as well see what you've done before I go."

"What d'you mean?" said I.

"Read that."

He handed me a letter. I laid down my instrument of torture and read as follows—

SIR,

I am directed by the Countess of Loganberry to acknowledge your communication of the 20th inst., and to say that she cannot recollect the inclusion of your name among those of the guests invited to assemble at Pride Langley the day after to-morrow.

In these circumstances I am to express the hope that you will not trouble to favour her with your attendance upon the 24th inst. or any other date, and that you will take immediate steps to prevent the dispatch of your luggage and of the four parasites, for which, should they arrive, she can accept no responsibility.

I am to add that the Countess is not interested in the acquisition of the animal to which you refer, or in the nature of the victuals with which it is your habit to console yourself of nights.

I am, sir,
Your obedient servant,
FREDERICK BOLETON.

I stroked my chin thoughtfully. Then—

"I don't want to say anything rash," said I, "but it looks as if a mistake had been made."

"But what a brain!" observed by brother-in-law. "What insight!" He glanced at his watch. "And it's not half-past nine yet."

"It is wonderful, isn't it? Now all we want is a line from Diana St. Martin to say how glad she is you're going to the lecture on January the 3rd. Do you agree, brother?"

"I am not here," said Berry loftily, "to discuss your crime. Have you anything to say why the Court should not give judgment?"

"Yes. First, this communication must be answered forthwith. Secondly, Mr. Boleton is clearly a menace to Society. It is therefore our painful duty, brother, to proceed with the operation, inadvertently begun, of pulling his leg until he will require a pair of field glasses to see his own foot."

With a grin Berry clapped me on the back.

"I leave it to you, partner. Make the telegram windy. Wind always inspires wind." He took the letter out of my hand and slipped it into his pocket. "You won't want this document. And now I must be going. See you to-morrow, laddie."

The next moment he was gone.

Within the hour the following telegram was on its way to Pride Langley—

Your letter not understood aaa cannot consent to cancel my arrangements at this hour aaa expect me to-morrow as arranged aaa four tons of luggage entrained last night aaa loose-boxes containing parasites due to arrive at 5.15 to-day aaa imperative these should be watered and fed within one hour of arrival aaa acknowledge.

*　*　*　*　*

Although the train had yet to make its appearance, the platform was crowded. Somewhere at the far end Jonah was waiting to see that our heavy baggage was placed in the van, while Daphne, Jill and I were standing beside such articles as we were proposing to take in the carriage, hoping feverishly that, when the train pulled in, we should find ourselves opposite to a first-class coach.

"Thath a nithe dog," said an unpleasant voice on my left.

I turned to see a very dark gentleman, clad in a light tweed overcoat and cloth-topped boots, with a soft grey hat on the back of his head, smoking an insanitary cigar and smiling unctuously upon Nobby, who was tucked under my arm.

"Yes," I said.

"A Thealyham, ain't he?"

"I believe so."

Undeterred by my evident reluctance to converse, the fellow bowed his head as if to examine the dog, at the same time expelling a cloud of disgusting smoke.

In the twinkling of an eye the terrier had sneezed, wriggled from under my arm, and slipped to the ground. I was just in time to see him scuttle in the direction of a crate of live turkeys which he had vainly struggled to approach when we passed them a few minutes earlier.

Suppressing a violent desire to choke his assailant, I thrust the rug I was carrying into Jill's arms, and started to elbow my way towards the turkeys.

A sudden stutter of barks, a fearful burst of gobbling, and a chorus of indignant cries suggested that the sooner I arrived to take charge, the better for all concerned.

As I pushed forward, the press swayed expectantly towards the edge of the platform, and I glanced round to see the train pulling in.

Thereafter my passage to the scene of the uproar was Homeric. Every step was contested, not actively, but with that jealous determination not to yield which distinguishes the prospective traveller who has bought an expensive ticket and, by no means certain that the supply of seats will be equal to the demand, interprets every movement as an attempt to secure an unfair advantage. I eventually arrived to find in progress a game which I prefer not to describe. Suffice it that, though Nobby was leading, two inspectors and a clergyman with an umbrella were running him pretty close, while the turkeys were simply nowhere.

With a well-timed dive I secured the terrier just as he evaded a left hook from the Church, and, disregarding the loud tones in which several intending passengers announced their conception of the qualifications of a dog-owner, fought my way back to where I had left the girls. The fact that the latter had managed to reserve and hold four seats did them, to my mind, infinite credit.

It was not until we were gliding out of the station that I looked round for my dispatch-case.

I did so in vain.

An investigation of the spaces between the seats and the floor proved equally fruitless.

I sank back in my seat with a groan.

"Where did you see it last?" said Daphne.

"I'm hanged if I know, but of course it was with the other things. I put it in the hall last night, and Falcon knows I always take it wherever I go."

"I'll swear nothing was left on the platform," said Jill.

"Nor in the car," said Jonah. "I looked there myself."

"I've not the slightest doubt it's been pinched," said I. "It's just the sort of thing that'd take a thief's fancy. By Jove!" I cried suddenly. "What about the swab in the light coat? I'll bet any money he took it."

"What swab?" said Jonah.

"Oh, a complete mobsman. Came and jawed about Nobby and then gassed him with his cigar till he did a bunk. That put me out of the way. With the girls trying to get a carriage, the rest was easy. Gad! Why doesn't one think of these things? It's locked, and there's nothing terribly valuable in it, but I do hate being stung."

"First stop Flail," said Jonah, looking at his watch. "You've got the best part of two hours to think it over. I should write out a synopsis of the crime in duplicate, with a description of the missing property——"

"And a plan of the station, I suppose, showing the all-red route I took to the crate of turkeys, with a signed photograph of Nobby. I've only got to attach my birth certificate, and there you are."

"Gentleman seems annoyed," said Jonah, unfolding the *Pall Mall*.

Jill laid a hand on my arm, and I laughed in spite of myself.

"He'll be fed to the teeth when he gets it open," I said. "I admit the cigars are not what he's accustomed to, but I'd like to meet the fence that'll take a nainsook pinafore and a couple of bibs."

This comfortable reflection in some sort consoled me. All the same, when we steamed into Flail I sent for the station-master and handed that gentleman two short descriptions—one of the dispatch-case, and the other of the thief. He promised readily to keep a look-out and inform the police.

"An' I'll telephone down the line, sir. You never know. He might be on the train, or even 'ave got out 'ere." I made as if to leave the compartment. "Ah, he'd be gone by now, an' you're just off. But I'll do what I can. Your address, Red Abbey. Very good, sir."

*　　*　　*　　*　　*

Diana St. Martin was at the station to meet us, in a fever of excitement and good-will. Her obvious disappointment at Berry's absence was allayed by our assurance that he would appear the next day.

"Of course," she announced, "I was thrilled to learn that you were going to the Loganberry's lecture, but I couldn't help feeling that there was some news, more relevant to your visit, which I ought to know. Hullo! Is he going to honour us?" she added, pointing to Nobby, who, with tail erect and eyes looking sideways, was considering whether or no to accept the advances of an Irish terrier in the spirit in which they were patently offered. "What a darling!"

"If you please," said I.

"Splendid. And now come along. We can all get in the limousine, and there's a van for your luggage."

During the drive from the station I told her the style of the letter she should have received, and disclosed the grave construction placed upon it by the actual recipient. When I told her that Mr. Boleton and I were now in telegraphic communication, she gave a little crow of delight.

"How priceless!" she cried. "Perhaps there'll be a wire when we get back."

She was wrong. But only by a few minutes. Before we had been at Red Abbey for a quarter of an hour, a telegram was handed to me. Falcon had forwarded it from London.

> Forced to regard your conduct as molestful delivery of your luggage will not be accepted parasites will remain boxed and receive necessary attention at your expense and risk

pending instructions regarding their removal which should be communicated to station-master direct any attempt on your part to enter Pride Langley to-morrow will be forcibly resisted.

At once I arranged for the dispatch of the following reply—

At great inconvenience have arranged to postpone arrival of luggage and parasites until to-morrow aaa impossible however to stop elephants seven of which should reach you by road before midnight and remainder by 2 a.m. aaa as already stated am unable at this juncture to cancel my visit but shall certainly never stay at Pride Langley again aaa if "molestful" means what I think it does I shall point you out to the large parasite.

We spent a hilarious evening.

The Irish terrier showed Nobby that hospitality for which the Isle is famous. He made him free of the house and grounds, showed him the way to the kitchen, and indicated by occupation the most comfortable chairs. Nobby returned the compliment by initiating his host into the mysteries of a game which consisted of making a circuit of the great hall, ascending the main staircase, entering and erupting from any bedroom of which the door stood open, and descending the staircase—all of this recurring—with the least possible delay. The Irish terrier proved an apt pupil, and, so far as can be judged, if Diana's maid had not encountered them in the midst of their seventh descent, and been upset, and of vexation nipped by an angry competitor for her pains, the game might have gone on for weeks. This incident, however, followed by the production of a hunting whip, brought the game to a close and the host to his senses. Hastily he repaired a grave omission, and a moment later Nobby was cowering in comparative, if inconvenient, safety beneath an enormous tallboy chest.

After dinner cards were brought forth and *vingt et un* was played. In a weak moment I volunteered to "carry" Jill, who played with an *abandon* which was at once exhilarating and extremely expensive. Her persistent refusal to "stand" on anything less than twenty-one commanded an admiration which, but for my presence, would have been universal. The only run of luck with which her audacity was favoured coincided with my tenure of the bank, during which period she took fifty-two shillings off me in seven minutes.

As I pushed her counters across—

"I've heard of robbing Peter to pay Paul," I said gloomily, "but never of robbing Charlie to pay Chaplin. Why couldn't you do this when some one else had the bank?"

"You shouldn't deal me such cards," was the ungrateful reply.

A moment later she turned up a "natural" with a dazzling smile.

There was a roar of laughter.

"Of course, this is Berry's luck," said I. "And it needs Berry's tongue to cope with it. A little more, and I shall ship for Australia before the mast. Yes, I'll have a brandy-and-soda, please. Of appropriate strength."

"In inverse proportion to your luck?" said my host.

I shook my head.

"That would require Berry's liver. Besides, to-morrow morning I'm going to help your wife to decorate the church. I admit I was a fool to promise, but it's done now, and——"

The chocolate which Diana threw at me ricocheted from my cheekbone on to the hearth, and was devoured by Nobby in the very teeth of his host.

I looked at my watch with a sigh.

"I suppose I ought to have told you that chocolates fall without the limit of his digestive powers. The last one took about four hours. And it's eleven now. I am glad I came."

My statement was received with ironical cheers. . . .

It may or may not have been the chocolate, but in the small hours of the following morning it became expedient that I should admit Nobby into the open air. And so it came about that I stood patient and shivering, in a fur coat and pyjamas, at a garden door, while a small white rough-haired thing heaved upon the lawn twelve decent yards away.

The sailing moon, clear-cut, issued her cold white light and showed the sleeping country silent but troubled. A pride of clouds rode high in heaven, and the same strong careless wind that bore them swept from the leafless boughs of earth below a boisterous melody, that rose and fell in league-long phrases, far as the ear could follow. Nature was in a royal mood. Her Cap of Maintenance was out, Pomp was abroad, the trump of Circumstance was sounding. A frown of dignity knitted her gentle brow, and meadows, roads, thickets and all her Court wore a staid look to do her honour. Only her favourite, water, dared to smile, and the flashing lake flung back the moonlight with long ripples of silvery laughter.

Somewhere close at hand an owl cried, and Nobby answered the challenge with a menacing bark. I whistled, and he came running, the very embodiment of health and spirits. Marvelling at a dog's recuperative powers, I opened the door. As I did so, I heard the stable clock striking. Three o'clock.

* * * * *

Twelve hours later a servant entered the library to arouse me from a refreshing sleep with the news that some one desired to speak with me upon the telephone. Heavily I made my way to the lobby and put the receiver to my ear, but the first sentence I heard drove the lingering rearguard of Slumber headlong from my system.

It was an Inspector of Police, speaking from Flail.

"I think we've got your case, sir. Pigskin, seventeen inches by ten, an' a blue line runnin' acrost it?"

"That's right," I said excitedly.

"An' it's still locked. No initials. But we'd like your formal identification. Besides . . . I don't know whether you could manage this afternoon, sir, but if you could . . . You see, it's a matter of a charge. We're detainin' a man in connection with the thef'."

"Oh, I don't want to proceed. So long as I get the case back . . ."

" 'Fraid we can't 'ardly do that, sir."

I groaned. Then—

"How far is Red Abbey from Flail?"

"Matter o' twelve mile, sir. Wouldn't take you no time in a car."

"I'll see what I can do. Good-bye."

Both cars were needed to meet incoming guests, but a Miss Doiran, who had arrived that morning in her own two-seater, offered to drive me to Flail and back before tea.

A quarter of an hour later we were on the road.

She listened attentively to the story of my loss. When I had finished—

"You'd little enough to go on, I must say. I'd never have dared to say that man had stolen it."

"It was a bow at a venture," I admitted. "But it seems to have come off. All the same, I don't want to charge the chap. He deserves six months, if only for his cigar, but I'd rather somebody else sent him down."

"I expect they'll make you. After all, it was a pretty smart capture, and the police'll be fed to the teeth if you don't go through with it."

"Considering it was stolen in London, I didn't see any sense in telling the police at Flail, but the station-master apparently knew his job."

With a temporarily disengaged hand Miss Doiran caressed Nobby, who was seated between us.

"I've always wanted a Sealyham," she sighed.

"You could have had one for nothing at three o'clock this morning."

"Did he have you up?"

I nodded.

"And down and out." I sighed. "It was a handsome night. Very cold, though. I thought of you all warm in bed."

"What a wicked story! You never knew of my existence."

"I thought of everybody. That embraced you. It's extraordinary how little women can wear without dying of exposure, isn't it?"

Miss Doiran glanced at her sleeve.

"This coat is lined with chamois leather," she said. "I don't know what more you want."

"Yes. But your stockings aren't. When you stepped into the car I was frightened for you."

My companion's chin rose, and she stared through the windscreen with compressed lips.

"I'm as warm as toast," she said defiantly.

"If you're no warmer than the toast I had for breakfast this morning——"

"You should get up earlier."

"I thought I told you I was up and about at three."

"That doesn't count."

"Doesn't it? All right. You get up at three to-morrow and think of me all warm in bed, and see whether it counts. By the way, don't say you wear pyjamas, because I can't bear it."

Miss Doiran addressed our companion.

"Is he often like this, Nobby?"

I explained.

"It's not idle curiosity. You see, I'm editing a directory to be called *That's That*. It's really a short list of a few nice people left who aren't anybody: with just a word or two about their manners, failings, virtues, if any, and the attire they usually effect when off duty. It won't say when they were born, but why they were born."

"That'll sell it," said Miss Doiran.

"So you see. May I know now, or must I wait outside the bathroom?"

"I'm afraid," said Miss Doiran, "that you must wait outside the bathroom."

I sighed.

"If it is pyjamas," said I, "I shall scream."

Some geese hissed as we swept by. The noise was inaudible, but the hostility of their gesture was patent. Its effect upon Nobby was electrical. Exasperated to madness by the gratuitous insult, he made the most violent attempts to leave the car, only pausing the better to lift up his voice and rave at his, by this time distant, tormentors. His dignity was outraged and, what was much worse, unavenged.

"D'you still want him?" I shouted, holding fast to his collar with one hand, while with the other I strove to muffle his cries with the rug.

"Every time."

I swallowed before replying.

"Of course, this is exceptional," I said weakly. "He can be very good if he likes."

Miss Doiran laughed.

"I believe you just dote on him."

I lugged the white scrap out of the welter of rug and set him up on my knees. Surprised, he stopped barking and looked me full in the eyes. Then he thrust a cold nose into my face. Almost roughly I put him away.

"I believe you're right," I said.

Ten minutes later we drove up to Flail Police Station.

I thrust Nobby under my arm and stepped out of the car. Then I turned to the girl.

"I'll be as quick as I can," I said.

"Right oh!"

Sure enough it was my dispatch-case. In some embarrassment I described the ridiculous contents. Then I produced the key and confirmed my own words.

"I must say," I said, "you haven't wasted much time. How did you recover it?"

The inspector in charge looked grave.

"'E's a nice little lot, what took this case, sir. I shouldn't wonder if there was 'alf a dozen warrants out for 'im. As plausible a rogue as ever I see, an' as full o' swank as a negg is o' meat. Told us the tale proper, 'e did. One o' the kind as gets through by sheer nerve. Now, nine out o' ten'd 'ave bin through this 'ere case last night and throwed it away. But 'e's not that sort. Walks through the town this afternoon with it under 'is arm, as bold as brass." A "plain-clothes" man entered and stood waiting. "All ready? Right." He turned again to me. "An' now sir, we'll be obliged if you'll step into the yard and see if you see anybody you recognize. I'd like the identification to be regular."

Perceiving my chance of doing the thief a good turn, I assented readily. It was my fixed intention to recognize no one.

I followed the policeman into a high-walled yard.

Variously attired, six men were drawn up in line.

"Do you see anybody you know?" repeated the inspector.

I did. *Standing third from the left, with a seraphic look on his face, was Berry.*

For a moment I stood spellbound. Then I began to laugh uncontrollably.

"Go on, you fool," said Berry. "Indicate the felon. I admit it's one up to you, but I'll get my own back. You wait. Why, there's Kernobby." The terrier slipped from under my arm and ran to where he stood. "Good dog. But I mustn't play with you till the gentleman in blue boxcloth says so. 'Sides, I'm a giddy criminal, I am." He addressed my companion. "Will you dismiss the parade, inspector? Or shall we do a little troop drill?"

I turned to the bewildered officer.

"It's all a mistake, inspector. This is my brother-in-law. He must have borrowed the case without my knowledge. For goodness' sake, get these men away, and we'll explain things."

The inspector hesitated, but Nobby's frantic efforts to lick the suspect's face settled the matter. Gruffly he acted upon my suggestion, and the little squad broke up.

In the charge-room we satisfied him of the sincerity of our statements and exonerated him from blame. To do the police justice, Berry was dressed more or less in accordance with my hazy description of the "thief", and it was my dispatch-case. Courtesies were exchanged, I signed a receipt for my property, and Berry, his effects restored, gave a poor devil, who was brought in to be charged with begging, enough to console the latter for his detention on Christmas Day.

A moment later I was introducing him to Miss Doiran.

"Thief and brother-in-law in one," I said. "A terrible combination."

Berry took off his hat and put a hand to his head.

"Whose reign is it?" he said dazedly. "When I entered the gaol it was King George."

* * * * *

With his back to the fire in Daphne's bedroom, Berry proceeded to clear the air.

"If any one of you four had a tenth of the instinct of a village idiot, it would have occurred to those diseased fungi which you call your minds that I had said I should want Boy's dispatch-case. But let that pass.

"I was walking through Flail according to plan, and following the tram-lines according to the drivelling advice given me by an outside porter with a suggestive nose. Need I say that before I had covered a hundred yards the lines branched? I was still praying for the soul of my informant, when I observed that a large blue constable, who was apparently lining the street, was staring at me as at an apparition. Courteously I gave him 'Good day'. In return he handed me a look which I shall try to forget, and asked me how I came by the dispatch-case.

" 'I didn't,' I said. 'I came by train.'

"Noticing that he seemed piqued by my reply, I made haste to suggest that we should repair to a neighbouring dairy and consume two small glasses of butter-milk and a sponge cake at my expense. Not to be outdone in hospitality, he made a counter-proposal, which, after some hesitation, I thought it discreet to accept. Our progress through the streets afforded the acme of gratification to the populace, most of whom accompanied us with every circumstance of enthusiasm and delight. Altogether it was most exhilarating.

"My reception at the police station was cordial in the extreme. They told me their theory, and I gave them my explanation. The fact that the beastly case was still locked was naturally in my favour. In fact, everything in the garden was lovely, and I was on the point of pushing off to catch my train, when that fool of an inspector asked if I'd leave my card, as a matter of form.

" 'I'm afraid I haven't one on me,' I said, 'but I dare say I've got an envelope,' and I started to feel in my pockets. There was only one paper there, and that wasn't an envelope. *It was Mr.*

Boleton's letter.

"The moment I saw what it was, I knew I was done. I couldn't put it away, or they'd get suspicious. If I showed it them, they'd regard me as first-class crook, and very big game. I suppose I hesitated, for the Inspector leaned forward and took it out of my hand.

"The rest was easy. I was reviled, searched, cautioned, examined, measured, described and finally told that I should be detained pending inquiries. I was then immured in a poisonous-looking dungeon, which, to judge from its atmosphere, had been recently occupied by an anti-prohibitionist, and, from its condition, not yet reached by the chambermaid.

"Yes," he concluded, "you have before you the complete gaol-bird."

"How did you spend your time?" said Jonah.

"B-b-beating my wings against the crool b-b-bars," said Berry. "My flutterings were most painful. Several turnkeys broke down. The rat which was attached to me for pay and rations gambolled to assuage my grief. Greatly affected by the little animal's antics, I mounted the plank bed and rang the b-b-bell for the b-b-boots. In due course they appeared full of the feet of a gigantic warder. I told him that I had not ordered vermin and should prefer a fire, and asked if they'd mind if I didn't dress for dinner. I added that I thought flowers always improved a cell, and would he buy me some white carnations and a b-b-begonia. His reply was evasive and so coarse that I told the rat not to listen, and recited what I could remember of 'The Lost Chord'." He turned to me. "The remainder of my time I occupied in making plans for the disposal of your corpse."

"You've only yourself to thank." said I. "You shouldn't have borrowed the goods. I acted in good faith."

"I wonder," said Berry, "where one gets quicklime."

*   *   *   *   *

It was during the interval between the third and fourth dances, both of which had been given me by Miss Doiran, that the latter consulted her programme.

"I'm dancing the fifth," she announced, "with the Duke of Blackpool." I started violently, but she took no notice. "I think you know him. He was released from prison this afternoon. As my aunt's secretary, I've had some correspondence with him under the name of Boleton."

My brain began to work furiously.

"I scent collusion," I said. "Diana is in this."

Miss Doiran laughed.

"She rang me up directly she got your note about the lecture. The rest sort of came natural. I believe you were responsible for the telegrams. I congratulate you. The elephants were a brain-wave. My aunt was tickled to death by them."

"How dreadful! I mean—it's very nice of her. I'm afraid it was all rather impertinent."

"If so, we were the first to offend, and, after all, Major Pleydell has expiated his crime."

"And he's fixed my murder for the first week in January. There's really only you left."

"Oh, I'm punished already," said Miss Doiran. "I've lost my heart. And he doesn't love me."

"Would it be indiscreet to ask his name?"

Miss Doiran looked round the room.

"When I last saw him," she said, "he was talking to an Irish terrier."

CHAPTER V

How Jill's Education was Improved, and Daphne gave her Husband the Slip

"As I have frequently observed," said Berry, "your education has been neglected. I'm not blaming those responsible. Your instruction must have been a thankless task."

"I should think the masters who taught you enjoyed their holidays."

Such a reply from Jill was like a sudden snowstorm in June, and Berry, who was in the act of drinking, choked with surprise. When he had recovered his breath—

"You rude child," he said. "My prizes are among my most cherished possessions."

"Where d'you keep them?"—suspiciously.

"Chancery Lane Safe Deposit," was the reply. "When I die I shall leave them to the Wallace Collection. The shoes I wore at the first night of *Buzz-Buzz* are already promised to the Imperial Institute."

"When you've quite finished," said Daphne, "I'll suggest that we go up for the day on Friday. I don't mean to-morrow, but the one after."

"It's a little early in the year," said I. "All the same, there's no reason why we shouldn't go up again later on. It's always open."

"If the weather holds," said Jonah, "it will be looking wonderful."

Oxford. Some reference had been made to the city while we sat at dessert, and in the midst of a banana Jill had confessed that she had never been there. The rest of us knew the place well. Berry had been at Magdalen, Jonah at New College, and I had fleeted four fat years carelessly as a member of "The House". But, while my sister had spent many hours there during my residence, Jill had not once visited her brother—largely, no doubt, because there was a disparity of eight years, in her favour, between their ages.

"I warn you," said Berry, "that I may break down. My return to the haunts of early innocence may be too much for me. Yes," he added, "I shouldn't be at all surprised if I were to beat my breast somewhere near The Martyrs' Memorial."

"An appropriate locality," said Jonah. "If my memory serves me, it was for a crime committed almost under the shadow of that monument that you were irrevocably sent down."

Berry selected a cigar before replying. Then—

"Only a malignant reptile would refer to that miscarriage of justice. It was not my fault that the animal which I employed exceeded its instructions and, as it were, pushed on after attaining its objective."

"You expected it to consolidate the position?" said I.

"Precisely. To dig itself in. It was like this. It was expedient—no matter why—that a large boar should be introduced into Balliol College shortly before 10 p.m. A gigantic specimen was accordingly procured and brought to the Broad street entrance in a hansom cab. It was then induced to take up a position commanding the wicket-door. The juxtaposition of two hurdles, held in place by my subordinates, frustrated any attempt at untimely evacuation. At a given signal the customary kick was administered to the gate, indicating that some person or persons sought admission to the foundation. Unhesitatingly the porter responded to the summons. The wicket was opened, and the pig passed in."

"I think it was very cruel," said Daphne.

"Not at all," said her husband. "There was more succulent grass upon the lawns of Balliol than was dreamt of in its ferocity. To continue. My mission accomplished, I entered the hansom and drove to the Club. It was during an unfortunate altercation with the cabman, who demanded an unreasonably exorbitant sum for the conveyance of the pig, that I was accosted by the proctor for being gownless. The cab was still redolent of its late occupant, and, although nothing was said at the time, it was this which afterwards led the authorities to suspect my complicity. Even so, nothing would have been said but for a most distressing development.

"I had expected that the pig would confine its attention to the quadrangles and gardens and to startling such members of the college as happened casually to encounter it. Fate, however, decreed otherwise. It appears that the creature's admission coincided with the opening of a door which led directly into the Senior Common Room, where the Master and Fellows were still discussing classical criticism and some '34 port. Attracted by the shaft of light and the mellow atmosphere of good cheer and hilarity which streamed into the comparative gloom of the quadrangle, the pig made a bee-line for the doorway, and a moment later the exclusive circle was enriched by the presence of this simple and unaffected guest. The details of what followed have never transpired, but from the Senior Proctor's demeanour at a subsequent interview, and the amount of the bill for damage which I was requested to pay, I am inclined to think that the pig must have been a confirmed Bolshevist."

"I hope you apologized to the Master."

"I did. I received in reply a letter which I shall always value. It ran as follows—

SIR,

I beg that you will think no more of the matter. Youth must be served. Many years ago I assisted your father in a somewhat similar enterprise. Till the other evening I had always believed that the havoc provoked by the introduction of a dancing bear into a concert-room could not be surpassed. I am now less certain.

Yours very faithfully,

. . . ."

" I think," said Jill, "he was very forgiving."

"It was deep," said Berry, "calling to deep. By the way, you'll all be pleased to hear that I have received peremptory instructions 'within one week to abolish the existing number by which this house is distinguished, and to mark or affix on some conspicuous part thereof a new number, and to renew the same as often as it is obliterated or defaced.' Selah."

"Whatever," said Daphne, "do you mean?"

"Sorry," said Berry. "Let me put it another way. Some genii, masquerading as officials, have got a move on. Snuffing the air of 'Reconstruction', they have realized with a shock that the numbers of the houses in this street have not been changed for over half a century. Thirstily they have determined to repair the omission. We've always been '38'. In a few days, with apologies to Wordsworth, we shall be '7'. A solemn thought."

"But can we do nothing?"

"Certainly. In that case somebody else will obliterate the existing number, and I shall be summoned to appear before a Justice of the Peace."

"It's outrageous," said Daphne. "It'll cause endless confusion, and think of all our notepaper and cards. All the dies will have to be scrapped and new ones cut."

"Go easy," said I. "After a decent interval they'll alter the name of the street. Many people feel that The Quadrant should be renamed 'The Salient', and Piccadilly 'High Street'. I'm all for Progress."

"Is this renumbering stunt a fact?" said Jonah. "Or are you just being funny?"

"It's a poisonous but copper-bottomed fact," said Berry. "This is the sort of thing we pay rates and taxes for. Give me Germany."

"Can't we refuse?"

"I've rung up Merry and Merry, and they've looked up the law, and say there's no appeal. We are at the mercy of some official who came out top in algebra in '64 and has never recovered. Let us be thankful it wasn't geography. Otherwise we should be required to name this house 'Sea View' or 'Clovelly'. Permit me to remark that the port has now remained opposite you for exactly four minutes of time, for three of which my goblet has been empty."

"I think it's cruel," said Jill, passing on the decanter. "I think——"

"Hush," said Berry. "That wonderful organ, my brain, is working." Rapidly he began to write upon the back of a *menu*. "We must inform the world through the medium of the Press. An attractive paragraph must appear in *The Times*. What could be more appropriate than an epitaph? Ply me with wine, child. The sage is in labour with a song." Jill filled his glass and he drank. "Another instant, and you shall hear the deathless words. I always felt I should be buried in the Abbey. Anybody give me a rhyme for 'bilge'? No, it doesn't matter. I have ingeniously circumvented the crisis."

He added one line, held the card at arm's length, regarded it as a painter a canvas, sighed, and began to read.

A painful tale I must relate.
We used to live at thirty-eight,
But, as we hope to go to heaven,
We've come to live at number seven.
Now, if we'd lived at number nine,
I'd got a simply priceless line—
I didn't want to drag in heaven,
But nothing else will rhyme with seven.

"Soldier, mountebank, and rhymester too!" said Jonah. "And yet we breathe the same air."

"I admit it's strange," said my brother-in-law. "But it was foretold by my predecessor. I think you'll find the prophecy in *Henry the Fifth*. 'And wholesome berries thrive and ripen best, Neighboured by fruit of baser quality.' My game, I think. What?"

* * * * *

As was fitting, St. George's Day dawned fair and cloudless. Her passionate weeping of the day before dismissed, April was smiling—shyly at first, as if uncertain that her recent waywardness had been forgiven, and by and by so bravely that all the sweet o' the year rose up out of the snowy orchards, dewy and odorous, danced in the gleaming meadows and hung, glowing and breathless, in every swaying nursery that Spring had once more built upon the patient trees.

The Rolls sailed through the country, proudly indifferent to hill or dale, melting the leagues to miles with such swift deadliness as made you sorry for the lean old road that once had been so much to reckon with.

I was on the point of comunicating this Quixotic reflection to Agatha Deriot, who was seated in front between Jill and myself, when there fell upon my reluctant ears that heavy sigh which only an expiring tyre can heave. As I slowed up, it occurred to me that the puissance of the roads of England was still considerable.

"Which is it?" said Agatha.

"Off hind, I fancy." We were in the midst of a pleasant beechwood, and I pulled in to the side of the road with a grunt. "If it had to be, it might have happened in a less pleasing locality."

"I gather," said Berry's voice, "I gather that something untoward has befallen the automobile. Should I be wrong, correct me and explain the stoppage."

"With that singular clarity of interest which never fails to recognize the obvious, you have correctly diagnosed the case. We have picked up a puncture."

"Speak for yourself," said Berry. "I always let them lie. I did gather a bunch of bursts once, but——"

"Sorry," said I. "I forgot how near we were to Oxford. What I meant was that some hostile body of a sharp nature had penetrated a tyre, thus untimely releasing the air hitherto therein confined."

"Thank you," said Berry. "Experience leads me to anticipate a slight delay, the while you effect the necessary repairs. I shall therefore compose myself to slumber and meditation. Possibly I shall toy with a cigarette. Possibly——"

"Your programme will, I fear, miscarry for more than one reason. In the first place, you're sitting on the jack. In the second place, clumsy fool though you are, Jonah can change the wheel quicker if you help him." With that I climbed out of the driver's seat, and lighted a cigarette. "Who," I added, "will come for a little walk?"

"I'm coming," said Daphne, setting aside the rug and rising from her seat between Jonah and her husband.

"I forbid you," said the latter, "to consort with that blasphemous viper."

My sister leaned down and kissed him.

"A little gentle exercise," she said, "will do you good. I expect it'll make you hot, so take your coat off. Then you'll have something to put on again."

Coldly Berry regarded her.

"How long," he said, "did it take you to work that out?"

As we strolled down the sun-flecked road in the wake of Miss Deriot and Jill, I turned and looked back at the car. Something was squatting on the tarmac close to the petrol tank. The fact that

Jonah was unstrapping a spare wheel suggested that my brother-in-law was taking exercise. . . .

My sister slid an arm through mine, and we walked idly on. The road curled out of the wood into the unchecked sunlight, rising to where its flashing hedgerows fell back ten paces each, leaving a fair green ride on either side of the highway. Here jacketed elms made up a stately colonnade, ready to nod their gay green crests at each stray zephyr's touch, and throwing broad equidistant bars of shadow across the fresh turf and the still moist ribbon of metalling beyond. Two piles of stones lay heaped upon the sward, and, as we drew near, we heard the busy chink of a stone-breaker's hammer, a melodious sound that fitted both morning and venue to perfection. Again I fell to thinking on the old coach road. . . .

The stone-breaker was an old, old man, but the tone in which he gave us "Good day" was blithe and good to hear, while he looked as fit as a fiddle.

"You work very fast," said I, as he reached for a mammoth flint.

"Aye," he said. "But it come easy, sir, after so many year."

"Have you always done this?" said Daphne.

The old fellow plucked the gauze from his brow and touched his battered hat.

"Naught else, m'm. Nine-and-seventy year come Michaelmas I've kep' the Oxford road. An' me father before me."

"That's a wonderful record," said I amazedly. "And you carry your years well."

"Thank you, sir. There's a many as tells me that. I'll be ninety-one in the month o' June. An' can't write me own name, sir."

"That's no shame," said I. "Tell me, you must remember the coaches."

"That do I. They was took off my road just afore I started breakin' meself, but long afore that I used to bring me father 'is dinner, an' I remember them well. Many a time I've watched the 'Tantivy' go by, an' Muster Cracknell drivin'. Always nodded to father, 'e did, an' passed the time o' day. An' father, 'e'd wave 'is 'ammer, an' call me an' tell me 'is name, an' what a fine coachman 'e were. 'Twas a Birmin'ham coach, the 'Tantivy', but Muster Cracknell used to 'and over at Oxford. London to Oxford was 'is stretch, sir. An' back."

"Isn't that wonderful?" said Daphne.

Agatha and Jill, who had joined us, agreed in awestruck

whispers.

The old fellow laughed.

"I've seen the coaches, m'm, and I've seen the motors, an' they can't neither of them do without the road, m'm. As it was in the beginnin', so ever it shall be. Soon I'll pass, but the road'll go on, an' others'll break for 'er. For she must needs be patched, you know, m'm, she must needs be patched. . . ."

We gave him money, and he rose and uncovered and pulled his white forelock with the antique courtesy of his class. As we turned away, I pinched Daphne's arm.

"I'll bet no man's ever done that to you before."

She shook her head, smiling.

"I don't think so. It was very nice of him."

"What would you call him?" said Jill. "A stone-breaker?"

I raised my eyebrows.

"I suppose so. Or roadman."

"I know," said Agatha softly. "He's a Gentleman of the Road."

"Good for you," said I. "The title never became a highwayman one half so well."

As I spoke, the Rolls stole up alongside. We climbed in, Jill and I sitting behind for a change. With a foot on the step, Daphne looked at her husband.

"Did you get very hot?" she said.

"I did," said Berry. "Every pore in my body has been in action. I always think it's so nice to start a day like that."

"How would you like to break stones," said I, "for seventy-nine years?"

Jonah let in the clutch.

"I perceive," said Berry, "that you are under the influence of drink. At the present moment I am more interested in the breaking of backs. Have you ever jacked up a car?"

"Often. You must stoop to conquer."

"Stoop? You must have a comic spine. My trunk kept getting in the way. And my nether limbs were superfluous. To do it properly you should be severed below the armpits."

"The correct way," said I, " is to face the jack, and then bend backwards till you face it again. Then it's simplicity itself. You work, as it were, between your own legs."

My brother-in-law sighed.

"I used to do my boots up like that, when an agent in Germany. In that way no one could assault me from behind. Those detailed to stab me in the back were nonplussed and in several cases shot for incompetence."

A quarter of an hour later we slid over Magdalen Bridge.

* * * * *

The venerable city was unchanged. That same peculiar dignity, which no impertinence can scathe, that same abiding peace, the handiwork of labouring centuries, that immemorial youth, which drains the cups of Time and pays no reckoning—three wonders of the world, rose up to meet us visitors.

Oxford has but two moods.

This day she was *allegro*. The Sunshine Holyday of Spring had won her from her other soberer state, and Mirth was in all her ways. Her busy streets were bright, her blistered walls glowed and gave back the warmth vouchsafed them, her spires and towers were glancing, vivid against the blue: the unexpected green, that sprawled ragged upon scaly parapets, thrust boldly out between the reverend mansions and smothered up the songs of architects, trembled to meet its patron: the blowing meadows beamed, gates lifted up their heads, retired quadrangles smiled in their sleep, the very streams were lazy, and gardens, walks, spaces and alleyed lanes were all betimes a-Maying.

Perhaps because it was St. George's Day, ghosts that the grey old stones can conjure up, at Fancy's whim came thronging. The state of Kings rode by familiar, shrewd virgin Majesty swayed in a litter down the roaring streets, and the unruly pomp of a proud cardinal wended its scarlet way past kneeling citizens. Cavaliers ruffled it in the chequered walks, prelates and sages loaded the patient air with discourse, and phantom tuck of drum ushered a praise-God soldiery to emptied bursaries. With measured tread statesmen and scholars paced sober up and down the flags, absorbed in argument, poets roamed absent by, and Law and bustling Physic, learned and gowned and big with dignity, swept in and out the gates of colleges whose very fame, that spurred their young intent, they lived to magnify.

After a random drive about the city, in the course of which we visited St. John's and Magdalen, we put the car in a garage and repaired to *The Mitre* for lunch.

Such other spectacles as we proposed to view lay more or less close together, and could be inspected more conveniently without the car, which claimed the constant vigilance of one of us just at the very times we least could spare it.

Fortified by the deference shown him by his scout, whom he

had encountered while visiting his old rooms overlooking the Deer Park, my brother-in-law had in some measure succeeded—so far as Jill and Agatha were concerned—in investing his sojourn at Magdalen with an ill-merited dignity; and Daphne, Jonah and I were quite justifiably delighted when a prosperous-looking individual, with a slip in his waistcoat and a diamond ring, left his table and laid a fat hand familiarly upon Berry's shoulder.

"Hullo, Pleydell, old man. How's things? Don't remember me, I suppose. Lewis." He mentioned the name of the minor college he had once adorned. "You were at Magdalen, weren't you?"

Taken completely by surprise, Berry hesitated before replying in a tone which would have chilled a glacier.

"Er-yes. I'm afraid my memory's not as good as yours. You must excuse me."

"That's all right," said the other, with a fat laugh. "I was one of the quiet little mice," he added archly, "and you were always such a gay dog." To our indescribable delectation he actually thrust a stubby forefinger into his victim's ribs.

"Er—yes," said Berry, moving his chair as far from his tormentor as space would permit. "I suppose you were. One of the mice, I think you said. You know, I still don't seem to remember your face or name. You're quite sure . . ."

"Anno Domini," was the cheerful reply. "We're both older, eh? Don't you remember the night we all—— But p'r'aps I oughtn't to tell tales out of school, ought I, old bean?" Again the forefinger was employed, and its owner looked round expectantly. Beads of perspiration became visible upon Berry's forehead, and Jonah and I burst into a roar of laughter.

Greatly encouraged by our mirth, Mr. Lewis beamed with geniality, and, slapping Berry upon the back with the diamond ring, commended the good old times, observed that the undergraduates of to-day were of a very different class to "me and you", and added that England was in such a rotten state that, if the Coal Controller had not personally begged him to "carry on", he would have "up stick and cleared out to Australia long ago."

At his concluding words Daphne sat up as if she had been shot. Then, administering to me a kick, which she afterwards explained had been intended for Berry, she smiled very charmingly.

"I suppose you're just up for the day, Mr. Lewis. As we are," she inquired.

With an elaborate bow Mr. Lewis agreed, and in a moment the two were carrying on an absurd conversation, to which Jonah and I contributed by laughing unfeignedly whenever a remark justified an expression of mirth. Jill and Agatha were on the edge of hysteria, and Berry sat sunk in a condition of profound gloom, from which he occasionally emerged to fix one or other of us with a stare of such malevolence as only served to throw us into a fresh paroxysm of laughter.

Had Mr. Lewis for one moment appreciated the true cause of our amusement, he would have been a broken man. Happily his self-confidence was sublime, and, when Daphne finally bowed and remarked with a dazzling smile that no doubt he and her husband would like to have a little chat after luncheon, he retired in a perfect ecstasy of gratification.

When he was out of earshot—

"Why not ask him to come and live with us?" said Berry. "He could go to the Loganberrys' ball on Tuesday, and Jonah and I can put him up for the Club. He might even stay for Ascot."

"I think he's a topper," said I.

"Old college pal, I suppose," said Jonah. "Let's call the Stilton after him."

"Listen," said Daphne. "Didn't you hear him say he was something to do with coal? Well, the moment he said it, I thought of what I've been trying to remember ever since yesterday morning. We've got three hundredweight left, and we've had more than our ration already. For goodness' sake, get him to do something for us."

"You wicked woman," said Berry. "You wicked, deceitful woman."

"Nonsense," said Daphne. "It's just a stroke of luck. Of course, he mayn't be able to help, but it's worth trying. If you want to do without a hot bath—let alone fires—for the next three months, I don't."

"And I am to be the cat's-paw?" said Berry. "I'm to have the felicity of hobnobbing with that poisonous bounder——"

"You've done it before," said I. "He remembers it perfectly."

"Vermin," said Berry, "you lie. My association with that little pet was confined to the two solitary occasions upon which I was so misguided as to be the guest of a club of which he was not a member, but which was, nevertheless, an institution of the college which he adorned. After dinner it was customary to pay a short but eventful visit to the rooms of the most unpopular man in college. On each occasion Mr. Lewis's rooms were unanimously selected."

"Nemesis," said I. "He's getting his own back."

"I rejoice to think," said my brother-in-law, "that it was I who conceived the idea of secreting Chinese figs in every pair of his boots and shoes that could be found. If I remember, we used the best part of two boxes."

"I depend upon you," said Daphne. "Be civil to him for five minutes, and we'll—we'll wait for you between St. Mary's and The Radcliffe."

"But how nice of you! I should hate to suggest that you were not taking any risks. Of course, a punt moored in midstream would be safer."

"He might be worse," said I. "I admit I could spare the diamond, but at least he's not wearing a cummerbund and sand shoes."

"Hush," said Jonah. "He's keeping them for Henley. You won't catch him out on dress. Ah me," he added with a sigh, "I love to see old chums meet again, don't you?"

"There's nothing so touching," said I, "as a reunion of souls. To revive the memory of boyhood's intimacy, of joys and troubles shared, of visits to the tuck-shop. . . . If the truth were known, I expect they were always together, sort of inseparable, you know."

"No doubt. Naturally, Berry's a bit shy at first, but that's often the way. Before the afternoon's out, he'll be calling him ' 'Erb' again, and they'll have changed hats."

"This," said Berry, "is intolerable. A little more and I shall burst into large pear-shaped tears. Let's pay the bill, will you?" He rose to his feet. "And now I'm going to remember more things in five minutes than Mr. Lewis has forgotten in thirteen years. Will two tons be enough?"

"Make it three," said Daphne.

"And we are to reassemble between St. Mary's and The Radcliffe. Or was it between The Radcliffe and St. Mary's?"

"We shall wait five minutes and no more," said I. "That gives you one minute forty seconds a ton, or five seconds a hundred-weight. Keep the home fires burning."

"Mathematician and imitation humorist," said Berry. "Isn't it wonderful? Don't forget to let me know what the bill comes to. Just as a matter of interest."

He sauntered in the direction of Mr. Lewis, who was watching him with the air of a terrier that hopes to be taken out for a walk. . . .

I called for the bill, and five minutes later the rest of us were strolling across the cobbles under the shadow of The Radcliffe Camera.

"As soon as he comes," said Jonah, "we'll go to New College. We can sit in the gardens there for a bit and suck soda-mints. When the process of digestion is completed, we can see the chapel and hall, and then one of us can borrow a gown, and we'll look in at The Bodleian."

The project seemed admirable, but, as has been frequently remarked, Man but proposes.

More than four minutes had elapsed, and we were casually sauntering towards The High, to see if Berry was in sight, when the latter swung round the corner of Brasenose with Mr. Lewis stepping joyously by his side.

Instead of his grey Homburg, my brother-in-law was wearing a soft clerical hat which was too small for him. The ludicrous effect created by this substitution of headgear can be more easily imagined than described.

For a moment we wavered. Then Jill gave a shriek of laughter, and we broke and scattered something after the manner of a mounted reconnoitring patrol that has unexpectedly "bumped into" a battalion of the enemy. Our retreat, however, was not exactly precipitate, and we endeavoured to invest it with a semblance of hypocrisy not usually thought necessary in warfare; but it was in no sense dignified, and only a child, too young to differentiate between right and wrong, could have failed to recognize the true motive which prompted our withdrawal.

Seizing Agatha by the arm I turned left about, pointed vehemently to the dome of the Camera, and hurried her in the direction of the gate which admitted to that institution. Simultaneously Jonah wheeled right about and, apparently imparting information of a startling character concerning the east front of Brasenose to his sister and cousin, began to hustle them towards the entrance. To Berry's repeated nominal exhortations we paid not the slightest attention. Coal or no coal, the combination of Mr. Lewis and my brother-in-law—the latter in a mood which the assumption of so ridiculous a garb made it impossible to mistake—was too awful to contemplate. There are things which are worse than a cold bath.

I did not stop until we were safely on the leads of the Camera. Considerably out of breath, we leaned cautiously upon the balustrade, if possible from our eminence to observe the manoeuvres of our terror. Look where we would, there was no one to be seen.

"The brute must have followed the others into B.N.C.," I panted. "I'd love to see them come out."

"I think he's a scream," said Agatha. "If he could only see himself in that hat . . ."

She dissolved into peals of laughter.

"I agree. But I'd rather watch from the stalls than assist him in one of his turns."

"Stalls? This is more like the gallery."

"True. But remember. 'Who sups with the devil should hold a long spoon.' All the same, if you can bear another proverb, 'It's an ill wind,' etc. If I hadn't been hard up for a refuge, I should never have thought of bringing you up here, and for any one to get an idea of Oxford it's as good a place as I know."

Miss Deriot gazed at the magnificent prospect before replying.

"It ought to make me feel very small," she said suddenly, "but somehow it doesn't. It's so terribly old and all that, but it's got such a kind look."

"That," said I, "is the quality of Oxford. And I congratulate you. You are articulate where wise men have stood dumb. Perhaps it's because you're so much alike."

"Who?"

"You and Oxford."

"Am I so terribly old?"

I shook my head.

"But you're beautifully built, and you've got a kind look and handsome ways, and your temples are a dream, and all our swains commend you, and——"

"Stop, stop. You're getting mixed."

"Not at all. My intellect was never less clouded. In spite of two glasses of ginger beer, my hand is like a spade—I mean a rock. Insert a fly in your eye, and I will remove it unhesitatingly."

"I'll take your word for it," said Agatha.

"One of these days I shall compare you to a burst of melody. At the present moment I am between your dimple and the deep sea."

"The dimple you are," said Agatha, with a smile that promised laughter with difficulty suppressed.

Amusedly I regarded her.

She was very tastefully dressed. A blue silk coat and a white laced blouse beneath it, a pale grey skirt of some soft stuff, grey silk stockings and small grey shoes—these with a hat of crocheted silk that matched her jersey—suited her pretty figure and the April day to rare perfection.

Leaning easily against the worn masonry of the balustrade, slight, lithe and graceful, she was the embodiment of vitality in repose. She stood so still, but there was a light shining in the brown eyes, that were cast down and over the parapet, keeping a careful watch for any indication of Berry's activity, a tell-tale quiver of the sensitive nostrils, an eagerness hanging on the parted lips, which, with her flushed cheeks, lent to a striking face an air of freshness and a keen *joie de vivre* that was exhilarating beyond description.

"I wonder what's happening," said Agatha, nodding down at the gateway. "Can they get out another way?"

"I'm not sure. There is another gate, but——"

"At last," said a familiar voice. "I wouldn't have missed those stairs for anything. Think of the fools who've trodden them before." The next moment Berry, followed by Mr. Lewis, made his appearance. "Why, here are our little playmates." He advanced beaming. "Don't be shy any longer. And what a storied retreat you have selected!" He indicated the building with a sweep of his arm. "You know, originally this was a helter-skelter lighthouse, but Henry the Eighth lost his mat half-way down the chute, and had it closed down in revenge. There was a great deal of feeling about it. Especially on the part of the King. He hunted from a litter for months."

I addressed myself to Miss Deriot.

"Wonderfully well-informed, isn't he? Scratch the buffoon and you get the charlatan."

Berry turned to Mr. Lewis.

"Much of my crowded life," he said, "has been devoted to research. I am, as it were, a crystal fount of knowledge. I beg that you will bathe in me."

Not knowing exactly what reply to make to this offer, Mr. Lewis laughed heartily, while Agatha, overcome with emotion, hurriedly turned away and stared over the roofs of Oxford, shaking with long spasms of laughter.

Stifling a desire to join her, I crossed to Mr. Lewis and engaged him in reasonable conversation, while Berry seized the opportunity of indicating to Agatha the main points of the city, accompanying his gesticulations with a series of inaudible remarks, which, to judge from their reception, concerned Mr. Lewis more nearly than Oxford, and were of a grotesque character. I was just leading up to the question of fuel, when a cry from my brother-in-law interrupted me.

"My hag," he announced, "is below. With a notorious wine-bibber. Where are the women police?"

The next moment he had slid an arm through Agatha's and had begun to descend. I followed with Mr. Lewis. . . .

I pass over the meeting in the street below, which I was just in time to witness. Berry's swoop was so sudden that his prey appeared to realize that the game was up, and made no attempt to fly. It was almost piteous. An apprehension of certain embarrassment to come extinguished the instant impulse to shriek with laughter which was written plain upon their faces, and my sister gave one wild glance about her before turning to face the delinquent.

As I came up she addressed him.

"Berry, I appeal to you to take off that hat."

"My tongue," was the reply, "I mean my hands, are clean. Bereft of my own headgear, I had no choice. Some absent-minded priest is now scandalizing his parishioners by parading in a pearl-grey Homburg which is four sizes too big for him, while I—would you have me go naked in the streets?"

Here the Vice-Chancellor passed, preceded by his Bedels with staves reversed, and Berry uncovered and fell upon his knees. Surprised by the unwonted attention, the dignitary raised his mortar-board and bowed.

"Let's go and touch him," said Berry excitedly. "Then we shan't get the King's Evil. That's the origin of inoculation."

"I implore you," said Daphne, "to behave yourself. As a personal favour——"

"You see in me," said her husband, "a huntleyed palmer seeking the tomb of Anne of Cloves. On finding it, I must scourge myself. Any one who directs me to it will be assaulted."

"She's buried at Oranges," said Jonah. "But don't let that stop you."

Berry replaced his wideawake and stared at him.

"To mock me," he said, "is most dangerous. Several people have been transformed for such an offence. Only yesterday I was compelled to change a taxi-driver into a Gorgonzola of military age."

Several clocks struck the half-hour. Half-past two.

"Look here," said I. "We want to go to New College and 'The House', but we can't push off if you're going to come with us looking like that. For Heaven's sake, go back to *The Mitre* and get your own hat. Mr. Lewis, won't you go and fix him up?"

Quick as a flash, Daphne threw her weight into the scale which I had slung.

"Yes, do," she implored. "You know, you oughtn't to have let him come out like that," she added, with a reproachful smile. "And then you can join us at New College."

Our manoeuvre was successful beyond all expectation. His vanity flattered, the gentleman addressed flung himself into the breach with every manifestation of delight, and, seizing my brother-in-law by the arm, haled him gleefully in the direction of The High, humouring his obvious reluctance with the familiar assurances which one usually associates with the persuasion of the unsober.

In silence we watched them till they had turned the corner. Then—

"Did I say New College?" said Daphne hurriedly.

"You did," said I. "So we'd better go straight to 'The House'."

Three minutes later we were exploring my old rooms in Peckwater Quadrangle, Christ Church.

* * * * *

In spite of its inauspicious beginning, we spent an enjoyable afternoon. By common consent New College was ruled out of our itinerary, but Oxford cannot be viewed in a day, and we found much to delight our senses south of the High Street. Finally, a languorous journey by punt from the Barges to Magdalen Bridge more than compensated us for the somnolent half-hour which we had been proposing to spend under the shadow of the City Wall.

Our return to *The Mitre*—a movement which was effected with great caution—was eagerly awaited by the hall-porter, who inquired anxiously regarding my brother-in-law, and produced his grey Homburg with a note addressed *To the Owner* stuck in the hatband.

"The gentleman as was of your party, sir, was inquirin' about 'is 'at an hour or two back, sir. 'E 'adn't 'ardly gone, when a reverend gent come in, all of a state, with this 'at in 'is 'and. Seems he took it away absent-minded like, instead of 'is own, sir. Though 'ow 'e can 'ave made such a mistake I can't think, 'is bein' a Church 'at as plain as plain. But they're like that up 'ere, sir, some o' them."

We stared at one another, frankly astonished to learn that Berry's fantastic explanation was founded strictly upon fact.

"Did the clergyman get his own back?" said I.

"Yes, sir. 'Ere it was in the 'all."

Apparently neither the porter nor the divine had any idea of the abuse to which the latter's wideawake had been put.

"Oh, well, our friend'll be in presently," said Jonah, taking the Homburg. "When he comes, tell him we've got his hat and are having tea."

"Very good, sir. You see there's a note there, sir? The reverend wrote it 'ere. I think 'e was 'opin' to 'ave seen your gentleman and told 'im 'ow sorry 'e was, but when 'e 'eard 'e was out, 'e sits down an' writes 'im a letter. 'E was in a state."

"Poor man," said Daphne, following after Jonah. "After all, there's no harm done."

"It was a near thing," said I. "But for my brainwave——"

"Nonsense," said Daphne, "I got him away."

"To be candid," said Jonah, "if anybody's to get a mention, I'm inclined to think it should be Mr. Lewis."

While we were waiting for tea, I read the letter aloud.

SIR,

I can never adequately express my regret for the distressing, if momentary, aberration unhappily responsible for my appropriation of a hat which in no way resembles my own.

I dare entertain no hope that inconvenience has not resulted to you, but I beg that you will accept, first, my fervid assurance that it was not of industry, but of case that I offended, and, secondly, my most humble apologies for the commission of so unfriendly a gest.

I am, Sir,
Your obedient Servant,
LUKE ST. J. BILDEW, B.D.

When I had finished—

"I don't understand half of it," said Jill.

"I confess it needs annotating, but it's worth keeping, for it's the real thing, my dear—a human document. You see, Oxford is the most wonderful backwater in the world, but—it's a backwater."

"And if you stay in it always," said Agatha, "and never come out into the stream——"

"You are liable to take the wrong hat and to write letters that would be the better for footnotes."

Berry arrived with the tea.

In silence he received his own hat, compared it with one which he had just purchased, and then handed the latter to the waiter. In silence he read Mr. Bildew's note. In silence he selected a piece of bread and butter and sank into a chair.

"I can't bear it," said Daphne. "Where's Mr. Lewis?"

"Happily he decided to catch a train twenty minutes ago. Otherwise it would have been murder. I should have pleaded guilty to manslaughter, committed under extreme provocation. That man oughtn't to be allowed. I suppose you forgot to go to New College. Yes, just so."

"And the coal?" said I. "Have you fixed that up?"

"Three tons of the best nuts are to be delivered *sub rosa* between two and three to-morrow afternoon. Nothing is to be said, nothing signed. Nobody is to know anything about it. The carter will simply take up the plate, shoot the stuff in, and push off. As I happened to have six pounds ten shillings upon me, the transaction will not be recorded." With a depreciatory hand he waved aside the involuntary buzz of grateful admiration. "I am not long for this world. I am, as it were, ear-marked for a more worthy sphere. My translation may occur any moment. I should like Lewis to have some trifle in memory of me. A personal effect, I mean. I've got a gun-metal sovereign-case somewhere. But anything useful will do."

*　*　*　*　*

We made a point of being in upon the following afternoon. It was not often that we all sat down to lunch together, but the satisfaction of witnessing the delivery of three precious tons of coal in the teeth of the authorities was more than we could forego. The butler was admitted to our confidence, and instructed to stifle any attempt to allay curiosity, by interpretation of the carman, that might originate in the servants' hall, and immediately after luncheon, which finished at three minutes to two, an O.P. was established by the side of one of the dining-room windows, in which Jill was posted with orders to advise us directly the convoy appeared.

In the library we spent a restless time. Berry, usually somnolent at this hour, sat upon the club kerb and toyed with *The Times*. Jonah fidgeted with a refractory pipe. Daphne glanced from the clock to her novel and the novel to the clock at intervals of fifteen seconds, and I wrote four letters to the War Office about my gratuity, and very properly destroyed them as incoherent one after another.

At a quarter past two, by common consent, I visited Jill to see if she was asleep. . . . When I made my report we reminded one another that Mr. Lewis had said between two and three, and agreed that it was early as yet.

At half-past two Daphne left the room and did not return.

At twenty minutes to three I made no attempt to disguise my uneasiness, and joined my cousin and sister in the dining-room.

Ten minutes later Jonah and Berry came in.

After a hurried consultation it was decided that, if the coal had not arrived in ten minutes' time, Berry should telephone to Mr. Lewis forthwith. Almost immediately it was found that nobody knew the man's number, initials, or address, and reference to the Directory showed that there were four columns of subscribers all bearing his name.

At five minutes past three the strain was telling, and every one's temper began more or less to show signs of wear and tear.

"Are you sure," said Daphne for the fourth time, "that it was to come between two and three?"

"No," said her husband. "That's why I've been waiting."

"Fool," said his wife.

Berry sighed.

"Some people are very hard to please. If I were you, I should take a course of ventriloquism. Then you can ask yourself questions and give yourself any perishing answers you like. At times you might even revile yourself."

Five minutes later Jonah announced that he was going to Ranelagh, and inquired whether any one wanted a round of golf. Berry accepted the invitation, and they left together.

The arrival of Fitch with the car at half-past three reminded my sister that she was going to call upon some one in Regent's Park, and she withdrew in a state of profound depression.

Jill, who was on the very brink of tears, refused to leave her post until a quarter to four, and, when that hour arrived, slow-treading but coalless, it was only my promise to take her to see Charlie Chaplin forthwith that could coax the ghost of a smile to play about her lips.

As I closed the front-door behind us, a neighbouring clock struck four.

Moodily we walked down the street, talking of cinemas and thinking of coal. Had our thoughts been otherwise employed, the condition of the pavement outside a house about a hundred and twenty yards down on the opposite side would have recalled them pellmell to our disappointment. It was obvious that a considerable quantity of coal had been recently delivered to a more fortunate *ménage*. Idly I looked at the number of the house. *From either pillar of the porch a freshly painted* "38" *grinned at me.* For a moment I stared at them blankly. Then Jill gave a choking cry and caught at my arm. . . .

I realized with a shock that, while Mr. Lewis had been as good as his word, my brother-in-law's recollection of our change of address was less dependable.

CHAPTER VI

How Nobby Attended a Wedding, and Berry Spoke Nothing but the Truth

"If I am to drive," said Jonah, "I won't be responsible for doing it in a minute under two hours." He looked down at Nobby, who, with a section of one of my shoe-trees in his mouth, was importuning him to play by the simple expedient of thrusting the bauble against the calf of his leg. "My good dog, if you expect me to interrupt an agreeable breakfast to join you in the one-sided game of which you never tire, you are doomed to disappointment. Go and worry your owner."

With a reproachful look the terrier took his advice and, trotting across to the sideboard, laid his toy at my feet and looked up expectantly. I hardened my heart.

"It is not my practice," said I, "to gambol upon an empty stomach. Try Jill."

Slowly the brown eyes sank from mine to the bottom button of my waistcoat. As I moved to my place, plate in hand, he gave a protesting bark, which was answered by a fox-terrier from the box-seat of a passing van. In a flash Nobby was upon the sill of the open window, hurling defiance at the intruder.

"Is he coming with us?" said Daphne.

"I don't see why he shouldn't. We can leave him at Hillingdon while we're at Church. By the way, what time does the balloon go up?"

"The marriage," said Jonah, "is to be solemnized at two o'clock. As I said a moment ago, it'll take us two hours to get there. If we start at eleven, that'll give us an hour to brush one another, lunch and rehearse the series of genial banalities with which it is the habit of wedding-guests to insult one another's intelligence."

"I believe," said Jill, "I heard the telephone."

I called upon Nobby to suspend his fury, and we all listened. Sure enough, a long spasm of ringing came simultaneously from the library and the lobby in the back hall.

"I shouldn't be surprised," said I, "if that was the Club, to tell me I've drawn a runner in the three-pound sweep." And, with that, I left my kidneys and repaired to the library.

"Can I speak to Major Pleydell?" said a voice.

"Who is it, please?"

"The Waddell Institute speaking."

"Oh, yes. Will you hold the line?"

I went to the foot of the stairs and shouted for Berry. There was no reply. In some annoyance I ascended the first flight and shouted again. From behind a closed door his voice answered me. It was with a malicious pleasure that I located its origin. . . .

A moment later I opened the bathroom door.

From the depths of a luxurious bath Berry regarded me.

"That's right," he said. "You come in. Don't take any notice of me. And don't shut the door, or the servants won't be able to see in."

"You are wanted," said I, "upon the telephone."

"How interesting!" said Berry. "I suppose you told them to hold on."

"I did."

He sank into a recumbent position and crossed his legs.

"What a marvellous thing," he said, "the telephone is. There's that fool, Heaven knows how many miles away, sitting with his ear glued to a piece of vulcanite, and here am I in the midst of an exacting toilet—d'you think he'd hear me if I were to shout? Or would you rather take a message?"

"It is," said I, "the Waddell Institute."

The savagery with which my brother-in-law invested a very ordinary expletive was quite remarkable.

"Why," he added, sitting upright, "cannot they ring up at a lawful hour? Why must they——"

The sentence was never finished. With the rush of a whirlwind, Nobby tore into the room. His delight at having run me to earth was transformed to ecstasy at encountering unexpectedly another member of the household, hitherto missing from his tale, and, observing that the latter's face was a reasonable distance from the ground, and so less inacessible than usual, the Sealyham leapt upon the rim of the bath to offer the lick of greeting which it was his practice to bestow.

The result was inevitable.

Nobby tried to save himself by reaching for Berry's shoulder with his forepaws, but at the critical moment his buffer flinched, the paws fell short of their objective, and with a startled grunt the terrier fell heavily into the bath, his desperate claws leaving two long abrasions upon his victim's ribs.

The scene that followed baffles description.

Berry began to roar like a wounded bull, while a bedraggled Nobby scrambled and blew and slipped and scratched, caring not at all what was his understanding, so long as it provided a foothold and kept his head above water.

"He thinks I'm a straw!" yelled Berry. "He's catching at me. Don't stand there like a half-baked corner-boy. Get him *out*!"

But I was helpless with laughter, from which I only recovered in time to rescue the offender, who, with the bath to himself, was swimming sturdily in the deep water and scrabbling fruitlessly on the porcelain, while Berry, in a bath-dressing-gown and a loud voice, identified and enumerated the several scratches upon his person.

"For Heaven's sake," said I, "go and answer the telephone."

"I shall die," said Berry, slipping his feet into a pair of pumps. "I shall get pneumonia (bis) and die. I got into that bath in the prime, as it were, the very heyday of life. And now . . . At least, I shall be in the fashion. 'The body of the deceased bore signs of extreme physical violence.' Any more for the crime wave?"

I wrapped Nobby in my brother-in-law's towel and followed the latter downstairs.

My sister was standing in the library's doorway.

"What on earth," she demanded, "has been the matter?"

I held up my hand.

"Listen."

Berry was speaking upon the telephone.

"Is that the Waddell Institute? I am so very sorry—I might almost say distracted—that you should have been kept waiting.

. . . You see, I've just been mauled. . . . No. Not 'called', mauled. Emma, ak, u, l for leather—I beg your pardon. Yes, isn't it tawful? Well, if you must know, it was bloodhound. They told me at the Dogs' Home that he'd lost his scent as a result of the air raids, but last night the charwoman gave him a sausage I'd left, and he pulled me down this morning. . . . Yes. This is Major Pleydell. . . . Oh, Walter Thomas Dale? Yes, I remember perfectly. . . . Received the requisite number of votes? Splendid. . . . Can be admitted on the fifteenth of June? Thanks very much. . . . What? . . . Oh, I shall pull round. Yes, thanks. I shall just get the wounds plugged, and . . . Good-bye."

"Hurray!" cried Daphne. "I am glad. That's a real load off my mind. Write and tell them this morning, will you?" I looked up from the operation of drying Nobby and nodded. "Poor people, they'll be so thankful. And now, what happened upstairs!"

"Mixed bathing," said I. "Your husband had not left the bath when Nobby entered it. Both were frightened, but neither was hurt."

As I spoke, Berry emerged from the library with a cigarette in his mouth.

"My milk-white skin," he said, "has been defaced. My beautiful trunk has been lacerated as with jagged nails. You know, I tremble for that dog's soul. It mayn't be his fault, but it's invariably my misfortune." He turned to my sister. "You heard about Walter Thomas? Good. And now I shall slip on some iodine and underclothes and come down as I am."

"Jonah says we must leave at eleven," said Daphne. "For goodness' sake, don't be late."

"My wedding garments are prepared and but await my entry. The sponge-bag trousers are unrolled, the elastic-sided boots untreed, the made-up tie dusted. Of course, we're taking Nobby?"

I looked up from my charge, who was by this time fairly dry and as full of beans as an egg is of meat.

"Of course."

"Of course. You never know. I might get run over. That'd give him an opening."

"Here," said I, "is your towel. He's all right now."

Carefully Berry fingered the fabric.

"He was wet, wasn't he?" he said. "Yes. I suppose I can dry myself on the curtains. I wonder which of us he would bite if I were to assault you." He hung the towel over his arm, picked up the terrier and looked into his eyes. "You wicked scrap! Why, he's not nearly dry yet." Nobby licked his face. "Come along up with uncle, and we'll share the bathmat."

The two disappeared up the staircase, wrangling amicably regarding my brother-in-law's right to pull the terrier's whiskers.

"You won't forget to write, will you?" said Daphne, as we returned to the dining-room.

"I promise," said I. "You shall see the letter."

Trooper Dale, W., had been in my squadron in the field, and for three weeks he had taken my first servant's place. Incidentally he had also taken two pounds ten shillings in notes, which I frankly admit I had no business to have left in my pocket. Taxed with the theft, he had broken down and told me a piteous tale.

A delicate wife and a little boy with curvature of the spine needed every honest halfpenny that could be turned—and more also. Between a chauffeur's wages and his Army pay there was fixed a great gulf, and—well, it was hard to know that the child was suffering for want of nourishment.

I caused inquiries to be made. A convenient aunt investigated the case and found it genuine. Between us we did what we could. Then, on her return from Egypt, my sister visited the family and reported that they would be most thankful if the child could be admitted to a first-class home. With the Waddell Institute Berry had influence, and at last a coveted vacancy had been obtained. . . .

Before we left for Monk's Honour I composed a suitable letter to the ex-trooper, telling him that his little boy could soon be received into an institution, from which there was every reason to believe that he would eventally emerge comparatively restored to health.

* * * * *

It was a lovely day. And we were glad of it, for at two o'clock my Cousin Madrigal was to be married from the old house where she was born, and in the old church in which she was baptized. A special train was being run from London, but Monk's Honour lay four miles from the nearest station, and it was doubtful if the supply of cars and carriages would prove equal to the demand. Therefore we had decided to go down by road. With my uncle's land marched the well-timbered acres of Hillingdon, where the Tanyons lived, and they had very kindly invited us to luncheon, so that we should not descend untimely upon a simmering household. In their keeping we proposed to leave Nobby and the car. The house was only five minutes' walk from the church and as many again from Madrigal's home, so that once we had reached the village we should need no conveyance until the time came for us to return to Town.

For a wonder we were all on time, and it was barely eleven o'clock when Jonah let in the clutch and the Rolls began to move. Daphne sat in front, and Jill between Berry and me on the back seat. The girls wore dust-cloaks to save their finery, and two large bandboxes concealed their respective hats. Berry, Jonah and I wore light overcoats above our morning-dress, and three tall hats, ironed to perfection, each in his stiff white hat-box, jostled one another on the mat at our feet. A smaller box by their side contained three blooming gardenias.

Once clear of London Jonah gave the Rolls her head, and we were soon floating through the midst of blowing cherry orchards and fragrant hop gardens, which of the great sun were quick with radiance.

The deeper we plunged into the countryside, the richer this became. Here was a treasure of woodland, and there a wealth of pasture: grey lichened walls hoarded a precious park, keeping the timid deer in generous custody: a silver stream stole between smiling hayfields, crept shadowed and cool under the dusty road and, beyond, braided a spreading cloth of golden buttercups, that glowed with a soft brilliancy, such as no handicraft on earth could coax from the hard heart of costly metal.

Presently we left the main road to sail up a curling hill, and over and down past a fair steading into a friendly valley, where the cattle stood drowsy under the shelter of giant chestnut trees, and luxuriant hawthorns in full blossom filled all the neighbouring air with timely sweetness. At the bidding of an aged finger-post Jonah turned to the left, and a moment later the car was scudding up a leafy lane, high-banked, narrow, and soon so screened and arched with foliage that in a little we were being swept through a veritable tunnel, seemingly driven through the living green. More than once the lane changed direction, but the tunnel held: the ground was rising, but we sailed on, the steady purr of the engine swelling into a low snarl as we swung to right and left between the cool green walls. . . .

As we slid through Marvel, the clock of the old grey church showed us that it was five and twenty to one. We were in good time, for now but a short seven miles lay between us and the village which we sought.

Jonah settled himself in his seat and prepared to cover the last lap at an easier pace. . . .

Before we had realized what was happening, it was all over.

The road which we were using ran at right angles into a better-class way by the side of an old oast-house. Here, for Monk's Honour, we must turn to the left. Jonah, prince of drivers, slowed for the turn and sounded his horn carefully, for ours was the lesser road. As we rounded the corner there was a deafening roar, a cry, a violent shock, a splintering crash, the Rolls quivered like a ship that has struck, and a great green touring car tore past and was gone in a cloud and a flurry of dust before we had come to rest with our near fore-wheel eighteen inches up the near-side bank.

Dazedly I watched a little white dog with a black patch take a flying leap into the road, stumble, pick himself up, and hurl himself in the wake of the monster, barking furiously. Then the whirling dust swallowed him up, and I saw him no more.

"LF 8057," said Daphne, "LF 8057. Write it down, somebody. Quick. LF 8057."

"That's right," said Jonah. "I got it too. LF 8057."

In silence I dragged a pencil out of my pocket and with trembling finger wrote down the precious figures on the back of an envelope.

"Anybody hurt?" continued Jonah, screwing himself round to look at the back seat.

"We're all right," said I. "But it was a close call."

"The brute!" cried Jill passionately. "The beastly stinking—"

Berry spoke between his clenched teeth in a voice shaken with choler.

"We'll have that blistered swine if we have to drag hell for him. For all he knows, the car's overturned and on fire, and we're pinned under it. It's German. Pure full-blooded German. It's the most verminous thing I've ever dreamed of. It's—— Burn it! Words fail me."

He rose and got out of the car. I followed him and helped Jill to alight. She was a little pale, and, when she saw the havoc on the off-side, her eyes began to fill with tears.

I put my arm about her.

"Don't worry, darling. It looks worse than it is. And we'll have that merchant's blood. We've got his number."

Daphne came up to comfort her, and Jonah, after a cursory

glance at the damage, limped to the opposite side of the road, sat down on the bank, and lighted a cigarette.

"What was he doing?" said Berry, his face still a dark red.

I shrugged my shoulders.

"Shouldn't like to say. Maybe seventy. Maybe more. But it was a frightful pace." I pointed along the road to the left and right. "See how it curves. And we're on the outside of the bend. To clear us at that pace, he'd 've had to go over himself."

"How can we hit him best?"

"All round. We can summon him under the Motor Car Acts and bring a civil action for damages. He ought to go down heavily."

"No escape?"

"I should say we've got him cold."

Berry heaved a long sigh and clapped me on the back.

"I feel better already," he said.

Before doing anything else, Jonah and I subjected the Rolls to a careful examination.

Both wings and the running-board on the off-side had been ripped off, and the front axle was bent by the side of the steering-pin. The off fore-wheel had apparently been struck on the tyre, and the fact that neither of the fore-wheels had collapsed spoke volumes for their sturdy construction. The shock, however, had put the steering-gear out of action. So far as we could tell, that was the extent of the damage. Whether any further injuries would later appear, it was impossible to say.

I crossed to the girls and Berry, who were seated disconsolate upon the bank on the opposite side of the road. Heavily I made my report.

"There's only one thing to do," I concluded. "I must leg it to Marvel and see if I can raise a couple of mechanics, some tools, and a car. I can drive back with them, and then we can leave them here and all go on in the hireling to Hillingdon. We shan't get any lunch, but we'll be in time for the wedding, with luck. By the time we get back from Monk's Honour, if the fellows know their job, we ought to be able to get the Rolls to Marvel under her own power. From there she'll have to come up to Town by rail. And we can go back by the special, whenever it leaves."

As I finished speaking, Jill gave a little cry, and I turned to see a small white scrap, way down the long white road, plodding wearily in our direction. It was our Champion. As he came nearer, it was obvious that he was much exhausted. More than once he stumbled, and a red tongue lolled from his gaping jaws; but his little tail was up, and, as he toiled gamely towards us, he wagged it to and fro by way of greeting. Of one accord we welcomed him with a cheer. Obviously gratified by our appreciation, Nobby smiled an unmistakable smile and, wagging his tail more vigorously than before, quickened his flagging steps. A moment later he thrust a dusty nose against my extended hand and, bowing his tousled head sideways by way of homage, rolled over on his back and lay panting in the shade at my feet.

"Good little chap," said I, stroking his heaving flank. "It didn't take you long to get a move on."

"You darling!" said Jill, stooping to caress him. "The way you went after that car was just heroic."

"I suppose," said Berry, "that if I were to suggest that he knew perfectly well that he couldn't catch it, and that it was nothing more than a brilliant display of eye-wash, I should be abused."

"What a shame!" cried Daphne and Jill in a breath. "What a beastly shame!"

"I said so," said Berry. "Now, if I'd got out and chased it, you'd have had me certified."

"I agree," I retorted. "And if you were to offer to walk to Marvel instead of me, I should have you watched."

"Don't be afraid," was the rejoinder. "The shock was severe, but I'm not as bad as that. How soon d'you think you'll be back?"

I turned to my sister.

"I'm banking on being able to get a car. But there mayn't be one. So, if you can get a lift, don't wait." I pointed to Nobby. "He'll want to come with me, so hang on to him. And if you could find some water"—I glanced at the oast-house—"I think he'd be glad of it."

"All right, dear. Take it as easy as you can."

A moment later I was striding along the Marvel road.

By the time I had covered the two miles it was a quarter past one, and I was unpleasantly hot. I was also conscious of being improperly dressed in an unusually loose grey overcoat, tweed cap, striped cashmere trousers and patent-leather boots. I had taken off my morning coat and waistcoat before starting to walk, but the heat was awful, and my stiff white shirt and collar were wilting visibly. . . .

I was fortunate to obtain the services of two mechanics, but I must confess that my face fell when the only car that was available proved to be a 1908 Ford. . . .

As we drew up at the fatal corner, the others came out of the oast-house to see what was making the noise. When they beheld their conveyance, they were profoundly moved.

"Do you mean to say," said Daphne, "that this is the best you could do?"

I nodded.

"And you'll have to look sharp if you want to be there before the service is over. One cylinder's missing."

"So's the skid-pan," said Berry. "And where's the back seat? I beg your pardon—I'd got it the wrong way round. It is facing that way, isn't it? Yes. Oh, but what a line. What finish! You know, all it wants is a board with 'Ancient Lights' on the radiator, and somebody to close its doors one day in every year, and then, whenever the fowls lay in it, you can turn them out."

During this eulogy Jonah had been busy transferring the hat-boxes from the Rolls, and two minutes later the mechanics had been given their instructions, and we were ready to start.

I took the wheel, with Jonah sitting beside me. Daphne and Jill sat upon the back seat, and Berry, in a standing position, Nobby, the hat-boxes, and the buttonholes more than occupied the remaining space.

"Right behind?" I inquired.

"Anything but," said Berry. "Still, the door that will shut is closed, so carry on."

As tenderly as I could, I let in the clutch.

Instantly, with a frightful jerk, the car leapt forward.

As it did so, Berry lost his balance and, with a yell of apprehension, fell heavily into the welter of hat- and bandboxes, the cardboard of which gave right and left. Construing his involuntary action as the demonstration of a new game, Nobby immediately leaped barking upon him and began to lick his face. Daphne and Jill clung to one another, convulsed with merriment and emitting such tremulous wails of laughter as the function of breathing would permit, while, with tears coursing down his cheeks, Jonah was trying to bellow a coherent description of the catastrophe into my ear. And all the time the good old car ground raving along the road, heaving herself over the macadam in a sickening series of lurches, to every one of which we found ourselves reluctantly compelled to conform. . . .

The bride was ten minutes late, and we beat her by a short head. As we were ushered, breathing heavily, into our places, there was a tell-tale stir at the porch, uprose the strains of a well-known hymn, the bridegroom glanced round and gave slightly at the knees, and the next moment his future wife had entered the aisle.

Furtively I felt my collar and wiped the perspiration from my face. . . . It was with something of a shock that, as the echoes of the "Amen" died away, I heard a familiar growl.

Hastily I turned in my seat to see Nobby three paces away. With back arched, one fore-paw raised, and his white teeth bared, he was regarding the trousers of an amateur sidesman, who had set a foot upon the broken string which trailed from his collar, with a menacing glare. . . .

By the time I had bestowed the terrier under lock and key and returned to the church, Madrigal was signing her maiden name for the last time.

* * * * *

Five days later Berry received the following letter:—

SIR,

Mr. Douglas Bladder of The Vines, Swete Rowley, has handed us your communication of the twenty-third inst.

We are instructed to say that, while there is no doubt that its number is LF 8057, Mr. Bladder's car did not leave the garage upon the day of the accident in which you were concerned, for the reason that he and his chauffeur were engaged in overhauling the engine.

It is therefore obvious that a mistake has been made, and that, unless some other car was bearing his number, which you will agree is improbable, in the natural confusion of the moment the letters or figures or both upon the offender's number-plate were misread.

Our client wishes us to add that, while the tone of your letter is not such as he is accustomed to, he appreciates that it was written while you were smarting under a sense of grave injury, and was indeed intended for somebody other than himself.

Yours faithfully,

BERTHEIM AND GROWTH.

This being the quarter in which the wind was sitting, we made our dispositions accordingly.

So far as the number of the car was concerned, Daphne and Jonah never wavered, and we were certain about its colour and style. Moreover, we were all agreed that, while the back seat was empty, there were two people in front, and that the one who was not driving was wearing a chauffeur's dress. Finally, the village of Swete Rowley lay but some twenty-two miles from the scene of the accident. But that was all. It was, of course, unthinkable that the offending car could have sustained no damage, but it was quite possible that it would have nothing more serious to show than a dented hub-cap and a battered wing; and, while hub-caps can be changed in five minutes, it is no great matter to straighten a bent wing, and any traces of battery which still survive can be unanswerably attributed to one or other of quite a variety of innocent mishaps.

Inquiries were set afoot, and the moment we learned that Mr. Bladder in fact possessed a large green high-powered touring car, which he was in the habit of driving himself at a notorious pace, we threw down the glove. Solicitors were instructed, counsel's opinion was taken, an information was sworn before a Justice of the Peace, and within one week of the date of his solicitors' letter, Mr. Douglas Bladder had become the recipient of a writ for four hundred pounds damages and four separate summonses under the Motor Car Acts. We were out for blood.

At Marvel's Police Court the defendant appeared by his solicitor, who asked that the hearing of the summonses might be adjourned, pending the action in the High Court. This request was granted.

Everything possible was done to expedite matters, and by great good fortune the case of *Pleydell* v. *Bladder* came into the Special Jury list during the last week of July.

* * * * *

There is about the High Court a signal air of gravity which to the layman is most compelling. The majesty of the Law is not apparent: of severity there is but a suggestion: something, indeed, of dignity, but less than a visitor will expect to find: something of silence. These are but equerries, subordinate. The Lady Paramount is Consequence.

Here seem to dwell those things that signify. Here lies that crucial junction which is at once the terminus of Cause, and of Effect the starting-point. Here are wise analysts, skilled to distil its meaning from the idle word, surgeons whose cunning probes will stir its motive from the deed, never so thoughtless. Whole walls of law books, ranged very orderly, calf-bound, make up a reverend pharmacopœia, where you shall find precepts of iron, smelted from trespasses and old-time bickerings, whose long-dead authors, could they but come to life, would gape and stare and scratch their humble heads to find their modest names become so notable.

Pursed lips, brows wrinkled in thought, and restless anxious eyes indorse the serious aspect of the place. The very bustle of counsel, the scurry of clerks, the dash of messengers, proclaim matters of moment to be afoot. The whispered consultation, the pregnant nod, the nervous litigant buttonholing his lawyer, his advisers urging a certain course upon an indignant suitor, the furtive fellowship of witnesses, the solemn tipstaves, the ushers commanding silence, and the still small voice of Justice, charge all the dusty atmosphere with such importance as ties up the ready tongues of chatterers, ushers the jest still-born, and renders the very self of Folly wide-eyed and breathless.

Punctually at half-past ten his lordship entered the Court, returned the bows of counsel, and took his seat upon the Bench. With a sharp jingle the usher drew the green curtains across the door which led into the Judge's corridor, descended into the well of the Court, and looked complacently about him. Two or three cases were mentioned, the jury was sworn, and the Associate, after inquiring nonchalantly whether the King's Counsel were prepared, called on the case of *Pleydell against Bladder*, and sank back in his seat with a look of resignation.

Daphne, Jonah, and Jill were seated behind the junior Bar, while Berry and I sat one upon either side of our attorney at the solicitors' table. Upon the same bench, a little further along, was sitting Mr. Bladder, a large bland gentleman, with an air of good-nature which in the circumstances was rather too pronounced to be natural, and a taste in dress which would have better become a younger and a slenderer man.

Briefly our leader opened the case. There was little to be said, and he was on his feet for less than a quarter of an hour, but in that space of time he had presented to the jury so vivid a word-picture of the accident, and had dwelt so convincingly upon the facts which pointed to the defendant's guilt, that it was actually difficult to believe that the issue of the action was any longer in doubt, and I began to speculate upon the amount of damages we should be awarded. Such is the art of pleading.

A plan of the spot at which the collision had taken place was produced and officially accepted by the defence. Then Jonah was called. He gave his evidence admirably, and all counsel's endeavours to shake his confidence regarding the identity of the number-plate were of no avail. Daphne followed her cousin. She was a little nervous at first, and the Judge requested her to raise her voice. She responded gallantly, and the conviction with which she told her story in corroboration of Jonah produced a noticeable effect upon the Court. The result of her cross-examination was in our favour. I came next. Counsel for the defence made a great effort to pin me to a certain estimate of the speed at which the offending car was moving, but I scented danger and refused to be tied down.

It was considered unnecessary and not altogether expedient to expose our artless Jill to the mercies of our opponent's team, and, when I stepped down from the box, my brother-in-law's name was at once called by our junior counsel—

"Major Pleydell."

His examination-in-chief was very short. As was to be expected, he made an excellent witness. I began to wonder whether the defendant would be so foolish as to appeal. . . .

Perhaps because the cross-examination of his predecessors had been so barren, the leader for the defence rose to deal with Berry with a menacing air. He was a "silk", whose obvious confidence in his ability was shared by few. Influence rather than merit had, I was told, won his admission to the Inner Bar, and the supercilious manner which he continually observed towards the Bench afforded a first-class exhibition of particularly bad form.

"This mysterious car," he began, "that we've all heard so much about—you say it was green?"

"I do," said Berry.

"What sort of green?"

"A bilious green."

There was a subdued titter, and one of the jurymen made no attempt to disguise his amusement. The frown upon counsel's face deepened.

"Was it a light or dark green, sir?"

"Light."

"Might it have been grey?"

"It might. It might have been a beautiful ruby pink. But it wasn't. It was just green."

A second titter, more pronounced than before, ran round the Court, and counsel flushed angrily.

"You have sworn that it was an open car?"

"So it was."

"And that there were two passengers?"

"So there were."

"And that the one who was not driving was wearing a chauffeur's uniform?"

"So he was."

"Listen. You saw its colour, you noticed its style, you swear to the number of passengers, and were actually able to observe how one of them was clad. How is it that you cannot speak to its number?"

"I will tell you. I was sitting——"

"On your oath, sir!"

"No, on the back seat." There was more than a ripple of laughter, and the Judge shot a quick glance at counsel before removing his *pince-nez* and sitting back in his chair. "The heads and shoulders of Mrs. Pleydell and Captain Mansel, who were seated in front, obscured my view."

"Wasn't it because the car was travelling too fast?"

"Certainly not. They saw it."

"That is a matter of opinion."

"It is a matter of fact," was the retort.

"It is easy to be rude, Major Pleydell."

"I'll take your word for it."

Counsel appealed to the Judge.

"My lord, I must ask your lordship——"

"I see no reason to interfere," was the cold reply.

Counsel swallowed before proceeding. He was one of those who cannot let ill alone.

"The truth is," he announced, as if by way of conclusion, "that your recollection of the whole matter is extremely hazy, isn't it?"

For a moment Berry regarded him. Then he leaned back in the box and folded his arms.

"You know," he said, slowly shaking his head, "you know, you can't be well."

There was a roar of laughter.

"Never mind my health, sir," was the heated reply.

"Oh, but I do," said Berry. "If you were to burst or anything, I should be all upset, I should."

Again the Court, which was now packed, rocked with merriment. The tone in which counsel put his next question reeked of the insolence of anger.

"You consider your recollection clear?"

"As daylight. Let me explain——"

Counsel held up a deprecatory hand.

"Pray spare us. There was, I believe, a lot of dust."

"There was."

"Any amount of it?"

"Any amount. The road was thick with it."

"And the air?"

"Any amount of that, too. For a windless day, I never——"

"No, no, *no!* Wasn't the air thick with dust?"

"After the car had gone by—yes. It swallowed up the dog completely."

"The dog?"

Berry started and looked round uneasily.

"Perhaps," he stammered, "I shouldn't have . . ."

Counsel rose at the bait like a carp upon the tenth of April.

"This is most interesting. You say the dust swallowed the dog?"

"Yes, and the dog swallowed the dust. It was quite remarkable."

Amid the tempest of laughter counsel stood glowering.

"What dog are you referring to?"

"A Sealyham. When the car had gone by, he jumped out into the dust it had made and ran after it."

Hurriedly counsel conferred with his client.

"Why didn't you mention this dog before?"

"I didn't think it necessary."

"Did you tell your solicitor about it?"

"Yes. He didn't think it necessary, either."

"Really! You know, I thought we should get at something presently. Now, if the defendant didn't happen to own a Sealyham, this would be rather a valuable piece of evidence to show that it wasn't his car, wouldn't it?"

"I don't think so. You see——"

"Come, come, sir. Up to now nothing has been said of the offending car which could not be said with equal truth of the defendant's."

"I cordially agree."

"Both are green, both open, both, according to your story, bear the same number."

Berry nodded.

"Unquestionably," he said.

"Wait. Supposing the defendant swears that he has never had a Sealyham or any other kind of terrier?"

"I don't know that I should believe him, but I shouldn't argue it. Perhaps he doesn't like dogs."

"You'd accept his statement?"

"For what it was worth."

"Exactly. And if he had no terrier, it's quite obvious that the car out of which the Sealyham jumped was not his, but somebody else's?"

"Undoubtedly," said Berry. "As a matter of fact, it was ours."

The explosion of mirth which this statement provoked showed that his headlong progress towards the pit which he had digged had been gleefully followed by nearly everybody in Court, and counsel turned very pale.

"Have you ever discussed this case with any one?"

"I have."

"Who with?"

Berry took a deep breath.

"Well, I haven't seen my dentist lately, but I think everybody else I know has had it."

"Have you discussed it with the other witnesses?"

"Ad nauseam."

"Have you indeed? Perhaps that explains why you all tell the same tale?"

"That," said Berry coolly, "is an infamous suggestion."

Somebody gave an audible gasp, and there was a breathless silence. Sitting back in his padded chair, the Judge might have been a graven image.

"Sir?" thundered counsel interrogatively.

"And one beneath the dignity of even a stuff gown."

For a long moment the two men looked one another full in the eyes. Then counsel sat down somewhat unsteadily. . . .

Berry was followed by an expert witness, called to substantiate our contention that two hundred pounds was a fair charge for the execution of such repairs to the Rolls as the accident had necessitated, and that another two hundred for the hire of a similar car for the month during which our own was in dock, was not excessive.

As he stepped down from the box—

"That, my lord," said our leader, "is the case for the plaintiff."

It was a quarter to one when Berry's antagonist rose again to his feet. Shortly he opened his case. Nothing, he said, was more difficult to prove than a negative. But for one thing, it might have gone hard with an innocent man. Everything looked very black, but, as luck would have it, most fortunately for himself, Mr. Bladder could prove incontestably that upon the twenty-second of May his car never left its garage, for the very good reason that its engine was down. "I shall call the defendant, and I shall call before you his chauffeur. Both will tell you in detail that the dismantling of the engine was commenced at ten in the morning, and that by half-past twelve—a few minutes before the actual time of the accident—the operation was completed." That the plaintiff had suffered an injury he did not attempt to deny. As a fellow-motorist, he had Mr. Bladder's whole-hearted sympathy. His annoyance was justified, but he could not expect Mr. Bladder to pay the penalty for somebody else's misdeeds. He had no doubt that the witnesses honestly believed that they had correctly memorized the letters and figures upon the number-plate. It was his duty to satisfy the Court that they were mistaken. . . .

As he sat down, I realized that it was not going to be a walk-over.

Mr. Douglas Bladder made a masterly witness. I have rarely seen a more accomplished liar. His regret was infinite. With horrified hands he deplored what he referred to as "the shocking affair". He thundered unsought denunciation of "the dastardly conduct of some fugitive cur". As a motorist, he "so well understood our feelings". But—at length and with a wealth of detail he described how he and his chauffeur had spent the twenty-second of May. With the exception of an hour for lunch, they had worked on the car in the garage from ten o'clock until five. "It seemed a shame," concluded the witness, "to waste such a beautiful day, but I had earmarked the twenty-second for the job, so we went through with it."

A most dangerous thing in the hands of any witness, detail is seldom employed by the dishonest. It is not difficult safely to embroider a lie, but it apparently requires more thought, patience, and rehearsal than ninety-nine rogues out of a hundred are prepared to spend. It soon became unpleasantly clear that Mr. Bladder was the hundredth knave, and that in return for his labour he had a story to tell which was as excellent an imitation of the truth as you might reasonably expect to hear in six whole months of Sundays.

I began to feel extremely uneasy.

To make matters worse, he came through his cross-examination untouched. For every question put to him he had a good natural answer, and, when he stepped down from the box and the Court rose at five-and-twenty minutes past one, it was with something of a shock that I found myself wondering whether by any possible chance a mistake had been made, and we were pursuing an innocent man.

Berry had engaged a table at the Savoy, and he and the others left immediately, for there was little time.

I stayed for a moment to speak with our advisers.

"It's no use disguising the fact," said counsel in a low tone, "that we are up against it. I believe that fellow to be a prize liar. He's too infernally suave. But he knows his job inside out, and he's shaken our case badly. I can't speak for the Judge, but he's impressed the jury, and you can't get away from it. If his chauffeur comes up to the scratch, I believe they'll stop the case." I groaned, and he touched me on the shoulder. "You go and get your lunch," he said.

Heavily I made my way out of the building.

I was waiting for the taxi to which I had signalled, when—

"I observe," said a quiet voice, "that you don't remember me."

I swung round to see a tall dark girl with grey-blue eyes and a charming smile regarding me amusedly. But a moment before I had passed her upon the steps, and, as I did so, wondered what was her business with the Supreme Court. I took off my hat. Now that I saw her properly, her face seemed faintly familiar.

"Forgive me," I said. "I was preoccupied."

The smile deepened.

"I defy you to say where we have met before."

I continued to rack my brain feverishly, but it was no good.

"I can't concentrate," I said desperately. "I can tell you where we shall meet again all right."

"That's not the point. Try Madrigal's wedding."

"Of course. You were one of her bridemaids."

"That's better. How's Nobby?"

The taxi was waiting, so I opened the door.

"I'll tell you about him at lunch. We'll find the others at the Savoy."

She hesitated.

"It's very good of you, but——"

"My sister," I said gravely, "would never forgive me."

The next moment we were rocketing past St. Clement Danes.

"And now," said I, "what have you been doing in the Palace of Lies? What incorruptible judge have you corrupted with your smile? What jury have you bewitched with your small mouth? Or are you just a ward in Chancery?"

My lady smiled.

"What a pity," she said, "you can't remember my name! However will you introduce me?"

"I shall call you Miss Prision of Treason," said I, "and chance it. And what may I say you were doing in yonder Fool's Paradise?"

"You're very bitter and terribly inquisitive," said my companion. "Still, if you must know, I came down to be taken to hear a case. I've got a brother at the Bar, and the little wretch told me to meet him there, and he'd get me in to hear a motor-car case." I started. "Of course he never appeared, and I—my father was a K.C., so I'm not frightened—I just walked in and sat down in the first court I came to. It wasn't very interesting, but there were three judges. All in red, too. By the way, what's arson?"

"Setting fire to a house. All on purpose like. But tell me. D'you know anything about the case you were to have heard?"

"Only that the head of Paul's chambers is in it. That's how he knew it would be interesting."

"Is he in Tristram's chambers?"

"How on earth did you know?"

As she spoke the taxi drew up at the entrance to the *Savoy*.

"Oh, it's our precious case. That's all." I handed her out twittering. "Didn't you know we'd had a smash on the day of the wedding?"

"I did hear something. You don't mean to say . . ."

I paid the driver and hurried her into the hall.

"If you want to be there," I said, "to see us go down, you'll have to have a pretty quick lunch."

We joined the others to find them in a state of profound despondency. My companion was immediately recognized by my sister and Jill, but, to my relief, Berry and Jonah were not quite so quick in the uptake.

"Came to hear our case," I explained, "and got swep' into the Court of Criminal Appeal."

"Talk as you eat," said Berry. "Converse and masticate simultaneously. You know. Like you used to do before you knew me. What's Tristram got to say?"

I swallowed a piece of salmon before replying.

"Frankly pessimistic," I said.

Berry raised his eyes to heaven and ground his teeth. A hard look came upon Jonah's face.

"And we've got to sit there and watch that liar laugh in his sleeve," he said bitterly.

"And pay his costs as well as our own," said I. "Jolly, isn't it?"

Daphne touched me upon the arm, and I looked up. She was very pale.

"D'you think it's hopeless?"

"I think, darling, we're up against it. And—and I'm terribly afraid."

"I see," she whispered. "Need Jill and I go back?"

"Jill needn't, but you must, dear. You're a witness."

As I spoke, I shot a glance at my cousin. The latter was unburdening her soul to Madge Lacey, the quondam bridesmaid, and, to judge from such fragments of the load as reached my ears, uttering sufficient slander regarding Mr. Douglas Bladder to maintain another dozen actions at law.

As some cold tongue was set before me—

"Everything was going so well," said Daphne miserably. "I thought Berry was splendid."

"He was," said I, sousing my brandy with soda. "So were you, sweetheart. Nobody could have done more. And they don't disbelieve you and Jonah. They just think you've made a mistake."

She nodded dully.

"I don't blame them," she said slowly. "That man is so terribly clever. His whole attitude——"

A cry from Jill interrupted her.

"Daphne! Boy! She saw the car! On the way to the wedding. It nearly ran into her too. And Nobby running after it."

"*What?*"

Four mouths—three empty and one full of tongue—framed the interrogative simultaneously.

"Mother and Dad and I," announced Miss Lacey, bubbling, "were driving to the wedding. As we turned out of Long Lane into the Buckler Road, a great green car went by like a flash of lightning. Fortunately we were on the other side, or we'd have been smashed up. And, miles behind, there was a little white dog running the same way. I saw him, because I was back to the engine. Of course we were going much faster than him, and I soon lost sight of him."

Nobby!

Berry was the first to recover.

"Thank Heaven I dragged him in." He glanced at his watch. "Counsel must know this at once. Come on. Never mind the bill: we can settle later."

No one who was that afternoon lunching at the Savoy will ever forget our eruption from the restaurant. The girls actually ran. Berry, Jonah, and I, pursued by frantic waiters, thrust in their wake, taking the carpeted steps three at a time, and generally evincing such symptoms of nervous excitement as are seldom seen save upon the screen of a cinematograph. Indeed, our departure would have done credit to any stage manager, and I firmly believe that the majority of the guests attributed our behaviour to the ingenious brain of a manufacturer of films.

Five minutes later we panted up the steep steps into the corridor which led to our Court. As luck would have it, our solicitor was in the act of pushing open the swing-doors.

I caught him by the arm and breathed into his ear.

"Important new evidence. Vital. We've got the witness here."

He was a man of few words.

"In there," he said shortly, pointing to a consulting room. "I'll get counsel."

We trooped into the apartment and shut the door.

In silence we waited for what seemed a century. Then there were hasty steps, the door opened, and the K.C., followed by his junior and the attorney, entered the room.

Briefly Berry related the story which Miss Lacey could tell.

"This is the lady," he concluded. "I know our case is closed, but surely she can be called?"

We hung upon the reply.

"Can she speak to the number?"

"No. But in corroboration——"

"My dear Major Pleydell," said Tristram, "you need no corroboration. The jury believe you. They believe you were smashed up. They believe it was done by a green touring car. The devil of it is, they believe the defendant too. And so they come to the very natural conclusion that, between the excitement of the moment and the pace at which the car was travelling, Mrs. Pleydell and Captain Mansell have made a mistake—perhaps only of one figure—in the number they saw. And, unless we can discredit that fellow's story, call evidence to show he *was* out on that day, or something, I'm very much afraid we shall go down. His counsel is certain to ask for the benefit of the doubt, and they'll give it him."

I never remember feeling so disappointed.

I think we all felt the weight of his words, but our collapse was pitiful. Lured by a treacherous hope into the belief that we were saved, we were fallen into a deeper Slough of Despond than before. Jill was hard put to it to restrain her tears. . . .

Listlessly we followed our advisers into Court, and a moment later the Judge took his seat.

One or two applications, which did not concern our case, were made. Then leading counsel for the defence rose to his feet and called his next witness—

"Walter Dale."

At the sound of the name I started violently. Then, open-mouthed and trembling with excitement, I twisted myself round to get a glimpse of the witness as he approached the box. Could it be possible that Fate with fiendish irony had selected the ex-trooper whom we had befriended to administer to our case the *coup de grâce*? It must be a man of another name. But Dale *was* a chauffeur....

There was a stir at the back of the crowded Court. Somebody was pushing his way forward. Somebody...

It *was* Dale.

The short, stockily-built figure, that I had not seen for more than three years, stepped out of the ruck of onlookers and took its place in the witness-box.

"Take the Book in our right hand...."

It was the Associate's voice. As in a dream I heard the oath administered.

"The truth.... The whole truth.... And nothing but the truth."

Dale's lips moved and he kissed the Testament.

He was very pale. As he laid the Book down, our eyes met, and he looked me full in the face. My heart began to thump violently.

"Your name is Walter Dale?" said counsel.

"Yes"—in a low voice.

"Speak up, please, so that his lordship and the jury may hear. You are a chauffeur in the employ of the defendant?"

"Yes."

"Do you remember the twenty-second of May?"

"Yes, sir."

"Now, I want you to tell the Court in your own words exactly what you did that day. First of all, on that day did your master's car leave the garage?"

"Yes, it did."

The Court gasped. Jurymen, counsel, officials, reporters—every one sat up as if they had been shot. Even the Judge started, and the defendant half rose from his seat and, when his solicitor laid a hand on his arm, sank back with bayed ferocity in his eyes and a face the colour of cigar-ash.

"I don't think you quite understood my question," purred counsel. "On the twenty-second of May, the day of the accident to the plaintiff's car, did Mr. Bladder's car, of which you were in charge, leave the garage?"

"Yes," said Dale sturdily, "it did."

"You understand what you're saying?" said the Judge.

"Yes, sir. An' if I was to say anythin' else, I'd not only be tellin' a lie, but I'd be doin' in the bes' friend as ever I 'ad." He pointed to me. "The Captain there. Little I knowed, when I took 'is money"—scornfully he nodded at the defendant—" 'oo it was we run into that day. Twenty-five pound it was, an' another twenty-five if we won the case."

"My lord," said counsel, protesting, "I——"

The Judge held up his hand and turned to the witness.

"Remember you are on your oath."

"I do that, sir. It's gospel truth what I'm sayin'. The accident 'appened exactly as you've heard them tell. 'E was drivin', an' me by 'is side. Tore by 'em, we did, an' 'it 'em an' left 'em. Sends me up to Town for a new 'ub-cap the nex' day. Lettin' 'er out, 'e was, to see 'ow she'd run after the over'aul. That was the day before."

He paused for lack of breath, and the Judge turned his head slowly and peered at counsel over the rim of his glasses.

I was looking at the defendant.

If any corroboration of Dale's story were needed, it was written upon his master's face for all to see. Guilt, fear, and beastly rage were horribly depicted. The close-set eyes shifted frantically from side to side. The mouth worked uncontrollably. . . .

As I looked, the fellow rose to his feet, swayed, put a hand to his throat, and stepped uncertainly towards the doors. The crowd parted, and he passed through. . . .

A thick voice shattered the silence.

"In the circumstances your lordship will appreciate that I can carry my case no further."

With a swish of silk, counsel resumed his seat.

As was to be expected, the jury delivered its verdict without leaving the box. As the applause subsided—

"I ask for judgment with costs," said Tristram.

The Judge nodded.

"And I direct," he said, "that the documents of the case be impounded and be sent to the Director of Public Prosecutions."

Amid the buzz of excitement which succeeded his words, I felt a touch on my shoulder. Our leader was smiling.

"Cast your bread upon the waters," he said. "For you shall find it after many days."

CHAPTER VII

How Jonah Obeyed his Orders, and Daphne and Katharine Festival Backed the same Horse

Berry laid down his knife and fork and raised his eyes to heaven.

"This," he said, "is the frozen edge. I'm getting used to the distemper which is brought me in lieu of soup, and, although I prefer salmon cooked to raw, you may have noticed that I consumed my portion without a word. But this . . ." Contemptuously he indicated the severed *tournedos* upon his plate. "You know, they must have been using the lime-kiln. Nobody could get such a withered effect with an electric cooker. Oh, and look at our olive. Quick, before it shuts up."

Jill began to shake with laughter.

"I can't help it," said Daphne desperately. "I know it's awful, but what can we do?"

"There must be some cooks somewhere," said I. "The breed isn't extinct. And they can't all be irrevocably suited. I always thought the Cooks' Brigade was one of the most mobile arms of domestic service."

"I've done everything," said my sister, "except advertise. Katharine Festival put me off that. She says she spent seven pounds on advertisements and never got a single answer. But I've done everything else. I've asked everybody I know, my name's on the books of every registry office I've ever heard of, and I've written and sent stamped addressed envelopes to every cook whose name I've been given. Three out of about sixty have replied, saying they were already suited. One came here, practically said she'd come, and then wrote to say she was frightened of the electric cooker. And another wanted a hundred a year and a private bathroom. It's simply hopeless."

"If," said Berry, "we survive this meal, I'll write to Jonah and tell him to bring one back with him. If he can't raise one in Paris, he ought to be shot. And now let's have a sweep on the savoury. I'll bet it tastes of paraffin and looks like a pre-War divot."

"Let's try advertising," said Jill. "Katharine mayn't have had a good one."

"I agree," said I. "I'll get one out to-night. A real snorter."

In silence the traces of the course which had provoked the outburst were removed, clean plates were set before us, and the footman advanced with a dish of nauseous-looking fritters.

Daphne instinctively recoiled.

"Hullo," said Berry. "Another gas attack?"

With an effort my sister recovered herself and took one with a shaking hand. Loyally Jill followed her example, and, with tears running down her cheeks, induced a glutinous slab to quit the silver, to which it clung desperately.

I declined the delicacy.

With compressed lips the servant offered it to my brother-in-law.

Berry shook his head.

"Mother wouldn't like me to," he said. "But I can see it's very tasty." He turned to his wife. "What a wonderful thing perfume is! You know, the smell of burnt fat always makes me think of the Edgware Road at dusk."

"Hush," said I, consulting the *menu*. "*De mortuis*. Those were banana fritters. That slimy crust enshrined the remains of a once succulent fruit."

"What?" said Berry. "Like beans in amber? How very touching! I suppose undertakers are easier than cooks. Never mind. It's much cheaper. I shan't want to be reminded of food for several days now." He looked across the table to Daphne. "After what I've just seen, I feel I can give the savoury a miss. Do you agree, darling? Or has the fritter acted as an *apéritif*?"

My sister addressed herself to Jill.

"Don't eat it, dear. It's—it's not very nice." She rose. "Shall we go?"

Gloomily we followed her into the library, where I opened all the windows and Berry lighted a huge cigar, in the hope of effacing the still pungent memory of the unsavoury sweet. Gradually it faded away. . . .

Three weeks had passed since the mistress of our kitchen, who had reigned uninterruptedly for seven years, had been knocked down by a taxi and sustained a broken leg. Simple though the fracture fortunately was, at least another nine weeks must elapse before she could attempt to resume her duties, and we were in evil case. Every day we became more painfully aware of the store which we had unconsciously set by decently cooked food. As time went on, the physical and mental disorder, consequent upon Mrs. Mason's accident, became more and more pronounced. All topics of conversation became subservient to the burning question of filling the void occasioned by her absence. Worst of all, dissatisfaction was rampant in the servants' hall, and Daphne's maid had hinted broadly that, if a cook was not shortly forthcoming, resignations would be—an intimation which made us desperate. Moreover, in another month we were due to leave Town and repair to White Ladies. There, deep in the country, with no restaurants or clubs to fall back upon, we should be wholly at the mercy of whoever controlled the preparation of our food, and, unless the situation improved considerably, the prospect was far from palatable.

Moodily I extinguished my cigarette and filled and lighted a pipe in its stead. Then I remembered my threat.

Berry was writing a letter, so I extracted a sheet of notepaper from the left-hand drawer and, taking a pencil from my pocket, sat down on the sofa and set to work to compose an advertisement calculated to allure the most suspicious and *blasée* cook that ever was foaled.

Jill sat labouring with her needle upon a dainty teacloth, pausing now and again to hold a whispered and one-sided conversation with Nobby, who lay at inelegant ease supine between us. Perched upon the arm of a deep armchair, my sister was subjecting the space devoted by five daily papers to the announcement of "Situations Required" to a second and more leisurely examination.

Presently she rose with a sigh and crossed to the telephone.

We knew what was coming.

Every night she and Katharine Festival communicated to one another their respective failures of the day. More often than not, these took the simple form of "negative information".

She was connected immediately.

"Hullo, that you, Katharine? . . . Yes, Daphne. Any luck? . . . Not much. You know, it's simply hopeless. What? . . . 'Widow with two boys of seven and nine'? Thank you. I'd rather . . . Exactly . . . Well, I don't know. I'd give it up, only it's so awful . . . . Awful."

"If she doesn't believe it, ask her to dinner," said Berry.

"Shut up," said Daphne. "It's all right, Katharine. I was speaking to Berry. . . . Oh, he's fed to the teeth."

"I cannot congratulate you," said her husband, "upon your choice of metaphor."

My sister ignored the interruption.

"Oh, rather . . . His food means a lot to him, you know."

"This," said her husband, "is approaching the obscene. I dine off tepid wash and raw fish, I am tormented by the production of a once luscious fillet deliberately rendered unfit for human consumption, and I am deprived of my now ravening appetite by the nauseating reek from the shock of whose assault I am still trying to rally my olfactory nerves. All this I endure with that unfailing good——"

"Will you be quiet?" said his wife. "How can I——"

"No, I won't," said Berry. "My finer feelings are outraged. And that upon an empty stomach. I shall write home and ask to be taken away. I shall——"

"Katharine," said Daphne, "I can't hear you because that fool Berry is talking, but Boy's getting out an advertisement, and we're going to . . . Oh, are you? I thought you said you'd given it up. . . . Another nineteen shillings' worth? Well, here's luck, anyway . . . Yes, of course. But I daren't hope . . . Good-bye." She replaced the receiver and turned to me. "Katharine's going to start advertising again."

"Is she?" I grunted. "Well, I'll bet she doesn't beat this. Listen.

> COOK, capable, experienced, is offered for three months abnormal wages, every luxury and a leisurely existence: electric cooker: constant hot water: kitchen-maid: separate bedroom: servants' hall: late breakfast: town and country: followers welcomed.—Mrs. Pleydell, 7, Cholmondeley Street, Mayfair: 'Phone, Mayfair 9999."

"That's the style," said Berry. "Let me know when it's going to appear, and I'll get a bedroom at the Club. When you've weeded the best out of the first hundred thousand, I'll come back and give the casting vote."

From behind, my sister put her arms about my neck and laid her soft cheek against mine.

"My dear," she murmured, "I daren't. Half the cooks in England would leave their situations."

"So much the better," said I. "All's fair in love and war. I don't know which this is, but we'll call it 'love' and chance it. Besides," I added cunningly, "we must knock out Katharine."

The light of battle leapt into my sister's eyes. Looking at it from her point of view, I realized that my judgment had been ill-considered. Plainly it was not a question of love, but of war—"and that most deadly". She drew her arms from my neck and stood upright.

"Couldn't you leave out my name and just put 'Box So-and-so'?"

I shook my head.

"That's so intangible. Besides, I think the telephone number's a great wheeze." Thoughtfully she crossed to the fireplace and lighted a cigarette. "I'll send it to-morrow," I said.

Suddenly the room was full of silvery laughter.

From Berry's side at the writing-table Jill looked up sparkling.

"Listen to this," she said, holding up the letter which my brother-in-law had just completed.

Dear Brother,

Incompetent bungler though you are, and bitter as has been my experience of your gaucherie in the past, I am once again about to prove whether out of the dunghill of inefficiency which, with unconscious humour, you style your "mind" there can be coaxed a shred of reliability and understanding.

It is within your knowledge that some three weeks ago this household was suddenly deprived of the services of its cook. This out of a clear sky and, if we may believe the police, in one of those uncharted purlieus which shroud in mystery the source of the Cromwell Road. After four lean days your gluttonous instincts led you precipitately to withdraw to Paris, from whence, knowing your unshakable belief in the vilest forms of profligacy, I appreciate that lack of means must ere long enforce your return.

Therefore I write.

For twenty-two unforgettable sultry days we have endured the ghastly pleasantries of charwomen, better qualified to victual the lower animals than mankind. To call the first meal "breakfast" is sheer blasphemy: lunch is a hollow mockery: dinner, the abomination of desolation. I do what I can with grape-nuts and the gas-stove in the bathroom, but the result is unhappy, and last night the milk was too quick for me.

I therefore implore you to collect a cook in Paris without delay. Bring it with you when you come, or, better still, send it in advance, carriage paid. Luxury shall be heaped upon it. Its slightest whim shall be gratified, and it shall go to "the movies" at my expense, whenever I am sent tickets. Can generosity go further? Wages no object: fare paid back to

Paris as soon as Mrs. Mason's leg can carry her.

Brother, I beseech you, take immediate action. The horror of our plight cannot be exaggerated. Do something—anything. Misrepresent facts, corrupt honesty, suborn the faithful, but—procure a cook.

My maw reminds me that it is the hour of grape-nuts, so I must go.

Berry.

P.S.—If you can't raise one, I shouldn't come back. Just go to some high place and quietly push yourself off. It will be simpler and avoid a scene which would be painful to us both.

"That's rather worse than the advertisement," said Daphne. "But, as Jonah is accustomed to your interpretation of the art of letter-writing, I suppose it doesn't much matter."

"When," said Berry, "you are making yourself sick upon *tête de veau en tortue* and *crêpes Suzette*, I shall remind you of those idle words."

* * * * *

The advertisement appeared for the first time on Thursday morning.

As I entered the dining-room at half-past nine—

"It's in," said Jill. "On the front page."

"Yes," said Berry, "it's most arresting. Applicants will arrive from all over the kingdom. It's inevitable. Nothing can stop them. Old and trusted retainers will become unsettled. The domestic upheaval will be unparalleled."

I read the advertisement through. In cold print my handiwork certainly looked terribly alluring. Then I laid down the paper and strolled to the window. It had been raining, but now the sun was out, and the cool fresh air of the June morning was sweet and winsome. As I looked into the glistening street—

"It's a bit early yet," continued Berry. "Give 'em a chance. I should think they'll start about ten. I wonder how far the queue will reach," he added reflectively. "I hope the police take it past The Albert Memorial. Then they can sit on the steps."

"Nonsense," said I a little uneasily. "We may get an answer or two to-morrow. I think we shall. But cooks are few and far between."

"They won't be few and they'll be anything but far between by twelve o'clock." He tapped the provocative paragraph with an accusing finger. "This is a direct incitement to repair to 7, Cholmondeley Street, or as near thereto as possible——"

"I wish to goodness we hadn't put it in," said Daphne.

"It's done now," said her husband, "and we'd better get ready. I'll turn them down in the library, you can stand behind the whatnot in the drawing room and fire them from there, and Boy'd better go down the queue with some oranges and a megaphone, and keep on saying we're suited right up to the last."

In silence I turned to the sideboard. It was with something of an effort that I helped myself to a thick slab of bacon which was obviously but half-cooked. From the bottom of a second dish a black and white egg, with a pale green yoke, eyed me with a cold stare. With a shudder I covered it up again. . . . After all, we did want a cook, and if we were bombarded with applications for the post, the probability of getting a good one was the more certain.

As I took my seat—

"Is Katharine's advertisement in?" I asked.

My sister nodded.

"She's put her telephone number, too."

"Has she? She will be mad when she sees we've had the same idea."

"Ah," said Berry. "I'd forgotten the telephone. That's another vulnerable spot. I shouldn't wonder if——"

The sentence was never finished.

The hurried stammer of the telephone bell made a dramatic irruption, and Jill, who was in the act of drinking, choked with excitement.

In silence we listened, to be quite sure. A second prolonged vibration left no room for doubt.

"They're off," said Berry.

"I—I feel quite nervous," said Daphne. "Let Falcon answer it."

But Jill was already at the door. . . .

Breathlessly we awaited her return.

Nobby, apparently affected by the electricity with which the air was charged, started to relieve his feelings by barking stormily. The nervous outburst of reproof which greeted his eloquence was so unexpectedly menacing that he retired precipitately beneath the table, his small white tail clapped incontinently between his legs.

The next moment Jill tore into the room.

"It's a cook!" she cried in a tempestuous whisper. "It's a cook! She wants to speak to Daphne. It's a trunk call. She's rung up from Torquay."

"Torquay!" I cried aghast. "Good Heavens!"

"What did I say?" said Berry. My sister rose in some trepidation. "Two hundred miles is nothing. Have another hunk of toast. It was only made on Sunday, so I can recommend it."

Daphne hastened from the room, with Jill twittering at her heels, and in some dudgeon I cut myself a slice of bread.

Berry turned his attention to the Sealyham.

"Nobby my lad, come here."

Signifying his delight at this restoration to favour by an unusually elaborate rotatory movement of his tail, the terrier emerged from his cover and humbled himself at his patron's feet. The latter picked him up and set him upon his knee.

"My lad," he said, "this is going to be a momentous day. Cooks, meet to be bitten, are due to arrive in myriads. Be ruthless. Spare neither the matron nor the maid. What did Mr. Henry say in 1415?—

> This day is call'd the feast of Sealyham:
> She that outlives this day, and comes safe home,
> Will sit with caution when this day is named,
> And shudder at the name of Sealyham.
> She that shall live this day, and see old age,
> Will yearly on the razzle feast her neighbours,
> And say, 'To-morrow is Saint Sealyham':
> Then will she strip her hose and show her scars,
> And say, 'These wounds I had on Nobby's day.'
> Old cooks forget; yet all shall be forgot,
> But she'll remember with a flood of talk
> What feats you did that day."

Nobby licked his face enthusiastically.

Then came a swift rush across the hall, and Daphne and Jill pelted into the room.

"She's coming up for an interview to-morrow," panted the latter. "Six years in her last place, but the people are going abroad. If we engage her, she can come on Monday. Sixty pounds a year."

Daphne was beaming.

"I must say I liked the sound of her. Very respectful she seemed. Her name's rather unusual, but that isn't her fault. Pauline Roper. I fancy she's by way of being an expert. She's got a certificate from some institute of cookery, and her sister's a trained nurse in Welbeck Street. That's why she wants to be in London. What's the return fare from Torquay?" she added. "I said I'd pay it, if I took up her reference."

"Oh, something under five pounds," said Berry.

"What!"

"My dear," said her husband, "if the expenditure of that sum were to ensure me a breakfast the very sight of which did not make my gorge rise, I should regard it as a trustee investment."

Reference to a time-table showed that the price of Pauline Roper's ticket would be two pounds nine shillings and fourpence halfpenny.

Somewhat to our surprise and greatly to our relief, the day passed without another application for the post of cook, personal or otherwise.

To celebrate the solitary but promising response to our S.O.S. signal, and the prospect which it afforded of an early deliverance from our state, we dined at the *Berkeley* and went to the play.

On returning home we found a telegram in the hall. It had been handed in at Paris, and ran as follows:

> Cook called Camille François leaving for Cholmondeley Street to-morrow aaa can speak no English so must be met at Dover aaa boat due 4.15 aaa Jonah.

* * * * *

The train roared through Ashford, and Berry looked at his watch. Then he sighed profoundly and began to commune with himself in a low tone.

"*Mille pardons, madame. Mais vous êtes Camille François? Non? Quel dommage! Dix mille pardons. Adieu.* . . . Deuce of a lot of 'milles', aren't there? I wonder if there'll be many passengers. And will she come first-class, or before the mast? You know, this is a wild mare's chest, and that's all there is to it. We shall insult several hundred women, miss the cook, and probably lose Pauline into the bargain. What did I come for?"

"Nonsense," said Jill stoutly. "Jonah's told her to look out for us."

"I'll bet he never thought I should be fool enough to roll up, so she won't expect me. As a matter of fact, if he's described any one, he's probably drawn a lifelike word-picture of Daphne."

"It's no good worrying," said I. "The only thing to do is to address every woman who looks in the least like a cook as she steps off the gangway. When we do strike her, Jill can carry on."

"It's all very well," said Berry, "but what does a cook look like, or look least like, or least look like? I suppose you know what you mean." Jill began to shake with laughter. "She'll probably be all dressed up to give us a treat, and, for all we know, she may have a child with her, and, if she's pretty, it's a hundred to one some fellow will be seeing her off the boat. You can't rule out any one. And to accost strange women indiscriminately is simply asking for trouble. Understand this: when I've been knocked down twice, you can count me out."

This was too much for Jill, who made no further efforts to restrain her merriment. Fixing her with a sorrowful look, my brother-in-law sank back in his corner with a resigned air.

Jonah's telegram had certainly complicated matters.

We had received it too late to prevent the dispatch of the cook whose services he had apparently enlisted. After a prolonged discussion we had decided that, while Daphne must stay and interview Pauline Roper, the rest of us had better proceed to Dover with the object of meeting the boat. It was obvious that Jill must go to deal with the immigrant when the latter had been identified, but she could not be expected to effect the identification. I was unanimously chosen for this responsible task, but I refused point-blank to make the attempt single-handed. I argued with reason that it was more than one man could do, and that the performance of what was, after all, a highly delicate operation must be shared by Berry. After a titanic struggle the latter gave in, with the result that Jill and he and I had left London by the eleven o'clock train. This was due to arrive at Dover at two minutes to one, so that we should have time for lunch and to spare before the boat came in.

But that was not all.

The coming of Jonah's *protégée* made it impossible for my sister to engage Pauline Roper out of hand. Of course the latter might prove impossible, which, in a way, would simplify the position. If, as was more probable, she seemed desirable, the only thing to do was to pay her fare and promise to let her know within twenty-four hours whether we would engage her or not. That would give us time to discover whether Camille François was the more promising of the two.

Whatever happened, it was painfully clear that our engagement of a cook was going to prove one of the most costly adventures of its kind upon which we had ever embarked.

The train steamed into Dover one minute before its scheduled time, and we immediately repaired to the Lord Warden Hotel.

Lunch was followed by a comfortable half-hour in the lounge, after which we decided to take the air until the arrival of the packet.

Perhaps the most famous of the gates of England, Dover has always worn a warlike mien. Less formidable than renowned Gibraltar, there is a look of grim efficiency about her heights, an air of masked authority about the windy galleries hung in her cold grey chalk, something of Roman competence about the proud old gatehouse on the Castle Hill. Never in mufti, never in gaudy uniform, Dover is always clad in "service" dress. A thousand threats have made her porterage a downright office, bluntly performed. And so those four lean years, that whipped the smile from many an English hundred, seem to have passed over the grizzled Gate like the east wind, leaving it scatheless. About herself no change was visible. As we leaned easily upon the giant parapet of the Admiralty Pier, watching the tireless waves dance to the *cappriccio* of wind and sun, there was but little evidence to show that the portcullis, recently hoist, had for four years been down. Under the shadow of the Shakespeare Cliff the busy traffic of impatient Peace fretted as heretofore. The bristling sentinels were gone: no craft sang through the empty air: no desperate call for labour wearied tired eyes, clawed at strained nerves, hastened the scurrying feet: no longer from across the Straits came flickering the ceaseless grunt and grumble of the guns. The wondrous tales of nets, of passages of arms, of sallies made at dawn—mortal immortal exploits—seemed to be chronicles of another age. The ways and means of War, so lately paramount, were out of sight. As in the days before, the march of Trade and caravan of Pleasure jostled each other in the Gate's mouth. Only the soldierly aspect of the place remained—Might in a faded surcoat, her shabby scabbard hiding a loose bright blade. . . .

The steamer was up to time.

When four o'clock came she was well in sight, and at fourteen minutes past the hour the rattle of the donkey-engine came to a sudden stop, and a moment later the gangways were thrust and hauled into their respective positions.

Berry and I stood as close the the actual points of disembarkation as convenience and discretion allowed, while Jill hovered excitedly in the background.

As the passengers began to descend—

"Now for it," said my brother-in-law, settling his hat upon his head. "I feel extremely nervous and more ill at ease than I can ever remember. My mind is a seething blank, and I think my left sock-suspender is coming down. However . . . Of course, it is beginning to be forcibly what they call 'borne in upon' me that we ought to have brought some barbed wire and a turnstile. As it is, we shall miss about two-thirds of them. Here's your chance," he added, nodding at a stout lady with a green suit-case and a defiant glare. "I'll take the jug and bottle department."

I had just time to see that the object of his irreverence was an angular female with a brown paper parcel and a tumbler, when my quarry gained *terra firma* and started in the direction of the train.

I raised my hat.

"Pardon, madame. Mois vous êtes Camille——"

"Reeang," was the discomfiting reply. "Par de baggarge."

I realised that an offer which I had not made had been rejected, and that the speaker was not of French descent.

The sting of the rebuff was greatly tempered by the reception with which Berry's advances were met.

I was too late to hear what he had said, but the resentment which his attempt had provoked was disconcertingly obvious.

After fixing my brother-in-law with a freezing stare, his addressee turned as from an offensive odour and invested the one word she thought fit to employ with an essence of loathing which was terrible to hear.

"Disgusting!"

Berry shook his head.

"The right word," he said, "was 'monstrous'."

He turned to accost a quiet-looking girl wearing an oil-silk gabardine and very clearly born upon the opposite side of the Channel.

With a sigh, I addressed myself to a widow with a small boy clad in a *pélérine*. To my embarrassment she proved to be deaf, but when I had stumblingly repeated my absurd interrogation, she denied the impeachment with a charming smile. During our exchange of courtesies the child stood staring at me with a finger deep in his mouth. At their conclusion he withdrew this and pointed it directly at my chin.

"Pourquoi s'est-il coupé, maman?" he demanded in a piercing treble.

The question was appropriate, but unanswerable.

His mother lugged him incontinently away.

Berry was confronting one of the largest ladies I have ever seen. As he began to speak, she interrupted him.

"Vous êtes Meestair Baxtair, n'est-ce pas? Ah, c'est bien ça.

J'avais si peur de ne pas vous trouver. Mais maintenant je suis tranquille. Mon mari me suit. Ah, le voilà!" She turned about, the better to beckon to a huge man with two bags and a hold-all. *"Pierre! Pierre!"*

Beneath the avalanche of good-will Berry stood paralysed.

Recognizing that something must be done, I sought to interfere.

"Leave me alone," said Berry weakly. "I've—I've got off."

It took all my energy and most of my French to convince his *vis-à vis* that she was mistaken.

During the interlude about fifteen "possibles" escaped us.

I threw a despairing glance in Jill's direction, wiped the sweat from my brow, and returned to the attack.

After four more failures my nerve began to go. Miserably I turned to my brother-in-law.

He was in the act of addressing a smart-looking girl in black, bearing a brand-new valise and some wilting roses.

Before she had time to appreciate his inquiry there was a choking yell from the gangway, and a very dark gentleman, with an Italian cast of countenance, thrust his explosive way on to the pier.

My knowledge of his native tongue was limited to *carissimo, spaghetti*, and one or two musical directions, but from the vehemence of his tone and the violence of his dramatic gestures it was plain that the torrent which foamed from his lips was both menacing and abusive. From the shape of the case which he was clutching beneath his left arm, I judged him to be an exponent of the guitar.

Advancing his nose to within an inch and a half of Berry's chin he blared and raved like a maniac, alternately pointing to his shrinking *protegée* and indicating the blue vault of heaven with frightful emphasis.

Berry regarded him unperturbed. As he paused for breath—

"In answer to your observations," he said, "I can only say that I am not a Mormon and have absolutely no connection with Salt Lake City. I may add that, if you are partial to garlic, it is a taste which I have never acquired. In conclusion, I hope that, before you reach the platform for which you are apparently making, you will stumble over one of the ridiculously large rings with which the quay is so generously provided, and will not only suffer the most hideous agony, but remain permanently lame as a result of your carelessness."

The calm dignity with which he delivered this speech had an

almost magical effect upon the jealous Latin. His bluster sank suddenly and died. Muttering to himself and staring at Berry as at a wizard, he seized the girl by the arm and started to move rapidly away, wide-eyed and ill at ease. . . . With suppressed excitement and the tail of my eye, I watched him bear down upon one of the stumbling-blocks to which Berry had referred. The accuracy with which he approached it was almost uncanny. I found myself standing upon one leg. . . . The screech of anguish with which he hailed the collision, no less than the precipitancy with which he dropped the guitar, sat down and began to rock himself to and fro, was irresistibly gratifying.

The muscles about Berry's mouth twitched.

"So perish all traitors," he said. "And now I don't know how you feel, but I've had about enough of this. My nerves aren't what they were. Something may snap any minute."

With one accord we proceeded to rejoin Jill, who had been witnessing our humilitaions from a safe distance, and was dabbing her grey eyes with a ridiculous handkerchief.

As we came up, she started forward and pointed a trembling finger in the direction of the boat. Berry and I swung on our heels.

Looking very well, Jonah was descending the gangway with a bored air.

My brother-in-law and I stared at him as at one risen from the dead. Almost at once he saw us and waved airily. . . . A moment later he limped to where we were standing and kissed his sister.

"I had an idea some of you'd turn up," he said coolly.

Berry turned to me.

"You hear?" he said grimly. "He had an idea some of us'd turn up. An idea . . . I suppose a little bird told him. Oh, take me away, somebody, and let me die. Let me have one last imitation meal, and die. Where do they sell wild oats?"

Jonah disregarded the interruption.

"At the last moment," he said calmly, "I felt there might be some mix-up, so I came along too." He turned and nodded at a nervous little man who was standing self-consciously a few paces away and, as I now observed for the first time, carrying my cousin's dressing-case. "That," he added, "is Camille."

His momentous announcement rendered us speechless. At length—

"You—you mean to say," I gasped, "that—that it's a man?"

Jonah shrugged his shoulders.

"Look at his trousers," he said.

"But—but of course we expected a woman," cried Jill in a choking voice. "We can't have a *chef*."

"Nothing," said Jonah, "was said about sex."

Berry spoke in a voice shaken with emotion.

"A man," he said. "A he-cook, called 'Camille'. And it actually occurred to you that 'there might be some mix-up'. You know, your intuition is positively supernatural. And it is for this," he added bitterly, "that I have dissipated in ten crowded minutes a reputation which it has taken years to amass. It is for this that I have deliberately insulted several respectable ladies, jeopardized the *Entente Cordiale,* and invited personal violence of a most unpleasant character. To do this I shall have travelled about a hundred and fifty miles, with the shade temperature at ninety, and lost what would have been an undoubtedly pleasant and possibly extremely fruitful day at Sandown Park. Don't be afraid. I wouldn't touch you for worlds. You're being reserved for some very special form of dissolution, you are. She-bears, or something. I should avoid woods, any way. And now I'm going home. To-morrow I shall start on a walking tour, with a spare sock and some milk chocolate, and try to forget. If that fails, I shall take the snail—I mean the veil."

He turned on his heel and stalked haughtily in the direction of the boat train.

Gurgling with merriment, Jill laid a hand on my arm.

"Daphne will simply scream," she said.

"If this little stunt has cost us Pauline," said I, "she won't leave it at that."

We turned to follow my brother-in-law.

Jonah beckoned to Camille.

"Venez. Restez près de moi," he said.

* * * * *

On arriving at Charing Cross we left Jonah and the cook to weather the Customs, and drove straight to Cholmondeley Street.

As we entered the hall, my sister came flying out of the library.

"Hello," she cried, "where's the cook? Don't say——"

Berry uncovered.

"Pardon, madame," he said, *"mais vous êtes Camille Franç*—— That's your cue. Now you say 'Serwine!' Just like that. 'Serwine!' Put all the loathing you can into it—you'll find it can hold quite a lot—and fix me with a glassy eye. Then I blench and break out into a cold sweat. Oh, it's a great game."

"Poor old chap," said Daphne. "It must have been awful. But haven't you got her?"

"It's a he!" cried Jill, squeaking with excitement. "It's a he. Jonah's bringing him——"

"A *what*?" said my sister, taking a pace backward.

"A male," said I. "You know. Like Nobby. Separate legs, and shaves on Thursdays."

"Do you mean to say that it's a *chef*?"

I nodded.

My sister collapsed into a convenient chair and closed her eyes. Presently she began to shake with laughter.

"It is droll, isn't it?" said Berry. "People wouldn't believe it. Fancy travelling a hundred and fifty miles to molest a lot of strange women, and then finding that for all the good you've done you might as well have spent the day advertising for 'The Lost Chord'."

My sister pulled herself together.

"Thank goodness, I had the sense to engage Pauline," she announced. "Something told me I'd better. But I waited before taking up her reference, on the off-chance of this one being a marvel. Where is the wretched man?"

"Jonah fetched up with him. He's stayed behind because of the Customs. They ought to be here any minute."

"Well, there's no place for him to sleep here," said Daphne. "Fitch will have to look after him for to-night, and to-morrow he'll have to go back."

Berry looked at his watch.

"Five past seven," he said. "As the blighter's here, why not let him sub-edit the dinner to-night? It'll shorten his life, but it may save ours. You never know."

My sister hesitated. Then—

"He'll never do it," she said. "I can suggest it, but, if he's anything of a cook, he'll go off the deep end at once."

"And give notice," said I. "Well, that's exactly what we want. Then we shan't have to fire him. He can just push off quietly to-morrow, Pauline will roll up on Monday, and everything will be lovely in the garden."

"That's it," said Berry. "If he consents, well and good. If he declines, so much the better. It's a blinkin' certainty. Whichever happens, we can't lose."

"All right," said Daphne. "I shall make Jonah tell him."

It took Jonah and M. François longer to satisfy the officers of

His Majesty's Customs and Excise than we had anticipated, and I had consumed a much-needed whisky and soda and was on the way to the bathroom when I heard them arrive.

Before I had completed a leisurely toilet, it was all over.

As we waited in the lounge of the *Carlton* Grill for a table, which we had been too late to reserve, my sister related the circumstances which had led to the *débâcle*.

"The wretched little man didn't seem to take to the idea of starting in right away, but I explained that he needn't do any more than just run his eye over the *menu*, and that, as they were going to have the same dinner in the servants' hall, it really only amounted to looking after his own food.

"Then I sent for Falcon, explained things, and told him to look after the man this evening, and that I was making arrangements for him to stay with Fitch over the garage. Then I had Mrs. Chapel up."

"That, I take it," said Berry, "is the nymph lately responsible for the preparation of our food?"

Daphne nodded.

"I told her about François, and that, as he was here, he would help her with dinner to-night. I said he was very clever, and all that sort of thing, and that I wanted her to show him what she was cooking, and listen to any suggestions he had to make."

"I suppose you added that he couldn't speak a word of English," said her husband.

"Be quiet," said Daphne. "Besides, he can. Several words. Any way, she didn't seem over-pleased, but, as Pauline's coming on Monday, that didn't worry me. So I sent her away, and rang up Fitch and told him he must fix the Frenchman up for the night."

"Did he seem over-pleased?"

"I didn't wait to hear. I just rang off quick. Then I went up to dress. The next thing I knew was that they'd tried to murder each other, and that Camille had bitten William, and Nobby'd bitten Camille. I don't suppose we shall ever know exactly what happened."

So far as we had been able to gather from the butler, who had immediately repaired to Daphne's room for instructions, and was labouring under great excitement, my sister's orders had been but grudgingly obeyed. Mrs. Chapel had been ill-tempered and obstructive, and had made no attempt to disguise her suspicion of the *chef*. The latter had consequently determined to be as nasty as the circumstances allowed, had eyed her preparations for dinner with a marked contempt, and had communed visibly and audibly with himself in a manner which it was impossible to mistake. Finally he had desired to taste the soup which she was cooking. Poor as his English was, his meaning was apparent, but the charwoman had affected an utter inability to understand what he said. This had so much incensed the Frenchman that the other servants had intervened and insisted on Mrs. Chapel's compliance with his request. With an ill grace she snatched the lid from the saucepan. . . .

Everything was now in train for a frightful explosion. In bitterness the fuse had been laid, the charge of passion was tamped, the detonator of spleen was in position. Only a match was necessary. . . .

Camille François, however, preferred to employ a torch.

After allowing the fluid to cool, the Frenchman—by this time the cynosure of sixteen vigilant eyes—introduced a teaspoonful into his mouth. . . .

The most sanguine member of his audience was hardly expecting him to commend the beverage. Mrs. Chapel herself must have felt instinctively that no man born of woman would in the circumstances renounce such a magnificent opportunity of "getting back". Nobody, however, was apparently prepared for so vigorous and dramatic an appreciation of the dainty.

For the space of two seconds the *chef* held it cupped in his mouth. Then with an expression of deadly loathing, intensified by a horrible squint, he expelled the liquid on to the kitchen floor. Ignoring the gasp which greeted his action, he was observed to shrug his shoulders.

"I veep my eyes," he announced, "for ze pore pig."

Here the steady flood of the butler's narrative became excusably broken into the incoherence of rapids and the decent reticence of disappearing falls. Beyond the fact that Mrs. Chapel had swung twice to the jaw, and that Camille had replied with an ineffectual kick before they were dragged screaming apart, few details of the state of pandemonium that ensued came to our ears. I imagine that a striking *tableau vivant* somewhat on the lines of Meissonier's famous painting was unconsciously improvised. That three maids hardly restrained Mrs. Chapel, that the footman who sought to withhold Camille was bitten for his pains by the now ravening Frenchman, that the latter was only saved from the commission of a still more aggravated assault by the timely arrival of the butler, that Nobby, attracted by the uproar, contributed to the confusion first by barking like a demoniac and then by inflicting a punctured wound upon the calf of the alien's leg, we learned more by inference and deduction than by direct report. That our impending meal would be more than usually unappetizing was never suggested. That was surmise upon our part, pure and simple. The conviction, however, was so strong that the repast was cancelled out of hand.

Mrs. Chapel was dismissed and straitly charged never to return. Camille was placed in the custody of the chauffeur and escorted to the latter's rooms above the garage, to be returned to France upon the following morning. Nobby was commended for his discrimination. Jonah was reviled.

All this, however, took time. The respective dismissal and disposal of the combatants were not completed until long past eight, and it was almost nine before we sat down to dinner.

"I think," said Daphne faintly, "I should like some champagne."

Berry ordered the wine.

It was abnormally hot, and the doors that were usually closed were set wide open.

From the street faint snatches of a vibrant soprano came knocking at our tired ears.

Mechanically we listened.

"When you come to the end of a perfect day . . ."

Berry turned to me.

"They must have seen us come in," he said.

*   *   *   *   *

It was with a grateful heart that I telegraphed the first thing on Saturday morning to Mrs. Hamilton Smythe of Fair Lawns, Torquay, asking *pro forma*, whether Pauline Roper, now in her service, was sober, honest and generally to be recommended to be engaged as cook.

As she had been for six years with the lady, and was only leaving because the latter was quitting England to join her husband in Ceylon, it was improbable that the reference would be unflattering. Moreover, Daphne had taken to her at once. Well-mannered, quiet, decently attired and respectful, she was obviously a long way superior to the ordinary maid. Indeed, she had admitted that her father, now dead, had been a clergyman, and that she should have endeavoured to obtain a position as governess if, as a child, she had received anything better than the rudest education. She had, she added, been receiving fifty pounds a year. Hesitatingly she had inquired whether, since the employment was only temporary, we should consider an increase of ten pounds a year unreasonable.

"Altogether," concluded my sister, "a thoroughly nice-feeling woman. I offered her lunch, but she said she was anxious to try and see her sister before she caught her train back, so she didn't have any. I almost forgot to give her her fare, poor girl. In fact, she had to remind me. She apologized very humbly, but said the journey to London was so terribly expensive that she couldn't afford to let it stand over."

We had lunch at Ranelagh, and were sitting in a quiet corner of the pleasant grounds, taking our ease after the alarms and excursions of the day before.

Later on we made our way to the polo-ground.

Almost the first person we saw was Katharine Festival.

"Hurray," said Daphne. "I meant to have rung her up last night, but what with the Camille episode and dining out I forgot all about it. When I tell her we're suited, she'll be green with envy."

Her unsuspecting victim advanced beaming. Being of the opposite sex, I felt sorry for her.

"Daphne, my dear," she announced, "I meant to have rung you up last night. I've got a cook."

The pendulum of my emotions described the best part of a semicircle, and I felt sorry for Daphne.

"I am glad," said my sister, with an audacity which took my breath away. "How splendid! So've we."

"Hurray," said Katharine, with a sincerity which would have deceived a diplomat. "Don't you feel quite strange? I can hardly believe it's really happened. Mine rejoices in the name of Pauline," she added.

I started violently, and Berry's jaw dropped.

"Pauline?" cried Daphne and Jill.

"Yes," said Katharine. "It's a queer name for a cook, but—— What's the matter?"

"But so's ours! Ours is Pauline! What's her other name?"

"Roper," cried Katharine breathlessly.

"Not from Torquay?"—in a choking voice.

Katharine nodded and put a trembling handkerchief to her lips.

"I paid her fare," she said faintly. "It came to ——"

"Two pounds nine and fourpence halfpenny," said my sister. "I gave her two pounds ten."

"So did I," said Katharine. "She was to come on—on Monday."

"Six years in her last place?" said Daphne shakily.

"Yes. And a clergyman's daughter," wailed Katharine.

"Did—did you take up her reference?"

"Wired last night," was the reply.

In silence I brought two chairs, and they sat down.

"But—but," stammered Jill, "she spoke from Torquay on Wednesday."

"Did she?" said Berry. "I wonder."

"Yes," said Katharine. "She did."

"You know she did," said Daphne and Jill.

"Who," said I, "answered the telephone?"

"My parlourmaid did," said Katharine.

"And Jill answered ours," said I. Then I turned to my cousin. "When you took off the receiver," I asked, "what did you hear?"

"I remember perfectly," said Jill. "Exchange asked if we were Mayfair 9999 and then said, 'You're through to a call office'. Then Pauline spoke."

"Precisely," said I. "But not from Torquay. In that case Exchange would have said, 'Torquay wants you', or 'Exeter', or something. Our Pauline rang up from London. She took a risk and got away with it."

"I feel dazed," said Daphne, putting a hand to her head. "There must be some mistake. I can't believe——"

" 'A thoroughly nice-feeling woman'," said Berry. "I think I should feel nice if I could make five pounds in two hours by sitting on the edge of a chair and saying I was a clergyman's daughter. And now what are we going to do? Shall we be funny and inform the police? Or try and stop Camille at Amiens?"

"Now don't you start," said his wife, "because I can't bear it. Jonah, for goodness' sake, get hold of the car, and let's go."

"Yes," said Berry. "And look sharp about it. Time's getting on, and I should just hate to be late for dinner. Or shall we be reckless and take a table at Lockhart's?"

We drove home in a state of profound melancholy.

Awaiting our arrival was a "service" communication upon a buff sheet, bluntly addressed to "Pleydell".

It was the official death-warrant of an unworthy trust.

Sir,

I beg leave to inform you that your telegram handed in at the Grosvenor Street Post Office at 10.2 a.m. on the 26th June addressed to Reply paid Hamilton Smythe Fair Lawns Torquay has not been delivered for the reason indicated below.

ADDRESS NOT KNOWN.

I am, Sir, Your obedient Servant,
W.B.,
Postmaster.

CHAPTER VIII

How Jill Slept Undisturbed, and Nobby Attended Church Parade

"What d'you do," said Berry, "when you want to remember something?"

"Change my rings," said Daphne. "Why?"

"I only wondered. D'you find that infallible?"

My sister nodded.

"Absolutely," she said. "Of course, I don't always remember what I've changed them for, but it shows me there's something I've forgotten."

"I see. Then you've only got to remember what that is, and there you are. Why don't I wear rings?"

"Change your shoes instead," said I drowsily. "Or wear your waistcoat next to your skin. Then, whenever you want to look at your watch, you'll have to undress. That'll make you think."

"You go and change your face," said Berry. "Don't wait for something to remember. Just go and do it by deed-poll. And then advertise it in *The Times*. You'll get so many letters of gratitude that you'll get tired of answering them."

Before I could reply to this insult—

"I suppose," said my sister, "this means that you can't remember something which concerns me and really matters."

In guilty silence her husband prepared a cigar for ignition with the utmost care. At length—

"I wouldn't go as far as that," he said. "But I confess that at the back of my mind, in, as it were, the upper reaches of my memory, there is a faint ripple of suggestion for which I cannot satisfactorily account. Now, isn't that beautifully put?"

With a look of contempt, Daphne returned to the digestion of a letter which she had that morning received from the United States. Reflectively Berry struck a match and lighted his cigar. I followed the example of Jill and began to doze.

With the exception of Jonah, who was in Somerset with the Fairies, we had been to Goodwood. I had driven the car both ways and was healthily tired, but the long ride had rendered us all weary, and the prospect of a full night and a quiet morrow was good to contemplate.

On the following Tuesday we were going out of Town. Of this we were all unfeignedly glad, for London was growing stale. The leaves upon her trees were blown and dingy, odd pieces of paper crept here and there into her parks, the dust was paramount. What sultry air there was seemed to be second-hand. Out of the pounding traffic the pungent reek of oil and fiery metal rose up oppressive. Paint three months old was seamed and freckled. Look where you would, the silver sheen of Spring was dull and tarnished, the very stones were shabby, and in the summer sunshine even proud buildings of the smartest streets wore but a jaded look and lost their dignity. The vanity of bricks stood out in bold relief unsightly, dressing the gentle argument of Nature with such authority as set tired senses craving the airs and graces of the countryside and mourning the traditions of the children of men.

"Adèle," said Daphne suddenly, "is sailing next week."

"Hurray," said Jill, waking up.

"Liverpool or Southampton?" said I.

"She doesn't say. But I told her to come to Southampton."

"I expect she's got to take what she can get; only, when you're making for Hampshire, it seems a pity to go round by the Mersey."

"I like Adèle," said Berry. "She never seeks to withstand that feeling of respect which I inspire. When with me, she recognizes that she is in the presence of a holy sage, and, as it were, treading upon hallowed ground. Woman," he added, looking sorrowfully upon his wife, "I could wish that something of her piety were there to lessen your corruption. Poor vulgar shrew, I weep——"

"She says something about you," said Daphne, turning over a sheet. "Here you are. *Give Berry my love. If I'd been with you at Oxford, when he got busy, I should just have died. All the same, you must admit he's a scream. I'm longing to see Nobby. He sounds as if he were a dog of real character. . . .*"

"Thank you," said her husband, with emotion. "Thank you very much. 'A scream', I think you said. Yes. And Nobby, 'a dog of character'. I can't bear it."

"So he is," said I. "Exceptional character."

"I admit," said Berry, "he's impartial. His worst enemy can't deny that. His offerings at the shrine of Gluttony are just as ample as those he lays before the altar of Sloth."

"All dogs are greedy," said Jill. "It's natural. And you'd be tired, if you ran about like him."

"He's useful and ornamental and diverting," said I. "I don't know what more you want."

"Useful?" said Berry, with a yawn. "Useful? Oh, you mean scavenging? But then you discourage him so. Remember that rotten fish in Brook Street the other day? Well, he was making a nice clean job of that, he was, when you stopped him."

"That was a work of supererogation. I maintain, however, that nobody can justly describe Nobby as a useless dog. For instance——"

The sudden opening of the door at once interrupted and upheld my contention.

Into the room bustled the Sealyham, the personification of importance, with tail up, eyes sparkling, and gripped in his large mouth the letters which had just been delivered by the last post.

As the outburst of feminine approval subsided—

"Out of his own mouth," said I, "you stand confuted."

Either of gallantry or because her welcome was the more compelling, the terrier made straight for my sister and pleasedly delivered his burden into her hands. Of the three letters she selected two and then, making much of the dog, returned a foolscap envelope to his jaws and instructed him to bear it to Berry. Nobby received it greedily, but it was only when he had simultaneously spun into the air, growled and, placing an emphatic paw upon the projecting end, torn the letter half-way asunder, that it became evident that he was regarding her return of the missive as a *douceur* or reward of his diligence.

With a cry my brother-in-law sprang to enlighten him; but Nobby, hailing his action as the first move in a game of great promise, darted out of his reach, tore round the room at express speed, and streaked into the hall.

By dint of an immediate rush to the library door, we were just in time to see Berry slip on the parquet and, falling heavily, miss the terrier by what was a matter of inches, and by the time we had helped one another upstairs, the medley of worrying and imprecations which emanated from Daphne's bedroom made it clear that the quarry had gone to ground.

As we drew breath in the doorway—

"Get him from the other side!" yelled Berry, who was lying flat on his face, with one arm under the bed. "Quick! It may be unsporting, but I don't care. A-a-ah!" His voice rose to a menacing roar, as the rending of paper became distinctly audible. "Stop it, you wicked swine! D'you hear? *Stop it!*"

From beneath the bed a further burst of mischief answered him. . . .

Once again feminine subtlety prevailed where the straightforward efforts of a man were fruitless. As I flung myself down upon the opposite side of the bed—

"Nobby," said Jill in a stage whisper, "chocolates!"

The terrier paused in his work of destruction. Then he dropped the mangled remains of the letter and put his head on one side.

"Chocolates!"

The next second he was scrambling towards the foot of the bed. . . .

I gathered together the *débris* and rose to my feet.

Nobby was sitting up in front of Jill, begging irresistibly.

"What a shame!" said the latter. "And I haven't any for you. And if I had, I mightn't give you them." She looked round appealingly. "Isn't he cute?"

"Extraordinary how that word'll fetch him," said I. "I think his late mistress must have——"

"I'm sure she must," said Berry, taking the ruins of his correspondence out of my hand. "Perhaps she also taught him to collect stamps. And/or crests. And do you mean to say you've got no chocolates for him? How shameful! I'd better run round and knock up Gunter's. Shall I slip on a coat, or will the parquet do?"

"There's no vice in him," I said shakily. "It was a misunderstanding."

With an awful look Berry gingerly withdrew from what remained of the envelope some three-fifths of a dilapidated dividend warrant, which looked as if it had been immersed in water and angrily disputed by a number of rats.

"It's—it's all right," I said unsteadily. "The company'll give you another."

"Give me air," said Berry weakly. "Open the wardrobe, somebody, and give me air. You know, this is the violation of Belgium over again. The little angel must have been the mascot of a double-breasted Jaeger battalion in full blast." With a shaking finger he indicated the cheque. "Bearing this in mind, which would you say he was to-night—useful or ornamental?"

"Neither the one, nor the other," said I. "Merely diverting."

Expectantly my brother-in-law regarded the ceiling.

"I wonder what's holding it," he said. "I suppose the whitewash has seized. And now, if you'll assist me downstairs and apply the usual restoratives, I'll forgive you the two pounds I owe you. There's a letter I want to write before I retire."

Half an hour later the following letter was dispatched—

Sir,

The enclosed are, as a patient scrutiny will reveal, the remains of a dividend warrant in my favour for seventy-two pounds five shillings.

Owing to its dilapidation, which you will observe includes the total loss of the date, signature and stamp, I am forced to the reluctant conclusion that your bankers will show a marked disinclination to honour what was once a valuable security.

Its reduction to the lamentable condition in which you now see it is due to the barbarous treatment it received at the teeth and claws of a dog or hound which, I regret to say, has recently frequented this house and is indubitably possessed of a malignant devil.

In fairness to myself I must add, first, that it was through no improvidence on my part that the domestic animal above referred to obtained possession of the document, and, secondly, that I made such desperate efforts to recover it intact as resulted in my sustaining a fall of considerable violence upon one of the least resilient floors I have ever encountered. If you do not believe me, your duly accredited representative is at liberty to inspect the many and various contusions upon my person any day between ten and eleven at the above address.

Yours faithfully,

etc.

P.S.—My cousin-german has just read this through, and says I've left out something. I think the fat-head is being funny, but I just mention it, in case.

P.P.S.—It's just occurred to me that the fool means I

haven't asked you to send me another one. But you will, won't you?

*　　*　　*　　*　　*

For no apparent reason I was suddenly awake.

Invariably a sound sleeper, I lay for a moment pondering the phenomenon. Then a low growl from the foot of the bed furnished one explanation only to demand another.

I put up a groping hand and felt for the dangling switch.

For a moment I fumbled. Then from above my head a deeply-shaded lamp flung a sudden restricted light on to the bed.

I raised myself on an elbow and looked at Nobby.

His body was still curled, with his small strong legs tucked out of sight, but his head was raised, and he was listening intently.

I put my head on one side and did the same. . . .

Only the hoot of a belated car faintly disturbed the silence.

I looked at my wrist-watch. This showed one minute to one. As I raised my eyes, an impatient clock somewhere confirmed its tale.

With a yawn I conjured the terrier to go to sleep and reached for the switch.

As I did so, he growled again.

With my fingers about the "push", I hesitated, straining my ears. . . .

The next moment I was out of bed and fighting my way into my dressing-gown, while Nobby, his black nose clapped to the sill of the doorway, stood tense and rigid and motionless as death.

As I picked him up, he began to quiver, and I could feel his heart thumping, but he seemed to appreciate the necessity for silence, and licked my face noiselessly.

I switched off the light and opened the door.

There was a lamp burning on the landing, and I stepped directly to the top of the stairs.

Except that there was a faint light somewhere upon the ground floor, I could see nothing, but, as I stood peering, the sound of a stealthy movement, followed by the low grumble of utterance, rose unmistakably to my ears. Under my left arm Nobby stiffened notably.

For a moment I stood listening and thinking furiously. . . .

It was plain that there was more than one visitor, for burglars do not talk to themselves, and Discretion suggested that I should seek assistance before descending. Jonah was out of Town, the men-servants slept in the basement, the telephone was downstairs. Only Berry remained.

The faint chink of metal meeting metal and a stifled laugh decided me.

With the utmost caution I stole to the door of my sister's room and turned the handle. As I glided into the chamber—

"Who's that?" came in a startled whisper.

Before I could answer, there was a quick rustle, a switch clicked, and there was Daphne, propped on a white arm, looking at me with wide eyes and parted lips. Her beautiful dark hair was tumbling about her breast and shoulders. Impatiently she brushed it clear of her face.

"What is it, Boy?"

I laid a finger upon my lips.

"There's somebody downstairs. Wake Berry."

Slowly her husband rolled on to his left side and regarded me with one eye.

"What," he said, "is the meaning of this intrusion?"

"Don't be a fool," I whispered. "The house is being burgled."

"Gurgled?"

"Burgled, you fool."

"No such word," said Berry. "What you mean is 'burglariously rifled'. And then you're wrong. Why, there's Nobby."

I could have stamped with vexation.

My sister took up the cudgels.

"Don't lie there," she said. "Get up and see."

"What?" said her husband.

"What's going on."

Berry swallowed before replying. Then—

"How many are there?" he demanded.

"You poisonous idiot," I hissed, "I tell you——"

"Naughty temper," said Berry. "I admit I'm in the wrong, but there you are. You see, it all comes of not wearing rings. If I did, I should have remembered that a wire came from Jonah just before dinner—it's in my dinner-jacket—saying he was coming up late to-night with Harry, and that if the latter couldn't get in at the Club, he should bring him on here. He had the decency to add 'Don't sit up.' "

Daphne and I exchanged glances of withering contempt.

"And where," said my sister, "is Harry going to sleep?"

Her husband settled himself contentedly.

"That," he said drowsily, "is what's worrying me."

"Outrageous," said Daphne. Then she turned to me. "It's too late to do anything now. Will you go down and explain? Perhaps he can manage in the library. Unless Jonah likes to give up his bed."

"I'll do what I can," I said, taking a cigarette from the box by her side.

"Oh, and do ask if it's true about Evelyn."

"Right oh. I'll tell you as I come back."

"I forbid you," murmured her husband, "to re-enter this room."

I kissed my sister, lobbed a novel on to my brother-in-law's back, and withdrew before he had time to retaliate. Then I stepped barefoot downstairs, to perform my mission.

With the collapse of the excitement, Nobby's suspicion shrank into curiosity, his muscles relaxed, and he stopped quivering. So infectious a thing is perturbation.

The door of the library was ajar, and the thin strip of light which issued was enough to guide me across the hall. The parquet was cold to the touch, and I began to regret that I had not returned for my slippers.

As I pushed the door open—

"I say, Jonah," I said, "that fool Berry——"

It was with something of a shock that I found myself looking directly along the barrel of a .45 automatic pistol, which a stout gentleman, wearing a green mask, white kid gloves, and immaculate evening-dress, was pointing immediately at my nose.

"There now," he purred. "I was going to say, 'Hands up'. Just like that. 'Hands up'. It's so romantic. But I hadn't expected the dog. Suppose you put your right hand up."

I shook my head.

"I want that for my cigarette," I said.

For a moment we stood looking at one another. Then my fat *vis-à-vis* began to shake with laughter.

"You know," he gurgled, "this is most irregular. It's enough to make Jack Sheppard turn in his grave. It is really. However . . . As an inveterate smoker, I feel for you. So we'll have a compromise." He nodded towards an armchair which stood by the window. "You go and sit down in that extremely comfortable armchair—sit well back—and we won't say any more about the hands."

As he spoke, he stepped forward. Nobby received him with a venomous growl, and to my amazement the fellow immediately caressed him.

"Dogs always take to me," he added. "I'm sure I don't know why, but it's a great help."

To my mortification, the Sealyham proved to be no exception to the rule. I could feel his tail going.

As in a dream, I crossed to the chair and sat down. As I moved, the pistol moved also.

"I hate pointing this thing at you," said the late speaker. "It's so suggestive. If you'd care to give me your word, you know . . . Between gentlemen . . ."

"I make no promises," I snapped.

The other sighed.

"Perhaps you're right," he said. "Lean well back, please. . . . That's better."

The consummate impudence of the rogue intensified the atmosphere of unreality, which was most distracting. Doggedly my bewildered brain was labouring in the midst of a litter of fiction, which had suddenly changed into truth. The impossible had come to pass. The cracksman of the novel had come to life, and I was reluctantly witnessing, in comparative comfort and at my own expense, an actual exhibition of felony enriched with all the spices which the cupboard of Sensation contains.

The monstrous audacity of the proceedings, and the business-like way in which they were conducted, were almost stupefying.

Most of the silver in the house, including a number of pieces, our possession of which I had completely forgotten, seemed to have been collected and laid in rough order upon rugs, which had been piled one upon the other to deaden noise. One man was taking it up, piece by piece, scrutinizing it with an eye-glass such as watchmakers use, and dictating descriptions and particulars to a second, who was seated at the broad writing-table, entering the details, in triplicate, in a large order-book. By his side a third manipulated a pair of scales, weighing each piece with the greatest care and reporting the result to the second, who added the weight to the description. Occasionally the latter paused to draw at a cigarette, which lay smouldering in the ash-tray by his side. As each piece was weighed, the third handed it to a fourth assistant, who wrapped it in a bag of green baize and laid it gently in an open suit-case. Four other cases stood by his side, all bearing a number of labels and more or less the worse for wear.

All four men were masked and gloved, and working with a rapidity and method which were remarkable. With the exception of the packer, who wore a footman's livery, they were attired in evening-dress.

"We find it easier," said the master, as if interpreting my thoughts, "to do it all on the spot. Then it's over and done with. I do hope you're insured," he added. "I always think it's so much more satisfactory."

"Up to the hilt," said I cheerfully. "We had it all re-valued only this year, because of the rise in silver."

"Splendid!"—enthusiastically. "But I'm neglecting you." With his left hand the rogue picked up an ash-tray and stepped to my side. Then he backed to the mantelpiece, whence he picked up and brought me a handful of cigarettes, laying them on the broad arm of my chair. "I'm afraid the box has gone," he said regretfully. "May I mix you a drink?"

I shook my head.

"I've had my ration. If I'd known, I'd have saved some. You see, I don't sit up so late, as a rule."

He shrugged his shoulders.

As he did so, my own last words rang familiarly in my ears: "I don't sit up so late" . . . "Don't sit up." . . .

Jonah! He and Harry were due to arrive any moment!

Hope leaped up within me, and my heart began to beat violently. I glanced at the silver, still lying upon the rugs. Slowly it was diminishing, and the services of a second suit-case would soon be necessary. I calculated that to complete the bestowal would take the best part of an hour, and began to speculate upon the course events would take when the travellers appeared. I began to pray fervently that Harry would be unable to get in at the Club. . . .

"Now, then, you three," said a reproving voice. "I'm surprised at you."

Daphne!

The rogues were trained to a hair.

Before she was framed in the doorway, the cold steel of another weapon was pressing against my throat, and the master was bowing in her direction.

"Madam, I beg that you will neither move nor cry out."

My sister stood like a statue. Only the rise and fall of her bosom showed that she was alive. Pale as death, her eyes riveted on the speaker, who was holding his right hand markedly behind him, her unbound hair streaming over her shoulders, she made a beautiful and arresting picture. A kimono of softest apricot, over which sprawled vivid embroideries, here in the guise of parti-coloured dragons, there in that of a wanton butterfly, swathed her from throat to foot. From the mouths of its gaping sleeves her shapely wrists and hands thrust out snow-white and still as sculpture.

For a moment all eyes were upon her, as she stood motionless. . . . Then the man with the eye-glass screwed it back into his eye, and resumed his dictation. . . .

The spell was broken.

The packer left his work and, lifting a great chair bodily with apparent ease, set it noiselessly by my side.

The master bowed again.

"I congratulate you, madam, upon your great heart. I beg that you will join that gentleman."

With a high head, My Lady Disdain swept to the spot indicated and sank into the chair.

"Please lean right back. . . . Thank you."

The cold steel was withdrawn from my throat, and I breathed more freely.

Nobby wriggled to get to my sister, but I held him fast.

"So it was burglars," said Daphne.

"Looks like it," said I.

I glanced at the leader, who had taken his seat upon the club-kerb. His right hand appeared to be resting upon his knee.

"I think," said my sister, "I'll have a cigarette."

I handed her one from the pile and lighted it from my own. As I did so—

"Courage," I whispered. *"Jonah ne tardera pas."*

"I beg," said the spokesman, "that you will not whisper together. It tends to create an atmosphere of mistrust."

My sister inclined her head with a silvery laugh.

"You have a large staff," she said.

"That is my way. I am not a believer in the lone hand. But there you are. *Quot homines, tot sententiæ*," and with that, he spread out his hands and shrugged his broad shoulders.

Daphne raised her delicate eyebrows and blew out a cloud of smoke.

" 'The fewer men,' " she quoted, " 'the greater share of—*plunder*.' "

The shoulders began to shake.

"Touché," was the reply. "A pretty thrust, madam. But you must read further on. 'And gentlemen in *Mayfair* now abed Shall

think themselves accursed they were not here.' Shall we say that —er—honours are easy?" And the old villain fairly rocked with merriment.

Daphne laughed airily.

"Good for you," she said. "As a matter of fact, sitting here, several things look extremely easy."

"So, on the whole, they are. Mind you, lookers-on see the easy side. And you, madam, are a very privileged spectator."

"I have paid for my seat," flashed my sister.

"Royally. Still, deadhead or not, a spectator you are, and, as such, you see the easy side. Now, one of the greatest dangers that can befall a thief is avarice."

"I suppose you're doing this out of charity," I blurted.

"Listen. Many a promising career of—er—appropriation has come to an abrupt and sordid end, and all because success but whetted where it should have satisfied." He addressed my sister. "Happily for you, you do not sleep in your pearls. Otherwise, since you are here, I might have fallen . . . Who knows? As it is, pearls, diamonds and the emerald bracelets that came from Prague—you see, madam, I know them all—will lie upstairs untouched. I came for silver, and I shall take nothing else. Some day, perhaps . . ."

The quiet sing-song of his voice faded, and only the murmur of the ceaseless dictation remained. Then that, too, faltered and died. . . .

For a second master and men stood motionless. Then the former pointed to Daphne and me, and Numbers Three and Four whipped to our side.

Somebody, whistling softly, was descending the stairs. . . .

Just as it became recognizable the air slid out of a whistle into a song, and my unwitting brother-in-law invested the last two lines with all the mockery of pathos of which his inferior baritone voice was capable.

"I'm for ever b-b-blowing b-b-bub-b-bles,
B-blinkin' b-bub-b-bles in the air."

He entered upon the last word, started ever so slightly at his reception, and then stood extremely still.

"Bubbles be blowed," he said. "B-b-burglars, what? Shall I moisten the lips? Or would you rather I wore a sickly smile? I should like it to be a good photograph. You know, you can't touch me, Reggibald. I'm in balk." His eyes wandered round the room. "Why, there's Nobby. And what's the game? Musical

Chairs? I know a better one than that." His eyes returned to the master. "Now, don't you look and I'll hide in the hassock! Then, when I say 'Cuckoo', you put down the musket and wish. Then—excuse me."

Calmly he twitched a Paisley shawl from the back of the sofa and crossed to his wife. Tenderly he wrapped it about her feet and knees. By the time he had finished a third chair was awaiting him, and Numbers Three and Four had returned to their work.

"Pray sit down," drawled the master. "And lean well back. . . . That's right. You know, I'm awfully sorry you left your bed."

"Don't mention it," said Berry. "I wouldn't have missed this for any thing. How's Dartmoor looking?"

The fat rogue sighed.

"I have not had a holiday," he said, "for nearly two years. And night work tells, you know. Of course I rest during the day, but it isn't the same."

"How wicked! And they call this a free country. I should see your M.P. about it. Or wasn't he up when you called?"

The other shook his head.

"As a matter of fact," he said, "he was out of Town. George, give the gentleman a match." The packer picked up a match-stand and set it by Berry's side. "I'm so sorry about the chocolates. You see, I wasn't expecting—— Hullo!"

At the mention of the magical word Nobby had leapt from my unready grasp and trotted across to the fireplace. There, to my disgust and vexation, he fixed the master with an expectant stare, and then sat up upon his hindquarters and begged a sweetmeat.

His favourer began to heave with merriment.

"What an engaging scrap!" he wheezed, taking a chocolate from an occasional table upon which the contents of a dessert dish had apparently been emptied. "Here, my little apostate . . . Well caught!"

With an irrational rapidity the Sealyham disposed of the first comfit he had been given for more than six months. Then he resumed the attractive posture which he had found so profitable. Lazily his patron continued to respond. . . .

Resentfully I watched the procedure, endeavouring to console myself with the reflection that in a few hours Nature would assuredly administer to the backslider a more terrible and appropriate correction than any that I could devise.

Would Jonah never come?

I stole a glance at the clock. Five and twenty minutes to two.

And when he did come, what then? Were he and Harry to blunder into the slough waist-high, as we had done? Impossible. There was probably a man outside—possibly a car, which would set them thinking. Then, even if the brutes got away, their game would be spoiled. It wouldn't be such a humiliating walk-over. Oh, why had Daphne come down? Her presence put any attempt at action out of the question. And why . . .

A taxi slowed for a distant corner and turned into the street. For a moment it seemed to falter. Then its speed was changed clumsily, and it began to grind its way in our direction. My heart began to beat violently. Again the speed was changed, and the rising snarl choked to give way to a metallic murmur, which was rapidly approaching. I could hardly breathe. . . . Then the noise swelled up, hung for an instant upon the very crest of earshot, only to sink abruptly as the cab swept past, taking our hopes with it.

Two-thirds of the silver had disappeared.

Berry cleared his throat.

"You know," he said, "this is an education. In my innocence I thought that a burglar shoved his swag in a sack and then pushed off, and did the rest in the back parlour of a beer-house in Notting Dale. As it is, my only wonder is that you didn't bring a brazier and a couple of melting-pots."

"Not my job," was the reply. "I'm not a receiver. Besides, you don't think that all this beautiful silver is to be broken up?" The horror of his uplifted hands would have been more convincing if both of them had been empty. "Why, in a very little while, particularly if you travel, you will have every opportunity of buying it back again in open market."

"But how comic," said Berry. "I should think you're a favourite at Lloyd's. D'you mind if I blow my nose? Or would that be a *casus belli*?"

"Not at all"—urbanely. "Indeed, if you would care to give me your word . . ."

Berry shook his head.

"Honour among thieves?" he said. "Unfortunately I'm honest, so you must have no truck with me. Never mind. D'you touch cards at all? Or only at Epsom?"

Beneath the green mask the mouth tightened, and I could see that the taunt had gone home. No man likes to be whipped before his underlings.

Nobby profited by the master's silence, and had devoured two more chocolates before Berry spoke again—this time to me.

"Gentleman seems annoyed," he remarked. "I do hope he hasn't misconstrued anything I've said. D'you think we ought to offer him breakfast? Of course, five is rather a lot, but I dare say one of them is a vegetarian, and you can pretend you don't care for haddock. Or they may have some tripe downstairs. You never know. And afterwards we could run them back to Limehouse. By the way, I wonder if I ought to tell him about the silver which-not. It's only nickel, but I don't want to keep anything back. Oh, and what about the dividend warrant? Of course it wants riveting and—er—forging, and I don't think they'd recognize it, but he could try. If I die before he goes, ask him to leave his address; then, if he leaves anything behind, the butler can send it on. I remember I left a pair of bed-socks once at Chatsworth. The Duke never sent them on, but then they were perishable. Besides, one of them followed me as far as Leicester. Instinct, you know. I wrote to *The Field* about it." He paused to shift uneasily in his seat. "You know, if I have to sustain this pose much longer, I shall get railway spine or a hare lip or something."

"Hush," said I. "What did Alfred Austin say in 1895?"

"I know," said Berry. " 'Comrades, leave me here a little, while as yet 'tis early morn.' Precisely. But then all his best work was admittedly done under the eiderdown."

The clock upon the wall was chiming the hour. Two o'clock.

Would Jonah never come?

I fancy the same query renewed its hammering at Berry's brain, for, after a moment's reflection, he turned to the master.

"I don't wish to presume upon your courtesy," he said, "but will the executive portion of your night's work finish when that remaining treasure has been bestowed?"

"So far as you are concerned."

"Oh, another appointment! Of course, this 'summer time' stunt gives you another hour, doesn't it? Well, I must wish you a warmer welcome."

"That were impossible," was the bland reply. "Once or twice, I must confess, I thought you a little—er—equivocal, but let that pass. I only regret that Mrs. Pleydell, particularly, should have been so much inconvenienced."

"Don't mention it," said Berry. "As a matter of fact, we're all very pleased to have met you. You have interested us more than I can say, with true chivalry you have abstained from murder and mutilation, and you have suffered me to blow my nose, when a less courteous visitor would have obliged me to sniff with desperate and painful regularity for nearly half an hour. Can generosity go further?"

The rogue upon the club-kerb began to shake with laughter again.

"You're a good loser," he crowed. "I'll give you that. I'm quite glad you came down. Most of my hosts I never see, and that's dull, you know, dull. And those I do are so often—er—unsympathetic. Yes, I shall remember to-night."

"Going to change his rings," murmured Berry.

"And now the highly delicate question of our departure is, I am afraid, imminent. To avoid exciting impertinent curiosity, you will appreciate that we must take our leave as artlessly as possible, and that the order of our going must be characterized by no unusual circumstance, such, for instance, as a hue and cry. Anything so vulgar as a scene must at all costs be obviated. Excuse me. Blake!"

Confederate Number One stepped noiselessly to his side and listened in silence to certain instructions, which were to us inaudible.

I looked about me.

The last of the silver had disappeared. The packer was dismantling the scales as a preliminary to laying them in the last suit-case. The clerk was fastening together the sheets which he had detached from the flimsy order-book. Number Three had taken a light overcoat from a chair and was putting it on. And the time was six minutes past two. . . .

And what of Jonah? He and Harry would probably arrive about five minutes too late. I bit my lip savagely. . . .

Again the chief malefactor lifted up his voice.

"It is my experience," he drawled, "that temerity is born, if not of curiosity, then of ignorance. Now, if there is one vice more than another which I deplore, it is temerity—especially when it is displayed by a host at two o'clock of a morning. I am therefore going to the root of the matter. In short, I propose to satisfy your very natural curiosity regarding our method of departure, and, incidentally, to show you exactly what you are up against. You see, I believe in prevention." His utterance of the last sentences was more silky than ever.

"The constables who have passed this house since half-past twelve will, if reasonably observant, have noticed the carpet which, upon entering, we laid upon the steps. A departure of guests, therefore, even at this advanced hour, should arouse no more suspicion than the limousine-landaulette which has now been waiting for some nine minutes.

"The lights in the hall will now be turned on, the front door will be opened wide, and the footman will place the suit-cases in the car, at the open door of which he will stand, while my colleagues and I—I need hardly say by this time unmasked—emerge at our leisure, chatting in a most ordinary way.

"I shall be the last to enter the car—I beg your pardon. To-night I shall be the last but one"—for an instant he halted, as if to emphasize the correction—"and my entry will coincide with what is a favourable opportunity for the footman to assume the cap and overcoat which he must of necessity wear if his closing of the front door and subsequent occupation of the seat by the chauffeur are to excite no remark. . . . You see, I try to think of everything."

He paused for a moment, regarding the tips of his fingers, as though they were ungloved. Then—

"Your presence here presents no difficulty. Major and Mrs. Pleydell will stay in this room, silent . . . and motionless . . . and detaining the dog. You"—nonchalantly he pointed an extremely ugly trench-dagger in my direction—"will vouch with your—er—health for their observance of these conditions. Be good enough to stand up and place your hands behind you."

With a glance at Berry, I rose. All things considered, there was nothing else to be done.

The man whom he addressed as "Blake" picked up Nobby and, crossing the room, laid the terrier in Berry's arms. Then he lashed my wrists together with the rapidity of an expert.

"Understand, I take no chances." A harsh note had crept into the even tones. "The slightest indiscretion will cost this gentleman extremely dear."

I began to hope very much that my brother-in-law would appreciate the advisability of doing as he had been told.

"George, my coat." The voice was as suave as ever again. "Thank you. Is everything ready?"

Berry stifled a yawn.

"You don't mean to say," he exclaimed, "that you're actually going? Dear me. Well, well . . . I don't suppose you've got a card on you? No. Sorry. I should have liked to remember you in my prayers. Never mind. And you don't happen to know of a good plain cook, do you? No. I thought not. Well, if you should hear of one . . ."

"Carry on."

Blake laid a hand on my shoulder and urged me towards the door. As I was going, I saw the master bow.

"Mrs. Pleydell," he said, "I have the honour——Dear me! There's that ridiculous word again. Never mind—the honour to bid *adieu* to a most brave lady."

With a faint sneer my sister regarded him. Then—

"Au revoir," she said steadily.

"So long, old bean," said Berry. "See you at Vine Street."

As I passed into the hall, the lights went up and a cap was clapped on to my head and pulled down tight over my eyes. Then I was thrust into a corner of the hall, close to the front door. Immediately this was opened, and I could hear everything happen as we had been led to expect. Only there was a hand on my shoulder. . . .

I heard the master coming with a jest on his lips.

As he passed me, he was speaking ostensibly to one of his comrades . . . ostensibly. . . .

"I shouldn't wait up for Jonah," he said.

* * * * *

Thanks to the fact that one of the Assistant Commissioners of Police was an old friend of mine, we were spared much of the tedious interrogation and well-meant, but in the circumstances utterly futile, attentions of the subordinate officers of the C.I.D.

Admission to the house had been gained without breaking, and there were no finger-prints. Moreover, since our visitors had worn masks, such descriptions of them as we could give were very inadequate. However, statements were taken from my sister, Berry and myself, and the spurious telegram was handed over. The insurance company was, of course, informed of the crime.

Despite the paucity of detail, our description of the gang and its methods aroused tremendous excitement at Scotland Yard. The master, it appeared, was a veritable Prince of Darkness. Save that he existed, and was a man of large ideas and the utmost daring, to whose charge half the great unplaced robberies of recent years were, rightly or wrongly, laid, little or nothing was known of his manners or personality.

"I tell you," said the Assistant Commissioner, leaning back and tilting his chair, "he's just about as hot as they make 'em. And when we do take him, if ever we do—and that might be to-morrow, or in ten years' time—we might walk straight into him next week with the stuff in his hands; you never know—well, when we do take him, as like as not, he'll prove to be a popular M.P., or a recognized authority on livestock or something. You've probably seen him heaps of times in St. James's, and, as like as not, he's a member of your own Club. Depend upon it, the old sinner moves in those circles which you know are above suspicion. If somebody pinched your watch at Ascot, you'd never look for the thief in the enclosure, would you? Of course not. Well, I may be wrong, but I don't think so. Meanwhile let's have some lunch."

For my sister the ordeal had been severe, and for the thirty hours following the robbery she had kept her bed. Berry had contracted a slight cold, and I was not one penny the worse. Jill was overcome to learn what she had missed, and the reflection that she had mercifully slept upstairs, while such a drama was being enacted upon the ground floor, rendered her inconsolable. Jonah was summoned by telegram, and came pelting from Somerset, to be regaled with a picturesque account of the outrage, the more purple features of which he at first regarded as embroidery, and for some time flatly refused to believe. As was to be expected, Nobby paid for his treachery with an attack of biliousness, the closing stages of which were terrible to behold. At one time it seemed as if no constitution could survive such an upheaval; but, although the final convulsion left him subdued and listless, he was as right as ever upon the following morning.

The next Sunday we registered what was to be our last attendance of Church Parade for at least three months.

By common consent we had that morning agreed altogether to eschew the subject of crime. Ever since it had happened we had discussed the great adventure so unceasingly that, as Berry had remarked at breakfast, it was more than likely that, unless we were to take an immediate and firm line with ourselves, we should presently get Grand Larceny on the brain, and run into some danger of qualifying, not only for admission to Broadmoor, but for detention in that institution till His Majesty's pleasure should be known. For the first hour or two which followed our resolution we either were silent or discussed other comparatively uninteresting matters in a preoccupied way; but gradually lack of ventilation began to tell, and the consideration of the robbery grew less absorbent.

As we entered the Park at Stanhope Gate—

"Boy, aren't you glad Adèle's coming?" said Jill.

I nodded abstractedly.

"Rather."

"You never said so the other night."

"Didn't I?"

"I suppose, if she comes to Southampton, you'll go to meet her. May I come with you?"

"Good heavens, yes. Why shouldn't you?"

"Oh, I don't know. I thought, perhaps, you'd rather . . ."

I whistled to Nobby, whose disregard of traffic was occasionally conducive to heart failure. As he came cantering up—

"Adèle isn't my property," I said.

"I know, but . . ."

"But what?"

"I've never seen Nobby look so clean," said Jill, with a daring irrelevance that took my breath away.

"I observe," said I, "that you are growing up. Your adolescence is at hand. You are fast emerging from the chrysalis of girlish innocence, eager to show yourself a pert and scheming butterfly." My cousin regarded me with feigned bewilderment. "Yes, you've got the baby stare all right, but you must learn to control that little red mouth. Watch Daphne."

Jill made no further endeavour to restrain the guilty laughter which was trembling upon her lips.

"I b-believe you just love her," she bubbled.

I thought very rapidly. Then—

"I think we all do," said I. "She's very attractive."

"I mean it," said Jill.

"So do I. Look at her ears. Oh, I forgot. Hides them under her hair, doesn't she? Her eyes, then."

"I observe," said Jill pompously, "that you are sitting up and taking notice. Your adol—adol—er—what you said, is at hand. You are emerging from the chrysalis of ignorance——"

"This is blasphemy. You wicked girl. And what are you getting at? Matchmaking or only blackmail?"

"Well, it's time you got married, isn't it? I don't want you to, dear, but I know you've got to soon, and—and I'd like you to be happy."

There was a little catch in her voice, and I looked down to see her eyes shining.

"Little Jill," I said, "if I marry six wives, I shall still be in love with my cousin—a little fair girl, with great grey eyes and the prettiest ways and a heart of the purest gold. And now shall we cry here or by The Serpentine?"

She caught at my arm, laughing.

"Boy, you're very—— Oh, I say! Where's Nobby?"

We had reached the Achilles Statue, and a hurried retrospect showed me the terrier some thirty paces away, exchanging discourtesies with an Aberdeen. The two were walking round each other with a terrible deliberation, and from their respective demeanours it was transparently clear that only an immediate distraction could avert the scandal of a distressing brawl.

Regardless of my surroundings, I summoned the Sealyham in my "parade" voice. To my relief he started and, after a menacing look at his opponent, presumably intended to discourage an attack in rear, cautiously withdrew from his presence and, once out of range, came scampering in our direction.

My brother-in-law and Daphne whom we had out-distanced, arrived at the same time.

As I was reproving the terrier—

"The very people," said a familiar voice.

It was the Assistant Commissioner, labouring under excitement which he with difficulty suppressed. He had been hurrying, and was out of breath.

"I want you to cross the road and walk along by the side of The Row," he said jerkily. "If you see any one you recognize, take off your hat. And, Mrs. Pleydell, you lower your parasol."

"But, my dear chap," said Berry, "they were all masked."

"Well, if you recognize a voice, or even——"

"A voice? My dear fellow, we're in the open air. Besides, what jury——"

"For Heaven's sake," cried the other, "do as I ask! I know it's a chance in a million. Think me mad, call me a fool—anything you like . . . but go."

His earnestness was irresistible.

I whistled to Nobby—who had seized the opportunity of straying, apparently by accident, towards a bull-terrier—and started to stroll in the direction of The Row. Jill walked beside me, twittering, and a glance over my shoulder showed me my sister and Berry a horse's length behind. Behind them, again, came the Assistant Commissioner.

We crossed the road and entered the walk he had mentioned.

It was a beautiful day. The great sun flamed out of a perfect sky, and there was little or no wind. With the exception of a riding-master and two little girls The Row was empty, but the walk was as crowded as a comfortably filled ball-room, if you except the dancers who are sitting out; for, while three could walk abreast with small inconvenience either to others or themselves, there was hardly a seat to spare.

I have seen smarter parades. It was clear that many *habitués* had already left Town, and that a number of visitors had already arrived. But there was apparent the same quiet air of gaiety, the same good humour which fine feathers bring, and, truth to tell, less *ennui* and more undisguised enjoyment than I can ever remember.

Idly I talked with Jill, not thinking what I said nor noticing what she answered, but my heart was pounding against my ribs, and I was glancing incessantly from side to side in a fever of fear lest I should miss the obvious.

Now and again I threw a look over my shoulder. Always Berry and Daphne were close behind. Fervently I wished that they were in front.

I began to walk more slowly. . . .

Suddenly I realized that I was streaming with sweat.

As I felt for my handkerchief—

"Look at Nobby," said Jill. "Whatever's he doing?"

I glanced at my cousin to follow the direction of her eyes.

Nobby was sitting up, begging, before a large elderly gentleman who was seated, immaculately dressed, some six paces away. He was affecting not to see the terrier, but there was a queer frozen look about his broad smile that set me staring. Even as I gazed he lowered his eyes and, lifting a hand from his knee, began to regard the tips of his fingers, as though they were ungloved. . . .

For a second I stood spellbound.

Then I took off my hat.

CHAPTER IX

How Adèle Feste Arrived, and Mr. Dunkelsbaum Supped with the Devil

"There she is!" cried Jill.

"Where?" said I, screwing up my eyes and peering eagerly at the crowded taffrails.

"There, Boy, there. Look, she's seen us. She's waving."

Hardly I followed the direction of my cousin's pink index finger, which was stretched quivering towards the promenade deck.

"Is that her in blue?"

But a smiling Jill was already nodding and waving unmistakably to the tall slim figure, advances which the latter was as surely returning with a cheerly wave of her slight blue arm. Somewhat sheepishly I took off my hat.

Adèle Feste had arrived.

More than fifteen months had elapsed since we had reluctantly seen her into the boat-train at Euston and wished her a safe journey to her American home. At the time, with an uneasiness bred of experience, I had wondered whether our friendship was to survive the battery of time and distance, or whether it was destined to slip into a decline and so, presently, out of our lives, fainting and painless. Touch, however, had been maintained by a fitful correspondence, and constant references to Miss Feste's promised visit to White Ladies—a consummation which we one and all desired— were made for what they were worth. Finally my sister sat down and issued a desperate summons. "My dear, don't keep us waiting any longer. Arrive in August and stay for six months. If you don't, we shall begin to believe what we already suspect—that we live too far away." The thrust went home. Within a month the invitation had been accepted, with the direct result that here were Jill and I, at six o'clock of a pleasant August evening, standing upon a quay at Southampton, while the Rolls waited patiently, with Fitch at her wheel, a stone's throw away, ready to rush our guest and ourselves over the odd fifteen miles that lay between the port and White Ladies.

With us in the car we could take the inevitable cabin-trunk and dressing-case. Adèle's heavy baggage was to be consigned to the care of Fitch, who would bring it by rail the same evening to Mockery Dale, the little wayside station which served five villages and our own among them.

Nobody from the quay was allowed to board the liner, and none of the passengers were allowed to disembark, until the baggage had been off-loaded. For the best part, therefore, of an hour and a half Jill and I hovered under the shadow of the tall ship, walking self-consciously up and down, or standing looking up at the promenade deck with, so far as I was concerned, an impotently fatuous air and, occasionally, the meretricious leer usually reserved for the photographer's studio.

At last—

"If they don't let them off soon," I announced, "I shall break down. The strain of being cordial with somebody who's in sight, but out of earshot, is becoming unbearable. Let's go and have a breather behind the hutment." And I indicated an erection which looked like a ticket-office that had been thrown together during the Crimean War.

But Jill was inexorable.

"It can't be long now," she argued, "and if we go away—— There!" She seized my arm with a triumphant clutch. "Look! They're beginning to get off."

It was true. One by one the vanguard of passengers was already straggling laden on to the high gangway. I strained my eyes for a glimpse of the slight blue figure, which had left the taffrail and was presumably imprisoned in the press which could be observed welling out of a doorway upon the main deck. . . .

A sudden and violent stress upon my left hand at once reminded me of Nobby's existence, and suggested that of a cat. Mechanically I held fast to the lead, at the opposite end of which the Sealyham was choking and labouring in a frenzied endeavour to molest a sleek tabby, which, from the assurance of its gait, appeared to be a *persona grata* upon the quay. The attempted felony attracted considerable attention, which should have been otherwise directed, with the result that a clergyman and two ladies were within an ace of being overrun by an enormous truck-load of swaying baggage and coarsely reviled by a sweating Hercules for their pains. As it was, the sudden diversion of the trolley projected several pieces of luggage on to the quay, occasioning an embryo stampede of the bystanders and drawing down a stern rebuke, delivered in no measured terms, from a blue-coated official, who had not seen what had happened, upon the heads of innocent and guilty alike. The real offender met my accusing frown with the disarming smile of childish innocence, and, when I shook my head, wagged his tail unctuously. As I picked him up and put him under my arm—

"So this is Nobby," said Adèle.

I uncovered and nodded.

"And he had a bath this morning, so as to be all nice and clean when Miss Feste arrived. I did, too."

"How reckless!" said Adèle. "You look very well on it."

"Thank you," said I, shaking hands. "And you look glorious. Hullo! You've let your hair grow. I am glad."

"Think it's an improvement?"

"If possible."

The well-marked eyebrows went up, the bright brown eyes regarded me quizzically, the faint familiar smile hung maddeningly on the red lips.

"Polite as ever," she flashed.

"Put it down to the bath," said I. "Cleanliness is next to—er—devotion."

"Yes, and he's been counting the days," broke in Jill. "He has really. Of course, we all have. But——Oh, Adèle, I'm so glad you've come."

Adèle drew my cousin's arm within her own.

"So'm I," she said quietly. "And now—I did have a dressing-case once. And a steamer-trunk. . . . D'you think it's any good looking for them?"

Twenty minutes later we were all three—four with Nobby—on the front seat of the Rolls, which was nosing its way gingerly out of the town.

"I wonder if you realize," said Adèle, "what a beautiful country you live in."

At the moment we were immediately between an unpleasantly crowded tram and a fourth-rate beer-house.

"Don't you have trams?" said I. "Or does alcohol mean so much to you? I suppose prohibition is a bit of a jar."

"To tell you the truth, I was thinking of the Isle of Wight. It looked so exquisite as we were coming in. Just like a toy continent out of a giant's nursery."

"Before the day is out," I prophesied, "you shall see finer things than that."

Once clear of the streets, I gave the car her head.

For a while we slid past low-lying ground, verdant and fresh and blowing, but flat and sparsely timbered, with coppices here and there and, sometimes, elms in the hedgerows, and, now and again, a parcel of youngster oaks about a green—fair country enough at any time, and at this summer sundown homely and radiant. But there was better to come.

The car fled on.

Soon the ground rose sharply by leaps and bounds, the yellow road swerving to right and left, deep tilted meadows on one side with a screen of birches beyond, and on the other a sloping rabble of timber, whose foliage made up a tattered motley, humble and odd and bastard, yet, with it all, so rich in tender tones and unexpected feats of drapery that Adèle cried that it was a slice of fairyland and sat with her chin on her shoulder, till the road curled up into the depths of a broad pine-wood, through which it cut, thin, and dead straight, and cool, and strangely solemn. In a flash it had become the nave of a cathedral, immense, solitary. Sombre and straight and tall, the walls rose up to where the swaying roof sobered the mellow sunshine and only let it pass dim and so, sacred. The wanton breeze, caught in the maze of tufted pinnacles, filtered its chastened way, a pensive organist, learned to draw grave litanies from the boughs and reverently voice the air of sanctity. The fresh familiar scent hung for a smokeless incense, breathing high ritual and redolent of pious mystery. No circumstance of worship was unobserved. With one consent birds, beasts and insects made not a sound. The precious pall of silence lay like a phantom cloud, unruffled. Nature was on her knees.

The car fled on.

Out of the priestless sanctuary, up over the crest of the rise, into the kiss of the sunlight we sailed, and so on to a blue-brown moor, all splashed and dappled with the brilliant yellow of the gorse in bloom and rolling away into the hazy distance like an untroubled sea. So for a mile it flowed, a lazy pomp of purple, gold-flecked and glowing. Then came soft cliffs of swelling woodland, rising to stay its course with gentle dignity—walls that uplifted eyes found but dwindled edge of a far mightier flood that stretched and tossed, a leafy waste of billows, flaunting more living shades of green than painters dream of, laced here and there with gold and, once in a long while, shot with crimson, rising and falling with Atlantic grandeur, till the eye faltered, and the proud rich waves seemed to be breaking on the rosy sky.

And over all the sun lay dying, his crimson ebb of life staining the firmament with splendour, his mighty heart turning the dance of Death to a triumphant progress, where Blood and Flame rode by with clouds for chargers, and Earth and Sky themselves shouldered the litter of their passing King.

An exclamation of wonder broke from Adèle, and Jill cried to me to stop.

"Just for a minute, Boy, so that she can see it properly."

Obediently I slowed to a standstill. Then I backed the great car and swung up a side track for the length of a cricket-pitch. The few cubits thus added to our stature extended the prospect appreciably. Besides, it was now unnecessary to crane the neck.

At last—

"If you're waiting for me to say 'Go'," said Adèle, "I shouldn't. I'm quite ready to sit here till nightfall. It's up to you to tear me away."

I looked at Jill.

"Better be getting on," I said. "The others'll be wondering where we are."

She nodded.

We did not stop again till the car came to rest easily before the great oak door, which those who built White Ladies hung upon its tremendous hinges somewhere in the 'forties of the sixteenth century.

*　　*　　*　　*　　*

"It is my duty," said Berry, "to inform you that on Wednesday I shall not be available."

"Why?" said my wife.

"Because upon that day I propose to dispense justice in my capacity of a Justice of the Peace. I shall discriminate between neither rich nor poor. Beggars and billionaires shall get it equally in the neck. Innocent and guilty alike——"

"That'll do," said Daphne. "What about Thursday?"

"Thursday's clear. One moment, though. I had an idea there was something on that day." For a second he drummed on the table, clearly cudgelling his brains. Suddenly, "I knew it," he cried. "That's the day of the sale. You know. Merry Down. I don't know what's the matter with my memory. I've got some rotten news."

"What?"

Daphne, Jill, Jonah and I fired the question simultaneously.

"A terrible fellow's after it. One Dunkelsbaum. Origin doubtful—very. Last known address, Argentina. Naturalized in July, 1914. Strictly neutral during the War, but managed to net over a million out of cotton, which he sold to the Central Powers *at a lower price than Great Britain offered* before we tightened the blockade. Never interned, of course. Well, he tried to buy Merry Down by private treaty, but Sir Anthony wouldn't sell to him. They say the sweep's crazy about the place and that he means to have it at any price. Jolly, isn't it?"

There was a painful silence.

Merry Down was the nearest estate to White Ladies, and was almost as precious to us as our own home. For over two centuries a Bagot had reigned uninterruptedly over the rose-red mansion and the spreading park, the brown water and the waving woods—a kingdom of which we had been free since childhood. Never an aged tree blew down but we were told of it, and now—the greatest of them all was falling, the house of Bagot itself.

One of the old school, Sir Anthony had stood his ground up to the last. The War had cost him dear. His only son was killed in the first months. His only grandson fell in the battles of the Somme. His substance, never fat, had shrunk to a mere shadow of its former self. The stout old heart fought the unequal fight month after month. Stables were emptied, rooms were shut up, thing after thing was sold. It remained for a defaulting solicitor to administer the *coup de grâce*. . . .

On the twelfth day of August, precisely at half-past two, Merry Down was to be sold by auction at *The Fountain Inn*, Brooch.

Berry's news took our breath away.

"D'you mean to say that this is what I fought for?" said I. "For this brute's peaceful possession of Merry Down?"

"Apparently," said my brother-in-law. "More. It's what Derry Bagot and his boy died for, if you happen to be looking at it that way."

"It'll break Sir Anthony's heart," said Daphne.

"But I don't understand," said Adèle. "How—why is it allowed?"

"I must have notice," said Berry, "of that question."

"Have you ever heard," said Jonah, "of the Society for the Prevention of Cruelty to Alien Enemies?"

Adèle shook her head.

"I think you must have," said Jonah. "Some people call it the British Nation. It's been going for years."

"That's right," said I. "And its motto is 'Charity begins at Home'. There's really nothing more to be said."

"I could cry," announced Jill, in a voice that fully confirmed her statement. "It's just piteous. What would poor Derry say? Can't anything be done?"

Berry shrugged his shoulders.

"If half what I've heard is true, Merry Down is as good as gone. The fellow means to have it, and he's rich enough to buy the county itself. Short of assassination, I don't see what anybody can do. Of course, if you like, you can reproduce him in wax and then stick pins into the image. But that's very old-fashioned, and renders you liable to cremation without the option of a fine.

Besides, as a magistrate, I feel it my bounden duty to——"

"I thought witchcraft and witches were out of date," said Adèle.

"Not at all," said Berry. "Only last week we bound one over for discussing the housing question with a wart-hog. The animal, which, till then, had been laying steadily, became unsettled and suspicious and finally attacked an inoffensive Stilton with every circumstance of barbarity."

"How awful!" said Adèle. "You do see life as a magistrate, don't you? And I suppose somebody kissed the wart-hog, and it turned into a French count? You know, it's a shame about you."

Berry looked round.

"Mocked," he said. "And at my own table. With her small mouth crammed with food, for which I shall be called upon to pay, she actually——"

"O-o-oh!" cried Adèle. "It wasn't. Besides, you shouldn't have asked me."

"I can only say," said Berry, "that I am surprised and pained. From the bosom of my family I, as the head, naturally expect nothing but the foulest scurrility and derision. But when a comparative stranger, whom, with characteristic generosity, I have made free of my heart, seizes a moment which should have been devoted to the mastication of one of my peaches to vilify her host, then indeed I feel almost unsexed—I mean unmanned. Are my veins standing out like cords?"

"Only on your nose," said I. "All gnarled, that is."

"There you are," said Berry. "The slow belly reviles the sage. The——"

Scandalized cries from Daphne and Jill interrupted him.

"You ought to be ashamed of yourself," said his wife, pushing her chair. "And now let's all have coffee on the terrace. That is, unless you three want to stay."

Jonah, Berry and I shook our heads, and she took Adèle's arm and led the way out of the room. . . .

It was a wonderful night.

While Nature slept, Magic, sceptred with a wand, sat on her throne.

The sky was rich black velvet, pricked at a million points, from every one of which issued a cold white brilliance, just luminous enough to show its whereness, sharp and clear-cut. No slightest breath of wind ruffled the shadows of the sleeping trees. With one intent, Night and the countryside had filled the cup of silence so that it brimmed—a feat that neither cellarer can do alone. The faint sweet scent of honeysuckle stole on its errant way, "such stuff as dreams are made on", so that the silken fabric of the air took on a tint of daintiness so rare, fleeting, and exquisite as made your fancy riot, conjuring mirages of smooth enchantment, gardens that hung luxuriant beneath a languorous moon, the plash of water and the soft sob of flutes. . . .

For a long moment all the world was fairy. Then, with a wild scrabble of claws upon stone, a small white shape shot from beneath my chair, took the broad steps at a bound and vanished into the darkness. The welter of barks and growls and grunts of expended energy, rising a moment later from the midst of the great lawn, suggested that a cat had retired to the convenient shelter of the mulberry tree.

The sudden eruption startled us all, and Berry dwelt with some asperity upon the danger of distracting the digestive organs while at work.

Menacingly I demanded the terrier's immediate return. Upon the third time of asking the uproar ceased, and a few seconds later Nobby came padding out of the gloom with the cheerful demeanour of the labourer who has done well and shown himself worthy of his hire. Wise in his generation, he had learned that it is a hard heart which the pleasurable, if mistaken, glow of faithful service will not disarm. Sternly I set the miscreant upon my knee. For a moment we eyed one another with mutual mistrust and understanding. Then he thrust up a wet nose and licked my face. . . .

For a minute or two there was no noise save the occasional chink of a coffee-cup against its saucer. Then—

"Since you ask me," said Berry, "my horoscope is of peculiar interest."

"What's a horoscope?" said Jill.

"A cross between a birth certificate and a conduct sheet," said I, nodding at Berry. "His is a wonder. You can get a copy of it for three and sixpence at Scotland Yard."

"I was born," said my brother-in-law, "when Uranus was in conjunction, Saturn in opposition, and the Conservatives in power. Venus was all gibbous, the Zodiac was in its zenith, and the zenith was in Charles's Wain, commonly called The Cart. My sign was Oleaqua—The Man with the Watering Pot. When I add that a thunderstorm was raging, and that my father had bet five pounds I should be a girl, and had decided to call me 'Hosannah', you will appreciate that it is no ordinary being who is addressing you. A singularly beautiful infant, it was at once obvious that I was born to rule. Several people said it was inevitable, among them an organ-grinder, who was ordered out of the grounds, to which during the excitement he had gained access. He didn't put it that way, but he explained at the police court that that was what he had meant."

"To whose good offices," said Jonah, "do you ascribe your pretty ways?"

"Uranus," was the airy reply. "From that deity came also meekness, an unshakable belief in human nature, and the fidgets."

"You ought to have been called after him," said Adèle.

"My godfathers thought otherwise. In a fit of generosity they gave me my name and a pint pot, which the more credulous declared to be silver, but whose hallmark persistently defied detection. Then the fount dried up. And now let me read your hand. Or would you rather I taught you the three-card trick?"

"It's too dark," I protested. "Besides, she's going to sing."

"Who said so?" said Adèle. "I was going to suggest that you told us a fairy-tale."

"A song for a tale," said I.

"Done."

"There was once a princess," said I, "with eyes like brown stars and a voice like the song of a silver brook. One day she was sitting all alone by the side of a shady trout-stream, when she heard a bell. For a moment she thought she was dreaming, for she was rather tired. Then she heard it again— a clear tinkle, which seemed to arise from the heart of the stream itself. This surprised the princess very much, because no bells were allowed in her father's kingdom. The old man was a bit of an autocrat, and one morning, when he had been rung up seven times running by subjects who wanted quite a different number, he just passed a law prohibiting bells, and that was that. Well, while she was wondering what to do the bell rang again rather angrily, and, before she knew where she was, she had said 'Come in.'

" 'At last,' said a voice, and a large frog heaved himself out of the water and sat down on a tuft of grass on the opposite bank. 'I shan't knock next time.'

" 'I didn't hear you knock,' said the princess.

" 'I didn't,' said the frog. 'I rang. How's your father?'

" 'Full of beans,' said the princess. 'And yours?'

" 'That's my business,' said the frog. 'Are you married yet?'

" 'No such luck,' said the princess. 'And, what's more, I never shall be.'

" 'Why?' said the frog. 'Half the kingdom goes with you, doesn't it?'

" 'Exactly,' said the princess. 'And there's the rub.'

" 'Where?' said the frog, looking round.

" 'Well, I'm all right,' said the princess, 'but who wants half a one-horse kingdom that's mortgaged up to the hilt and a bit over?'

"At this the frog looked so wise that the princess felt quite uncomfortable, and began to think he must be a waiter at the Athenæum who had had a misunderstanding with a witch. Suddenly—

" 'Which of your suitors do you like best?' said the frog.

" 'Albert the Watchguard,' said the princess. 'He's a bit of a fool, but you ought to see him dance.'

" 'No, I oughtn't,' said the frog. 'It would be extremely bad for me. Listen. Tell Albert to come down here with a sieve to-morrow morning. He may be a bit of a fool, but, if he doesn't apply for you before lunch, he's a congenital idiot.' And with that he took a short run and dived into the stream.

"The princess did as she was bid, and at eleven o'clock the next morning Albert the Watchguard appeared, complete with sieve, upon the bank of the trout-stream. Twenty-five minutes later, with a cigarette behind his ear and *a nugget of gold in each boot*, he made formal application for the hand of the princess and half the kingdom—a request which was immediately granted.

"Two days later they were married.

"What Albert the Watchguard said, on learning that his half of the kingdom did not include the territory watered by the trout-stream, is not recorded.

"If you remember, he was a bit of a fool."

"Good for you, old chap," said Daphne.

Jill's hand stole out of the darkness and crept into mine.

Berry turned to Adèle.

"A blinking wonder," he said, "is not he? Fancy turning out a comic cameo like that on demand. But then for years he's been on the staff of *Chunks*. He does the *Gossipy Gobbets* column."

Adèle laughed musically.

"It was very nice of him to do as I asked," she said. "And as a bargain's a bargain . . ."

She rose and turned to the open windows. . . .

I saw her settled at the piano, and then stole back.

A moment later the strains of her beautiful mezzo-soprano

floated out into the darkness.

It is doubtful whether *Printemps Qui Commence* ever enjoyed a more exquisite setting.

It was a wonderful night.

* * * * *

If we had driven straight to Brooch the incident would not have occurred.

We had lunched early, for Berry and I were determined to attend the sale of Merry Down. Sir Anthony, who was sure to be there, would need comforting, and we had, moreover, a feeling that we should like to see the last of an old friend. Once the place had passed into the power of the dog, we should try to forget. It was Adèle's suggestion that she should accompany us. "I'd like to see Brooch," she had said, "and I want to get a new piece of silk for my wristwatch. Besides, I can sit in the car while you and Berry are at the sale. That'll save your taking the chauffeur." We agreed readily enough.

Because Adèle was with us we started in good time, so that we could go by way of Hickory Hammer and Three Horse Hill. That way would bring us on to the London road at a point five miles from Brooch, and, while the view from the hill was as fine as any in the neighbourhood, Hickory Hammer was not only extremely ancient, but generally accounted one of the most picturesque villages in the whole of England.

I was driving, with Nobby beside me, while Adèle and Berry sat on the back seat. Our thoughts were not unnaturally dwelling upon the sale, and now and again I caught fragments of conversation which suggested that my brother-in-law was commenting upon the power of money and the physiognomy of Mr. Dunkelsbaum—whose photograph had appeared in the paper that very morning, to grace an interview—with marked acerbity. Once in a while a ripple of laughter from Adèle came to my ears, but for the most part it was a grave discourse, for Berry felt very bitter, and Adèle, whose father's father was the son of an English squire, had taken to heart the imminent disseizure with a rare sympathy.

It was five minutes to two when we slid out of Lullaby Coppice and on to the London road. A furlong ahead the road swung awkwardly to the left—a bend which the unexpected *débouchement* of a by-road rendered a veritable pitfall for the unwary motorist. I slowed for the turn cautiously, for I knew the place, but I was not surprised when, on rounding the corner, we found ourselves confronted with a state of affairs presenting all the elements of a first-class smash.

What had happened was transparently clear.

Huddled between a trolley and the nearside bank, which was rising sheer from the road, was a large red limousine, listing heavily to port and down by the head. Both vehicles were facing towards Brooch. Plainly the car had sought to overtake the trolley, which was in the act of emerging from the by-road, and pass it upon the wrong side. The former, of course, had been travelling too fast to stop, and the burden which the latter was bearing had made it impossible for the other to pass upon the right-hand side. Three sturdy oaks, new felled, one of them full fifty swaying feet in length, all of them girt by chains on to the trolley's back, made a redoubtable obstruction. The chauffeur had taken the only possible course and dashed for the narrowing passage on the left. A second too late, the car had been pinched between the great wain and the unyielding bank, like a nut between the jaws of the crackers. But for the action of the carter, who had stopped his team dead, the car would have been crushed to flinders.

The two occupants of the limousine were apparently unhurt, for, when I first saw them, they were standing in the middle of the road, looking anxiously in our direction. The next moment they were signalling to us violently, spreading out ridiculous arms, as if the treetrunks were not putting our passage of the road for the present out of the question.

As I brought the Rolls to a standstill, I heard a stifled cry. The next moment Berry's voice hissed in my ear.

"Talk of the devil. . . . Look at the cove on the right. *It's Dunkelsbaum himself.*"

A lightning glance showed me the truth of his words. The original of the photograph over which we had pored that morning was standing before us in all the grossness of flesh.

Almost before I had recovered from the shock, the other—a long sallow creature with a false grin and a cringing air—was at my elbow.

"You mutht eckthcuthe me," he lisped, uncovering, "but could you pothibly give uth a lift ath far ath Brooch? Thith gentleman"—he indicated Mr. Dunkelsbaum—"hath a motht important engagement there at half-patht two, and, ath you thee, we have been unfortunate. Tho, if you could thee your way to accommodating uth, we thould be greatly obliged."

Before I could reply—

"We can get there by half-past two," said Berry, speaking slowly and distinctly, "if—*if we go through Ramilly*."

Now, Ramilly was a great enclosure, and could be entered from the by-road down which the trolley had come. *But it was not on the way to Brooch.*

With the greatest difficulty I repressed a start. Then I leaned forward as if to examine the dash, but in reality to conceal my excitement. . . .

Apparently guileless, my brother-in-law's protasis was nothing less than a deliberate direction to me to postpone Mr. Dunkelsbaum's arrival at Brooch until Merry Down was no longer in the market.

My heart began to beat violently. . . .

Berry was speaking again.

"Wait half a minute, and we'll change over." He turned to Adèle. "Will you sit in front with Boy?"

As the change was being made, Mr. Dunkelsbaum advanced.

I have seldom set eyes upon a less prepossessing man. To liken him to a vicious over-fed pug is more than charitable. Smug, purse-proud and evil, his bloated countenance was most suggestive. There was no pity about the coarse mouth, which he had twisted into a smile, two deep sneer lines cut into the unwholesome pallor of his cheeks, from under drooping lids two beady eyes shifted their keen appraising glance from me to Berry and, for a short second, to Adèle. There was about him not a single redeeming feature, and for the brute's pompous carriage alone I could have kicked him heartily.

The clothes were like unto the man.

From beneath a silk-faced overcoat, which he wore unbuttoned, the rich contour of a white waistcoat thrust its outrageous way, spurning the decent shelter of a black tail-coat and making the thick striped legs look shorter than ever. A diamond pin winked in the satin tie, and a black bowler hat and patent-leather boots mercifully covered, the one his crown, and the others his short fat feet.

My gentleman raised his hat and removed a cigar from his mouth before speaking in a thick voice and with a strong foreign accent.

"My segretary 'as tol' you of my agsident, yes. I voz much oblige' vor a lif' to Brrrrooch. These gattle"—contemptuously he pointed to the waggoner and his great beasts, to whose common sagacity he owed his life—"should not allowed be on der roats, no.

Ach, so. It voz all wrong."

"Quite so," said Berry. "I think they're worse than pedestrians. If I had my way, nothing but high-powered cars would be allowed on any high road. If people can't afford cars, let them keep to the lanes."

"So 'ave I say often. What vor are der baths an' lanes else? Bah!"

By now Adèle had taken her seat in front, and my brother-in-law, who had descended, was ushering Mr. Dunkelsbaum into the place she had left. With a grunt the fellow made to hoist himself in, when Nobby took a flying leap from the front seat and planted himself in the intruder's path, barking furiously.

Immediately withdrawing the foot which he had set upon the carpet, Mr. Dunkelsbaum descended anyhow on to his secretary, who was not expecting him and so too late to recede. The scream of agony which the unfortunate creature emitted, no less than the convulsive way in which he clung to the wing, while standing upon one leg and protesting with a horrible leer that he was unhurt, gave the lie to his words.

His employer spoke at once and to the point.

"Den, if you 'ave no 'urt, what vor 'ave you yell in mine ear-'ole? Bah!" He turned to me. "You vill blease gondrol der 'ound."

Mastering a desire to do the man violence, I leaned out and over the back of my seat and, taking Nobby by the scruff of his neck, hauled him struggling and growling across the barrier. Adèle received him tenderly and endeavoured to soothe him. But the Sealyham was mourning a lost opportunity and would not be comforted.

Bluntly commanding his creature to stay with the car and arrange for its salvage, Mr. Dunkelsbaum once more heaved himself into the Rolls and sank upon the back seat. Berry followed, and a moment later I had let in the clutch and turned up the by-road.

By the time we had reached the entrance to the enclosure it was ten minutes past two, and, as Berry got out to open and hold the gate, I saw our passenger bring out a handsome timepiece and, after a glance at the dial, replace it in some uneasiness.

"Your dime voz der same as London?" he inquired.

"Five minutes ahead," I replied maliciously.

"Ach!"

"We shall do it all right," I said airily. "Your appointment's at three, isn't it?"

Mr. Dunkelsbaum went a rich green colour, half rose from his seat, and clawed at the air before replying.

"Three?" he raved. "Three? No, no! 'Alf-pas' doo, man, 'alf-pas' doo! 'Oo 'as say it voz three? In a quarder of an hour ve mus' be dere. It is fital, yes."

Adèle began to shake with laughter.

"Right oh," I said casually. "I dare say we can manage it." The gate was open, and I let in the clutch with a bang. With a startled grunt, Mr. Dunkelsbaum was projected violently on to the seat he had left. As I slowed up for Berry to rejoin us, "But I may have to go rather fast," I added.

"Like der devil," was the reply.

The going was good, and the road was unfrequented, so I let the car out. We tore down an avenue of firs, great rugged banks of rhododendrons sprawling on either side, scudded into a beech-wood—pillars all silver-grey, set in a ruffled mass of whispering green, swam through a sea of bracken, rippling and feathery. And all the time I was racking my brain. . . .

To the best of my recollection, we had another three miles to cover before we should emerge from Ramilly on to the King's highway. But at the very point at which we should leave the enclosure there were crossroads and, I was sure, a finger-post announcing the way to Brooch in a plain manner which there was no mistaking.

In the face of this direction, which our passenger would be certain to see, it would be impossible to take another road, and, though we should undoubtedly reach *The Fountain* after the appointed hour, it was quite possible that the proceedings might not be punctually conducted, and that the essential business of the sale would not have been completed before our arrival. Of course, there was nothing to prevent us from throwing off the mask, stopping the car, and politely intimating our inability to carry Mr. Dunkelsbaum any further. But his reception of such an open declaration of war was certain to be unsuitable for Adèle's eyes and ears, and the subsequent action which a man of his calibre would undoubtedly take might prove troublesome, if profitless.

Again, our eventual arrival at Brooch, however belated, would be better avoided. Berry and I were well known in the town, as was also our close friendship with Sir Anthony. Our identification, therefore, would be only a matter of time, and since, in the absence of a burst or a puncture, our progress to Brooch could only be delayed by pretended engine trouble, the suspicions which this would be sure to arouse in our passenger's mind would very soon be confirmed.

Sooner or later the fellow would gather that he had been befooled, but, provided that we preserved our incognitos, that did not matter. If we could possibly leave him uncertain whether we were as cunning as serpents or as simple as doves, so much the better.

In no sort of order all these reflections elbowed and jostled one another before my mind's eye, which was itself searching feverishly for a solution. Then we floated round a long curve, and I saw the splash.

We were at the top of a short steep hill in the midst of a dense wood of tender years. At the foot of the hill our road was overrun by a fair-sized stream, so that while there was a little footbridge, vehicles that were wishing to pass this way must do so by way of the ford. Beyond the water the ground rose sharply again, making the whole place a bottom or hollow, such as was commonly encountered in this part of England.

I slowed up, and we slid down the hill at a reduced speed.

With the utmost caution I put the Rolls at the splash, making no attempt to disguise my uneasiness. Mr. Dunkelsbaum would naturally conclude that I was anxious lest the water was deep. As a matter of fact, I was fearful lest the ford should prove shallow.

But luck was with us.

Very gently the great car entered the brown water, which was flowing slowly and steadily over its gravel bed. With my heart in my mouth, I watched the water rise. . . . It was half-way to the running-board. . . . It was level—above. . . . It was lapping the spare wheel, and—we were in the deepest part. Quick as a flash I changed into top and let in the clutch with a bang. Instantly the engine stopped, and the car came to rest in mid-stream.

I took out my handkerchief and wiped my face.

There was an electric silence. Then—

"What's the matter?" said Berry.

"Flooded out," I said shortly, hoping that Mr. Dunkelsbaum was not an engineer.

As I spoke, I heard a choking sound at my shoulder. I turned sharply, and there was my gentleman in a terrible toss. His eyes were protruding, and he could hardly speak.

"To Brrrooch!" he screamed. "To Brrrooch! Ve mus' go on. I 'ave say it is fital. Sdard der gar, man, sdard der gar! What vor do you vaid?"

"I'll try," I said coolly. "But you'll have to get out. Our only chance is to make her as light as possible."

With a saintly look Berry opened the off-side door and sprang nimbly on to the foot-bridge. Then he turned to the other.

"Come along, sir."

Mr. Dunkelsbaum stared at the water as if it had been boiling oil. As he estimated the distance he was to cover, a bead of perspiration began to course down his face. It was the first of many. . . .

Berry extended his hand.

"Come along, sir."

The fellow threw one despairing glance about him, hung out of the car till he could reach Berry's hand, and then, with a frightful grunt, goose-stepped into space. . . .

The sight of Mr. Dunkelsbaum, still hand-in-hand with Berry, endeavouring by the latter's direction to step out of twelve inches of water on to the foot-bridge—a feat which only a contortionist could have accomplished—was diverting in the extreme. But when the unfortunate creature did by some superhuman effort get the elongated toe of his right elastic-sided boot upon the plank, and Berry found himself unable to do more than haul him half-way to safety, so that for one long hectic moment he hung writhing convulsively, frantically waving his left leg in quest of a footing and alternately calling upon Heaven and frenziedly charging his betrayer not to let go; when, as a result of muscular vibration, his left boot worked loose and fell into the water with a derisive plop; when Nobby, who had been watching the efforts of the storming party in a fever of excitement, leapt from Adèle's arms on to my shoulders and thence into the flood, and, beating its raving owner by a matter of inches in a rush for the errant footgear, splashed his triumphant way to the bank and, amid a hurricane of execration, bore his waterlogged trophy into the undergrowth; then I bowed my head upon the steering-wheel and, throwing decency to the winds, ran before the tempest of Titanic laughter. . . .

A wail of merriment from Adèle and a pressure upon my left arm brought me to my senses.

Watch in hand, Mr. Dunkelsbaum was dancing upon a strip of turf by the edge of the stream, bellowing at me to start the car.

'I do nod gare vor my bood, no. But der abboinmen'. . . . It vill nod vaid, I say. An' it is now vive minute to begin. Ach! What vor 'ave you sid dere an' laugh? My 'eart pleeds vor you. Ten tousand devil! But *vill you sdard ub der auto*?"

The yell with which he delivered the last sentence changed to a howl as his bootless foot alighted heavily upon an odd pebble, and Nobby peered out of some long grass, boot in mouth, to see whether the situation was affording further opportunities. Apparently it was not, for he lay down where he was and proceeded with the dismemberment of his spoil.

Adèle turned her head away and held her handkerchief to her eyes.

I set my foot upon the self-starter. . . .

The moment the engine started, Nobby abandoned his treasure and leapt barking to the side of the car, fearful, as usual, lest he be left behind. Muttering hideously, Mr. Dunkelsbaum seized the opportunity of retrieving his boot, whose present condition was apparently even worse than he had expected, for a hurried examination of the same elicited an involuntary cry of torment, and he shook his fist at the terrier in a fit of ungovernable fury.

Slowly I brought the Rolls out of the splash, and when, as I judged, about six feet lay between the back wheels and the stream, again I stopped the engine. . . .

For a moment I thought Mr. Dunkelsbaum would offer me violence. His mouth worked uncontrollably, and there was a suspicion of foam upon the thick lips. A sudden violent tug at the boot, which was still in his right hand awaiting replacement, mercifully diverted his attention, but the savagery with which he launched a kick at Nobby, who was once more in possession and already out of range, was terrible to witness.

" 'Ell-ound!" he screamed. " 'Ell-'ound! You vould dare! I vill throw you oud of der vindow with one 'and. I vill gig der eyes from your 'ead." In the midst of the paroxysm he turned to me, wild-eyed and gesticulating. "What vor 'ave you stay still? You mus' sdard again an' again, yes. To Brrrooch! To Brrrooch!" He snatched his watch from his pocket and dabbed at its face with a shaking forefinger. "Der glogs vill berhaps be wrong. I vill give you dwendy bounds if ve shall 'ave arrive in dime!"

The rearguard of my compunction, which had been putting up a fight, vanished into thin air. The sweep had offered me money. I was prepared to twist his tail indefinitely.

"If you pushed behind," I said coldly, "we might get her going. If we do, you must get in while she's moving. I daren't stop, or we may have to begin all over again."

Mr. Dunkelsbaum eyed me suspiciously, and Berry, who had been hitherto afraid to trust his voice, took up the running with a dash.

"That's the ticket. Come on, Herr Stunkenblotch. Never mind your boot. Think of the purchase you'll get with a bare foot." He stepped behind the car. "Now, you do as I do, and, when I say 'Go,' drop your bullet head and try to shove the old 'bus into the middle of next fortnight."

With a snarl, Mr. Dunkelsbaum slunk limping to the back of the car. . . .

A moment later—

"Go!" said my brother-in-law.

Maliciously I waited the best part of thirty seconds. Then—

"Are you ready?" I inquired, innocently enough.

The explosion which my question provoked was truly terrible.

The panting alien and Berry immediately reappeared, one upon either side of the car, the latter protesting with an injured air that he was not so young as he was, and that, if I wanted him to survive the summer, I had better keep my ears open, while to judge from his behaviour, the reflection that his recent output of vigour had been rendered nugatory by my unreadiness was hurrying Mr. Dunkelsbaum into the valley of insanity. Purple in the face from the unwonted violence of his physical and mental exercise, streaming with perspiration and shaking with passion, the fellow stormed and raved like a demoniac, and, if Berry had not stepped in front of the bonnet and, taking him by the arm, led him again to the back of the car, I believe he would have fallen down in a fit.

"Are you ready?" I called.

A hurricane of affirmatory invective answered me.

I started the engine, changed into first and let in the clutch. As I changed into second, uprose a medley of cries and barking. I leaned out, exhorting the pedestrians by words and gestures to come aboard. . . .

Head up, teeth bared, fists clenched and arms working, Mr. Dunkelsbaum was running like a stag. Berry was loping along just behind, apparently offering encouragement and advice, while the Sealyham was alternately running and jumping up and down in front of the frantic alien, barking as if he were possessed. Even as I looked, the inevitable happened. Nobby miscalculated his distance and landed too close to the object of his attentions, Berry gave a warning, but belated, shout, and Mr. Dunkelsbaum made a desperate effort to avoid the stumbling-block, tripped, recovered himself, crossed his legs, and with an unearthly cry fell heavily to the ground.

I changed into third speed.

As we swung round the corner at the top of the hill, I threw a glance over my shoulder.

Berry was sitting on the bank by the side of the road with his head in his hands, Mr. Dunkelsbaum had risen to his feet and was in the act of hurling himself in the direction of Nobby, and the latter, with his small tail well over his back, was circling delightedly about his victim, still barking like a fiend and ricocheting like a roulette ball.

The next moment we were out of sight, and I changed into top speed.

Adèle caught at my arm.

"You're not going to leave them?"

I nodded.

"Best way out," I said. "Berry'll understand and pull out somehow. You see, we're too well known about here to take any chances. And now I think we'll slip along to *The Fountain* and find Sir Anthony."

"You tell me I speak good English," said Adèle.

"So you do."

"Well, I don't want to spoil my record. What's the Anglo-Saxon for 'a thaw-proof nerve'?"

"Can't be done," said I. "But I can put your mouth into Italian. *Bocca bella carissima.* Now, isn't that nice?"

The sweet pretty lips began to tremble with laughter.

"You're incorrigible," she announced. "Fifteen long months, and you haven't changed a bit."

"Long months, Adèle?"

The soft rose of her cheeks was glowing as she turned to reply.

"The longest I've ever spent," she said softly. "That—that's the worst of cutting your hair. I thought it was never going to grow."

"They've been very long ones for me, Adèle."

Up went the delicate eyebrows.

"Have they?"

I nodded.

"A close scrutiny will reveal that my hair, once a rich mud colour, is now flecked with grey."

"I should attribute that to the march of Time."

I shook my head.

"The responsibility," I said, "rests with the United States of America. Seriously, I missed you terribly."

"That," said Adèle, "I refuse to believe. If you had, you would have paid us a visit."

"I was not invited."

Adèle shrugged her shoulders.

"Any old way," she announced, "I'm here now. And, while we're on the subject of hair, please remember that since you last saw me, I've put mine up."

"Which means?"

"That I am a dangerous woman of the world, who gives nothing and takes everything—with a grain of salt. I warn you, I've changed."

"Unquestionably," said I, "you have had a violent love-affair. That is as plain as is the dainty nose upon your charming face."

Adèle regarded me with a dazzling smile.

"I forgot," she said, "that I was addressing an expert. Tell me, d'you think I shall get over it?"

"If you don't," said I, "it shan't be my fault."

"You're very good."

"Not at all," said I. "Can you spell 'homœopathy'?"

* * * * *

For a man who had just parted with the home of his fathers, poor old Sir Anthony was in high spirits. Lock, stock and barrel, Merry Down had been sold to the highest bidder. Of that there was no manner of doubt. What was more to the point was that the purchaser, who had paid a good price, was of English blood, and had known Derry Bagot at Eton, and soldiered with him first in South Africa and afterwards in France. The place had passed into good clean hands and was to be well cared for.

"A very civil fellow," said Sir Anthony, whom we had brought back to White Ladies to tea, "and a sportsman. I'm truly thankful. Spoke so nicely of Derry—said he'd always looked up to him and he was proud to think he was to carry on his—his home." His voice faltered, and something of the old stricken look hung for an instant in the keen grey eyes. The next moment it was ousted by the flash of victory, and they were bent upon me. "So you deported the alien to Ramilly? Gad, but I'd 've liked to see the terrier bring him down."

As he spoke there was the noise of a familiar scamper, and a moment later Nobby had hurled himself across the terrace into my lap and was licking my face with an enthusiastic violence which could not have been more pronounced if he had not seen me for years.

And in his wake came Berry.

I had told Sir Anthony that, if he desired to thank any one, he must thank my brother-in-law, because, but for the latter's quick wit, Merry Down would have fallen into the enemy's hands. But, when the old baronet had clapped him upon the back, Berry nodded at me.

"I believe," he said, "I was the first to conceive the felony. That comes of being a magistrate. But that's the merchant who carried it out. Largely at my expense, I admit. But that's a matter for him and me to settle. I tell you, Sir Anthony, you must thank him—and the—er—hell-hound. A more masterly display of devilry I never witnessed." He sank into a chair. "Let refreshment be brought me."

Daphne blew him a kiss.

"One moment, old chap. Did the servants see you come in?"

Her husband nodded.

"Then there'll be some fresh tea in a moment. And now, what happened? We're simply wild to hear."

"Yes," cried Jill eagerly. "And did you really call him 'Stunkenblotch'? And what happened to his boot? And where——"

"The last thing we saw," said Adèle, "was the fellow get up and go for Nobby. You were sitting by the side of the road."

"And before you begin," said I, "let me say that I wouldn't have left you, brother, if I could have thought of any other way out. But it seemed the only thing to do."

Berry put up his hand.

"Strange as it may seem," he said, "for once I don't blame you. If I hadn't been so weak with laughter I might have boarded the car, but it was then or never. I didn't expect you to wait."

"How did you get on?"

"I fear," said Berry, "that Mr. Dunkelsbaum did expect the car to be waiting at the top of the hill. What he said when he found that the road, which we could see for about five furlongs, was unoccupied, I shall try to forget. Suffice it that he perspired with great freedom, and for a long time appeared to be afflicted with an impediment in his speech. Occasionally he addressed me in Patagonian, but since the only words I could remember were *schloss, ausgang* and *bahnhof*, my replies, judging from their reception, were unsatisfactory and sometimes, I grieve to think, even irrelevant.

"Presently I suggested that we should return for his boot. For this he sought, whilst I detained Nobby. I had recommended that the latter's services should be employed in the search, but the bare suggestion provoked such a shocking outburst of profanity that I said no more. When, after exploring the undergrowth for nearly half an hour, he suddenly descried his footgear lodged in the branches of a neighbouring ash, Mr. Dunkelsbaum's behaviour gave me cause to fear for his reason. My theory that some dim-sighted fowl must have mistaken the truant for a piece of refuse met with a furious dismissal, and, from the perfectly poisonous stare with which he declined my offer of assistance to secure his quarry, I was forced to the conclusion that he associated me with its elevation. This discovery caused me much pain, but the rude man was soon to pay dearly for his foul suspicion. True, he got it down: but it seemed as if the ravages of wear and tear, to say nothing of its immersion, had heavily discounted the value of the boot as an article of wearing apparel, for, after several agonized endeavours to replace it upon his foot, Mr. Dunkelsbaum screamed, flung it down, spat upon it, and offered up what I took to be a short prayer for immediate death.

"After this horrible exhibition of temper, I felt that no useful purpose could be served by remaining within sight or earshot of the abandoned creature, so I released the terrier and made ready to depart.

" 'Herr Splodgenblunk,' I said, 'I must now leave you. Should you be still anxious to arrive at Bloat, you cannot do better than——'

"He interrupted me with a terrible cry.

" 'I vos neffer vant to 'ave arrive at Bloat!'

" 'But you said——'

" 'No! No!' he raved. 'It vos *Brrrooch*, I 'ave say—*Brrrooch*!'

"I affected the utmost surprise.

" 'Oh, Brooch. Why, we came miles out of our way. Brooch is over there. Back the way we came, out of the enclosure, and the first on the right. That's the worst of a Scotch accent.' "

Berry paused for the laughter to subside. As it died down—

"That," said I, "was refined cruelty."

"I confess," said Berry, "that, compared with the paroxysm which succeeded my statement, its predecessors were pale and colourless. Indeed, but for a timely diversion, I believe the gent would have gone up in smoke.

"You see, it was like this.

"Ever since his release, Nobby had evinced a pardonable

curiosity regarding Mr. Dunkelsbaum's bootless foot. Unknown to its owner, he had subjected this remarkable member to the closest scrutiny, and it was in the midst of the other's spirited study of 'A Lost Soul' that he decided to remove the objectionable cloak or covering, which it is charity to describe as a sock.

"It was, of course, unmannerly. The dog should have controlled his morbid thirst for knowledge. But there you are. Still, it was imprudent of Mr. Dunkelsbaum to kick him in the ribs. I felt that instinctively. Had the gentleman remained to argue, I should have said as much. But he didn't.

"Going extremely short upon the near fore, he rocketed down the hill, with Nobby in the immediate future, barking like a fiend and striving, so to speak, to take Time by the forelock. From the fragment of cashmere with which he presently returned, I fear that he was successful.

"And there you are. All things considered, if he's still alive, I should think he'd make Brooch about half-past eight."

"He may get a lift," said Jonah.

"Not he. Once bitten, twice shy. After all, he asked for it, didn't he? And now shall I have some tea? Or would that be greedy?"

Sir Anthony wiped his eyes.

"If he'd known you," he crowed, "as well as I do, he'd 've been more careful. Who sups with the devil should hold a long spoon."

"I don't know what you mean, sir," said Berry. "I'm a respectable——"

"Exactly," said I. "And meek. Thanks to Uranus."

CHAPTER X

How Adèle Broke her Dream, and Vandy Pleydell took Exercise

"What, again?" said I, staring at the breakfast-cup which Jill was offering me, that I might pass it to Daphne. "How many more cups is he going to drink? He's had three to my knowledge."

"That vessel," said Berry, "was passed to you for information and immediate action. So, as they say in the Army, close your perishin' head and get down to it."

"What you want," said I, "is a bucket. Or a private urn."

"What's the matter with a trough?" said Jonah. "That'd be

more in keeping."

Berry turned to Adèle.

"You see?" he said. "Two putrid minds with but a single snort. But there you are. Don't dwell on it. Pass the marmalade instead." He turned to his wife. "And what's the programme for to-day? The glass has gone up, it's already raining, 'all's right with the world'. Anybody like to play ping-pong?"

"Fool," said his wife. "As a matter of fact, I don't think it would be a bad idea if we went over to Broken Ash for tea." Berry made a grimace, and Jill and I groaned. Even Jonah looked down his nose at the suggestion. "Yes," my sister continued, "I didn't think it'd be a popular move, but I'd like Adèle to see the pictures, and we haven't shown a sign of life since we left Town."

At Broken Ash lived the other branch of the Pleydell family, consisting of our Cousin Vandy and his two sisters. Between them and us there was little love lost. Of their jealousy of us, they made but an open secret. But for our grand-father's birth, White Ladies would have been theirs: and then, to make matters worse, the terms of our grand-father's Will had ruled out for ever such hopes as they might have had. And Berry's marriage to my sister had finished everything. The conventions were, however, observed, Calendars were exchanged at Christmas, birthdays were recognized with a cold espistolary nod, and occasional calls were paid and invitations issued. Their possession of all but two of the family portraits was undoubted, and with nine points of the law in their favour they were well armed. It was an open question whether the tenth point, which was ours, was sufficiently doughty to lay the other nine by the heels. Years ago counsel had advised that the law was dead in our favour, but it was certain that Vandy and his sisters would resist any claim we made with great bitterness, and the settlement of a family quarrel in the public ring of the High Court was more than we could stomach.

Still, the pictures were worth seeing. There were a Holbein, a Van Dyck, three Gainsboroughs, and two from the brush of Reynolds among them, and, so soon as she had learned of their existence, Adèle Feste, who was on a visit from the United States, had evinced an eagerness to be shown the collection.

There was a moment's silence. Then—

"I'd hate to think you were going for my sake," said Adèle.

"We're not, dear," said Daphne. "Even if you weren't here, we should have to go some day soon."

"Yes," said Berry. "We hate one another like poison, but we've never declared war. Consequently, diplomatic relations are still maintained, and in due season we meet and are charmingly offensive to one another. When war broke out they were very sticky about billeting a few Yeomanry chargers, and crawled and lied about their stabling till the authorities got fed up and commandeered all they'd got. Therefore, whenever we meet, I chivvy the conversation in the direction of horseflesh. In the same way, having regard to the burglary which we suffered last month, Vandy will spread himself on the subject of old silver. The moment they heard of it, they sent us a triumphant telegram of condolence."

My sister laughed.

"If you say much more," she said, "Adèle will be afraid to come with us. I admit it's a duty call, pure and simple. All the same, there won't be any bloodshed."

"I'm ready for anything," said Adèle thoughtfully. "Shall I wear a red or white rose?"

"Don't tell us you can control your cheeks," said I. "It's unheard of. And why are you so pensive this morning? Is it because of Ireland? Or have you trodden on your sponge?"

"I believe she's broken the soap-dish," said Berry, "and is afraid to tell us."

"Don't tease her," said Jill. "Why shouldn't she be quiet if she likes?"

But Adèle was bubbling with laughter.

"The truth is," she announced, "I'm trying to remember a dream I had last night." She looked across the table at me. "You know what it is to dream something rather vivid and interesting, and then not to be able to remember what it was?"

I nodded.

"But you can't do anything," I said. "It's no good trying to remember it. Either you'll think of it, or you won't."

"Exactly," said my brother-in-law. "There's no other alternative. It's one of the laws of Nature. I well remember dreaming that I was a disused columbarium which had been converted into a brewery and was used as a greenhouse. I was full of vats and memorial tablets and creeping geraniums. Just as they were going to pull me down to make room for a cinema, Daphne woke me up to say there was a bat in the room. I replied suitably, but, before turning over to resume my slumbers, I tried to recapture my dream. My efforts were vain. It was gone for ever."

"Then how d'you know what it was about?" said Jill.

"I don't," said Berry. "What I have told you is pure surmise.

And now will you pass me the toast, or shall I come and get it?"

Choking with indignation, Jill stretched out a rosy hand in the direction of the toast-rack. . . . Suddenly the light of mischief leapt into her grey eyes, and she called Nobby. In a flash the Sealyham—never so vigilant as at meal-time—was by her side. Cheerfully she gave him the last piece of toast. Then she turned to Berry with a seraphic smile.

"I'm afraid there's none left," she said.

* * * * *

Before we had finished lunch, the rain had ceased, and by the time we were under way, *en route* for Broken Ash, the afternoon sun was turning a wet world into a sweet-smelling jewel. Diamonds dripped from her foliage, emerald plumes glistened on every bank, silver lay spilt upon her soft brown roads. No scentbag was ever stuffed with such rare spicery. Out of the dewy soil welled up the fresh clean breath of magic spikenard, very precious.

Punctually at half-past four we swept up the avenue of poplars that led to our cousins' house.

The visit had been arranged by Daphne upon the telephone, and Vandy and his two sisters were ready and waiting. . . .

The *réunion* was not cordial. Ease and Familiarity were not among the guests. But it was eminently correct. The most exacting Master of Ceremonies, the most severe authority upon Etiquette, would have been satisfied. We were extraordinarily polite. We made engaging conversation, we begged one another's pardon, we enjoyed one another's jokes. The dispensation and acceptance of hospitality did the respective forces infinite credit.

After tea we were taken to see the pictures.

Vandy, as showman, naturally escorted Adèle. The rest of us, decently grouped about his sisters, followed like a party of sightseers in the wake of a verger.

To do our host justice, he knew his own fathers. For what it was worth, the history of the Pleydell family lay at his fingers' ends. Men, manners and exploits—he knew them all. Indeed, years ago he had collected his knowledge and had it published in the form of a book. We had a copy somewhere.

We were half-way along the gallery, and our cousin was in full blast, when Adèle, to whom he was introducing the portraits with triumphant unction, started forward with a low cry.

"That's the very man," she exclaimed, pointing at the picture of a middle-aged gentleman in a plum-coloured coat, which, I seemed to remember, was unsigned but attributed—without much confidence—to the brush of Gonzales Coques. "What an extraordinary thing! I've broken my dream."

In the twinkling of an eye Vandy's importance was snatched from him, and the prophet's mantle had fallen upon Adèle. Where, but a moment before, he had been strutting in all the pride of a proprietor, she held the stage. More. Neither our discomfited host nor his sisters could divine what was toward, and the fact that their guests crowded eagerly about Adèle, encouraging her to "let them have it", was more disconcerting than ever.

"It was in a garden," said Adèle, "a quiet sort of place. I think I was walking behind him. I don't know how I got there, but he didn't see me. All the same, he kept looking round, as if he was afraid he was being watched. Presently we came to a place where there was a stone pedestal standing. It wasn't exactly a pillar—it wasn't high enough. And it was too high for a seat. Well, he stared at this for a moment; then he looked around again, very cautiously, and then—it sounds idiotic, but he began to prod the turf with his stick. At first he did it just casually, here and there: but, after a little, he started prodding at regular intervals, methodically. The ground was quite soft, and his stick seemed to go in like a skewer. Suddenly he seemed to hear something or somebody, for he listened very carefully, and then walked on tiptoe to the pedestal and leaned up against it as if he were resting. The next moment somebody—some man in ordinary clothes came out of . . ." She hesitated. "I don't know whether it was some bushes or a wall he came out of. Some bushes, I guess. Any way, he appeared, and—don't laugh—gave him a green tomato. Then I woke up."

"And this is the man you saw?" cried Daphne, pointing.

Adèle nodded.

"Dress and everything. He was wearing the same plumed hat and that identical coat, buttoned all down the front, with the pockets low down on either side. And I'll never forget his face. That's a wonderful picture. It's life-like."

"What an extraordinary thing!" said I. Then I turned to Vandy. "Has this portrait ever been reproduced?"

He did not seem to hear me.

With dropped jaw and bulging eyes, the fellow was staring at Adèle, staring . . .

Suddenly, as with an effort, he pulled himself together.

"Was that all you saw?" he said hoarsely.

Adèle pondered.

"I think so," she said slowly. "Except that there were some words carved on the pedestal. PER . . . IMP . . . PERIMP. . . . No. That wasn't it. Something like that. Not English. I can't remember."

"Ah!"

Berry took up the running.

"You say the merchant was prodding the ground?" he said.

"That's right. It sounds silly, but——"

"Not at all," said Berry excitedly. "He was looking for something. It's as clear as daylight." He turned to the picture. "That's William Pleydell, isn't it, Vandy? Seventeenth-century bloke. The one Pepys mentions."

My cousin nodded abstractedly. With unseeing eyes he was staring out of a window. It was patent that Adèle's recital had affected him strangely. . . .

Berry laid a hand on his arm.

"Where's the book you wrote?" he said gently. "That may throw some light on it."

One of our hostesses turned, as though she would fetch the volume.

"It went to be rebound yesterday," cried Vandy in a strained, penetrating voice.

His sister stopped and stood still in her tracks. A moment later she had turned back and was murmuring a confirmation.

Jonah, who had been busy with a pencil and the back of an envelope, limped towards us from one of the windows.

"The pedestal was a sundial," he said. Vandy looked at him sharply. He turned to Adèle. "PER . . . IMP . . . you said. Try PEREUNT ET IMPUTANTUR. Latin. 'The hours pass and are charged against us.' You'll find the phrase on five sundials out of six."

A buzz of excited applause greeted this admirable contribution.

Adèle looked at the written words.

"You are clever," she said. "Of course, that's it. It must be."

Vandy's reception of Jonah's discovery convinced me that it had already occurred to him. He applauded theatrically. The fellow was playing a part, feverishly. Besides, I did not believe his rotten book was being rebound. That was a lie. There was something there which he did not want us to see. Not a doubt of it. Well, we had a copy at White Ladies. No! Our copy was in Town. Hang it! What a sweep the man was!

With a horse-laugh he interrupted my reflections.

"Well, well, Miss Feste, I confess you gave me a shock. Still, if you had to meet one of our forefathers, I could have wished it had been any other than the notorious William. We enjoy his portrait, but we deplore his memory. Ha! Ha! Now, we're really proud of the next one—his cousin, James Godstow Pleydell. He it was who was responsible——"

"Forgive me," purred Daphne, "but I'm going to say we must fly. I'd no idea it was so late. People are coming to dinner, and we must go back by Brooch, because we've run out of ice."

Our host protested—not very heartily—and was overruled. Mutual regret was suitably expressed. Without more ado we descended into the hall. Here at the front door the decencies of leave-taking were observed. The host and hostesses were thanked, the parting guests sped. A moment later, we were sliding down the avenue to the lodge-gates. As we swung on to the road—

"Where's the book?" said Daphne. "That man's a liar."

"At Cholmondeley Street," said I. "But you're right about Vandy. He's trying to keep something back."

"He's so excited he doesn't know what to do," said Daphne. "That's clear."

"Well, what the deuce is it?" said Berry. "I've read the blinkin' book, but I'll swear there's nothing in it about buried treasure."

"Whatever it is," said I, "it's in that book. I'll get it to-morrow. D'you really want any ice?"

Daphne shook her head.

"But I couldn't stay there with that man another minute."

Adèle lifted up her sweet voice.

"I feel very guilty," she said. "I've upset you all, I've given everything away to your cousin with both hands, and I've——"

"Nonsense, darling," said Daphne. "You did the natural thing. How could you know——"

Jonah interrupted her with a laugh.

"One thing 's certain," he said. "I'll bet old Vandy's cursing the day he rushed into print."

* * * * *

Upon reflection it seemed idle for any of us to journey to London and back merely to fetch a volume, so the next morning one of the servants was dispatched instead, armed with a note to the housekeeper at Cholmondeley Street, telling her exactly where the book would be found.

The man returned as we were finishing dinner, and *The History of the Pleydell Family* was brought to Berry while we sat at dessert.

Nuts and wine went by the board.

As my brother-in-law cut the string, we left our places and crowded about him. . . .

Reference to the index bade us turn to page fifty-four.

As the leaves flicked, we waited breathlessly. Then—

"Here we are," said Berry. " 'WILLIAM PLEYDELL. In 1652 Nicholas died, to be succeeded by his only child, William, of whom little is known. This is perhaps as well, for such information as is to hand, regarding his life and habits, shows him to have been addicted to no ordinarily evil ways. The lustre which his father and grandfather had added to the family name William seems to have spared no effort to tarnish. When profligacy was so fashionable, a man must have lived hard indeed to attract attention. Nevertheless, Samuel Pepys, the Diarist, refers to him more than once, each time commenting upon the vileness of his company and his offensive behaviour. Upon one occasion, we are told, at the play-house the whole audience was scandalized by a *loose drunken frolic*, in which *Mr. William Pleydell, a gentleman of Hampshire*, played a disgraceful part. What was worse, he carried his dissolute habits into the countryside, and at one time his way of living at the family seat White Ladies was so openly outrageous that the incumbent of Bilberry actually denounced the squire from the pulpit, referring to him as "a notorious evil-liver" and "an abandoned wretch". If not for his good name, however, for the house and pleasure-gardens he seems to have had some respect, for it was during his tenure that the stables were rebuilt and the gardens decorated with statuary which has since disappeared. *A sundial*' "—the sensation which the word produced was profound, and Jill cried out with excitement—" '*a sundial, bearing the date 1663 and the cipher W.P., still stands in the garden of the old dower-house, which passed out of the hands of the family early in the nineteenth century.*' "

Berry stopped reading, and laid the book down.

"The dower-house?" cried Daphne blankly.

Her husband nodded.

"But I never knew there was one. Besides——"

"Better known to-day as 'The Lawn, Bilberry'."

"Quite right," said Jonah. "A hundred years ago that stood inside the park."

"The Lawn?" cried Jill. "Why, that's where the fire was. Years and years ago. I remember old Nanny taking me down to see it the next day. And it's never been rebuilt."

"To my knowledge," said I, "it's had a board up, saying it's for sale, for the last fifteen years. Shall we go in for it? They can't want much. The house is gutted, the garden's a wilderness, and——"

A cry from Adèle interrupted me. While we were talking, she had picked up the volume.

"Listen to this," she said. " 'William Pleydell died unmarried and intestate in 1667, and was succeeded by his cousin Anthony. Except that during the former's tenure a good deal of timber was cut, White Ladies had been well cared for. The one blot upon his stewardship was the disappearence of the greater part of the family plate, which Nicholas Pleydell's will proves to have been unusually rare and valuable. *There used to exist a legend, for which the author can trace no foundation, that William had brought it from London during the Great Plague and buried it, for want of a strong-room, at White Ladies.* A far more probable explanation is that its graceless inheritor surreptitiously disposed of the treasure for the same reason as he committed waste, viz., to spend the proceeds upon riotous living.' "

Dumbly we stared at the reader. . . .

The murder was out.

Berry whipped out his watch.

"Nine o'clock," he announced. "We can do nothing to-night. And that sweep Vandy's got a long lead. We haven't a moment to lose. Who are the agents for The Lawn?"

"It's on the board," said I, "and I've read it a thousand times, but I'm hanged if I can remember whether it's Miller of Brooch, or a London firm."

"Slip over there the first thing in the morning," said Jonah. "If it's Miller, so much the better. You can go straight on to Brooch. If it's a London man—well, there's always the telephone."

"I hope to heaven," said Daphne, "it's—it's still for sale."

"Vandy's got Scotch blood in him," said Berry. "He won't lay out fifteen hundred or so without looking round."

"More like three thousand," said Jonah.

"It's a lot of money to risk," said Daphne slowly.

"Yes," said Adèle anxiously. "I feel that. I know it's your affair, but, if it hadn't been for my dream, this would never have happened. And supposing there's nothing in it. . . . I mean, it would be dreadful to think you'd thrown away all that money and gotten nothing in exchange. And they always say that dreams are contrary."

"Let's face the facts," said my brother-in-law. "Taking everything into consideration, doesn't it look like a vision, or second sight?"

We agreed vociferously. Only Adèle looked ill at ease.

Berry continued.

"Very well, then. Less than a month ago all our silver was taken off us by comic burglars. Doesn't it look as if we were being offered the chance of replacing it by something better?"

Again we agreed.

"Lastly, the insurance company has paid up to the tune of four thousand pounds, which amount is now standing to the credit of my deposit account at Coutts'. I tell you, if we don't have a dart, we shall be mad."

"I agree," said I.

"So do I," cried Jill. "I'm all for it."

Only Daphne and Jonah hesitated.

I laid my hand upon the former's shoulder.

"Supposing," I said, "we take no action, but Vandy does. Supposing he strikes oil and lands the stuff under our noses. . . . Wouldn't you cheerfully blow the four thousand just to avoid that?"

My sister's eyes flashed, and Jonah's chin went up.

"Anything," said Daphne emphatically, "anything would be better than that."

So was the decision made.

We adjourned to the drawing-room, and for the rest of the evening discussed the matter furiously.

The suggestion that Vandy would not wait to buy, but had already got to work at The Lawn, was summarily dismissed. Our cousin was too cautious for that. He knew that the moment we had the book, we should be as wise as he, and that, since we were at loggerheads, we should certainly not sit quietly by and permit him to enrich himself to our teeth, when a word to the owners of The Lawn would compel him to disgorge any treasure he found. No, Vandy was no fool. He would walk circumspectly, and buy first and dig afterwards.

It was Jonah who raised the question of "treasure trove". In some uneasiness we sought for a book of law. Investigation, however, satisfied us that, if the plate were ever unearthed, the Crown would not interfere. Evidence that an ancestor had buried it was available, and reference to the will of Nicholas would establish its identity. Whether it belonged to us or to Vandy was another matter, but Reason suggested that Law and Equity alike would favour the party in whose land it was found.

We ordered breakfast early and the car at a quarter to nine, but, for all that, it was past midnight before we went to bed.

The next morning, for once in a way, we were up to time. Two minutes after the quarter we were all six in the car, and it was not yet nine o'clock when Jonah pulled up in the shade of a mighty oak less than a hundred paces from the tall iron gates which stood gaunt, rusty and forbidding, to mar the beauty of the quiet by-road.

So far as we could see there was no one about, but we were anxious not to attract attention, so Berry and I alighted and strolled casually forward.

The object of our visit was, of course, to learn from the board in whose hands the property had been placed for sale. But we had decided that, if it were possible, we must effect an entrance, to see whether the turf about the sundial had been disturbed. Moreover, if we could get Adèle inside, it would be highly interesting to see whether she recognized the place.

Wired on to the mouldering gates, a weather-beaten board glared at us.

FREEHOLD
with immediate possession
TO BE SOLD
This Very Desirable
OLD-WORLD MANSION
Standing in three acres of pleasure grounds
And only requiring certain structural repairs
To be made an ideal modern residence.
F. R. MILLER, Estate Agent, High St., Brooch.

Considering that the house had been gutted nearly twenty years ago, and had stood as the fire had left it from then until now, the advertisement was euphemistic.

By dint of peering between the corrupted bars, it was possible to see for ourselves the desolation. A press of nettles crowded about the scorched and blackened walls, square gaping mouths, that had been windows, showed from the light within that there was no roof, while here and there charred timbers thrust their unsightly way from out of a riot of brambles, wild and disorderly. What we could see of the garden was a very wilderness. Tall rank grass flourished on every side, carriage-way and borders alike had been blotted into a springing waste, and the few sprawling shrubs which we could recognize hardly emerged from beneath the choking smother of luxuriant bindweed.

The gates were chained and padlocked. But they were not difficult to scale, and in a moment Berry and I were over and standing knee-deep in the long wet grass.

Stealthily we made our way to the back of the house. . . .

The sundial was just visible. The grass of what had once been a trim lawn rose up about the heavy pedestal, coarse and tumultuous. But it was untouched. No foot of man or beast had trodden it—lately, at any rate.

Simultaneously we heaved sighs of relief.

Then—

"Adèle'll never recognize this," said Berry. "It's hopeless. What she saw was a lawn, not a prairie." I nodded. "Still," he went on, "there used to be a door in the wall—on the east side." As he spoke, he turned and looked sharply at the haggard building. "Thought I heard something," he added.

"Did you?"

I swung on my heel, and together we stared and listened. Eyes and ears alike went unrewarded. The silence of desolation hung like a ragged pall, gruesome and deathly. . . .

Without a word we passed to the east of the ruin. After a little we came to the door in the wall. Here was no lock, and with a little patience we drew the bolts and pulled the door open. It gave on to a little lane, which ran into the by-road at a point close to where the others were waiting.

I left Berry and hastened back to the car.

Exclamations of surprise greeted my issuing from the lane, and I could read the same unspoken query in four faces at once.

"We're first in the field so far," I said. There was a gasp of relief. "Come along. We've found a way for you."

Adèle and Jill were already out of the car. Daphne and Jonah made haste to alight.

"Think we can leave her?" said Jonah, with a nod to the Rolls.

"Oh, yes. We shan't be a minute."

Hurriedly we padded back the way I had come. Berry was still at the door, and in silence we followed him to where he and I had stood looking and listening a few minutes before.

"O-o-oh!" cried Jill, in an excited whisper.

"What about it, Adèle?" said Berry.

Adèle looked about her, knitting her brows. Then—

"I'm afraid to say anything," she said. "It may be the place I saw. I can't say it isn't. But it's so altered. I think, if the grass was cut..."

"What did I say?" said my brother-in-law.

"But the pedestal was exactly that height. That I'll swear. And it stood on a step."

"What did the words look like?" said I.

"They were carved in block letters on the side of the cornice."

As carefully as I could, I stepped to the sundial. As I came up to it, my foot encountered a step....

The column was unusually massive, and the dial must have been two feet square. Lichened and weather-beaten, an inscription upon the cornice was yet quite easy to read.

PEREUNT ET IMPUTANTUR

And the words were carved in block lettering....

A buzz of excitement succeeded my report. Then Daphne turned quickly and looked searchingly at the house.

"I feel as if we were being watched," she said, shuddering. "Let's get back to the car."

As Jonah followed the girls into the lane—

"What about bolting the door?" said I.

Berry shook his head.

"Doesn't matter," he said. "Any way, we've trodden the grass down. Besides, there's nothing to hide."

We dragged the door to and hastened after the others.

As we climbed into the car, Jonah started the engine.

"What are the orders?" he said. "Is Miller the agent? You never said."

"Yes," said I. "We'd better go straight to Brooch."

Our way lay past the main entrance of The Lawn.

As we approached this, Jonah exclaimed and set his foot on the brake.

Leaning against the wall was a bicycle, and there was a man's figure busy about the gates. He appeared to be climbing over....

As we came up alongside, he looked at us curiously. Then he went on with his work.

A moment later he slid a pair of pliers into his pocket and, wringing the board clear of its fastenings, lowered it to the ground.

We were too late.

The Lawn was no longer for sale.

* * * * *

Our chagrin may be imagined more easily than it can be described.

We returned to White Ladies in a state of profound depression, alternately cursing Vandy and upbraiding ourselves for not having sent for the book upon the evening of the day of our visit to Broken Ash.

Jonah reproached himself bitterly for giving our cousin the benefit of his detective work, although both Daphne and I were positive that Vandy had identified the pedestal from Adèle's description before Jonah had volunteered the suggestion that it was a sundial.

As for Adèle, she was inconsolable.

It was after lunch—a miserable meal—when we were seated upon the terrace, that Berry cleared his throat and spoke wisely and to the point.

"The milk's spilt," he said, "and that's that. So we may as well dry our eyes. With that perishing motto staring us in the face, we might have had the sense to be a bit quicker off the mark. But it's always the obvious that you never see. Vandy's beaten us by a foul, but there ain't no stewards to appeal to, so we've got to stick it. All the same, he's got some digging to do before he can draw the money, and I'm ready to lay a monkey that he does it himself. What's more, the last thing he'll want is to be disturbed. In fact, any interference with his work of excavation will undoubtedly shorten his life. Properly organized innocent interference will probably affect his reason. Our course of action is therefore clear.

"Unable to procure his beastly book—our copy cannot be found—we have forgotten the incident. It comes to our ears that he has bought The Lawn and is in possession. What more natural than that some of us should repair thither, to congratulate him upon becoming our neighbour? We shall roll up quite casually—by way of the door in the wall—and, when we find him labouring, affect the utmost surprise. Of our good nature we might even offer to help him to—er—relay the lawn or tackle the drains, or whatever he's doing. In any event we shall enact the *rôle* of the village idiot, till between the respective gadflies of suspicion—which he dare not voice—and impatience—which he dare not reveal—he will be goaded into a condition of frenzy. What about it?"

The idea was heartily approved, and we became more cheerful.

Immediate arrangements were made for the entrance to The Lawn to be watched for the next twenty-four hours by reliefs of out-door servants whom we could trust, and instructions were issued that the moment Mr. Vandy Pleydell put in an appearance, whether by day or night, we were to be informed.

At eight o'clock the next morning Berry came into my room.

"They're off," he said. "Thirty-five minutes ago Vandy and Emma and May arrived, unaccompanied, in a four-wheeled dog-cart. He'd got the key of the gates, but the difficulty of getting them open single-handed appears to have been titanic. They seem to have stuck, or something. Altogether, according to James, a most distressing scene. However. Eventually they got inside and managed to shut the gates after them. In the dogcart there was a scythe and a whole armoury of tools."

I got out of bed and looked at him.

"After breakfast?" I queried.

My brother-in-law nodded.

"I think so. We'll settle the premises as we go."

*   *   *   *   *

As we were approaching The Lawn, I looked at my watch. It was just a quarter to ten.

The little door in the wall was still unbolted, and a very little expenditure of energy sufficed to admit my brother-in-law, Nobby, and myself into the garden.

So far as the Sealyham was concerned, "the Wilderness was Paradise enow". Tail up, he plunged into the welter of grass, leaping and wallowing and panting with surprise and delight at a playground which surpassed his wildest dreams. For a moment we watched him amusedly. Then we pushed the door to and started to saunter towards the house.

It was a glorious day, right at the end of August. Out of a flawless sky the sun blazed, broiling and merciless. There was nowhere a breath of wind, and in the sheltered garden—always a sun-trap—the heat was stifling.

As we drew near, the sound of voices, raised in bitterness, fell upon our ears, and we rounded the corner of the building to find Vandy waist-high in the grass about the sundial, shaking a sickle at his sisters, who were seated upon carriage cushions, which had been laid upon the flags, and demanding furiously "how the devil they expected him to reap with a sweeping motion when the godforsaken lawn was full of molehills."

"Quite right," said Berry. "It can't be done."

Emma and May screamed, and Vandy jumped as if he had been shot. Then, with a snarl, he turned to face us, crouching a little, like a beast at bay. Before he could utter a word, Berry was off.

Advancing with an air of engaging frankness, which would have beguiled the most hardened cynic, he let loose upon our cousin a voluminous flood of chatter, which drowned his protests ere they were mouthed, overwhelmed his inquiries ere they were launched, and finally swept him off his feet into the whirlpool of uncertainty, fear and bewilderment before he knew where he was.

We had only just heard of his purchase, were delighted to think we were to be neighbours, had had no idea he was contemplating a move, had always said what a jolly little nook it was, never could understand why it had been in the market so long, thought we might find him here taking a look round, wanted to see him, so decided to kill two birds with one stone. . . . What about the jolly old book? Had it come back from the binders? We couldn't find ours, thought it must be in Town. . . . The girls were devilling the life out of him to look it up. Was it William or Nicholas? He thought it was William. Hadn't Vandy said it was William? What was the blinking use, any old way? And what a day! He'd got a bet with Jonah that the thermometer touched ninety-seven before noon. What did Vandy think? And what on earth was he doing with the pruning-hook? And/or ploughshare on his left front? Oh, a scythe. Of course. Wouldn't he put it down? It made him tired to look at it. And was he reclaiming the lawn? Or only looking for a tennis-ball? Of course, what he really wanted was a cutter-and-binder, a steam-roller, and a gang of convicts. . . .

I had been prepared to support the speaker, but, after three minutes of this, I left his side and sat down on the flags.

At last Berry paused for breath, and Emma, who had hurriedly composed and been rehearsing a plausible appreciation of the state of affairs, and was fidgeting to get it off her chest, thrust her way into the gap.

Well, the truth was, they were going to take up French gardening. There was no room at Broken Ash, and, besides, they must have a walled garden. Building nowadays was such a frightful expense, and suddenly they'd thought of The Lawn. It was sheltered, just the right size, not too far away, and all they had to do was to clear the ground. And Vandy was so impatient that nothing would satisfy him but to start at once. "He'll get tired of it in a day or two," she added artlessly, "but you know what he is."

For an improvised exposition of proceedings so extraordinary, I thought her rendering extremely creditable.

So, I think, did Vandy, for he threw an approving glance in her direction, heaved a sigh of relief, and screwed up his mouth into a sickly smile.

"Took up gardening during the War," he announced. "I—we all did. Any amount of money in it. Quite surprised me. But," he added, warming to his work, "it's the same with gardening as with everything else in this world. The most valuable asset is the personal element. If you want a thing well done, do it yourself. Ha! Ha!"

My brother-in-law looked round, regarding the howling riot of waste.

"And where," he said, "shall you plant the asparagus?"

Vandy started and dropped the sickle. Then he gave a forced laugh.

"You must give us a chance," he said. "We've got a long way to go before we get to that. All this"—he waved an unbusiness-like arm, and his voice faltered—"all this has got to be cleared first."

"I suppose it has," said Berry. "Well, don't mind us. You get on with it. Short of locusts or an earthquake, it's going to be a long job. I suppose you couldn't hire a trench-mortar and shell it for a couple of months?"

Apparently Vandy was afraid to trust his voice, for, after swallowing twice, he recovered the sickle and started to hack savagely at the grass without another word.

With the utmost deliberation, Berry seated himself upon the flagstones and, taking out his case, selected a cigarette. With an equally leisurely air I produced a pipe and tobacco, and began to make ready to smoke. Our cousins regarded these preparations with an uneasiness which they ill concealed. Clearly we were not proposing to move. The silence of awkwardness and frantically working brains settled upon the company. From time to time Emma and May shifted uncomfortably. As he bent about his labour, Vandy's eyes bulged more than ever. . . .

Nobby, whom I had forgotten, suddenly reappeared, crawling pleasedly from beneath a tangled stack of foliage, of which the core appeared to have been a rhododendron. For a moment he stared at us, as if surprised at the company we kept. Then his eyes fell upon Vandy.

Enshrined in the swaying grass, the latter's knicker-bockers, which had been generously fashioned out of a material which had been boldly conceived, presented a back view which was most arresting. With his head on one side, the terrier gazed at them with such inquisitive astonishment that I had to set my teeth so as not to laugh outright. His cautious advance to investigate the phenomenon was still more ludicrous, and I was quite relieved when our cousin straightened his back and dissipated an illusion monstrously worthy of the pen of Mandeville.

But there was better to come.

As the unwitting Vandy, after a speechless glance in our direction, bent again to his work, Nobby cast an appraising eye over the area which had already received attention. Perceiving a mole-hill which had suffered an ugly gash—presumably from a scythe—he trotted up to explore, and, clapping his nose to the wound, snuffed long and thoughtfully. The next moment he was digging like one possessed.

Emma and May stiffened with a shock. With the tail of my eye I saw them exchange horror-stricken glances. Panic fear sat in their eyes. Their fingers moved convulsively. Then, with one consent, they began to cough. . . .

Their unconscious brother worked on.

So did the Sealyham, but with a difference. While the one toiled, the other was in his element. A shower of earth flew from between his legs, only ceasing for a short moment, when he preferred to rend the earth with his jaws and so facilitate the excavation.

The coughing became insistent, frantic, impossible to be disregarded. . . .

As I was in the act of turning to express my concern Vandy looked up, followed the direction of four starting eyes, and let out a screech of dismay.

"What on earth's the matter?" cried Berry, getting upon his feet. "Been stung, or something?"

With a trembling forefinger Vandy indicated the miscreant.

"Stop him!" he yelled. "Call him off. He'll—he'll spoil the lawn."

"Ruin it," shrilled Emma.

"Where?" said Berry blankly. "What lawn?"

"*This* lawn!" roared Vandy, stamping his foot.

"But I thought——"

"I don't care what you thought. Call the brute off. It's my land,

and I won't have it."

"Nobby," said Berry, "come off the bowling green."

Scrambling to my feet, I countersigned the order in a peremptory tone. Aggrievedly the terrier complied. My brother-in-law turned to Vandy with an injured air.

"I fear," he said stiffly, "that we are unwelcome." Instinctively Emma and May made as though they would protest. In some dignity Berry lifted his hand. "I may be wrong," he said. "I hope so. But from the first I felt that your manner was strained. Subsequent events suggest that my belief was well founded." He turned to Vandy. "May I ask you to let us out? I am reluctant to trouble you, but to scale those gates twice in one morning is rather more than I care about."

Fearful lest our surprise at our reception should become crystallized into an undesirable suspicion, short of pressing us to remain, our cousins did everything to smooth our ruffled plumage.

Vandy threw down the sickle and advanced with an apologetic leer. Emma and May, wreathed in smiles, protested nervously that they had known the work was too much for Vandy, and begged us to think no more of it. As we followed the latter round to the quondam drive, they waved a cordial farewell.

The sight of the four-wheeled dogcart, standing with upturned shafts, a pickaxe, three shovels, a rake, two forks, a number of sacks, and a sieve piled anyhow by its side, was most engaging; but, after bestowing a casual glance upon the paraphernalia, Berry passed by without a word. Vandy went a rich plum colour, hesitated, and then plunged on desperately. Tethered by a halter to a tree, a partially harnessed bay mare suspended the process of mastication to fix us with a suspicious stare. Her also we passed in silence.

After a blasphemous struggle with the gates, whose objection to opening was literally rooted and based upon custom, our host succeeded in forcing them apart sufficiently to permit our egress, and we gave him "Good day".

In silence we strolled down the road.

When we came to the lane, Berry stopped dead.

"Brother," he said. "I perceive it to be my distasteful duty to return. There is an omission which I must repair."

"You're not serious?" said I. "The fellow'll murder you."

"No, he won't," said Berry. "He'll probably burst a blood-vessel, and, with luck, he may even have a stroke. But he won't murder me. You see." And, with that, he turned down the lane towards the door in the wall.

Nobby and I followed.

A moment later we were once more in the garden.

The scene upon which we came was big with promise.

Staggering over the frantic employment of a pickaxe, Vandy was inflicting grievous injury upon the turf about the very spot at which the terrier had been digging. Standing well out of range, his sisters were regarding the exhibition with clasped hands and looks of mingled excitement and apprehension. All three were so much engrossed that, until Berry spoke, they were not aware of our presence.

"I'm so sorry to interrupt you again"—Emma and May screamed, and Vandy endeavoured to check his implement in mid-swing, and only preserved his balance and a whole skin as by a miracle—"but, you know, I quite forgot to ask you about the book. And, as that was really our main object in——"

The roar of a wild beast cut short the speaker.

Bellowing incoherently, trembling with passion, his mouth working, his countenance distorted with rage, Vandy shook his fist at his tormentor in a fit of ungovernable fury.

"Get out of it!" he yelled. "Get out of it! I won't have this intrusion. It's monstrous. I won't stand it. I tell you——"

"Hush, Vandy, hush!" implored his sisters in agonized tones.

Berry raised his eyebrows.

"Really," he said slowly, "anybody would think that you had something to hide."

Then he turned on his heel.

I was about to follow his example, when my cousin's bloodshot eye perceived that Nobby was once more innocently investigating the scene of his labour. With a choking cry our host sprang forward and raised the pick. . . .

Unaware of his peril, the dog snuffed on.

One of the women screamed. . . .

Desperately I flung myself forward.

The pick was falling as I struck it aside. Viciously it jabbed its way into the earth.

For a long time Vandy and I faced one another, breathing heavily. I watched the blood fading out of the fellow's cheeks. At length—

"Be thankful," said I, "that I was in time. Otherwise——"

I hesitated, and Vandy took a step backwards and put a hand to his throat.

"Exactly," I said.

Then I plucked the pick from the ground, stepped a few paces apart, and, taking the implement with both hands, spun round and threw it from me as if it had been a hammer.

It sailed over some lime trees and crashed out of sight into some foliage.

Then I called the terrier and strode past my brother-in-law in the direction of the postern.

Berry fell in behind and followed me without a word.

* * * * *

"But why," said I, "shouldn't you tell me the day of your birth? I'm not asking the year."

"1895," said Adèle.

I sighed.

"Why," she inquired. "do you want to know?"

"So that I can observe the festival as it deserves. Spend the day at Margate, or go to a cinema, or something. I might even wear a false nose. You never know. It's an important date in my calendar."

"How many people have you said that to?"

I laughed bitterly.

"If I told you the truth," I said, "you wouldn't believe me."

There was a museful silence.

It was three days and more since Berry and I had visited The Lawn, and Vandy and Co were still at work. So much had been reported by an under-gardener. For ourselves, we had finished with our cousins for good and all. The brutal attack upon our favourite was something we could not forget, and for a man whom beastly rage could so much degrade we had no use. Naturally enough, his sisters went with him. Orders were given to the servants that to callers from Broken Ash Daphne was "not at home", and we were one and all determined, so far as was possible, never to see or communicate with Vandy or his sisters again. It was natural, however, that we should be deeply interested in the success or failure of his venture. We prayed fervently, but without much hope, that it might fail. . . . After all, it was always on the cards that another had stumbled long since upon the treasure, or that a thief had watched its burial and later come privily and unearthed it. We should see.

"I wonder you aren't ashamed of yourself," said Miss Feste. "At your age you ought to have sown all your wild oats."

"So I have," I said stoutly. "And they weren't at all wild, either. I've never seen such a miserable crop. As soon as the sun rose, they all withered away."

"The sun?"

I turned and looked at her. The steady brown eyes held mine with a searching look. I met it faithfully. After a few seconds they turned away.

"The sun?" she repeated quietly.

"The sun, Adèle. The sun that rose in America in 1895. Out of the foam of the sea. I can't tell you the date, but it must have been a beautiful day."

There was a pause. Then—

"How interesting!" said Adèle. "So it withered them up, did it?"

I nodded.

"You see, Adèle, they had no root."

"None of them?"

"None."

Adèle looked straight ahead of her into the box-hedge, which rose, stiff and punctilious, ten paces away, the counterpart of that beneath which we were sitting. For once in a way, her merry smile was missing. In its stead Gravity sat in her eyes, hung on the warm red lips. I had known her solemn before, but not like this. The proud face looked very resolute. There was a strength about the lift of the delicate chin, a steadfast fearlessness about the poise of the well-shaped head—unworldly wonders, which I had never seen. Over the glorious temples the soft dark hair swept rich and lustrous. The exquisite column of her neck rose from her flowered silk gown with matchless elegance. Her precious hands, all rosy, lay in her lap. Crossed legs gave me six inches of black silk stocking and a satin slipper, dainty habiliments, not half so dainty as their slender charge. . . .

The stable clock struck the half-hour.

Half-past six. People had been to tea—big-wigs—and we were resting after our labours. It was the perfect evening of a true summer's day.

Nobby appeared in the foreground, strolling unconcernedly over the turf and pausing now and again to snuff the air or follow up an odd clue of scent that led him a foot or so before it died away and came to nothing.

"How," said Adèle slowly, 'did you come by Nobby?"

Painfully distinct, the wraith of Josephine Childe rose up

before me, pale and accusing. Fragments of the letter which had offered me the Sealyham re-wrote themselves upon my brain. . . . *It nearly breaks my heart to say so, but I've got to part with Nobby. . . . I think you'd get on together. . . . if you'd like to have him.* . . . And there was nothing in it. It was a case of smoke without fire. But—I could have spared the question just then. . . .

Desperately I related the truth.

"A girl called Josephine Childe gave him to me. She wanted to find a home for him, as she was going overseas."

"Oh."

The silence that followed this non-committal remark was most discomfiting. I had a feeling that the moments were critical, and —they were slipping away. Should I leap into the tide of explanation? That way, perhaps, lay safety. Always the quicksand of *Qui s'excuse, s'accuse*, made me draw back. I became extremely nervous. . . . Feverishly I tried to think of a remark which would be natural and more or less relevant, and would pilot us into a channel of conversation down which we could swim with confidence. Of all the legion of topics, the clemency of the weather alone occurred to me. I could have screamed. . . .

The firebrand itself came to my rescue.

Tired of amusing himself, the terrier retrieved an old ball from beneath the hedge and, trotting across the sward, laid it down at my feet.

Gratefully I picked it up and flung it for him to fetch.

It fell into a thick welter of ivy which Time had built into a bulging buttress of greenery against the old grey wall at the end of the walk.

The dog sped after it, his short legs flying. . . .

The spell was broken, and I felt better.

"You mustn't think he's a root, though," I said cheerfully, "because he isn't. When did you say your birthday was?"

"I didn't," said Adèle. "Still, if you must know I was born on August the thirtieth."

"To-day! Oh, Adèle. And I've nothing for you. Except . . ." I hesitated, and my heart began to beat very fast. "But I'd be ashamed—I mean. . . ." My voice petered out helplessly. I braced myself for a supreme effort. . . .

An impatient yelp rang out.

"What's the matter with Nobby?" said Adèle in a voice I hardly recognized.

"Fed up, 'cause I've lost his ball for him," said I, and, cowardly glad of a respite, I rose and stepped to the aged riot of ivy, where the terrier was searching for his toy.

I pulled a hole in the arras and peered through.

There was more space than I had expected. The grey wall bellied away from me.

"What's that?" said Adèle, looking over my shoulder.

"What?" said I.

"There. To the right."

It was dark under the ivy, so I thrust in a groping arm.

Almost at once my hand encountered the smooth edge of masonry.

I took out a knife and ripped away some trails, so that we could see better.

There was nothing to show that the pedestal which my efforts revealed had ever supported a statue. But it was plain that such was the office for which it had been set up. Presumably it was one of the series which, according to Vandy's book, had displayed imaginative effigies of the Roman Emperors, and had been done away in 1710. The inscription upon the cornice upheld this conclusion.

PERTINAX IMPERATOR.

I looked at Adèle.

"PER . . . IMP . . ." said I. "Does the cap fit?"

"Yes," she said simply. "That's right. I remember it perfectly. The other seemed likely, but I was never quite sure." Trembling a little, she turned and looked round. "And you came out of that break in the hedge with the tomato, and—— Oh!"

She stopped, and the colour came flooding into her cheeks. . . .

Then, in a flash, she turned and sped down the alley like a wild thing. As in a dream, I watched the tall slim figure dart out of sight. . . .

A second impatient yelp reminded me that Nobby was still waiting.

* * * * *

The firm of silversmiths whom we employed to clean the collection, after it had been disinterred, valued it for purposes of insurance at twenty-two thousand pounds.

We saw no reason to communicate with Vandy. The exercise was probably doing him good, and he had shown a marked antipathy to interruption. A tent had been pitched at The Lawn, and the work of excavation went steadily on. Not until the twenty-eighth of September did it suddenly cease.

Three days later we had occasion to drive into Brooch. We returned by way of The Lawn. As we approached the entrance, I slowed up. . . .

From the tall gates a brand-new board flaunted its black and white paint.

But the legend it bore was the same.

Mr. Miller was evidently a Conservative.

CHAPTER XI

How Nobby met Blue Bandala, and Adele gave Jonah a Kiss

"Listen to this," said Berry.

> "Sir,—Shortly before six o'clock this evening an extremely valuable Chow, by name Blue Bandala, which I purchased last March for no less a sum than six hundred pounds, was brutally attacked in Bilberry village by a rough-haired mongrel, which was accompanying two girls. I am given to understand that this animal belongs to you. I was at first determined to issue a summons, but I have now decided to give you a chance before doing so. If it amuses you to keep such a cur about your house, there is nothing to prevent you from so doing. But you must understand that once it leaves your property it must be under proper and effective control, and if it ever attacks a dog of mine again, I shall either destroy it upon the spot or apply to the Bench for its destruction. I may say that Blue Bandala is not only very well bred, but a very quiet and friendly dog, and was in no way to blame for what occurred.
>
> Herbert Bason.
>
> B. Pleydell, White Ladies."

The explosion which the reading of this letter provoked is indescribable.

"It's a lie!" cried Jill in a choking voice. "It's a beastly lie. His dog started it. Nobby would never have touched him. He wasn't paying any attention. The Chow came up from behind and just fell upon him. And how dare he say he's a mongrel? It's just one lie after another, isn't it, Adèle?"

"It's outrageous," said Miss Feste. "Directly I saw the other dog I thought he meant mischief, but before I could tell Jill, he'd started in. Nobby didn't even know he was there."

The door opened, and dinner was announced.

"Falcon," said Berry.

"Sir," said the butler.

"Who brought this note?"

"It was a chauffeur, sir. I don't know 'im by sight, sir."

We filed out of the library, smouldering with resentment.

"But what an awful man he must be," said Daphne. "Even if our dog had been in the wrong, that's no reason for writing a letter like that."

"It's unpardonable," said I. "It's quite bad enough to have him living in the neighbourhood, but if this is the way he's going to behave . . ." I turned to Adèle. "Was his manner very bad at the time?"

"He seemed more rattled than anything else. He was clearly afraid to interfere. Jill and I got them apart, as I told you. He got very red in the face, but beyond muttering with his teeth clenched, he never said a word."

"Must have gone straight home and got it off his chest," said Jonah. "I expect he's awfully proud of that letter, if the truth were known."

"Well, don't let's dwell on it," said Berry, regarding the oysters which had been set before him. "After dinner will do. You hardly ever go down with typhoid within six hours." He turned to Adèle. "Bet you I've got more strepsicocci than you have," he added pleasantly.

"Shut up," said Daphne. "Adèle dear, d'you like oysters? Because, don't you eat them if you don't."

"No don't," said Berry. "If you don't, whatever you do, don't. And whatever you don't, I will."

Adèle looked at him with a mischievous smile.

"I couldn't bear," she said, "to have your blood on my head."

Then she glanced gratefully at Daphne and picked up a fork.

Mr. Herbert Bason had arisen out of the cloud of War. The time had produced the man. The storm had burst just in the nick of time to save the drooping theatrical interests which he controlled, and the fruit which these had borne steadily for the best part of five long years had been truly phenomenal. A patriot to the backbone, the bewildered proprietor obtained absolute exemption from the Tribunal, turned the first six rows of all his pits into stalls, and bought War Loan with both hands. It was after the second air-raid upon London that he decided to take a house in the country. . . . Less than a year ago he had disposed of his music-halls and had settled near Bilberry for good.

"By the way," said Daphne, "did I tell you? The laundry's struck."

"Thank you," said her husband, "for that phrase."

"Don't mention it," said my sister. "But I thought you'd like to know. Heaven knows when they'll go back, so I should go easy with your stiff collars and shirts."

"What, have the saws stopped working?" said Berry. "I can't bear it."

"What about my trousers?" said I. "I've only one clean pair left."

Daphne shrugged her white shoulders.

"What about my tablecloths?" she replied.

Berry addressed himself to Adèle.

"We live in pleasant times, do not we? Almost a golden age. I wonder what the trouble is now. Probably some absent-minded *blanchisseuse* has gone and ironed twenty socks in ten minutes instead of ten socks in twenty minutes, without thinking. And the management refuse to sack her for this grievous lapse into the slough of pre-War Industry, out of which a provident Trade Union has blackmailed her to climb."

"I've no doubt you're right," said I. "The question is, where are we going to end? It's the same everywhere. And the mere thought of Income Tax sends my temperature up."

"Ah," said Berry. "I had a quiet hour with the Book of the Words, issued by that Fun Palace, Somerset House, this afternoon. *Income Tax, and How to Pay it.* Commonly styled, with unconscious humour, The Income Tax Return. By the time I was through I had made out that, if I render a statement according to the printed instructions, my tax will exceed my income by one hundred and forty-four pounds. If, on the other hand, I make an incorrect return, I shall be fined fifty pounds and treble the tax payable. You really don't get a look in."

"If you say much more," groaned Jonah, "you'll spoil my appetite. When I reflect that in 1913 and a burst of piety I sent the Chancellor of the Exchequer a postal order for eight and sixpence by way of Conscience Money, I feel positively sick."

"Not piety," corrected my brother-in-law. "Drink. I remember you had some very bad goes about then."

"What a terrible memory you have!" said Adèle. "I feel quite uneasy."

"Fear not, sweet one," was the reply. "Before I retail your indiscretions I shall send you a list of them, with the price of omission clearly marked against each in red ink. The writing will be all blurred with my tears." Here Adèle declined a second vegetable. "There, now. I've gone and frightened you. And marrow's wonderful for the spine. Affords instant relief. And you needn't eat the seeds. Spit them over your left shoulder. That'll bring you luck."

There was an outraged clamour of feminine protest.

"I won't have it," said Daphne. "Disgusting brute!"

"And that," said Jonah, "is the sodden mountebank who dares to cast a stone into the limpid pool of my character. That is the overfed sluggard——"

"Take this down, somebody," said Berry. "The words'll scorch up the paper, but never mind. Record the blasphemy. Capital 'M' for 'mountebank'. 'Sluggard' with an 'H'. And I'm not overfed."

"You're getting fatter every day," said Jill, gurgling.

"That's right," said my brother-in-law. "Bay the old lion. And bring down these grey hairs in——"

"Talking of mountebanks," said I, "who's going to Fallow Hill Fair?"

"Adèle ought to see it," said Daphne. "Why don't you run her over in the car?"

"I will, if she'd like to go. It's a real bit of old England."

"I agree," said Berry. "What with the cocoa-nut shies and the steam roundabouts, you'd think you were back in the Middle Ages. I think I'll come, too."

"Then you go alone," said I. "I don't forget the last time you went."

"What happened?" said Adèle, her eyes lighted with expectation.

Berry sighed.

"It was most unfortunate," he said. "You see, it was like this. B-behind a b-barrier there was a b-booth with a lot of b-bottles, at which you were b-bothered to throw b-balls. If you b-broke three b-bottles——"

"This nervous alliteration," interposed Adèle, "is more than I can b-bear."

"—you received a guerdon which you were encouraged to select from a revolting collection of bric-à-brac which was displayed in all its glory upon an adjacent stall. Laden with munitions, I advanced to the rails. . . . Unhappily, in the excitement of the moment, I mistook my objective. . . . It was a most natural error. Both were arranged in tiers, both were pleading for destruction."

"Nonsense," said Daphne. "You did it on purpose. You know you did. I never saw anything more deliberate in all my life."

"Not at all," replied her husband. "I was confused. A large and critical crowd had collected to watch my prowess, and I was pardonably nervous."

"But what happened?" said Adèle.

"Well," said I, "naturally nobody was expecting such a move, with the result that the brute got off about six balls before they could stop him. The execution among the prizes was too awful. You see, they were only about six feet away. The owner excepted, the assembled populace thought it was the funniest thing they'd ever seen."

"Yes," chimed in Jill. "And then he turned round and asked the man how many bottles he'd won."

"I never was so ashamed," said Daphne. "Of course, the poor man was nearly off his head."

"And I paid for the damage," said Jonah.

I looked across at Adèle.

"So, if he comes with us," I said, "you know what to expect."

My lady threw back her head and laughed.

"I suppose you're to be trusted," she said.

"Once past the pub," said Berry, "he'll be all right. But if he says he feels faint outside the saloon-bar, don't argue with him, but come straight home."

"At any rate," said Adèle, "I shall have Nobby."

The reference brought us back to Mr. Bason with a rush.

In spite of our resolution to eschew the subject, that gentleman's letter was heatedly discussed for the remainder of dinner.

To-day was the third of September, and on the eleventh a dog-show was to be held at Brooch. I had not entered Nobby, because I felt that his exhibition would probably cause us more trouble than the proceeding was worth. It now occurred to us that Mr. Bason would almost certainly enter—had probably long ago entered his precious Chow. Any local triumph, however petty and easy for a man of means to procure, would be sure to appeal to one of his calibre, and the chance, which the show would afford, of encountering, if not accosting, one or two County people would be greatly to his relish. Supposing we did enter Nobby. . . .

The idea of beating Mr. Bason in the face for first prize with the "rough-haired mongrel" which "it amused us to keep about our house" was most appealing.

As soon as dinner was over, Berry rang up the Secretary.

Our surmise was correct. Blue Bandala was entered.

"Well, am I too late to enter a Sealyham?"

"Not if you do it to-morrow," came the reply.

"You shall have the particulars before mid-day."

"Right-oh."

Berry replaced the reciever.

"Little Herbert will take the first prize for Chows," he said. "That can't be helped. But he's entered his dog for the 'All Comers', and that's our chance. If we can't lift that goblet from under his ugly nose, I'll never smile again."

"What exactly's 'All Comers'?" said Jill.

"The best all-round specimen of any breed. Manners, carriage —everything's taken into consideration."

"If personality counts," said Jonah, "Nobby'll romp home."

I regarded our unconscious representative with an appraising eye. Supine upon the sofa, with his head out of sight behind Adèle, there was little to recommend him as a model of deportment. With a sigh I resumed the composition of a reply to Mr. Bason's remarkable letter.

When I had finished the draft, I gave it to Berry. The latter read it through, nodding solemn approval. Then he repaired to the writing-table and copied my sentences, word for word, on to a sheet of notepaper.

As he laid down his pen, he rose to his feet.

"I'll tell you what," he said. "If the blighter replies, and Nobby comes off at the show, we'll send this correspondence to the local Press."

"Let's have it," said Jonah.

Berry handed me the letter, and I read it aloud.

Sir,

I have received your note.

As an alloy of misrepresentation of fact, arrogant bluster and idle menaces, I doubt whether it has ever been equalled upon this side of the Rhine.

Indeed, its legibility would appear to be its only merit.

Not that I care for your style of handwriting, but in these degenerate days it is, you will agree, a relief to receive a letter which can be easily read.

You did go a bust on Blue Banana, didn't you?

Pray act upon your first impulse and apply for a summons. The Bench will not grant your application, but—again you will agree—it is the effort, and not the result, which counts.

It is nice of you to inquire after my Sealyham. He is none the worse, thanks, and I fancy he made old Blue Banana sit up.

Yours faithfully,
Berry Pleydell.

H. Bason, Esq.

P.S.—You must forgive me for addressing you as "Esquire", but it is difficult to break a foolish habit of courtesy which I formed as a child. B. P.

* * * * *

"Fifteen thirty," cried Adèle, making ready to serve. "Hullo!" She pointed with her racket over my shoulder. "Nobby's gone lame."

I swung on my heel to see the terrier limping apologetically towards me, and going dead lame upon the near fore.

As he came up, I dropped my racket and fell upon one knee, the better to search for the cause of the trouble. Carefully I handled the affected limb. . . . My fingers came to his toes, and the Sealyham winced. With a sigh of relief, I laid him upon his back.

"Got it?" said Adèle.

I looked up into the beautiful face three inches from mine.

"I fancy so." I bent to peer at the small firm foot. "Yes. Here we are. He's picked up a puncture."

The next moment I plucked a substantial thorn from between two strong black toes. A warm red tongue touched my restraining fingers in obvious gratitude.

"Will he be all right?"—anxiously.

"He shall speak for himself," said I, releasing my patient.

With a galvanic squirm the latter regained his feet, spun into the air, gyrated till I felt dizzy, and then streaked round the tennis-lawn, his hind feet comically overreaching his fore, steering a zigzag course with such inconsequence as suggested that My Lord of Misrule himself was directing him by wireless.

It was not worth while finishing our interrupted game, so we strolled back to the house. At the top of the stairs we parted, to go and change. Directly after lunch we were to leave for the fair.

Six days had elapsed since Nobby's scuffle with the apple of Mr. Bason's eye. Life had slipped by uneventfully. The Sealyham had been put upon a strict diet and was thoroughly groomed three times a day : my store of clean starched linen had dwindled to one shirt and two collars, which, distrusting my brother-in-law, I kept under lock and key : and Mr. Bason had been stung by our letter into sending a reply which afforded us the maximum of gratification. It ran as follows—

Sir,

Your insulting letter to hand.

I stand by every word of my previous letter.

The sooner, therefore, that you realize that I am not to be trifled with, the better for all concerned.

You are evidently one of those people who believe that impudent bluff will carry them anywhere, and that, with your birth and upbringing behind you, you can do as you please. But you are wrong. Among men who are men, as distinct from pedantic popinjays, you go for nothing. Pshaw.

Herbert Bason.

B. Pleydell, Esq.

P.S.—Be good enough to note that my dog's name is "Blue Bandala", not "Blue Banana".

H. B.

Our reply was dispatched within twenty-four hours.

Sir,

Many thanks for your masterly appreciation of my character.

We all think "pedantic popinjays" simply splendid. Is it your own?

Don't tell old Banana Skin, but I've had the nerve to enter my Sealyham for the "All Comers" event at Brooch.

So glad you're not to be trifled with. Selah.

Yours faithfully,

Berry Pleydell.

H. Bason, Esq.

In two days' time we should meet at Philippi.

It must be confessed that there were moments when we remembered our precipitancy in some uneasiness. Nobby was well bred, but he had not cost six hundred pounds. Always he looked his best, and his best was extremely good. His many excellent points were set off by a most attractive air and a singular charm and sprightliness of manner. Every movement and pose was full of grace, and he had the brightest eyes that I have ever seen. But Blue Bandala was clearly a "show" animal. Could our little David beat this very Goliath among dogs, and that upon the latter's own ground? Could our little amateur take on a plus-four professional and beat him at his own game? There was no manner of doubt that angels would at least have walked delicately where we had rushed in. However, it was too late now. Even if we would, we could not draw back. Beyond doing what we could to keep him as fit as a fiddle, there was nothing to be done.

After a bath I put on a tweed suit, concealed my discarded and sole surviving pair of white trousers from the rapacious eye of a random housemaid, and descended to lunch.

An hour later Adèle and Nobby and I were all in the Rolls, sailing along the soft brown roads *en route* for Fallow Hill.

It was a day of great loveliness, and the forest ways were one and all beset with a rare glory.

Thirty-six hours before, the first frost of autumn had touched the breast of Earth with silver finger-tips. 'Twas but a runaway knock. The mischief-loving knave was gone again, before the bustling dame had braced herself to open to her pert visitor. Maybe the rogue was beating up his quarters. The time of his dreaded lodgment was not yet. His apprehensive hostess was full of smiles. Summer was staying on. . . .

Yet on the livery of the countryside the accolade of Frost had wrought a wonder. Two days ago the world was green. To-day a million leaves glanced, green as before, yet with a new-found lustre —something of red in it, something of gold, something of sober brown. But the wonder was not to the trees. It was the humble bracken that had been dubbed knight. The homespun of the forest was become cloth of pure gold, glittering, flawless. In the twinkling of an eye the change had come. Here was an acre spread with the delicate fronds, and there a ragged mile, and yonder but shreds and patches—yet all of magic gold, flinging the sunlight back, lighting the shadows, making the humblest ride too rich for kings to trample till the green roofs and walls looked dull beside it, and the ephemeral magnificence took Memory by the throat and wrung a lease of life from that Reversioner.

"Tell me," I said, "of Mr. Bason. He interests me, and I've never seen him."

"Mr. Bason," said Adèle, "is short and fat and—yes, I'm afraid he's greasy. He has bright yellow hair and a ridiculous moustache, which is brushed up on end on each side of his nostrils. He has very watery pale blue eyes, and all the blood in his face seems to have gone to his nose."

"Muscular rheumatism," I suggested.

"I guess so. Of course, he knows best, and I don't pretend to say what men should wear, but white flannel suits aren't becoming to every figure, are they? Most of the rest of him was mauve—shirt, socks and handkerchief. Oh, and he had a tie on his pin."

"But how lovely!"

"Yes, but you should have smelt the lilac. He was just perfumed to death. If he isn't careful, one of these days he'll get picked."

"One of the old school, in fact. Well, well. . . ." We swept round a corner, and I nodded ahead. "See that ridge in front of us? Well, that's Fallow Hill. The village lies close, just on the other side."

"What are you going to do with the car?" said Adèle.

"They'll let me lock her up—don't be shocked—at the brewery. I know them there."

"You'll admit it sounds bad."

"Yes, but it smells lovely. You wait. For that reason alone, I should vote against Prohibition. The honest scent of brewing, stealing across the meadows on a summer eve, is one of the most inspiring things I know."

"But what a man!" said Adèle. " 'Books in the running brooks, *Virtue in vats*, and good in everything.' Nobby," she added reproachfully, "why didn't you tell me he was a poet?" The Sealyham put his head on one side, as if desiring her to repeat the question. "Oh, you cute thing!" And, with that, my lady bent and kissed the terrier between the bright brown eyes.

I put the wheel over hard, and the car swerved violently.

"For Heaven's sake!" cried Miss Feste. "What are you doing?"

"It's your fault," said I. "I'm only human. Besides he doesn't deserve it."

Adèle flung me a dazzling smile, made as though she would say something, and then, apparently changing her mind, relapsed into a provoking silence. . . .

A quarter of an hour later the Rolls had been safely bestowed at the brewery, and my companion and I were making our way amusedly past booths and tents and caravans, where chapmen, hucksters, drovers, cheapjacks, gipsies and bawling showmen wrangled and chaffered and cried their wares or entertainments, making with the crude music of the merry-go-rounds much the same good-humoured uproar which had been faithfully rendered at the village of Fallow Hill every September for the last five hundred years.

"Blessings on your sweet pretty face, my lady!" cried an old voice.

We turned to see a very old gipsy, seated a little apart upon a backless chair, nodding and smiling in our direction.

Adèle inclined her head, and I slid a hand into my pocket.

"Come hither to me, my lady," piped the old dame, "and let your man cross my old palm with silver, and I'll tell you your fortune. Ah, but you have a happy face."

Adèle looked at me, and I nodded.

"They're a good folk," I said, "and you'll get better stuff for your money than you would in Bond Street. But don't, if you don't want to."

My words could not have been heard by the gipsy. Yet, before Adèle could reply—

"Aye," she said, "the pretty gentleman's right. We're a good folk, and there be some among us can see farther than the dwellers in towns." Adèle started, and the crone laughed. "Come hither, my lady, and let me look in your eyes."

She was an old, old woman, but the snow-white hair that thrust from beneath her kerchief was not thin: her face was shrunken and wrinkled, yet apple-cheeked: and her great sloe-black eyes glowed with a strange brilliance, as if there were fires kindled deep in the wasted sockets.

Adèle stepped forward, when, to my amazement, the gipsy put up her hands and groped for the girl's shoulders. The significance of the gesture was plain. She was stone blind.

For a while she mumbled, and, since I had not gone close, I did not hear what she said. But Adèle was smiling, and I saw the colour come flooding into her cheeks. . . .

Then the old dame lifted up her voice and called to me to come also.

I went to her side.

An old gnarled hand fumbled its way on to my arm.

"Aye," she piped. "Aye. 'Tis as I thought. Your man also must lose ere he find. Together ye shall lose, and together gain. And ye shall comfort one another."

The tremulous voice ceased, and the hands slipped away.

I gave her money and Adèle thanked her prettily.

She cried a blessing upon us, I whistled to Nobby, and we strolled on. . . .

"Look at that baby," said Adèle. "Isn't he cute?"

"Half a second," said I, turning and whistling. "Which baby?"

"There," said Adèle, pointing. "With the golden hair."

A half-naked sun-kissed child regarded us with a shy smile. It was impossible not to respond. . . .

Again I turned and whistled.

"Where can he be?" said Adèle anxiously.

"Oh, he always turns up," I said. "But, if you don't mind going back a little way, it'll save time. With all this noise . . ."

We went back a little way. Then we went back a long way. Then we asked people if they had seen a little white dog with a black patch. Always the answer was in the negative. One man laughed and said something about "a dog in a fair", and Fear began to knock at my heart. I whistled until the muscles of my lips ached. Adèle wanted us to search separately, but I refused. It was not a place for her to wander alone. Feverishly we sought everywhere. Twice a white dog sent our hopes soaring, only to prove a stranger and dash them lower than before. Round and about and in and out among the booths and swings and merry-go-rounds we hastened, whistling, calling and inquiring in vain. Nobby was lost.

* * * * *

We had intended to be home in time for tea.

As it was, we got back to White Ladies, pale and dejected, at a quarter to eight.

As she rose to get out of the car, Adèle gave a cry and felt frantically about her neck and throat.

"What's the matter?" I cried.

"My pearls," she said simply. "They're not here."

For what it was worth, I called for lights, and we took the cushions out and looked in the car.

But there was no sign of the necklace. It was clean gone.

* * * * *

The lamentations with which the news of our misfortunes was received were loud and exceeding bitter.

Jill burst into tears; Daphne tried vainly to comfort her, and then followed her example; Berry and Jonah vied with each other in gloomy cross-examination of Adèle and myself concerning our movements since we had left White Ladies, and in cheerless speculation with regard to the probable whereabouts of our respective treasures.

After a hurried meal the Rolls was again requisitioned, and all six of us proceeded to Fallow Hill. Not until eleven o'clock would the fun of the fair be suspended, and it was better to be on the spot, even if for the second time we had to come empty away, than to spend the evening in the torment of inactivity.

Of the loss of the Sealyham we could speak more definitely than of that of the necklace. Nobby had been by my side when the gipsy hailed us, so that there was no doubt but that he was lost at the fair. Regarding her pearls, Adèle could speak less positively. In fact, to say that she had had the necklace before breakfast that morning was really as far as she could go. "I know I had it then," she affirmed, "because I always take it off before taking my bath, and I remember putting it on afterwards. As luck will have it, I was rather late this morning, and I couldn't fasten the safety-chain, so after two or three shots I gave up trying, intending to do it later on. And this is the result." She had not bathed again.

It was a sweet pretty gaud. So perfectly matched were its hundred and two pearls that many would have believed it unreal. It had belonged to her great-grandmother, and was not insured.

Arrived at Fallow Hill, we went straight to the police. The loss of the jewels we communicated to them alone. Somewhat shamefacedly and plainly against Adèle's will, I described the old gipsy and commended her to their vigilance. When they learned that she had laid hands upon Adèle, the two inspectors exchanged glances which there was no mistaking. . . .

So far as Nobby was concerned, as well as informing the police, we enlisted the sympathy of the Boy Scouts. Also we engaged six rustics to perambulate the fair and cry the loss of the Sealyham for all to hear. Information leading to his recovery would be rewarded with the sum of five pounds, while the crier to whom the communication was made would receive five more for himself. Our six employees went about their work with a will, bellowing lustily. Daphne and Jonah sat in the car, rejecting the luckless mongrels which were excitedly paraded before them, one after another, from the moment that our loss was made known. The rest of us hunted in couples—Adèle with Berry, and Jill with me—scouring the maze of temporary alleys and lanes and crooked quadrangles, till we knew them by heart.

The merry-go-rounds had stopped whirling, and the booths were being shrouded or dismantled, as Jill and I made our way to the car for the last time.

As we came up—

"That you, Boy?" cried Daphne. "Here's a waggoner who thinks he saw Nobby being taken away."

A little knot of men parted, and Jill and I thrust our way forward.

"Oi wouldden be sure," said a deep rough voice, "but a was a lil white chap of a dog on en' of a string. 'Twas a grume, simly, a-leadin' 'im Brooch way. An' a didn't want for to go, neither, for a stook toes in, a did, an' collar was 'alf-way over 'ead. Just come forth from *The Three Bulls*, Oi 'ad, oop yonder o' Bear Lane, an' the toime were nigh three o' the aafternoon."

We questioned him closely, but he could tell us no more.

Slight as the clue was, it was infinitely better than none at all. If it was indeed Nobby that the waggoner had seen, the thief was taking him out of the village, at least in the direction of White Ladies. This was encouraging. That any one making for the railway station would take the same road was a less pleasant reflection.

I took our informant's name and address and those of the crier who had brought him to the car. Then we dispensed some silver, and left for home.

Of Adèle's necklace we had heard nothing.

We determined to concentrate upon the recovery of the pearls upon the following day.

* * * * *

All through a wretched night the pitiful vacancy at the foot of my bed reminded me brutally of my loss. My poor little dog—where was he passing these dark hours? How many more must drag their way along before the warm white ball lay curled again in the crook of my knees? Had he rested there for the last time? With a groan I thrust the thought from me, but always it returned, leering hideously. Miserably I recited his qualities—his love for me, his mettle, his beauty, his unfailing good humour. . . . What naughtiness there was in him seemed very precious. Painfully I remembered his thousand pretty ways. He had a trick of waving his little paws, when he was tired of begging. . . .

Small wonder that I slept ill and fitfully.

Early as I was, the others were already at breakfast when I came down. Only Adèle had not appeared.

It was a melancholy meal.

Jonah said not a word, and Berry hardly opened his mouth. There were dark rings under Jill's grey eyes, and Daphne looked pale and tired.

A communication from the Secretary of the Brooch Dog Show, enclosing a pass for the following day, and informing me that my Sealyham must arrive at the Show in the charge of not more than one attendant by 11 a.m., did not tend to revive our drooping spirits.

We had nearly finished, when, with a glance at the clock, my sister set her foot upon the bell.

As the butler entered the room—

"Send up and see if Miss Feste will breakfast upstairs, Falcon. I think——"

"Miss Feste has breakfasted, madam."

"Already?"

"Yes, madam. Her breakfast was taken to her before eight o'clock."

"Where is she?"

"I think she's out bicycling, madam."

"Bicycling?"

The inquiry leapt from five mouths simultaneously.

"Yes, madam. She sent for me and asked if I could find 'er a lady's bicycle, an' Greenaway was very 'appy to lend 'er 'ers, madam. An' Fitch pumped up the tyres, an' she went off about 'alf-past eight, madam."

We stared at one another in bewilderment.

"Did she say where she was going?" said Berry.

"No, sir."

"All right, Falcon."

The butler bowed and withdrew.

Amid the chorus of astonished exclamation, Berry held up his hand.

"It's very simple," he said. "She's unhinged."

"Rubbish," said his wife.

"The disappearance of Nobby, followed by the loss of her necklace, has preyed upon her mind. Regardless alike of my feelings and of the canons of good taste, she rises at an hour which is almost blasphemous and goes forth unreasonably to indulge in the most hellish form of exercise ever invented. What further evidence do we need? By this time she has probably detached the lamp from the velocipede and is walking about, saying she's Florence Nightingale."

"Idiot," said Daphne.

"Not yet," said her husband, "but I can feel it coming on." He cast an eye downward and shivered. "I feared as much. My left leg is all unbuttoned."

"For goodness' sake," said his wife, "don't sit there drivelling——"

"Sorry," said Berry, "but I haven't got a clean bib left. This laundry strike——"

"I said 'drivelling', not 'dribbling'. You know I did. And what are we wasting time for? Let's do something—anything."

"Right-oh," said her husband. "What about giving the bread some birds?" And with that he picked up a loaf and deliberately pitched it out of the window on to the terrace.

The fact that the casement was not open until after the cast, made his behaviour the more outrageous.

The very wantonness of the act, however, had the excellent effect of breaking the spell of melancholy under which we were labouring.

In a moment all was confusion.

Jill burst into shrieks of laughter; Jonah, who had been immersed in *The Times*, cursed his cousin for the shock to his nerves; in a shaking voice Daphne assured the butler, whom the crash had brought running, that it was "All right, Falcon; Major Pleydell thought the window was open"; and the delinquent himself was loudly clamouring to be told whether he had won the slop-pail outright or had only got to keep it clean for one year.

Twenty minutes later Jonah had left for Brooch to see the Chief Constable about the missing jewels and arrange for the printing and distribution of an advertisement for Nobby. The rest of us, doing our utmost to garnish a forlorn hope with the seasoning of expectation, made a diligent search for the necklace about the terrace, gardens and tennis-lawn. After a fruitless two hours we repaired to the house, where we probed the depths of sofas and chairs, emptied umbrella-stands, settles, flower-bowls and every other receptacle over which our guest might have leaned, and finally thrust an electric torch into the bowels of the piano and subjected that instrument to a thorough examination.

At length—

"I give it up," said Daphne, sinking into a chair "I don't think it can be here."

"Nor I," said I. "I think we've looked everywhere."

"Yes," said Berry. "There's only the cesspool left. We can drag that before lunch, if you like, but I should prefer one more full meal before I die."

"Boy! Boy!"

Somewhere from behind closed doors a sweet excited voice was calling.

I sprang to the door.

"Yes, Adèle, yes?" I shouted.

A moment later my lady sped down a passage and into the hall.

"Get the car quick. I've found Nobby."

"Where?" we yelled.

"That man Bason's got him."

Her announcement momentarily deprived us of breath. Then we all started, and in the next two minutes sufficient was said about the retired music-hall proprietor to make that gentleman's pendulous ears burst into blue flame.

Again want of breath intervened, and Adèle besought us to make ready the car.

We explained vociferously that Jonah had taken the Rolls and would be back any minute. Whilst we were waiting, would she not tell us her tale?

Seating herself upon the arm of a chair, she complied forthwith.

"None of you seemed to suspect him, and, as I'm usually wrong, I decided to say nothing. But last night I asked a Boy Scout where he lived. Curiously enough, the boy had a brother who was a gardener in Bason's employ. That made me think. I asked him whether I could have a word with his brother, and he told me he lived at a cottage close to his work, and was almost always at home between nine and half-past in the morning.

"When he came home this morning, I was waiting for him. He seemed a nice man, so I told him the truth and asked him to help me. Thorn—that's his name—doesn't like Bason a bit, and at once agreed that he was quite capable of the dirtiest work, if any one got in his way. He hadn't, he said, seen Nobby, but that wasn't surprising. If the dog was there he'd probably be in the stables, and with those Thorn has nothing to do.

"Bason doesn't keep horses, but he uses one of the coach-houses as a garage. The chauffeur seems to be rather worse than his master. He's loathed by the rest of the staff, and, while he and Bason are as thick as thieves, neither trusts the other an inch.

"The first thing to do, obviously, was to find out if Nobby was there. Everything was always kept locked, so I determined to try the 'Blondel' stunt—yes, I know a lot of English History—and try and make Cœur de Lion speak for himself.

"First we synchronized our watches. Then Thorn showed me the house and told me exactly where the garage and stables were—close to the gates, happily. Then we arranged that in ten minutes' time he should try to get the chauffeur out of the way, while I took a look round. More than that we couldn't fix, but it was understood that, if there was a dog there and Thorn got an opening, he was to undo his collar and give him a chance to make good on his own. That wouldn't involve Thorn, for he could fasten the collar again and make it look as if Nobby had slipped it."

"But what a brain!" said Berry. "One short month of my society and the girl——"

An avalanche of protest cut short the speaker.

Adèle continued, gurgling.

"At first everything went all right. At twenty minutes to ten I put my head round the corner to see the chauffeur and Thorn disappearing at the other end of the yard. I stepped out of my cover and had a look round. There were stables on one side, and a coach-house and garage on the other, and the yard, which was open at both ends, lay in between. I was just going to try the loose-boxes—I was going to 'miaow' like a cat and see what answer I got—when I heard Bason's voice calling Banana. . . .

"There was only one door open, and that was the garage. I dashed for it and looked round for somewhere to hide. The place was as bare as your hand. But there was nothing the matter with the limousine, so I got inside and sat down on the floor.

"I was only just in time.

"Bason came stamping into the yard, shouting for 'Arthur', and the next moment Nobby gave tongue.

"I just had to look.

"There was Blue Banana with his nose to the door of the loose-box immediately opposite, snarling and showing his teeth, Bason was hammering on the door, yelling 'Shut up, you brute!' and Nobby, of course, was barking to beat the band."

As she spoke, a faint familiar cough from the drive announced the return of Jonah from Brooch.

In less time than it takes to record, I had flown to the front-door and put him wise. Two minutes later we were all in the Rolls, which was scudding at an unlawful speed along the Fallow Hill road.

"There's nothing much more to tell," said Adèle, as we clamoured for her to proceed. "I thought Bason would never go, and, when at last he did, the chauffeur took the opportunity of changing the two front tyres.

"For over two hours I sat in that car. At last the man shut the place up and, I suppose, went to his dinner.

"I had meant to borrow the limousine, but he'd taken the key of the switch, so I couldn't do that. And I couldn't get at Nobby, for the stable was locked. So I just pelted back to Thorn's cottage, told his wife to tell him my news, picked up the bicycle and came right back."

For a moment no one said anything. Then—

"I shall recommend you," said Berry, "for the Most Excellent Order of the Beer Engine. A very coveted distinction. The membership is limited to seven million."

"Yes," said I, "for a most daring reconnaissance behind the enemy's lines. You know, this ranks with the penetration of the Kiel Canal. Seriously, Adèle, I'm terribly grateful."

My lady looked at me with a shy smile.

"What did the gipsy say?" she said. "After all, I'm only obeying orders. And now——"

A cry from Jonah interrupted her, and the rest of us started inquiringly as he clapped on the brakes.

As the car came to a standstill—

"What's the matter?" I cried.

By way of answer my cousin took off his hat and, producing a silk handkerchief, deliberately wiped his forehead with the utmost care. Then he replaced his hat and looked up and over his right shoulder. . . .

From the top of a mossy bank by the side of the road Nobby was regarding us wide-eyed. Apparently he had broken prison and was on his way home. Time was nothing to him, and the roots of a wayside beech upon an attractive rise cried aloud for inspection. Besides, there was a serious loss of liberty which had to be made good. . . .

For a moment rescue-party and prize looked one another in the face. Then the latter hurled himself panting into the road and leapt into the arms which I stretched out of the car.

No prodigal ever received such an ovation. There was literally a fight for his person. Jill snatched him from me and pressed his nose to her face; Berry dragged him from her protesting arms and set him upon his knee; Daphne tore him away and hugged him close. Such of us as were temporarily disseized, stroked and fondled his limbs and cried endearing epithets. Only our fair American looked on with a wistful smile.

"So, you see," she said, "he's done without me, after all."

I took hold of her hand.

"My dear," I said, "your argument would be more forcible if he was wearing a collar."

There was a buzz of excitement as my statement was feverishly confirmed.

"I agree," said Berry. "What's more, he's brought us a souvenir."

As he spoke, he plucked something which was adhering to the terrier's beard.

It was a tuft of slate-grey hair.

* * * * *

The "All Comers" Event was won by Nobby, who beat a French bulldog by a short head.

Neither Blue Bandala nor his owner put in an appearance. For this a particularly curt note, bluntly requiring the return of the Sealyham's collar, may have been responsible.

The waggoner and the lad who found him received their rewards.

So also did Thorn. His letter of acknowledgment was addressed to Adèle.

Dear Madam,

Thank you kindly for the 5 lbs. I got to the dog by way of the ayloft which were in one of the stalls I undone is coller and here he run out the first dore as was open and appening on Blew Bandarlerer did not harf put it acrost him and Mr. Bason says I command you to seperate them dogs Arthur he says and Arthur fetches Blew B. one what he ment for your dog and Mr. Bason fetches him another what he ment for Arthur so the chough cort it proper.

Yours respectfully,

G. Thorn.

But for the loss of the pearls, we should have been jubilant.

* * * * *

Three days had elapsed since the dog show.

The whole of the morning and part of the afternoon I had spent in a bathroom, supervising the disconnection, severance and inspection of the waste-pipe which served the basin. When, hot and dejected, I made my report at half-past three, Adèle thanked me as prettily as if I had found the pearls.

I retired to wash and change into flannels.

It must have been two hours later when I looked up from the operation of combing Nobby and took my pipe from my mouth.

"Oh, Adèle," I said simply, "I do love you so."

Adèle put out a hand and touched my hair.

"I'm glad you do," she said gently.

As I got upon my feet, one end of her necklace hung trailing over the edge of my trousers where I had turned them up. They were the pair I had worn at tennis the day we had gone to the fair, and it must have fallen into the fold when we were finding the thorn.

Adèle saw it too, but, when I would have stooped, she shook her head.

Then I looked into her eyes, and there found such a light that I forgot the pearls and the rolling world with them.

As she slipped into my arms, she threw back her head.

"Once, at Port Said, you kissed me," she whispered. "And again at Rome." I nodded. "But this is your own home."

"Yes," I said steadily. "And here I plight thee my troth."

The brown eyes closed, and a glorious smile swept into the beautiful face.

For a moment I gazed at her. . . .

Then I kissed the red, red lips.

So we comforted one another.

* * * * *

The unexpected arrival of the laundry van at five minutes to eight, with, amongst other things, a month's table-linen, had pardonably dislocated the service of dinner.

Whilst the table was being relaid we spent the time in the library, gathered about the violet-tongued comfort of a chestnut-root fire.

"You know," said Jonah, looking up from an armchair, "if we don't—— Good Heavens!" His exclamation was so violent that we all jumped. "Why," he cried, staring at Adèle, "you've found them!"

A common cry of amazement broke from Daphne, Berry and

Jill, and our guest started guiltily and put a hand to her throat.

"O-o-oh, I"—she shot an appealing glance at me—"we quite forgot. Boy found them in the garden, whilst he was combing Nobby."

Berry looked round.

"You hear?" he said. "They quite forgot. . . . They stumble upon jewels worth a month of strike pay—baubles whose loss has stupefied the County, and forget to mention it. And I spent two hours this afternoon in a gas-mask studying the plan of the drains and calculating whether, if the second manhole was opened and a gorgonzola put down to draw the fire, Jonah could reach the grease-trap before he became unconscious." He raised his eyes to heaven and groaned. "The only possible excuse," he added, "is that you're both in . . ."

His voice tailed off, as he met Adèle's look, and he got suddenly upon his feet.

Jonah stood up, too.

Daphne took Adèle's hands in hers and turned to me a face radiant with expectation.

Jill caught at my sleeve and began to tremble. I put my arm about her and looked round.

"We plead that excuse," I said.

For a moment nobody moved.

Then Jonah limped to my dear and put her hand to his lips. Adèle stooped and kissed him.

"You beautiful darling," breathed my sister. "Sargent shall paint you, and you shall hang at the foot of the stairs."

The two kissed one another tenderly.

Then Adèle stretched out her white arms to grey-eyed Jill. My little cousin just clung to her.

"Oh, Adèle," she whispered, "I'm so glad. B-but you won't go away? He and you'll stay with us, won't you?"

"If you want me, darling."

Berry cleared his throat.

"Of course," he said, "as the head of the family—the overlord—I should have come first. However, I shall kiss her 'Good night' instead. Possibly I shall ker-rush her to me." He turned to me. "This will be the second time within my memory that a Pleydell has married above him."

"Very true," said I. "When was the first?"

"When I married your sister."

I nodded dreamily.

"I think," I said, "I think I was born with a silver spoon in my mouth."

Berry shook his head.

"Not a spoon," he said. "A soup-ladle."

THE END